The High Mage

"I cannot read your heart," Kileontheal whispered. "What have you done to yourself, Araevin?"

He had thought long and hard about how to answer that question, if the high mages asked him. In the end he could see that nothing except the truth would serve.

"I performed a rite devised by the star elf Morthil, once the Grand Mage of Sildëyuir. He was a student of Ithraides of Arcorar. The rite has fitted me to wield high magic in a tradition that Evermeet has forgotten."

For a growing number of elves, the ancient forests of Cormanthyr call for a Return, leaving their would-be neighbors to choose between a powerful elven realm in Myth Drannor, or a cabal of demonic half-breeds ruling the same. And that is not as easy a choice as it may seem. For one elf mage the Crusade has given him power beyond imagining, but that power has cost him a part of his soul, and the trust of the People.

Forever.

FORGOTTEN REALMS®

THE LAST MYTHAL
Forsaken House
Farthest Reach
Final Gate

Realms of the Elves
Edited by Philip Athans

Also by Richard Baker

R.A. Salvatore's War of the Spider Queen, Book III
Condemnation

The City of Ravens
The Shadow Stone
Easy Betrayals

STAR·DRIVE®
Zero Point

From Wiley Publishing
Dungeons & Dragons® for Dummies®
(with Bill Slavicsek)

FORGOTTEN REALMS

FINAL GATE

THE LAST MYTHAL
BOOK III

RICHARD BAKER

FINAL GATE
The Last Mythal, Book III

©2006 Wizards of the Coast, Inc.

All characters in this book are fictitious. Any resemblance to actual persons, living or dead, is purely coincidental.

This book is protected under the copyright laws of the United States of America. Any reproduction or unauthorized use of the material or artwork contained herein is prohibited without the express written permission of Wizards of the Coast, Inc.

Published by Wizards of the Coast, Inc. FORGOTTEN REALMS, DUNGEONS & DRAGONS, WIZARDS OF THE COAST, and their respective logos are trademarks of Wizards of the Coast, Inc., in the U.S.A. and other countries. FOR DUMMIES is a trademark of John Wiley & Sons, Inc. and/or its affiliates in the U.S. and other countries.

Printed in the U.S.A.

The sale of this book without its cover has not been authorized by the publisher. If you purchased this book without a cover, you should be aware that neither the author nor the publisher has received payment for this "stripped book."

Cover art by Adam Rex
First Printing: June 2006
Library of Congress Catalog Card Number: 2005935517

9 8 7 6 5 4 3

ISBN-10: 0-7869-4002-6
ISBN-13: 978-0-7869-4002-8
620-95533740-001-EN

U.S., CANADA,	EUROPEAN HEADQUARTERS
ASIA, PACIFIC, & LATIN AMERICA	Hasbro UK Ltd
Wizards of the Coast, Inc.	Caswell Way
P.O. Box 707	Newport, Gwent NP9 0YH
Renton, WA 98057-0707	GREAT BRITAIN
+1-800-324-6496	Save this address for your records.

Visit our web site at www.wizards.com

For Kelly and Dan
Why are you so surprised?

Acknowledgements

All the big pieces of this story were put in place by a handful of authors who were hard at work building the Realms long before I came onto the scene—namely, Ed Greenwood, Eric Boyd, Elaine Cunningham, Steven Schend, and Troy Denning. *The Last Mythal* would have been a much different (and much diminished) story without the foundations these talented writers laid down for me.

I'd also like to thank Phil Athans, my editor, and former Wizards of the Coast Director of Book Publishing Peter Archer for their encouragement and confidence in my work over the last few years.
It's been a pleasure working with them both.

Finally, a very special thanks to my wife Kim for her patience and support. Taking on an assignment as big as *The Last Mythal* means many, many evenings spent in front of the computer instead of helping around the house. I owe her big time.

PROLOGUE

*6 Flamerule, the Year of Stern Judgment
(666 DR)*

Blood ran in the streets of Myth Drannor. Fflar Starbrow Melruth stared at the bodies of elf and human alike, cut down in the square before the ruined Rule Tower. Crowds of angry partisans loyal to a dozen different noble Houses quarreled over the bodies of the fallen, shouting and brandishing steel at each other.

"Someone else is going to be killed here before long," Fflar said. "We need to put a stop to this."

"I don't see how we can," Elkhazel Miritar replied. "We'd need a hundred warriors to disperse this crowd and prevent any more bloodshed." The young sun elf shook his head, appalled by the senselessness of the scene. "Have we all gone mad, Fflar?"

"The answer lies in the streets before you," Fflar murmured. He was young as the People counted it, a tall moon elf of only sixty years. In a different day he would not yet have been accepted into the Akh Velar, the army of Myth Drannor, but in the short years since the coronal's death many things had changed in the city of his birth. "They are killing each other for the privilege of dying with their hands on the Ruler's Blade."

Across the square a diademed high lady of some sun elf House spoke the words of a flying spell and ascended. She soared up toward a great globe of golden energy that hovered over the spot where the Rule Tower had stood. Inside the shimmering sphere the silver Ruler's Blade hung in the air, point to the sky, spinning slowly as it awaited the hand of the elf who could claim it. Around the royal sword five high mages floated in the air, safeguarding the ancient rite of choosing. Until an elf set his hand on the hilt of the Ruler's Blade and lived, Cormanthyr had no coronal.

"Is that Tiriara Haladar?" Elkhazel asked, gazing up at the noblewoman who ascended toward the blade hundreds of feet above.

Fflar peered closer, not sure which of the Haladars soared toward the waiting test. But it did not matter; when the lady approached the sphere of magic, some mage amid the crowd of onlookers hurled a deadly green orb of crackling energy at her. With a shriek of dismay, the Haladar claimant dropped to the ground, her golden robes fluttering around her. A furious scuffle broke out in the crowd, as Haladar-sworn warriors leaped after the mage who had brought down their lady. Adherents of other Houses shouted defiance or even cheered the fall of the would-be coronal, who lay broken in the center of the plaza amid her beautiful robes.

"Corellon, have mercy," Elkhazel whispered.

Fflar stared in stunned amazement; he'd just seen murder done in broad daylight in the heart of Myth Drannor. With a sick feeling in his stomach, he started to push his way through the crowd toward the place where the lady had fallen. As a warrior of the Akh Velar, he was supposed to keep order in the city—though how he could hope to calm the chaos around him, he had no idea.

"Stop!" he shouted. "All of you, stop! There is to be no more killing today!"

"This is no business of the Akh Velar!" a bold human bravo snarled. The man shook his heavy rapier in Fflar's face. "Where were you when Lord Erithal was murdered? Do you think to tell me that the life of a human lord is less than that of some sun elf sorceress?"

Someone behind the human swordsman drew steel, and Fflar took half a step back and swept his own blade from its sheath. We should have a full company of Akh Velar swords here to put a stop to this, he fumed silently. But the Akh Velar barracks were three-quarters empty, as warriors of all races had answered the calls of their own native Houses and causes.

"You will not tell us what to do, moon elf!" the human hissed at Fflar. "We will make our own justice today!"

"Wait!" cried Elkhazel Miritar. "Wait! The Srinshee speaks!"

Fflar lowered his sword and looked up into the sky. All around him, noble-sworn blades did the same, enmity forgotten for a moment. The great golden sphere of magic in which the Srinshee and the four masked high mages hovered grew brilliant, throwing off gleams of golden light. The shadows of evening fled, and dusk brightened into bright daylight beneath the radiant orb overhead. Fflar could distinctly make out the Srinshee herself, in her elegant robes of black, floating a few feet above the Ruler's Blade itself.

"Attend me, people of Myth Drannor!" the Srinshee said, and by some artifice of magic her voice, high and clear, rang out over the whole city. "Look on what you have done today, and despair! A great gift was given to you, and it lies in shambles!"

Fflar let his gaze drop to the shattered stump of the Rule Tower, smoldering a bowshot beneath the great mage's feet. His heart ached at the sight. *This is not who we are,* he told himself. This is not what Myth Drannor stands for. What madness has stolen over us? From somewhere in the ranks of the Maendellyn House blades, he heard an elf sob openly at the Srinshee's words.

"Two score elves have reached for this blade with arrogance, with ambition, with hate or division in their hearts," the Srinshee continued. "All have been found wanting. The tower of the coronal's rule lies ruined under my feet! You have spurned the blessing of the Seldarine! Do you not understand what has been lost here today?

"I can bear no more. I will attempt the blade myself, because your madness must be made to stop. Should I prove less than worthy, the Claiming will continue. Decide your own fate thereafter!"

Robes swirling with the magic she wielded, the great archmage confronted the sword floating in the air over the shattered tower.

"Corellon's wrath!" Elkhazel murmured. "Does she mean what she says?"

"She must," Fflar answered.

The Srinshee had stood beside Cormanthyr's throne for as long as anyone he knew had lived, six centuries or more. In all that time she had been content to aid, advise, and serve. The magical might she wielded had never been employed in her own service. Fflar was terrified that she would be destroyed by the sword, incinerated as so many others had been in the last few days. How could Myth Drannor survive without the Srinshee to counsel and protect the city?

Or, worse yet—what might happen if she succeeded? Who could gainsay the Srinshee in anything? Power such as she wielded, unfettered by bonds of fealty and service . . . that way lay tyranny so black and desperate that Fflar quailed to consider it. No one possessed the wisdom to wield that sort of power. No one!

"Someone must stop her!" shouted a highborn noble in the street.

"The Srinshee will save us!" cried another. "She brings us hope, you fool!"

"She cannot draw the Ruler's Blade!" cried the human rake who stood by Fflar.

Dozens of shouts of reproach, of acclaim, of protest filled the air, but the Srinshee paid them no mind. With only a moment's hesitation, she reached out her slender hand and grasped the hilt of the mighty sword.

A great white gleam shot from the blade in the Srinshee's grasp, and the mighty orb of magic hovering above the wreckage of the Rule Tower glimmered white in response. Fflar felt the shock of the blade's acceptance even where he stood, the tremendous magic of the Claiming taking his breath away like a hammer blow.

"She has done it!" he gasped.

Thunder pealed through the streets of the city, and slowly died away. The Srinshee, her face streaked with tears, turned the Ruler's Blade point down and drew it close to her dark robes.

"I have proven worthy," she whispered. Magic again carried her words clearly to everyone in the city. "But I will not be coronal. I will not rule from the throne."

"But she drew the Ruler's Blade," Elkhazel murmured. "Now she refuses it?"

Other voices nearby muttered in consternation, but the Srinshee continued. "When peace rules your hearts, and you remember the dream of this place, I will return. When Oacenth's Vow is fulfilled, I will return."

Return? Fflar thought. *What does she mean to do?*

The Srinshee paused, and the Ruler's Blade grew bright as a star in her slender hands. "Now, people of Myth Drannor, attend. Look upon what I do today, and remember hope."

She released the Ruler's Blade, and the silver-glowing sword plunged down into the rubble of the Rule Tower. For a moment, Fflar could not perceive anything other than a single sheet of dancing white lightning that darted and crackled over the place where Cormanthyr's heart had stood. And he saw the rubble begin to shift, to move, the broken stones mounting to the sky like autumn leaves blown before a whirlwind. Thunder rumbled throughout the city, so heavy and strong that he felt it through the stone beneath his feet. He staggered back from the majesty of the sight, finding himself shoulder-to-shoulder with the swordsmen and rakes who had defied him only a few moments before.

There was one more peal of thunder, and the brilliant lightning faded. At the center of the square stood the magnificent Rule Tower, completely intact, as if nothing had ever happened to it. Fflar glanced up to the spot where the Srinshee and the high mages attending her hovered, the Ruler's Blade restored to their midst. The great golden sphere of magic surrounding them grew dimmer, fading even as he watched.

"What is happening?" the man near him asked in a whisper. "What does this portend?"

No one replied. But in the air above the restored tower, the Srinshee and her mages silently faded into nothingness. The royal sword gleamed once in the dusk and was gone. Stillness governed the square. Elf, human, noble, commoner, all stood quiet and stared at the white tower gleaming in the summer dusk.

"We have been given one more chance," Fflar answered the man. "The Seldarine and the Srinshee have put it in our hands, and no others can carry our fate. That is what it portends, friend. That is what it portends."

With a sigh, he sheathed his sword and moved forward to see to the dead.

CHAPTER ONE

*18 Flamerule, the Year of Lightning Storms
(1374 DR)*

Moonlight danced on the waters of Lake Sember as Araevin Teshurr landed on the Isle of Reverie. He commanded the graceful elven boat to remain fast by the shore, and leaped lightly to the pebble-strewn shore. Wet gravel crunched beneath his fine suede boots, and he paused to study the wooded islet around him.

Araevin was tall even for a sun elf, nearly six and a half feet, with a lean build and long hands and legs. In the moonlight his bronzed skin glowed with a golden hue, almost as if he were a ghostly image of himself. That was the work of the *telmiirkara neshyrr,* the rite of transformation he had performed two tendays ago in the darkness of Mooncrescent Tower. He was still becoming accustomed to the rite's effects—the changes in his perceptions, the magic that flowed through his veins, and the sheer wild *otherness* that he felt sleeping restlessly in his heart. Simply standing on the moonlit lakeshore, he felt almost lost in the simple delight of the wavelets caressing the beach and the creaking and rustling of the islet's ancient trees in the warm summer wind.

He climbed a winding path that led away from the landing. Despite the serenity of the Isle, Araevin was armed for battle. He wore a light shirt of fine mithral mail beneath his crimson cloak, and his sword Moonrill rode on his left hip, next to a holster carrying three wands of his own devising. Peril was never far off in that summer of wrath and fire, and even in the heart of Semberholme the daemonfey or their minions might strike.

Araevin soon found that the Isle was not large at all, little more than a small, rocky retreat nestled close to the northern shore of forest-guarded Lake Sember. It was an old place, a sacred place. He could feel the deep forgotten magic that slumbered beneath its ivy-grown colonnades and fragrant trees. In the days when Semberholme had been the heart of an elven kingdom, the small islet in the forest lake had served as its tower of high magic, and the stones, trees, and waters still dreamed of spells from days long past.

The soft breeze strengthened and shifted, whispering in the boughs of the white sycamores that grew among the ruins. Araevin climbed a winding set of stone stairs and found himself at the island's little hilltop, in an open shrine or chamber formed by a ring-shaped colonnade surrounding a floor of old moss-grown marble.

"I am here," he said to the old stones, and he composed himself to wait.

As it turned out, he did not wait for very long at all. Only a few minutes after he arrived, a feather-light touch of powerful sorcery caught his attention. Araevin glanced around the colonnaded shrine, and fixed his eyes on an old archway in the ruins. A silvery light blossomed in the arch. Then a slender sun elf woman in a stately robe of white stepped out of the light and into the Isle's ancient close. She looked around at the ivy-wreathed pillars and the softly rustling sycamores, pausing in the doorway.

"I have not set foot on the Isle of Reverie in four hundred years," she said softly, drawing a deep breath of the fragrant summer night.

"Good evening, High Mage Kileontheal," Araevin replied.

Kileontheal stepped away from the portal, and another elf followed her—a silver-haired moon elf in a simple gray silk tunic, whose dark eyes danced with warmth and wry humor.

"High Mage Anfalen," Araevin said, offering a shallow bow.

Anfalen nodded back at him and moved aside, joining Kileontheal. After him came another sun elf, the Grand Mage Breithel Olithir. Olithir wore elegant robes of green and gold, and carried the tall white staff of Evermeet's chief wizard. The grand mage inclined his head to Araevin as he stepped through, and Araevin bowed in response.

The grand mage has come? Araevin wondered. He did not think he had ever heard of a grand mage leaving Evermeet, even for a short time, but then again, he hadn't known many grand mages.

"Grand Mage. I am honored," Araevin began. "I did not mean to summon you from your duties on Evermeet. I would have been happy to journey to Evermeet to speak with you."

"This is probably better, Mage Teshurr," Olithir answered. Behind him the portal's silver light faded, leaving the four elves alone in the shadows beneath the white trees and old stones. "We would prefer that you do not attempt to set foot in Evermeet for now."

Araevin had not expected that. He stared at Olithir in amazement, and realized that the grand mage was thoroughly warded by subtle and powerful spell-shields. So, too, were Kileontheal and Anfalen.

"What?" Araevin managed. "But why?"

"Some among the high mages believe that the Nightstar has mastered you, and that you are a very clever Dlardrageth high mage who has managed to fool us all by walking around in Araevin's body," Anfalen answered. "High Mage Haldreithen has petitioned for Queen Amlaruil to ban you by royal edict, but I don't think she would do that without giving you an opportunity to respond first. Still, we think you should stay away from Evermeet for a time."

"I am standing here before you," Araevin said. He reached into his shirt and drew out the *selukiira* that had once been the Nightstar. In place of the virulent lambent hue the gemstone had once possessed, it gleamed with a pure white radiance. "This is what remains of the Nightstar. Look at me. Handle the stone for yourself. Do you think that I am Saelethil Dlardrageth?"

Kileontheal approached Araevin. Small and frail as she appeared, to Araevin's eyes the power in her blazed like a bonfire. She studied his features for a long moment, frowning a little as she took in the aura that played faintly over his skin and the opalescent brilliance of his eyes. They were no longer blank orbs of many-colored light, as they had been for a time after Araevin had completed the *telmiirkara neshyrr,* but his irises still shimmered with a striking, shifting hue that few others could look at for long. Araevin had taken to wearing hoods for the comfort of the people around him.

"I cannot read your heart," she whispered. "What have you done to yourself, Araevin?"

He had thought long and hard about how to answer that question, if the high mages asked him. In the end he could see that nothing except the truth would serve.

"I performed a rite devised by the star elf Morthil, once the Grand Mage of Sildëyuir. He was a student of Ithraides of Arcorar. The rite has fitted me to wield high magic in a tradition that Evermeet has forgotten."

The three high mages did not look at each other, but

Araevin felt the swift, subtle exchange of thoughts among them. *If I had achieved high magic by following their way I would understand what they are saying,* he told himself. *But it seems that my path has led me in a different direction.*

The Evermeetian mages finished their silent conversation. "There is a good reason why our high magic spells require more than one high mage, Araevin," the grand mage said. "Our spells *require* consensus, cooperation. No one person should have the responsibility of wielding such power. Do you not see how dangerous you have become? How can you resist the temptation to act when you can, instead of when you must?"

"I had little choice," Araevin countered. "The *telmiirkara neshyrr* gave Ithraides the power to defeat the daemonfey when they first arose in Arcorar, more than five thousand years ago. How else could we hope to defeat Sarya and her corruption of our old mythals?"

"Haven't you simply emulated the methods of our enemies by suiting yourself to wield high magic as they do?" Anfalen asked.

"I cannot unlearn what I have learned, High Mage. All I can do is put my knowledge to the best use I can find for it. What else would you have me do?"

"Make no works of high magic without our consent," Olithir said. "That would be a start."

Araevin sighed. "I can't make that promise, Grand Mage."

Olithir frowned, and the humor in Anfalen's eyes faded. "Tell him about the visions, Kileontheal," the moon elf said.

"Araevin, there is something more." The small sun elf folded her hands into her sleeves. "High Mage Isilfarrel has warned us that great danger attends you. She is a seer of no small skill, as you know. She doubts you because you have featured prominently in her visions of late. The specter of some awful disaster hangs over you, and she fears that you will bring it down on all of us."

Araevin stood silent for a moment, digesting her warning. "I can't say that I am pleased to hear that, but I am not surprised," he finally said. "That is why I asked to speak with you in the first place. I have discovered a terrible peril that threatens all of us, not just Cormanthor or the Crusade. Isilfarrel must have seen this, too."

"It seems that these days are full of terrible perils," Olithir said wearily. "Speak, then."

"Have you heard of the *Fhoeldin durr*?" Araevin asked.

Olithir and Anfalen frowned, shaking their heads, but Kileontheal nodded and said, "The Waymeet? It is a place where hundreds, perhaps thousands, of doorways meet. Magical portals, leading to many different places in Faerûn, the farther lands of Toril, and even other planes. Some human sages call it the Nexus."

"That is almost correct," said Araevin. "The Waymeet is not the place where the doorways meet; it is the *cause* of the doorways. Many of the old elven portals that crisscross Faerûn are emanations or earthly manifestations of the Waymeet. It is the Last Mythal of Aryvandaar."

Kileontheal looked up at Araevin. "I did not know that it was a work of Aryvandaar," she said.

"The high mages of Aryvandaar broke kingdoms and erased armies with the war-mythals they created," Araevin said. "The *Fhoeldin durr* was their final work, perhaps their greatest work."

"But how does the Waymeet present an imminent peril?" Anfalen asked. "If you are correct, it has existed for ten thousand years, perhaps more, and its purpose is benign. Magical portals have linked elven kingdoms together for ages."

"It is not simply a device for creating portals," Araevin replied. "The Vyshaanti lords who ruled over Aryvandaar secretly made it into a weapon as well. Not only would the Waymeet allow Aryvandaaran armies to invade any land at any time, but any place one of the Waymeet portals touched could be attacked directly with destructive magic of awesome power. I believe the Vyshaanti created the Waymeet as a weapon of last resort. They would have laid waste to the world rather than admit defeat in the last Crown War."

The high mages frowned, thinking on his words. Araevin continued, "Some of the myriad portals surrounding Myth Drannor, and likely other old elven ruins as well, are constructs of the Aryvandaaran mythal. Sarya Dlardrageth has already mastered Myth Drannor's corrupted mythal. She is on the verge of gaining control of the Waymeet as well. If she does, she will be able to employ all of the device's powers, anywhere she wishes to. She could open doors between Evermeet and the Nine Hells, erase Evereska as if it had never existed, or shatter the wards and bonds of every vault and prison where we have entombed evil things since the world began. That is what we face, High Mages."

Kileontheal paled. Anfalen looked away to the moonlit waters, glinting beneath the trees, and Olithir stood still, his face graven from stone, before he raised his staff and took a half-step closer to Araevin. "Are you certain of this?" the grand mage demanded.

"The *selukiira* that was the Nightstar preserves lore inscribed by the Vyshaanti mages of ancient Aryvandaar. I know what Saelethil Dlardrageth knew about the Waymeet and its uses." Araevin hesitated, then added, "What I do not know is exactly how close Sarya is to gaining mastery over the device, or even how she is doing it. I had thought that the Nightstar was the only place where that lore was still preserved, but clearly she knows more than she did even a few tendays ago."

"What do you propose, then?" Kileontheal asked.

"I need more high mages to study the *selukiira*. Some of you will have to master what is in the Nightstar. I believe that we may be able to undo Sarya's manipulations if we combine the strength of Evermeet's cooperative high magic with the lore of ancient Aryvandaar."

Olithir frowned. "I am hesitant to do that without a very thorough study of the rite you performed and the risks involved."

"With all due respect, Grand Mage, I doubt that we have the time to deliberate on the issue. You have wasted days in debate over the question of whether to even hear me out. How much more time do you need?"

"Works of high magic are not to be rushed into, Araevin," Kileontheal said. "You have always lacked patience with us, but the damage that can be done with a moment's carelessness is unspeakable. We cannot trust your judgment alone in this matter."

Araevin took a deep breath and reminded himself to remain calm. "I understand that you have reason to doubt my judgment," he said. "But if a fool warns a village of a forest fire, it doesn't mean that the warning can be disregarded simply because he's a fool. I hope you don't think I am a fool, but even if you do, you must examine this for yourself. The Waymeet has the potential to cause terrible harm."

"We hear you, Araevin," Olithir said. The grand mage turned back to the stone archway through which the three high mages had come, and woke it again with a gesture and a whispered word. "We will do as you ask, and study this threat. I promise you that no other question has greater priority."

"Very well." Araevin stilled his protests, recognizing that it would not help to be any more insistent than he had been. "I would be eager to present the evidence in the *selukiira* to any who wish to see it."

"Haldreithen would warn us against any contact at all with that loregem," Olithir remarked.

"I am sure that he would, but I think I trust Araevin," Kileontheal said. She turned and inclined her head to Araevin. "Sweet water and light laughter until we meet again, High Mage."

Araevin smiled. "And to you, Kileontheal." He watched

the three Evermeetian wizards step back through the silver door, standing in the moonshadows beneath the sycamore trees. Then he found his way back down to the shore where the boat waited.

☙ ☙ ☙ ☙ ☙

At sunrise, Seiveril Miritar found Adresin's body.

The captain of the elflord's guard had died fighting alone, trapped in the wreckage of an old watchtower at Semberholme's eastern border. Seiveril couldn't begin to guess when Adresin had become separated from the banner, or how he had found his way to this silent ruin. But the manner of his death was all too clear. Cruelly thorned vines of purple-black had burst through his body, piercing him from the inside out. Nearby the foul winged bodies of two vrock demons lay hacked to pieces, attesting to the fury of Adresin's last fight.

"Vrock spores," murmured Starbrow. He shook his head and turned away, leaving unvoiced the thought that ached under Seiveril's heart like a dull knife: Gods, what an awful way to die. In the last few tendays Seiveril had seen far too many elves fall to the foul malevolence of demons and their ilk, each seemingly gifted with its own particular poison or black sorcery to end the lives of mortals. But spores that took root in living flesh and bored their way slowly through muscles, bones, and organs . . . it was hideous beyond belief.

"Burn the body where it lies," Seiveril said wearily to the survivors of his guard. "Be careful of the vines, or you may share his fate."

He followed Starbrow out of the old tower and into the clean woodland outside. When things were ready, he would go back in to speak the funeral prayers himself, but until then he needed to feel sunlight on his face and think of anything other than what the young warrior's last moments must have been like.

He found Starbrow leaning against a fallen menhir, absently oiling the long white blade of Keryvian. The sword had served its purpose a hundred times over since the Crusade had come to Cormanthor. Starbrow was strong for an elf, taller than most humans but almost as sturdy in his build. He also had the quickness of a cat and the best instincts for battle that Seiveril had ever seen in his own four hundred years. In the moon elf's hands, the ancient baneblade was a weapon without peer.

Starbrow looked up as Seiveril limped to his side. He brushed his russet hair from his eyes and said, "We fought well last night, Seiveril. You know that, don't you?"

"Apparently not well enough for Adresin." Seiveril drew off his armored gauntlets and reached up to loosen his pauldrons. He looked down at the greaves of his left leg, where a set of deep furrows had creased the elven steel—the mark of a canoloth's jaws. He'd been lucky not to have had his leg torn off.

For the better part of a month, ever since leading the Crusade into the forest of Cormanthor, Seiveril's host had endured battle after battle—skirmishes against the daemonfey, clashes with the mercenaries of the Sembians, a smashing blow struck against the Zhentarim, and endless running fights against the demons, devils, yugoloths, and other infernal monsters conjured up out of the pits of the nether planes and set loose by Sarya Dlardrageth. The past night's battle had been a desperate struggle to repel a warband of fiendish creatures from the refuge of Semberholme, and Seiveril's elves and their Dalesfolk allies had driven off the raid. But he did not doubt that another one would follow in a day or two.

"Is there any end to this, my friend?"

Starbrow looked up sharply. "If you give in to despair, Seiveril, there will be exactly one end to this. I didn't come back to see another Weeping War."

"I do not mean to despair, Starbrow. But something has to change." He ran a hand through his silver-red hair, and grimaced. "Sooner or later, you'd think that even the Hells must be emptied."

The clatter of horses' hooves caught Seiveril's attention, and he looked up as a pair of riders cantered into the clearing by the tower. His daughter Ilsevele, dressed in the colors of a captain of the queen's spellarchers, reined in her mount.

"I've been looking all over for you, Father," she said.

"Ilsevele," Seiveril said warmly. He pushed himself upright and embraced his daughter after she dismounted. "I am glad that you are not hurt. And you too, Lord Theremen."

"Lord Miritar," the ruler of Deepingdale replied. "You should have sent to us. We could have spared a few swords for you." Theremen Ulath was a handsome man whose pale skin and fine features clearly showed more than a little elf blood. The folk of Deepingdale had welcomed the Crusade's arrival in the great forest with few reservations. For his own part, Seiveril had been somewhat surprised to find a strong, secure, and friendly Dale at his back when the Crusade marched into Semberholme. Deepingdale's archers and riders were a welcome addition to the Crusade's strength. Lord Theremen swung himself down from his warhorse and clasped Seiveril's arm.

Ilsevele frowned at Seiveril's awkward stance, and her eyes fell on the bloody creases in his greaves. "Father, you're hurt!"

"It is nothing." Seiveril settled himself back on the fallen menhir. "I am afraid that there were many who needed my healing spells more than I did last night. I take it things were quiet on the eastern marches?"

"For us, yes," Theremen answered. "But my scouts reported that the Sembians entrenched in Battledale had a furious time of it. The daemonfey aren't shy about sharing their fury with everyone around them, it seems."

"Sarya hates us more, but the Sembians are an easier target," Starbrow remarked. "If there's a strategy to her attacks, I can't see it. If I were her, I'd choose one enemy at a time."

In the ruins of the watchtower, a pillar of gray smoke started up. Ilsevele glanced over, and her face tightened. "Who fell?" she asked.

"Adresin," Seiveril answered quietly. "We were separated in the fighting last night. We found him only a short time ago."

Ilsevele looked down at the ground. "I am sorry, Father. He was a courageous warrior, faithful and good. I know you will miss him."

"He will not be the last, I fear," Seiveril said. He sighed and looked away from the smoke twisting into the sky. "Well, we have gone to ground in Semberholme, and Sarya seems unable or unwilling to push us any farther. So what do we do now? How do we bring some sort of hope out of this horror?"

"Seek aid from Cormyr?" said Ilsevele. "I would think that Alusair might be disposed to help us."

"You forget, we are currently at odds with Sembia as well as the daemonfey," Theremen said. "Alusair can't afford to be drawn into a war against Sembia by helping us in the Dales. Cormyr is still recovering from the troubles attending Azoun's death."

"Find Archendale's price and buy their help?" said Starbrow.

"You face the same problem," Theremen said. "The swords of Archendale don't want to stand opposite Sembia unless Sembia itself threatens them."

Seiveril looked up into the smoke-streaked sunrise. "We can't deal with the Shadovar, not after the way they treated Evereska. Is there some friendly great power nearby that I am forgetting about, Lord Ulath? Otherwise I am out of ideas."

A distant birdsong filled the silence as the elves and the Dalelord examined their own thoughts. Then, slowly, Ilsevele said, "We have to make common cause with Sembia. It's the only course of action that makes sense."

"Not while they're holding three Dales under their fist,"

Theremen countered. "I will not countenance any deal that concedes Battledale, Featherdale, or Tasseldale. We dare not feed that beast, not even once. They'd be swallowed whole in a generation, and we'd be feeding Mistledale or Deepingdale to Sembia next."

"Better the Sembians than the daemonfey," Starbrow pointed out.

"Some of my neighbors would say that it's better to die sword in hand than to live on as chattel in their own homes," Theremen snapped.

Seiveril raised his hand for calm. "It's an academic question anyway, isn't it? Sembia and Hillsfar have determined to carve up the Dales between them. We simply can't go along with that."

"But that was before the daemonfey fell out with Hillsfar," said Ilsevele. "We don't know if that accord still stands, do we? And even if it does, well, I'm willing to lay aside my differences with the Sembians long enough to end the daemonfey threat. How do we know that the Sembians wouldn't feel the same? After all, Sarya's triumph would be a disaster that none of us could stand for."

The lord of Deepingdale shook his head. "The Sembians hold more Dales than the daemonfey at the moment."

"But we don't know that the Sembians would insist on keeping those lands," Ilsevele answered. "As far as we know, they might be asking themselves what price *we* will insist on before we consent to aid *them*."

Starbrow studied Ilsevele for a long moment, deep in thought. "You know, Seiveril, we would find it harder to fight a war with the Sembians once we've fought alongside them. If Ilsevele is right, they'd find it hard too."

"But we would have to, if they tried to absorb the Dales their soldiers hold," Theremen warned. "What if it proved easier to lay down our swords and let them have what they've taken, instead of making them give it back?"

"I hear you," Starbrow said. "But we don't have the strength to beat the daemonfey and the Sembians both, so there's damned little we can say about Sembians in Featherdale right now anyway. As long as things stay the way they are, we aren't about to throw the Sembians out."

Seiveril leaned forward to rest his head in his hands, thinking. He hadn't picked the fight with the Sembians, and it made him sick to his stomach to even begin a conversation with humans who'd seen fit to throw an army between him and Myth Drannor. But for all the maneuvering, marching, and sharp skirmishes of the past two months, he had yet to try the Crusade against the Sembian army. And the real challenge thrown in his face had come from Hillsfar, not Sembia.

Corellon, guide me, he prayed silently. The Sembians have feared and envied us for a thousand years. How can we hope to set that aside now? He straightened and looked up at the sunrise again, watching the smoke of the burning tower—Adresin's funeral pyre, he reminded himself—glowing in the early light.

"Seiveril?" Starbrow asked quietly. "What do you think?"

"I agree with Ilsevele," Seiveril said. "We will send an embassy to the Sembians, and see if we can set aside our quarrel long enough to defeat the daemonfey. I will leave tomorrow."

"No, not you, Father," Ilsevele said. "The Crusade would be lost without you. I will go and speak for you."

"Absolutely not!" Seiveril stood up so fast that his injured leg almost buckled under him. He grunted in pain and sat back down again almost as fast as he had stood up. "The Sembians may prove treacherous, Ilsevele! The Hillsfarians certainly are. I can't let anyone else shoulder the risk."

"No, she's right, Seiveril," Starbrow sighed. "You can't go, and if you can't, there is no one better than Ilsevele. Besides, it was her idea."

"If the Sembians used her as a hostage against me, there is nothing I would not do."

"I know," said Starbrow. "I will go with her and make

sure that does not happen. I promise you, my friend, I will keep her safe."

Ilsevele crossed her arms. "I don't think—"

"I didn't ask you," Starbrow said firmly. "I'm going for your father's sake. Now, when do you want to leave?"

⊙ ⊙ ⊙ ⊙ ⊙

Sunlight and warm pine scent filled the forest glade when Araevin appeared. He ghosted into solidity, his hand resting on the battered old stone marker that stood in the center of the clearing. He felt the mossy stone cool and damp under his fingertips and allowed himself a small smile.

"I suppose they haven't barred me yet," he murmured.

It was late afternoon in Evermeet, a perfect summer day with just the faintest whisper of the ever-present sea somewhere far off beyond the forest. The glade stood high in the rugged hills overlooking the isle's northern shore, not far from the House of Cedars, where Araevin had grown up. He closed his eyes and inhaled deeply, momentarily lost in the memories of childhood years spent wandering in these hills.

"Well, this is a pleasant enough spot, but I was beginning to wonder why you'd asked me to come here."

Araevin turned at the sound of the voice. Quastarte, the ancient loremaster of Tower Reilloch, sat with his back to a tree trunk, resting in the shade. Araevin smiled and waved in the human manner.

"Quastarte!" he called. "I did not know if you would puzzle out my sending or not."

"They call me a loremaster for a reason," the old sun elf muttered. He squinted, looking closer at Araevin. "Now, why the secret summons to this place? And what has happened to your eyes? Unless I miss my guess, you have walked some strange roads indeed since we last met."

"First question first," Araevin answered. "I have been asked to stay away from Evermeet for a time. Given that,

Final Gate • 21

it hardly seemed like a good idea to rap on your door in Tower Reilloch."

"But this seemed like a less flagrant act of defiance?"

Araevin shrugged. "I needed to speak with you, and I felt that it could not wait." He sat down by a boulder near the loremaster, and dropped his rucksack to the ground at his feet. He rooted around in the sack and drew out a wineskin and two wooden mugs. "I have much to tell you, and I hope you will share some of your wisdom with me."

"I have no other business to attend this afternoon," Quastarte said. He poured himself some of the wine, and settled back against the tree. "Start at the beginning."

"That would be about eleven thousand years ago. . . ." Araevin drew in a deep breath, and he told Quastarte the story of his search for the secret of the *telmiirkara neshyrr,* the strange twilight quest in the fading world of Sildëyuir, and his subsequent conquest of Saelethil Dlardrageth's malevolent presence in the *selukiira* known as the Nightstar. He explained what he had learned from the ancient loregem and how that had illuminated what he had seen of Sarya's works in his visit to Myth Drannor's mythal. The better part of the afternoon passed as Araevin recounted his tale to the loremaster, while Quastarte listened attentively, frowned, and swirled the last swallow of wine in the bottom of his cup, thinking hard on Araevin's story.

"And you spoke with the high mages?" he asked Araevin after the mage finished.

"Yes. I asked them to help me expel Sarya's influence from Myth Drannor and the Waymeet, but they wish to study the threat more carefully before they employ high magic against the daemonfey."

"And you think that no such study is necessary?"

"I do not think that we have the luxury of deliberation. If Sarya succeeds while we still are pondering how to stop her, there will be no end to the damage she causes." Araevin took a swallow of his own wine. "I can't overthrow her by myself, and I can't wait for the help of the high mages."

"And so one old loremaster will have to serve in place of a circle of Evermeet's most powerful mages." Quastarte set down his cup. "All right, then. As I see it, Araevin, you need the Gatekeeper's Crystal."

"The same device Sarya used to open Nar Kerymhoarth, and free her fey'ri legion? It's powerful enough to destroy the Waymeet?"

"I suppose it might be, but that's not what it's for. The Gatekeeper's Crystal is the key to the Waymeet."

Araevin looked at him with a blank expression.

The loremaster shook his head. "See, that's what you get for drinking your knowledge from ancient loregems. If you had studied honestly, you would know this. The Gatekeeper's Crystal is not just a weapon, Araevin. It is intimately connected to the Waymeet. Now, we never had the whole crystal at Tower Reilloch, only one of the three shards, so I never had the opportunity to experiment with it. But we learned long ago that the crystal we guarded drew its power from the Waymeet."

"I never knew," Araevin said.

Quastarte sighed. "Trust me, I understand. I did not know that the Waymeet itself was a mythal of old Aryvandaar until you told me just now, and I have had centuries to figure it out."

"Sarya Dlardrageth holds the Gatekeeper's Crystal. I doubt she would let me borrow it to deal with the Waymeet."

"She had the crystal when she rent the wards of the Nameless Dungeon, yes. But she has it no more."

"How do you know?" Araevin demanded.

"It's the limitation of the crystal. When its full power is employed—as Sarya did when she opened Nar Kerymhoarth—its component shards fly apart and scatter themselves across the face of the world. She has not had the crystal since the day she freed her fey'ri."

Araevin leaped to his feet, and gathered up his rucksack. "Thank you, old friend. I think you've given me more hope than I've had in a long time."

Quastarte rose more slowly. "If you intend to assemble the Gatekeeper's Crystal again, start at the Nameless Dungeon. When the weapon shatters, it often leaves one of its component shards near the place where it was last employed."

Araevin clasped Quastarte's arm. "If you could neglect to mention to the high mages that I was here, I would appreciate it."

The old loremaster gestured at the forested hillside. "I went for a long walk in the woods on a fine summer day, and that is all. No one needs to know any more than that."

CHAPTER TWO

21 Flamerule, the Year of Lightning Storms

At sunset of the day following his illicit visit to Evermeet, Araevin rode into Highmoon, the chief settlement of Deepingdale. It was a handsome town that climbed a small hill alongside the East Way, the road that skirted the southern flanks of the great forest. Stands of trees hundreds of years old shaded much of the town, and lanterns suspended from the branches gave the place the look of an elven town—which was not far from the truth. Those few elves of Cormanthyr who hadn't Retreated had lingered in the forests near Deepingdale, befriending and mixing with the humans of the Dale. Only in Aglarond had Araevin encountered a land where elf and human ways were so intertwined.

He stopped by an inn advertising itself as the Oak and Spear, and swung himself down from his saddle with a pat for his horse's neck. The Oak and Spear at least seemed to be doing a fair business; music drifted from the taproom's open door into the warm night. Araevin led his horse into the stable, took his saddlebags, and headed into the common room. A single lutist strummed her instrument softly by the cold fireplace. Few Deepingdalesfolk were drinking that night; most of the able-bodied men were standing guard at the Dale's borders or serving with Theremen Ulath up in the forests around Lake Sember.

"About time you got here!"

Araevin glanced to his right, and found Maresa Rost leaning back in her chair as she nursed a small goblet of wine. The genasi wore crimson, as she often did; it made for a striking contrast with her perfect white complexion and drifting halo of silver-white hair. She had commandeered a big round table in an alcove of the taproom. Beside her sat the Aglarondan Jorin Kell Harthan, who had guided Araevin and his friends to the secret realm of Sildëyuir, and next to him the star elf Nesterin, who had accompanied them back to Faerûn. Donnor Kerth, the Lathanderite crusader, sat opposite, his fist around a mug of ale.

"We were starting to wonder if you had forgotten about us," Maresa said.

"I had to confer with some friends in Semberholme, and in Evermeet. I hurried back as quickly as I could." Araevin took a seat at the table next to Donnor and poured himself some wine from a flagon on the table. "Has Ilsevele arrived yet?"

"No, we have not seen her for several days," Nesterin said. The star elf was dressed in pale gray and white, with silver embroidery at the collar and sleeves. He attracted more than a few odd looks in the Oak and Spear. Deepingdalesfolk were familiar with most kindred of the elf race, but star elves were a different story. "As far as I know, she is with her father."

Araevin glanced at the door, half-expecting Ilsevele to follow on his heels, but she did not appear. "She knows we are gathering here," he mused. "I suppose she will be here when she can."

"What news of the daemonfey army?" Donnor asked. He was a thickly built human almost as tall as Araevin himself, but better than eighty pounds heavier than the sun elf. He kept his scalp shaved down to stubble, and wore a closely cropped beard. His tunic was emblazoned with the sunrise emblem of Lathander, Lord of the Dawn, the deity to whom Kerth had pledged his sword and his service.

"Sarya's demons and devils harry the borders of Semberholme every day. I don't know if or when Seiveril will try to take the battle to the daemonfey again."

"Glad we're here," Maresa muttered. "Wars are bad for the health, you know."

"We're not done with ours," Donnor growled. "The daemonfey have much to answer for."

"I haven't forgotten." The genasi hid her glower in her goblet, drinking deeply.

Jorin looked across the table to Araevin. "What did your 'friends' say about the threat you perceived in Sildëyuir?" the half-elf asked in a low voice. "Can they counter it?"

"They are going to study the question."

Nesterin raised an eyebrow. "I thought the matter was urgent."

"In my estimation, it is. But my friends in Evermeet have always been hesitant to move recklessly. They do not think it wise to exercise their power until they know precisely what will happen when they do."

"No one can foresee all outcomes. If you wait until you think you can, you will never act at all," the star elf said. "Sometimes it is wiser not to wait."

"That is what I fear. As my human friends like to say, he who hesitates is lost."

"So what are we going to do while your 'friends' are thinking things over?" Maresa asked.

Araevin allowed himself a small smile. Maresa had struck the nail on the head. "I think I know how to slam

Final Gate • 27

shut the doors that Sarya and her allies are trying to open. At the beginning of this war, Sarya used a weapon called the Gatekeeper's Crystal to open the ancient dungeon of Nar Kerymhoarth, freeing her fey'ri legion. I can use that same device to stop her from destroying the boundaries between the planes."

"How do we get the device away from her?" Jorin asked.

"We may not have to. Quastarte—one of my friends on Evermeet—reminded me that the crystal does not remain intact after use. It breaks into its component shards, three of them, and hurls its pieces across the world, sometimes even across the planes. I mean to find it, assemble it again, and use it to seal the Waymeet—the Last Mythal of Aryvandaar."

"These three pieces could be anywhere?" Donnor asked. "Where do we begin?"

"The place where Sarya Dlardrageth last employed the crystal. The Gatekeeper's Crystal often leaves at least one of its shards near the place where it was last used. It's not much, but it's a start."

"Back to the High Forest again." Maresa shook her head. "You don't let the moss grow under your feet, do you, Araevin?"

"We'll retrace our steps through the portals back to Myth Glaurach. I don't think that Nar Kerymhoarth is more than two days' ride from there." Araevin glanced at each of his companions, and added, "It may be a long, dull, or dangerous task to reassemble the Gatekeeper's Crystal. None of you should feel obligated to come with me."

"Is this the best way you can think of to slip a knife between Sarya's ribs?" Maresa asked. Araevin nodded. "Then I'm in."

"And I," said Donnor.

"Sildëyuir is in your debt, Araevin Teshurr," Nesterin answered. "I will help you."

Araevin looked to Jorin. The Aglarondan shrugged. "I haven't traveled these lands before. I have a notion that

I'd like to see more of the west, or wherever your search leads you."

"Thank you, my friends," Araevin said. "We'll set out first thing in the morning."

He raised his goblet to his companions and drank deeply; the others followed suit. Briefly, he explained as much as he felt comfortable telling them about the Waymeet and the crystal. He glanced at the door often, expecting Ilsevele to appear at any moment, but still she did not come. Finally, it grew late, and the companions said their goodnights to one another.

The innkeeper showed Araevin to his room, and Araevin spent some time double-checking his belongings, making sure that he was ready for another long journey. Then he stretched out on the bed to rest, slipping in and out of Reverie. He did not need as much as he used to—an odd side-effect of the *telmiirkara neshyrr,* one that he just as soon would have done without, since it left him wakeful and alert most of the night. Eventually he found himself simply sitting at the window seat in the little room, gazing out over the sleeping town while he grappled with wheels, fonts, and bonds of magic in his mind, reflecting on the artifices of high magic he had encountered in the last few tendays.

Shortly after midnight, his reflections were disturbed by the lonely clip-clop of a horse's hooves in the street outside his window. He shook himself and looked down. A rider in green approached, riding a small dapple-gray mare. The rider stopped before the Oak and Spear, and drew back her hood. Ilsevele shook out her copper-red hair and turned her face up to him.

"Keeping watch for me?" she asked with a small smile.

"Simply taking in the night," he told her. "I'll be down in a moment."

He slipped down from the window seat, pulled on his boots, and headed down the stairs to the dark and empty common room. Ilsevele came in a moment later, still dressed in her riding cloak.

"Do you want me to rouse the innkeeper?" Araevin asked. "It's late, but they might have something you could eat."

"Don't trouble the fellow. I am not hungry." She hesitated in the doorway, studying the room. "Are the others here?"

"Yes. We were only waiting for you." Araevin took her in his arms, and held her close, but she returned his embrace half-heartedly. When he frowned at her, she disentangled herself from his arms and stepped back. "What is it, Ilsevele?"

"Araevin," she said, "I cannot go with you."

"What? But why?"

"I have something else I need to do. I am leaving in the morning for the Sembian camp in Battledale. I am going to try to persuade them to make peace with us, so that we can turn our full attention against the daemonfey."

"It's too dangerous," he said automatically. "You would be too valuable as a hostage. The Sembians will try to use you against your father."

"I do not think they will." Ilsevele raised her hand to forestall his response. "If the daemonfey and the Sembians were still allied, you would certainly be right. But Sarya turned her demons and devils against the Sembians, too. We have a common foe, and I understand that counts for much in human diplomacy."

"Ilsevele, you don't understand—"

"Starbrow will come along to safeguard me, Araevin. And I'll have a trick or two up my sleeve, just in case. But we have to take the chance that the Sembians can be reasoned with, before all the Dales are laid to waste."

He started to protest but gave up with a grimace. "Very well. But promise me you will be careful, Ilsevele."

"Only if you do the same." She smiled thinly. "Do not worry for me, Araevin. Our paths will cross again before long."

"I am not as certain of that as I once was." He sighed and brushed a hand over his eyes. "We are heading back to the High Forest."

"The High Forest? Why?"

"Because the Gatekeeper's Crystal—or a piece of it, anyway—may remain somewhere near Nar Kerymhoarth. I think I will need it to deal with Sarya's wards at Myth Drannor, and her influence over the Waymeet." He quickly explained what he had learned about the Waymeet and the disaster he feared. "Will you stay to see us off?" he finished. "Morning is not long now."

"I can't. We are riding for Battledale at first light. I need to get back."

"Maresa will take it hard. She likes you more than she lets on."

"I am fond of her, too. Take good care of them, Araevin." Ilsevele allowed him to embrace her one more time, and she turned to go. But in the doorway, her steps slowed, and she looked back over her shoulder at him. "Araevin, there is one more thing . . . I heard that you spoke with the high mages on the Isle of Reverie."

"I did."

"I heard that they are giving careful consideration to your warning, and are deliberating on the best way to meet the danger you have seen."

Araevin briefly wondered how the story was reaching Ilsevele. High mages rarely discussed their business with others. Could it be Amlaruil herself? Ilsevele had served as a captain in the Queen's Guard, after all. He decided that it would be unseemly to interrogate his betrothed over the question.

"I don't know anything about the course of their deliberations," he said, "but I hope they intend more than just talk."

"So instead of waiting or conferring with the high mages, you are setting out after the Gatekeeper's Crystal immediately?" Disapproval gathered in her face.

"I don't think we have time to wait," Araevin answered. He paced in a small circle, trying to keep his frustration with the glacial pace of the high mages to himself, and not entirely succeeding. "While the high mages debate and ponder the right course of action, I feel doom approaching. Someone has to act now."

"That is always the way it is with you," Ilsevele murmured. "Something is always the only thing that matters. You are almost human in that, Araevin. You lose yourself in the moment. You always have, and since you . . . *changed* . . . in Mooncrescent Tower, I think it has become even more pronounced."

"This is important," he protested. "You know what I've seen. We can't defeat the daemonfey until we can deal with Sarya's wards in Myth Drannor, and we can't defeat the wards without the Gatekeeper's Crystal."

"You cannot even see it anymore, can you?" Ilsevele was as pale and perfect as a memory in the moonlight. "I can't feel your presence, Araevin. You are standing before me, but I don't feel your thoughts, I can't sense your mood. You have become a wall that I cannot see through."

Araevin shrugged awkwardly. "It may pass," he offered. It was true enough that he did not sense her as clearly as he had before the *telmiirkara neshyrr*. All elves shared a bond, a communion of sorts, that allowed them to feel what other elves nearby felt, especially those whom they loved. It was not unknown for the link to wax or wane in strength. Doubtless it had something to do with changing his nature to suit himself for high magic, but what choice had he had? He took a step toward her and reached for her hand. "Come with me, Ilsevele. I need you at my side."

"You haven't needed me in a long time, Araevin—and my place is here, at least for now." She touched the side of his face, and she drew back. "I think I should go now. Good luck in your journeys. I will pray for your success."

"Ilsevele, wait—" Araevin began, but she just shook her head and left him standing in the doorway.

❂ ❂ ❂ ❂ ❂

"This," snarled Sarya Dlardrageth, "is an abomination." She paced fretfully, her eyes aglow with hate. Sarya's face was heartbreakingly beautiful, her supple figure the very image of desire, but in her anger—and Sarya was indeed angered—her demonic heritage was inescapable. Ruby skin and great black wings overwhelmed her noble elf's features, and her slender serpentine tail coiled and uncoiled with agitation. "Tell me, Mardeiym, why haven't you destroyed it yet?"

Mardeiym Reithel was a lord of the fey'ri, and Sarya's most trusted general. Unlike many of Sarya's minions, he knew her well enough to sense that her anger was not directed at him, and he did not quail before her rage.

"Strong old magic guards it, my queen. I would not presume to destroy something of such antiquity without consulting you first."

"Antiquity?" Sarya snorted. "I am four times as old as this shameful stone. Don't speak to me of its antiquity!"

The daemonfey queen stood before the old monument the humans called simply the Standing Stone. It stood thirty miles south of Myth Drannor, at the spot where the road leading south to Sembia met the Moonsea Ride. Twenty feet tall, the gray obelisk was covered with old runes and hidden Elvish script that proudly—*proudly!* Sarya marveled—described how the great elven realm of Cormanthyr had given over the governance of its unforested lands to dirt-grubbing human squatters.

The flyspeck lands known as the Dales dated back to that day, growing up in and among the vales of the mighty forest . . . and the coronals of Myth Drannor had given the humans their *blessing*. Of course, time had demonstrated the folly of that decision. The coronals of Myth Drannor were dead, and their kingdom was no more. But Sarya could see clearly that this shameful monument in front of her marked the day that the elves' decline in Cormanthor had begun.

"Dlardrageth coronals would never have descended to such degrading pacts with humans," she spat. With a flick of her wings, she turned her back on the Standing Stone and confronted her chief general. "You have now consulted me. Have it pulled down and broken into rubble. Use whatever power is necessary to overcome its wards. I never want to see this . . . emblem of weakness again."

"It shall be as you say, my queen." Mardeiym bowed his horned head in acknowledgment. He paused, and added, "The drow emissary still awaits."

"I absolutely will not receive him standing in front of *that*," she said, flicking her tail at the Standing Stone. "He is at the ruined keep?"

"He is, my lady," Mardeiym affirmed.

"Come with me, then," Sarya said.

She reached out and took Mardeiym's hand, then teleported away from the road. There was an instant of darkness, of cold, and she stood in the courtyard of a ruined human keep, long abandoned. The place stood atop a rocky hill a few miles from the Standing Stone, overlooking the road. Less than a month before Seiveril Miritar had used that very keep for his headquarters while he hesitated on the doorstep of Myth Drannor, but since then the leader of Evermeet's Crusade cowered in the supposed safety of Semberholme, a hundred miles to the south. Well, she would deprive him of that refuge soon enough.

A party of four drow waited for her, surrounded by her fey'ri and yugoloths. It was a blazingly hot day, but the dark elves wore long hoods to shade their eyes. Bright sunlight was more than a little uncomfortable to them; they much preferred the gloom of the forest, or better yet, the cool darkness underground. Sarya could have invited them to step into the shadows of the keep's remaining buildings, but she decided that she had no particular need to make the drow comfortable.

She approached the dark elves, and studied them for a time. "I am Sarya Dlardrageth," she said. "To whom am I speaking?"

One of the drow limped forward. A brace of leather and iron encased his left leg. "I am Jezz, of House Jaelre," he answered. "Sometimes called Jezz the Lame, for reasons which should be obvious. These are my kinsmen Tzarrat, Dreszk, and Zilzin."

Sarya frowned in distaste. Before the ancient quarrel of House Dlardrageth with the rulers of Arcorar, before the war of great Aryvandaar against the lesser elf nations, all other elves had stood against the drow. Daemonfey and drow had rarely met, as far as she knew, but she had no reason to think well of the traitorous dark elves.

"I see you have earned the special disapproval of your spider-goddess," she said, looking at the clumsy brace. Any highborn drow should have had the resources to have such an injury healed with magic.

Jezz gave a short bark of laughter. "Well, I suppose Lolth doesn't think well of me at all, or any of my kin, for that matter. We turned our backs on the Spider Queen centuries ago, and follow Vhaeraun instead."

"Ah. You are the drow who hide in the Elven Court, then."

"We are. The cursed light-elves abandoned this realm; we decided to claim it for our own."

"I think you will find that I have already done so."

Jezz shrugged. "We are a practical race, Lady Sarya. We recognize strength when we see it. You are clearly the master of Myth Drannor, at least for now."

"For now, and for centuries to come." Sarya folded her arms and flicked her tail in irritation. "Now what is it that you want with me, drow?"

"We want to come to some understanding with you," Jezz answered. "We share a common enemy, after all. Should the Crusade succeed in evicting you from Myth Drannor, we have no illusions about who would be next. It would seem to be simply logical to agree to leave each other in peace . . . or, possibly, to consider how we profitably might work together against our mutual foes."

Final Gate • 35

Sarya snorted. "In other words, you have determined that I hold the winning hand, and so now you hope to share in the spoils."

Jezz inclined his head. "As I said, Lady Sarya—we are a practical race."

"Why should I share my conquests with you, drow? Why should I not have you thrown from the battlements for your presumption?"

"How many more enemies do you need, Sarya Dlardrageth?" the drow countered. "We do not have your strength, but we have *some* strength, and I think you would find us a more difficult conquest than the fat human farmers of Mistledale. If you are so strong that you can crush us at the same time that you fight against Sembia, Hillsfar, the Dales, and Seiveril Miritar's army, then you should do so, and dictate your terms to us. If, perhaps, you think it might be prudent to save just a little more of your strength for your true enemies, then hear me out."

The daemonfey queen measured the drow lord, thinking. Mardeiym would certainly advise her to avoid starting more wars, at least until they successfully concluded one of the wars they already had. The forest drow were not as strong as her fey'ri legion, but they could muster hundreds of skilled and stealthy warriors . . . at the very least, it would seem to make sense to leave them alone in the eastern forest, if they were willing to concede the rest of Cormanthor to her.

Besides, agreements could always be amended later, she reminded herself. She would not permit the drow to remain in Cormanthor unless they accepted her suzerainty, but that was a question she did not have to resolve that day.

"I agree that we need not fight each other," Sarya told the drow. "I will not send my legions against your holds in the Elven Court. And I admit that I am intrigued by the possibilities of cooperation."

Jezz sketched an awkward bow. "Then may I suggest that we find some place out of the sun to further develop our arrangement?"

◈ ◈ ◈ ◈ ◈

From Highmoon, Araevin and his small company rode north, to a lonely mausoleum in the depths of the Sember woods. Seven tendays past they had discovered the place while exploring a network of magical portals whose entrance was buried under the former daemonfey stronghold at Myth Glaurach. Seiveril Miritar had used the portals to traverse a thousand miles in the course of a few short days, bringing the Crusade from the Delimbiyr Vale to the deep woods of Cormanthor. Araevin retraced their steps, passing back to the long-abandoned City of Scrolls by means of the magical doorways that he and his friends had explored.

They found Myth Glaurach guarded by a company of wood elves from the nearby High Forest, reinforced by several wizards of Silverymoon's spell-guard. The daemonfey had shown no sign of returning to their original stronghold, but the folk of the High Forest and the Silver Marches intended to make sure that evil did not return to the old city.

Araevin and his friends enjoyed a fine lantern-lit dinner under the sighing firs of the wood elf camp on Myth Glaurach's forested shoulders, and spent no small amount of time telling the tale of the Crusade's efforts in Cormanthor. After that, Araevin asked the wood elves about the best way to the old stronghold of Nar Kerymhoarth. They did not answer right away, but instead summoned a slender elf huntswoman to the feast. She was lithe and handsome, with copper skin and the russet hair of her people, which she wore in a single long braid behind her.

"I am Gaerradh," the wood elf said to Araevin. "You are Araevin? The mage who took this mythal from the daemonfey?"

"I am," Araevin answered. "These are my companions Maresa, Donnor, Nesterin, and Jorin. I understand you know the way to Nar Kerymhoarth?"

Gaerradh nodded. "I know the place well. I'm the one who discovered what the daemonfey did there."

"You were there?"

"Yes. That was several months ago, of course. The daemonfey magic ripped the place in half. It looked like a mountain giant had struck off a whole hillside with his axe."

"Did you see the daemonfey assault on the dungeon?"

"No, I came upon the scene about two days after they had left."

Maresa leaned forward. "I don't suppose you found a big magical crystal lying around, did you?"

Gaerradh looked at her blankly. "I am afraid I saw no such thing. What sort of crystal?"

The genasi sat back. "It was worth a try," she sighed.

"It is about this long—" Araevin held up his hands, six inches apart— "and pale white, with a hint of violet light in its depths."

"Is it important?

"I think so," said Araevin. He went on to sketch out what he knew of the Gatekeeper's Crystal, explaining how he hoped to use it to put an end to the manipulations of the daemonfey. "So, we hope to find a shard of the crystal somewhere near Nar Kerymhoarth. Can you tell us where to start?"

Gaerradh shook her head. "We keep people away from the place because it has always been dangerous. But your efforts speak for you, Araevin. If you need to go to Nar Kerymhoarth, I'll take you and your companions there."

"Thank you." Araevin bowed.

Gaerradh returned such a stiff and formal parody of a sun elf bow that he couldn't help but laugh. "Sun elves are so solemn about everything," she said with a smile. Then she hurried off while Maresa and Nesterin were still holding their sides, and even dour Donnor was laughing softly.

In the morning, they set out toward the southwest, leaving the tree-grown ruins of Myth Glaurach behind them. They left their mounts in the care of the elves there, since the terrain was better suited to travel afoot. For most of the day they picked their way through the steep foothills and stream-filled gorges of the Talons, the swift cold mountain streams that formed the headwaters of the mighty Delimbiyr River. Then they veered west and skirted the forest verge, staying well to the north of the fuming crevasse where Hellgate Keep once stood.

"Turlang the Treant stands watch over the place, but it isn't safe to go any nearer," Gaerradh explained. "The Scoured Legion of Kaanyr Vhok lurks in the pits deep below the ruins of the keep."

Gaerradh led them to a well-hidden wood elf shelter, concealed high in the branches of a mighty shadowtop, where they camped for the night. Then, a little after sunrise, they continued on their way. Satisfied that they'd circled far enough around Hellgate Keep, the wood elf turned southward and led them into the depths of the High Forest. Araevin was struck by how different the woodland was from the forests of Evermeet or even Cormanthor. The High Forest was *old,* with a high, thick canopy so dense that sunlight did not reach the forest floor. While summer in Cormanthor had been humid, even sweltering at times, the air beneath the mighty boles was so chilly and damp that he could not believe the month was Flamerule.

"The trees don't like us," Donnor muttered when they halted for a brief rest. "I can feel it."

"They sleep more deeply here than they do in the Yuirwood, but they dream of dark things," Jorin agreed. "If I were you, I would avoid giving them offense."

The Lathanderite grimaced and wrung out the hood of his cloak. "I won't speak ill of them if they extend the same courtesy to me."

Shortly before sunset, they finally reached the rocky tor of Nar Kerymhoarth, the Nameless Dungeon. A low hill of ancient stone rose up through the forest mantle, its sides draped with young evergreens. Without Gaerradh's aid, they might easily have missed it altogether. Approaching from the north, there was nothing to indicate that a buried vault lay beneath the hill. The wood elf led them around the base of the tor and finally brought them out into a valley between two arms of the hill.

"Here," said Gaerradh. "This is the place where the daemonfey opened Nar Kerymhoarth."

Araevin frowned. All he saw was a desolate clearing in the forest between the rocky arms of the hillside. But then he realized that the defile in which they stood was not a natural valley, but instead a titanic bite taken out of the hillside. Clover and blackberries covered much of the bare dirt, but shorn tree trunks marked the edges of the vast wound, and great boulders lay tumbled out of place all around them. The defile ended in a deep cleft in the hillside, where a dark cave mouth awaited.

"Let me guess," Maresa said. "In there? That would be our luck. Trolls, demons, devils, whatever in the Nine Hells that monster Grimlight was . . . I just can't wait."

"It may not be inside," Araevin told her. "The crystal might be lying on the forest floor a mile or two away."

The genasi eyed the beckoning darkness under the hill. "Care to wager on that?"

Nesterin looked to Araevin. "You said that this was an old elven stronghold," the star elf said. "Who delved it, and why? What is the story of this place?"

"Its name is Nar Kerymhoarth. My people do not like to speak of it," Gaerradh answered for Araevin. "Because we don't tell its name to outsiders, the place became known as the Nameless Dungeon. It's one of the Seven Citadels of ancient Siluvanede.

"Long ago, three elven kingdoms shared this forest: Eaerlann, Siluvanede, and Sharrven. Siluvanede was the strongest of the three realms. It was a sun elf kingdom whose people hoped to build a realm to rival long-lost Aryvandaar.

"But a new shadow fell over Siluvanede. The sun elves grew proud and ambitious. Many were seduced into swearing allegiance to the daemonfey—though the Dlardrageths remained hidden for a long time, guiding the kingdom's affairs in secret. Finally war broke out among the three kingdoms; Eaerlann and Sharrven stood together against Siluvanede. That was the Seven Citadels' War." Gaerradh glanced at Donnor and Maresa, hesitating, but then she continued. "In the last years of the war, the fey'ri legions appeared. The foulness of the daemonfey was revealed for all to see. But Eaerlann and Sharrven together overcame Siluvanede.

"My ancestors bound the fey'ri and their masters in timeless magical prisons, buried beneath their ancient strongholds. The people of Eaerlann and Sharrven vowed to keep an eternal watch over these places."

Araevin picked up Gaerradh's tale. "Sharrven fell not long after Siluvanede," he said. "Eaerlann endured for many centuries more but was overthrown five hundred years ago, when demonic hordes emerged from Hellgate Keep and destroyed all the lands nearby."

Gaerradh nodded. "Our watch failed. By the time my people returned to this part of the forest, we'd forgotten the story of the old prisons. We knew that something old and evil slept in the secret strongholds of the forest, and so we kept watch. But we didn't know why."

"You seem to have pieced it all together now," Jorin observed.

"Only because the daemonfey showed us what we'd forgotten." Gaerradh shrugged. "I only learned the beginning of the story—the story of the fey'ri and the Seven Citadels' War—after speaking with the sages and scribes of Silverymoon this summer."

"So Sarya Dlardrageth's fey'ri army was imprisoned

right in there—" Donnor Kerth nodded at the ruined hillside— "after some ancient elven civil war?"

"Yes, you are right," the wood elf answered.

"Any idea of what lies buried here? What sort of magic or guardian monsters we might find?"

Gaerradh shook her head. "We never set foot in the deeper halls of the Nameless Dungeon. They were sealed so thoroughly we didn't even know they existed."

Araevin checked the wands he carried holstered on his left hip, and studied the dark opening in the hillside. "I suspect that Sarya emptied the place when she freed her legion. But there's only one way to be sure, isn't there?"

CHAPTER THREE

25 Flamerule, the Year of Lightning Storms

Maresa peered down each of four branching hallways, keeping her crossbow pointed in the direction she was looking. The deep halls of Nar Kerymhoarth were still as death, and the air was heavy with a damp, musty scent.

"Another intersection," the genasi said softly over her shoulder. "This place goes on forever, Araevin. Which way now?"

Araevin studied their surroundings, stretching out with his senses as he attempted to discern any glimmer of the crystal. So far, the artifact had resisted any effort to magically determine its location. Either the stone was protected by its own powerful concealing enchantments, or the remaining wards of the Nameless Dungeon itself were sufficient to deflect any attempt to scry out the shard's hiding place. After a moment, he gave up.

"Your guess is as good as mine," he told Maresa.

"That's hardly reassuring," the genasi muttered. She looked for a moment more and turned to the passageway on her left. "This way first, then."

Maresa led the way as they followed the passage. Donnor and Jorin stayed close behind her, swords at the ready. They soon came to a series of alcoves or niches in the vault. The first few they passed were empty, but then they found one occupied by a tall statue of iron. It was shaped like a proud sun elf warrior, dressed in the same sort of ancient armor that Araevin had seen many of the fey'ri wear. This was no fey'ri; for one thing, the statue lacked wings, horns, or any other demonic features. Heavy, spiked gauntlets encased its fists.

"That thing is built to fight," Donnor said. The cleric looked up and down the hall at the empty niches to each side. The company had already passed thirty or forty of them. "I wonder if all these alcoves used to have statues in them . . . and where they all went, if more of them were here once."

"Leave it alone," Araevin decided. "It doesn't seem to be active now." The mystery of the abandoned war-construct could wait.

He turned away to follow his companions deeper into the dungeon. They were ten paces farther down the hallway when the squeal of rusted metal in motion stopped him in his tracks.

"I do not like the sound of that," Nesterin said to Araevin.

Together the elves turned, and found themselves staring at the iron statue as it ponderously stepped forth from its alcove and swiveled to face them. It raised one arm slowly, as if to accuse them of some crime. Brilliant blue sparks abruptly sprang into life in its blank eyes and the joinings between its armored plates. From its outstretched gauntlet a great stroke of lightning leaped down the hallway with a terrible booming thunderclap.

Araevin threw himself aside but was still caught and spun around to the hard stone floor by the force of the bolt. His muscles jerked and kicked, leaving him writhing on the flagstones with searing white pain all along his right side and smoke rising from his cloak. Nesterin fell nearby, singed as badly as Araevin. Maresa ducked out of the way with an oath, but the lightning stroke bent toward Donnor in his plate armor and struck him with its full force. Blue sparks flew from the Lathanderite's body, and he was flung ten yards down the hall, spinning through the air as his sword clattered to the floor.

"Donnor's hurt!" Maresa cried.

She snapped a single shot from her crossbow at the advancing statue, but the bolt simply clattered away into the darkness like a matchstick thrown at an anvil.

"Help him," Araevin gasped.

He picked himself up, trying to keep his trembling legs underneath him, and looked up just in time to see the statue standing over him, drawing back its ogrelike fist. He scrambled back out of the way as the ancient war-construct pulverized a head-sized chunk of the masonry wall where he had been lying just a moment before.

With a quick gesture of his hand and an arcane syllable, Araevin blasted back at the statue with a spinning globe of magical force that struck the machine in the center of its black iron torso. The blow would have crushed the chest of a giant, but other than bludgeoning a good-sized dent in the thing's armor and knocking it back a step, the spell had little effect.

"Not good enough, Araevin," he hissed at himself, thinking furiously of spells that might be better suited to the task.

With a rush, Jorin hurtled past him and hammered at the construct's waist with his flashing swords. The Yuir ranger quickly realized that he couldn't get through the ancient armor plate either, and shifted targets. Weaving his blades in front of the statue's blank gaze and jamming sword points in any gap or joint he could find, he drew its attention away from the others.

"This way, you! Come on!" he called.

Gaerradh appeared behind the statue, fighting with a long axe in one hand and a short-hafted one in the other. Her axe-blows rang like hammers on an anvil against the statue's back, but she kept it off-balance. With one high leaping blow she struck it hard on the side of the helm, knocking its head slightly askew, but the war-construct responded by dropping to one knee and slamming its huge fist into the ground at her feet, blue sparks flying from the blow.

The flagstone floor erupted in a jagged line through the center of the hallway, knocking Araevin and Nesterin back down and bouncing Gaerradh head-over-heels. The wood elf landed flat on her back, stunned. The war-construct reached out one powerful hand to crush her.

Lying on the shattered floor, Araevin threw out his hand and barked out the words of another spell. A thin green ray sprang from his finger and struck the construct's arm. Wherever its sinister emerald light played, iron simply vanished into glittering black dust. Most of the machine's right arm disintegrated before the green ray winked out again.

"Well done, Araevin!" Nesterin cried.

As the war-construct reeled back, the star elf gathered his strength and gave voice to a single deep note that cracked stone and crumpled iron plate, hammering the statue over backward. The ancient machine fell heavily to the floor, landing on its back at Jorin's feet.

The Yuir ranger cast away one sword and gripped the other in both hands, capping his palm over the pommel. Then he dropped to a knee and drove the blade straight through the war-statue's visor. Brilliant blue sparks exploded from the device, hurling Jorin away—but then the azure light flickered and faded, leaving nothing but a wisp of smoke and a sharp, bitter smell in the air. The statue lay still, its helmet transfixed by Jorin's sword.

Araevin picked himself up wearily and looked around. "Maresa? How is Donnor?"

"Dazed, but still here," the genasi said. She helped the human knight to sit up. Donnor rubbed his head and groaned, but said nothing.

"Evidently, the construct still works," Nesterin said. He looked at the empty niches lining the hallway, and frowned. "Where are the rest of them, I wonder?"

"I don't know. Perhaps the fey'ri removed them after they escaped." Araevin rubbed his burned side. "Of course, if Sarya had had any number of those things at her command, we certainly would have seen them used against us in the battles near Evereska or in the High Forest."

"It wasn't very fast," Gaerradh observed. "Maybe she had a hard time getting them to her battles."

Araevin studied the wreckage of the war-construct a moment longer, and turned away. "Let's continue. We'll pass a warning to Seiveril Miritar to watch out for war-machines like this one when we finish our work here."

Moving more cautiously, they continued on past the last of the alcoves—eighty-eight of them, if Araevin had counted correctly—and came to a high gallery, overlooking a large shrine below. The Nameless Dungeon had proved much more extensive than Araevin had ever suspected. Vast lightless halls, dizzying shafts, and long passageways seemed to run on for miles in the darkness underneath the hill. Its armories and barracks could have accommodated an army.

Which is exactly what they did, he reminded himself. Sarya's fey'ri legion slumbered here in magical stasis for the better part of fifty centuries.

They descended from the gallery to the floor of the shrine by means of a stone slab levitated in midair by some ancient magic. Then they proceeded through an ornate archway into another hall, this one with a whole forest of thick stone columns, entwined by carvings of flowering vines and serpents.

The room smelled of death.

Araevin frowned and moved forward cautiously, glancing into each row of pillars as they passed. Then he discovered the source of the sickly scent hanging in the chamber. Half a dozen bodies were sprawled on the floor near the room's center: four lean, ruby-skinned warriors with broken black wings, and two green-scaled serpentine creatures. Signs of a furious battle were evident all around the pillared hall—the black scorch-marks of fire spells, pockmarks of broken stone in the walls and pillars, even a shattered sword on the floor.

"Those are fey'ri," Donnor said flatly. "What are they doing here?"

Araevin studied the scene carefully before answering. "The same thing we are," he decided. "Searching for the shard of the Gatekeeper's Crystal."

"How can you be sure?"

"I can see lingering auras of magic." Araevin pointed to an empty dais at the far end of the room. "Something powerful rested there not long ago, but now it is gone. I think it must have been the shard. Besides, Sarya Dlardrageth knew enough about the Crystal to steal it in the first place. It makes sense that she eventually would have sent some of her minions to recover the device."

"What about the snake creatures?" Maresa asked. She suppressed a shiver of distaste. "Were they looking for the shard too? For that matter, what are they?"

"I've seen those serpent monsters before," Gaerradh said. "They are called ophidians—clever and vicious creatures. Some are sorcerers, too. They haunt the upper reaches of the dungeon."

"If the shard was here at some point, where is it now?" Nesterin asked. The star elf studied the battle scene, his mouth set in a thoughtful frown. "Did other fey'ri survive the battle and take it from this place?"

"I do not think so," Jorin said. The Yuir ranger moved over to the dais, studying the floor closely. "There's very little dust here, but there is enough blood on the floor to tell an interesting tale. A snake-creature like those two over there slithered over this dais, leaving a smear of blood—there, and there." He followed the faint traces away from the dais, to another one of the thick pillars in the chamber, and circled it several times, frowning. Then he looked up and smiled. "Our missing serpent monster left the room through this pillar. There's a hidden door here."

"How long ago did these fey'ri and the serpent creatures die?" Araevin asked.

Jorin and Gaerradh exchanged glances. "It's hard to tell in the cold, dry air of a place like this," Gaerradh said. "But the blood's dry and brown, not at all sticky. I'd guess several days."

"Then there's little reason to hurry." Araevin moved to the far end of the pillared hall, well away from the grisly battle scene. He shrugged his rucksack from his shoulder, unbuckled his sword belt, and sat down with his back to the wall. "Let's get some rest before we follow the serpent monster into its lair."

❦ ❦ ❦ ❦ ❦

Accompanied by an escort of two wood elf scouts and eight lancers of the Silver Guard, Fflar and Ilsevele rode northeast from Deepingdale, following the narrow, swift Glaemril. By the end of their first day's ride they passed from Deepingdale into the wide, thinly settled borderlands that lay north of Tasseldale and west of Battledale. Long ago more people had lived in these parts; the small company rode past the lonely stumps of abandoned watchtowers and rambling old manors whose lands were sectioned off by long fieldstone walls, overgrown by thick briars.

They made camp for the night in the ruins of a fine old manor house not far from the Pool of Yeven, the place where the Glaemril and Semberflow joined the Ashaba. Fflar looked carefully to his mount, a fine roan stallion called Thunder, while Ilsevele tended her own horse Swiftwind, a gray destrier her father had brought from Evermeet. The night was warm, and she quickly discarded her leather doublet and arming coat, working in the thin white tunic she wore beneath her armor. Fflar found himself admiring her over his horse's back; she was strikingly pretty, with a graceful figure and eyes of brilliant green, shadowed by some unspoken concern that creased her brow.

She's spoken for, he reminded himself. Araevin is my friend. Besides, she's the *granddaughter* of Elkhazel Miritar. I died five centuries before she was even born. But . . . if you didn't count the years that I was in Arvandor, that would make us close to the same age, wouldn't it? I've only lived about a century and a half in this world, even if most of that was hundreds of years ago, before she was born.

Fflar scowled at himself, and decided that it was long past time to redirect his thoughts. "How do you think Araevin and the others are faring?" he asked.

"I don't know," she answered, a little more sharply than he might have expected. Fflar paused, brush in hand, and waited. After a moment, Ilsevele sighed and looked up to meet his eyes. "He said that he was going to start his search in the ruins of Nar Kerymhoarth. I suppose they're exploring the Nameless Dungeon even as we speak."

Fflar sensed something unspoken in her reply. Then he puzzled it out. "You wonder if your place is with Araevin, don't you?"

"I am concerned for him. And the rest of our companions, too. But I do not doubt my decision, Starbrow." Ilsevele returned to rubbing down Swiftwind. The small gray mare nickered in pleasure, and nuzzled Ilsevele's back. "I am certain that we must not fight the humans of these lands, not if there is any chance of making peace."

"If you are confident in your decision, then what troubles you?"

Ilsevele shook her fine copper hair out of her eyes and arranged her tack and saddle neatly on the ground. Then she looked away across the overgrown fields surrounding the old manor. Glimmers of sunset still played in the clouds high overhead, but the forest shadows were dark and impenetrable in the deepening dusk. "I know I am doing what is right, but . . . I didn't *want* to go with Araevin."

"Didn't want to go with him?" Fflar frowned. "There is nothing to trouble you there, Ilsevele. You see your duty differently than he sees his. There is no fault in that."

"That isn't what I meant, Starbrow." Ilsevele glanced over her shoulder at him, and looked away. He thought he saw the glimmer of a tear on her cheek. "Araevin has changed, and I am not speaking of the color of his eyes or the high magic in his heart. The last few months have awakened him from some long Reverie. I think I only really knew him when he was dreaming away his days in Evermeet."

"Someone had to do what he did," Fflar said. "It's a good thing that he was the equal of the challenge, isn't it? Without Araevin's skill, his determination, I do not know if we could have beaten the daemonfey at the Lonely Moor."

"I know. But have you seen how Mooncrescent Tower marked him?" Ilsevele shook her head. "I can't help but think that it's dangerous to want to be something other than what you are. You may get exactly what you want."

Fflar shrugged awkwardly. He was beginning to fear that he might not be the right person to hear out Ilsevele's heartache, but that was his problem, not hers.

"Give him time, Ilsevele," he managed. "He will remember himself, when better days are here."

She gave him a half-hearted smile and brushed the back of her hand across her eyes. "I hope they come swiftly, then," she said. She gave herself a small shake and fixed her eyes on him. "Enough of my foolish worries. You still haven't told me who you are, Starbrow. I think it's time you stopped dodging my questions."

"Starbrow is good enough."

"No, it's not." Ilsevele faced him, her arms folded across her chest. "You know Cormanthor like the back of your hand. You are one of the most skillful warriors I have ever seen. You carry the last Baneblade of Demron—a sword that my father kept safe for centuries. Where are you from? Do you have a family? How did you come to know my father?"

Fflar shook his head. "I told you once before, you'll need to ask your father about that."

"I am not asking him. I am asking you," Ilsevele retorted. "I trust my father implicitly, but I won't let you hide behind that blind any longer. We've shared deadly danger, and we've fought and bled together. I want to hear what you have to say for yourself."

He did not try to meet her eyes. "It's not my tale to tell."

Ilsevele waited. Then, saying nothing, she turned and left the broken hall. Fflar sighed, and finished tending to his horse—he'd been done for some time, really. Then he brushed his hands together and stood, looking out at the night. Ilsevele had trusted him with the trouble in her heart, but he hadn't shared anything in return, had he? She was right to be angry with him. He didn't think that Ilsevele would be awed by his story, or that she would tell anyone else if he asked her not to. It just seemed simpler, easier, to approach this new life of his without any of the encumbrances of the old one.

"Ah, damn it," he muttered softly. When it came down to it, refusing to speak openly was almost as bad as lying, and he hated falsehoods. Especially ones devised for his own comfort and convenience. She'd said it well enough, hadn't she? It was dangerous to want to be someone other than who you were.

He checked on the sentries, making sure that the small campsite was secure. Then he went in search of Ilsevele.

He found her sitting by a still pool in what had once

been the garden of the old manor. She did not look up as he approached. Without invitation, he sat down next to her and began to speak. "My name is Fflar Starbrow Melruth," he said. "I was born in Myth Drannor in the Year of the Turning Leaf, a little less than eight hundred years ago.

"I served in the Akh Velar, the city's guard. When I was eighty, I married Sorenna Alydyrrin, and a few years later, she bore me a son, whom we named Arafel. I loved them more than all the stars in the sky."

"You are the Fflar of whom the legends speak?" Ilsevele asked softly.

"I don't know of any legends. But I was captain of the Akh Velar in Myth Drannor's final days, and I carried Keryvian in many battles that last summer. I died on a summer afternoon, fighting the nycaloth lord Aulmpiter.

"After that . . . I walked in Arvandor for a time, though I do not now remember much of the Elvenhome. Your father called me back a few months ago, hoping that I could lead his Crusade to victory over the daemonfey."

Ilsevele stared at him. "My father raised you from the dead?" She grappled with the thought. "But . . . why? The Seldarine do not give away that magic lightly. How could my father have even known you would be willing to return?"

"Elkhazel Miritar—your grandfather, I suppose—was a good friend in my first life. I think he must have filled Seiveril's ears with wild tales about me when your father was a young fellow." Fflar permitted himself a small smile. "So now I am here."

Ilsevele studied him closely, her brow knit. "But you're so young," she managed. "You're not much older than I am."

"I was a little more than one hundred and thirty when I died."

She shook her head. "Of course," she murmured. "Of course. But . . ."

He patted her knee and stood up. "You asked. That's all I have to say. I can't make any more sense of it than you can, though I guess that I must have wanted to come back, or your father could not have called me out of Arvandor."

Ilsevele managed to shake off her amazement long enough to speak. "Starbrow—Fflar—"

"Starbrow is fine, if you're used to it."

"Starbrow, then—What became of your family?"

He hesitated, his heart aching. Strange, that such an innocuous question could hurt so much! "I don't know for certain. Sorenna escaped Myth Drannor with my son before the city fell. I know she lived for a time in Semberholme. But she is gone now, too. I hope that Arafel lived a long and happy life somewhere." He tried to laugh without bitterness, and almost succeeded. "I may have grandchildren or great-grandchildren around who are older than I am. That would be hard to explain, wouldn't it?"

"I don't know what to say," Ilsevele managed.

"Nor do I," Fflar answered truthfully. He could see the questions gathering in her face, but he could feel fresh hurt welling up in his heart. He had no more answers. With an effort he found a small smile for Ilsevele. "I suppose we should rest. We have a hard day's ride ahead." Then he retreated, leaving her wrapped in her own thoughts in the moonlit garden.

❧ ❧ ❧ ❧ ❧

The secret door in the pillar led to a narrow, black stairway that wound upward for quite a distance through the cool gloom of Nar Kerymhoarth. A faint but unsettling musky smell lingered in the close air of the stairs. The stairs ended in a small landing with blank walls on all sides, but with a few moments of searching, they discovered another secret door. This one opened out into a low-ceilinged hall of more pillars—blocky and square this time—with several large, still pools of water rimmed by foot-high lips of smooth masonry. Water dripped somewhere in the dark distance, echoing in the stone hall.

"Which way, Jorin?" Araevin asked.

The Aglarondan knelt, resting his fingertips on the paving blocks of the floor. "Straight ahead."

They came to the end of the square pillars and pools, and found a great doorway carved in the image of a serpent's head. Long stone fangs framed the archway, and the whole thing had been crudely painted in peeling green and yellow. Araevin studied the doorway for a moment, and decided that no magical traps lingered in the area. But he could feel danger nearby.

"Carefully, now," Araevin whispered to the others.

Maresa and Jorin led the way, ducking under the jutting fangs of the great serpent head. The passage beyond was fashioned to resemble a snake's gullet, with curved stone ribbing at even intervals and a floor of glossy tile. They followed the eerie passageway for a short time and emerged onto a balcony above another large hall.

Scores of ophidians slowly writhed and coiled together on the cold stone floor below, tangled in a scaly heap before a great serpentine idol at the far side of the room.

Stifling a gasp of surprise, Araevin quickly backpedaled down the passage they'd just emerged from. His friends retreated as well. Only when he judged that they were out of easy earshot did Araevin allow himself to breathe a sigh of relief.

"I quit," muttered Maresa. "I am *not* going in there."

"Do you think they spotted us?" Jorin whispered.

"I don't think so," Araevin said. "I think they would have let us know if they'd seen us."

"Did you see the idol?" Nesterin asked Araevin. "Was that crystal the one you seek?"

Araevin shook his head. "I saw the idol, but I didn't notice any crystal. Better show me."

Leaving the others at a safe distance up the passageway, Araevin and Nesterin crept softly back to the edge of the balcony. The mage studied the great serpent statue at the far end of the room closely. At first he didn't see anything, but he clearly sensed the presence of strong magic. Beside him, Nesterin tapped his arm and pointed toward a small offering dish that sat in the middle of the great stone serpent's coils.

A milky white crystal the size of a man's hand lay atop a heap of old coins in the dish. Araevin looked to Nesterin and nodded. Then, before they withdrew, he quickly looked around the rest of the room. The balcony ran along only the back wall of the shrine. To his left and right, stairs descended to the mosaic floor below, where the ophidians gathered around their sinister idol. There was a great dark pool in the center of the room, similar to the ones in the hall of the square pillars but much larger—and evidently inhabited. He caught the subtle stirring of something large moving in the water. He nodded to the star elf, and the two retreated back down the passage again.

"Is that it?" Nesterin asked.

"Yes. I'm pretty sure that is a shard of the Gatekeeper's Crystal."

"So how do we get it away from the serpent men?"

"There's more of them than I want to fight," Jorin said.

"It's worse than you think. There's some sort of creature in the big pool in the middle of the room, too," Araevin said. "I thought I sensed sorcery other than the crystal's aura."

"Then we steal it," Maresa said. "Since we don't have any particular quarrel with the ophidians, let's not fight them if we can help it." The genasi looked to Araevin. "Do you have any spells that might help?"

"I thought you wanted nothing to do with the ophidians."

"If we're going to have to do this anyway, I might as well make sure we do it right."

Araevin smiled at her. "I can make you invisible for a short time."

"That will do." Maresa quickly divested herself of her pack, crossbow, and bandolier of quarrels, keeping only her rapier and her fire wand for defense. "Be ready to discourage pursuit if things go badly."

"We'll be ready."

"Then let's go, before I change my mind."

Maresa led the way as they returned to the balcony overlooking the den of the ophidians. Araevin paused as close as he dared to the open balcony itself before casting his invisibility spell on Maresa. She smirked at him as she faded out of sight. Then, silently, the company stole back out to the doorway leading to the balcony, crouching low to stay out of sight. Jorin, Nesterin, and Gaerradh knelt with bows in their hands and arrows on the string. Donnor simply waited in the darkness, his sword in his hand.

Araevin murmured a soft word and wove a spell to give himself the ability to see Maresa despite her invisibility. He watched her steal quickly across the balcony to the steps on the right-hand side, and start down the wide, shallow steps. The great hall was weirdly quiet, disturbed only by the occasional soft hiss or the faint rasp of scales sliding over scales.

Keeping her shoulder to the wall, Maresa reached the bottom of the steps and started forward. Even though she was invisible, she made an effort to stick to the shadows of the room's thick stone buttresses and alcoves. Then she came to a place where several of the ophidians lay tangled, with coils of their bodies actually touching the wall she was moving along.

Maresa paused and looked for a way around, but if she moved left toward the middle of the room she would be in the middle of the creatures—and too near to the hidden menace in the pool for Araevin's comfort. Squaring her shoulders, she stepped over one ophidian, then actually set her foot in the coil of another's tail before stepping across its body as well. The monster shifted and began to move as Maresa tiptoed among its coils. She jumped two more steps to get away from it.

The ophidian turned with startling swiftness and hissed at the empty air where the genasi had stood just a moment before. Its long blue tongue flickered in and out, tasting the air, as Maresa backed away, hand on the hilt of her sword.

"Get ready," Araevin breathed to his companions.

The archers straightened and went to a three-quarters draw, sighting on serpent men in the tangled mass below. But before Araevin gave the order to shoot, the ophidian near Maresa lowered its head and returned to its somnolence.

"It's safe," he said softly, and the bows relaxed again. The genasi darted one quick glance back up toward the balcony where her companions waited, and headed for the idol.

She reached the statue of the serpent god, and climbed carefully up into its coils. Araevin held his breath as her foot slipped on the slick stone, but she recovered easily and reached the broad stone bowl where the crystal glittered. Maresa loosened a small leather pouch from her belt, and brought it up to where the shard lay. Smart girl, he realized. A crystal bobbing around in midair would be a lot more likely to attract attention than one that simply and quietly vanished. With one confident motion, Maresa swept the shard into the pouch and slid back down the side of the idol.

"There it goes," Nesterin whispered. "She has it."

Behind Maresa, one of the old bronze coins in the stone bowl slid off the shallow mound and clattered to the stone floor.

Ophidians raised their heads from the floor and peered at the idol. In the space of three heartbeats hisses of anger arose throughout the hall, and the serpent folk thrashed in agitation. Some surged upright, balancing on thick, scaly torsos as they looked around the chamber. Others slithered toward the great statue, forked tongues darting.

Maresa did not delay an instant. She dashed at once back toward the steps, dodging between writhing coils and leaping over those that lay on the ground. The ophidians still could not see her, but they sensed something brushing past, and the genasi left a wake of rearing torsos and snapping fangs in her wake.

From the pool in the center of the room, a powerful hooded serpent slowly rose up, its back gleaming with a brilliant black-and-red pattern of diamond scales. It glanced around at Maresa, and Araevin saw that its face was almost human, with cold yellow eyes and deadly fangs. A naga! he realized. It spotted the fleeing genasi at once and said something to its followers in a harsh, hissing speech. Ophidians threw themselves forward, trying to cut off her escape.

"Araevin!" Maresa cried. "Do something!"

Bowstrings sang as Jorin, Nesterin, and Gaerradh loosed their arrows at the ophidians below. The naga started to spit out the words of a spell, but at that moment Maresa leaped up the first few steps of the staircase. Araevin saw the chance he had been waiting for. Quickly intoning his own spell, he raised a great barrier of glittering white ice across the steps and the great hall, walling off the naga and its ophidian minions. White frost motes sparkled in the gloom as his companions' arrows rebounded from the icy wall.

Maresa reached the balcony and risked a quick glance behind her. "That should keep them. Nicely done," she said to Araevin.

"And you as well," he told the genasi.

"Hardly. If I'd done it right, they never would have known I was there."

"It was good enough," he reassured her. Then he looked to his companions. "Come on, my friends. We should make sure that we are well away from here by the time the ophidians find another way up to this balcony."

CHAPTER FOUR

27 Flamerule, the Year of Lightning Storms

To make sure that they outdistanced any pursuit from the ophidians or their masters, Araevin and his companions marched hard for a long time after climbing back up from the from the depths of the Nameless Dungeon. Only when the tor of Nar Kerymhoarth was lost to sight in the green sea behind them did Araevin signal for a halt.

"This should be safe enough," he said to his friends. "I don't think the serpent folk will follow us so far from their lair, but I'll weave some spells to hide us from them just in case."

"Good," Donnor said wearily. The human knight was soaked with sweat. He'd kept up with the long-striding elves despite the fifty pounds of steel he wore, but he heaved a deep sigh of relief as he began to unbuckle the straps and fastenings of his heavy armor. "Once I sit down, I won't be getting up for a long time, not even if the king of all serpent men himself comes to murder me in my sleep."

Maresa sat down nearby, loosed the collar of her scarlet-dyed leather coat, and shrugged her satchel off her shoulder. "Before we get too comfortable, maybe Araevin had better make sure that we got the right crystal. If we have to go back and try it again, I'd rather know right now."

She handed the satchel to Araevin, who drew out the shard and unwrapped it from the dark cloth Maresa had used to hide it. The piece was smooth and cool to the touch, roughly daggerlike in shape, and a little more than half a foot from tip to tip. In his hands it seemed to stir, as if it recognized the magic in his touch, and a bright violet-white gleam appeared in its depths. He turned it slowly in his hand, studying it closely.

"Well?" the genasi demanded.

"It's a piece of the Gatekeeper's Crystal. I saw the shard we kept in the vaults of Tower Reilloch years ago. I don't know for certain if this is the same one, but if it isn't, it's an exact copy."

"Can you sense the presence of the second or third shards, Araevin?" Nesterin asked.

Araevin allowed his perception to sink into the shard, absorbing the faint pearlescent glimmers that danced in its depths, groping for a spark of recognition or acknowledgment. Unlike the *selukiira* of Saelethil Dlardrageth, there was no guiding consciousness preserved in the Gatekeeper's Crystal. He could feel the power of the thing, a hidden wellspring of living magic waiting to be tapped, but the shard was not aware of itself or its surroundings.

While his companions watched, Araevin whispered the words of a finding spell and fixed his attention on the gleaming white crystal in his hand. At once he felt a sharp jolt of *connection*, as if the shard had sent some intangible call echoing out from the small clearing in the great forest, a call that swept swiftly and silently across the miles. And he felt an answer, a keen ringing tone somewhere far to the east and north. It was the sort of shrill, high tone he might have expected if he'd struck the shard in his hand with a small hammer. He scrambled to his feet without even noticing, and looked in the direction of the sound.

"There," he breathed. "Did you feel that?"

Maresa and Donnor simply shrugged, but Nesterin frowned. "I thought I sensed something, but I could not tell you what it was I felt," the star elf said.

"That direction," Araevin said, pointing. "Very far, I think. Possibly hundreds of miles."

"Hundreds?" Maresa picked up a handful of pine needles from the forest floor and threw them down again with a snort of disgust. "I'm getting tired of crisscrossing Faerûn chasing after your intuition, Araevin. Could you just for once go looking for an ancient elven gemstone that's been left out in some close-by, cheerful spot? For that matter, I'm tired of chasing after gems. Why is everything a damned gem or crystal?"

"Durability," Araevin answered. "The sun elves of old knew ways to fashion crystal that remains almost indestructible today, thousands of years after it was cast. We've been chasing after crystals because that's the form in which magical power and knowledge from elder days was preserved."

"It was a rhetorical question," Maresa grumbled. "So how far east do we have to go? Back to Cormanthor? Thay? Kara-Tur?"

"I am not certain," Araevin admitted. He could clearly sense the direction, but the distant ringing of the crystal had held an odd note, something he could not easily put into words. Somehow he doubted that it would be as simple as riding toward the dawn until they found the second shard. "We'll make for Myth Glaurach before we do anything else. We need to collect our mounts and provision ourselves for a long journey."

The short summer night passed quietly, and in the morning they retraced their steps back toward the conquered fey'ri stronghold. They reached the ruined city in the hills late in the day, and passed the night among the wood elves who guarded the place. Beneath the lanterns and starlight, Myth Glaurach's overgrown ruins did not seem as sad as they once did—but then again, the songs of the wood elves had a way of dispelling the gloom. They rested for the night in the small chapel where they had stayed a few tendays before, when the whole of Seiveril's Crusade was encamped in the ruins.

Early the following day, Gaerradh took her leave of the small company. "I must go visit Lady Morgwais in the High Forest and tell her what happened in Nar Kerymhoarth," she said. "And after that, I should go see Alustriel and Methrammar in Silverymoon. But I wish you luck in your search for the remaining shards."

"Thank you for your help, Gaerradh," Araevin said. "Sweet water and light laughter until we meet again."

He bowed to the wood elf, but she shook her head and caught him in a rib-cracking embrace. "Sun elves," she laughed. "Would it hurt you to smile?" Then she treated Jorin, Nesterin, and Maresa the same way, and even Donnor Kerth too, which left the fierce Tethyrian blushing—he was chivalrous to a fault and had firmly fixed ideas about how a devout man should act in the presence of the fairer sex. But he rallied enough to timidly pat her back before letting her go.

They spent the rest of the morning gathering provisions and seeing to their mounts, and rode out of Myth Glaurach in the afternoon. This time Araevin determined to head north into the wilds of Turnstone Pass. The day was warm and mild, and they were high enough in the hills that even in midsummer it would not grow uncomfortably hot, certainly not compared to the depths of the Yuirwood or Cormanthor.

The road climbed into the foothills north of the old city, winding between steep hills covered in thick pine forest. Sometimes the white ribbon of a waterfall slicing from the rocky heights above appeared through the trees. After a few miles, the road rose steadily higher along the shoulders of the hills, and the trees thinned out, offering broad views of the country to the east and south. Nesterin, riding beside Araevin, spent much of his time admiring the view.

"This is striking country," the star elf observed. "Those are the Nether Mountains?"

"Yes, on both sides of the pass." Araevin pointed toward the northeast, where the peaks rose bare and brown above the green mantle of forest covering their shoulders. "Netheril once stood on the far side of the mountains. The desert Anauroch lies there now."

Nesterin glanced at Araevin. "Our path leads us into the desert?"

"Not if I can help it," Araevin said. "I think our journey should begin at the House of Long Silences. There is a portal only a few miles farther up this road that will take us there."

"The House of Long Silences?"

"It's a meeting place of portals in the Ardeep Forest, near Waterdeep. I believe that some of the doors there lead into the Waymeet itself, and that in turn is a place where thousands of portals come together. I think that if we look there, we may find a gate that will take us much closer to the place where the second shard awaits."

After a while, they reached a place where a small side trail zigzagged up toward a lonely watchtower overlooking the pass. Little remained of the old tower, only a hollow ring of stone standing less than twenty feet tall. Mounds of stone blocks gathered around the stump, hinting at the height the tower had once possessed.

"A guard post for the pass raised by the humans of Ascalhorn," Araevin explained to the others. "I think it was razed by the fiends of Hellgate Keep soon after they overran the city."

He dismounted, and took his horse's reins in hand, leading his friends past the stump of the tower to the broken remains of a small shrine. Here, a doorway of stone with a lintel carved in the shape of a flowering vine stood incongruously in the steep hillside.

"That looks like portals we saw beneath Myth Glaurach," Donnor said.

"Yes, it's the work of elves. I never determined whether the portal was placed here after Ascalhorn raised the watchtower, or if Ascalhorn raised the tower at this spot because the portal was here." Araevin studied the old portal, seeking out the old activating words the builders had hidden in the decorative carvings around its edges. "Remember, once I activate the door, it will not stay open long. Lead your horses through on foot. All you need to do is keep the reins in hand while you touch the stone within the archway. You will appear in the Ardeep Forest."

After one quick look to make sure his companions were ready, Araevin woke the portal with his spells. The blank stone in the center of the archway did not vanish, but it took on a shimmering, liquid appearance. He paused for a moment, admiring the artistry of the long-dead mage who had fashioned its skein of enchantments and abjurations. Then he set his hand on the cool stone, murmured the ancient passwords, and was gone.

❧ ❧ ❧ ❧ ❧

The smoke of forges and foundries always hung thickly over the lower quarters of Zhentil Keep, filling the city with an acrid reek. Scyllua Darkhope, castellan and captain of the city's armies, clattered through the streets astride her fearsome white nightmare, with six of her elite Castellan's Guard riding after her. She hardly even noticed as common tradesmen and guttersnipes scattered from her path. Her eyes remained fixed on great and distant things.

The riders came to the new bridge spanning the Tesh, and turned north toward the black battlements of the keep from which her city took its name. By some lucky accident, the great castle was rarely troubled by the fuming stink of the city's industries. The westerly winds usually carried the smoke out over the dark waters of the Moonsea, away from the low hill where the castle stood guard above the cheerless streets.

"Make way for the castellan!" called one of the guards who followed her.

As Scyllua rode beneath the iron portcullis of the river gate, soldiers in black and yellow sprang to attention, striking the butts of their halberds on the flagstones. Somewhere far overhead, the long yellow whiptail of the castellan's pennant broke from a flagpole atop the keep, signaling the arrival of the castle's commander. Cries of "The castellan returns!" echoed from watchpost to watchpost along the walls.

Scyllua swung herself down from her pale steed, giving it a single pat of her gauntleted hand before the hell-horse vanished back into the infernal realms with a single shriek. It would come again at her call, to serve when she needed it. Then she finally acknowledged the sergeant-at-arms who stood with his arm across his chest in salute.

"Lord Fzoul summoned me?"

"Yes, High Captain. He awaits you in his chambers."

Scyllua nodded absently and strode into the keep's lower hall. She took the steps quickly despite her armor of black plate, and her Castellan's Guards labored to keep up with her. Five flights of stairs later, she came to a great double door of black adamantine, emblazoned with the symbol of a mighty gauntleted fist. Ten warriors stood guard before the door, as well as a fearsome beholder.

She did not look at the creature as she said, "Announce me, Tharxul."

The many-eyed monster drifted idly in the air, regarding Scyllua with several of its writhing eyes. "Of course, Lady Scyllua," the creature gurgled in a deep, wet voice. "We have been expecting you. You may enter."

The castellan took three strides past the floating monster

before she paused, her fist on the door. She frowned and looked back at the beholder. Her eyes lost their distant distraction as she fixed them on the monster. Bright and cold as steel they shone.

"What did you say, Tharxul?" she asked softly.

The endless weaving of the creature's eyestalks slowed. "You are expected," it wheezed. "You may enter."

"No, that is not what you said," Scyllua replied. She took two strides toward the hovering monster. "You said 'we' have been expecting you. Am I to understand that you presume to have me at your beck and call? Do you believe that you command some small measure of the authority of the Chosen Tyrant of Bane? Do Lord Fzoul's actions now require your sanction, Tharxul? Do you think to offer your *approval?*"

"You misunderstand me, Castellan—"

"I misunderstand *nothing!*" With a single swift motion Scyllua swept her broadsword from its sheath and struck off one of the beholder's weaving eyestalks. Black ichor spurted on the flagstones as the monster howled in outrage and dismay. "You do not approve, Tharxul! You submit, you serve, you *obey!*"

The beholder recovered from its shock and retreated, turning to bring more of its eyes to bear. For a moment incandescent death in the form of half a dozen blights, curses, and slaying spells at the monster's command gleamed in the eyes it trained on Scyllua, but the short woman's fierce glower did not waver for an instant. Tharxul seethed on the edge of rebellion and destruction, its blood dripping to the floor . . . and it blinked. Sinking down to the floor, it closed its eyes and inclined its round skull.

"I submit, I serve, I obey," the monster said thickly.

Scyllua stared at the creature for a moment longer, and slammed her sword back into its sheath. She deliberately turned her back on the beholder and said to no one in particular, "Have a cleric tend its wound." Then she pushed open the door of adamantine and entered the lair of her master.

Final Gate • 67

Fzoul Chembryl, master of Zhentil Keep and Chosen Tyrant of Bane, saw no reason to pretend to any false austerity. His personal chambers were literally palatial, the floor covered in exotic carpets from distant Semphar, the walls decorated with silk arrases and trophies of a dozen dark triumphs. Scyllua found her lord reclining on a golden couch by a window looking out over the Moonsea, reading from various scrolls.

At once she knelt and lowered her head. "I have come as you commanded, Lord Fzoul."

Fzoul took no notice for a moment, but then he finished the scroll he was looking at and set it aside. "So I see," he said. He swung his feet from the couch and stood up slowly. He was a tall man with long, luxurious red hair, broad-shouldered and strong. "You were quite stern with Tharxul, my dear. Beholders are somewhat hard to come by, you know."

"I submit myself for correction."

"Oh, I did not mean to rebuke you, Scyllua. In fact, I approve. You have taken to heart the instruction I provided you in the Citadel of the Raven, a few tendays past." The lord's mouth twitched up in a cold ghost of a smile. "Besides, Tharxul has become presumptuous of late. It is your duty to instruct any who stand beneath you in the Great Lord's service. The loss of an eye will perhaps encourage him to adopt a more appropriate attitude as he serves Bane with his remaining ten."

Scyllua did not presume to reply. After a moment Fzoul nodded. "You may rise."

She stood, her armor creaking, and awaited his command.

"Is your army prepared to march again?" Fzoul asked.

"It is, my lord."

"I expected nothing less. Attend me for a moment." The tyrant drifted over to a table nearby, on which a map of the Moonsea and the Dalelands lay. Scyllua followed him, focusing her gaze on the familiar lines and marks. Fzoul muttered the words of a spell prayer and brushed one hand over the yellow parchment. Beneath his touch the parchment came to life. The forests became a rolling sea of green, the waters of the Moonsea turned dark and glittered as if in the sunlight, roads and towns awoke to life.

"The new masters of Myth Drannor have driven the army of Evermeet all the way back to the southwest corner of the forest," Fzoul began. Tiny white banners glimmered beneath the trees, beset by dark roiling hordes of hellspawned monsters. "Sembia's army is melting like last winter's snows, retreating across the Blackfeather Bridge." Small rivers of disorganized troops pressed and bunched by the miniature bridge spanning the waters of the Ashaba.

"And here," the lord of Zhentil Keep continued, "and here, we see that Hillsfar's army near Mistledale has been routed completely . . . while Maalthiir's tower lies in rubble, where Sarya Dlardrageth and her demonic legions tore it to pieces." Under his fingertips the walled city of Hillsfar smoldered, and distant cries of pain and terror rose up from the image. "What observation do you draw from this, my castellan?"

Scyllua examined the map for only a moment before answering. "The daemonfey fight all our enemies. Sarya Dlardrageth has broken the elves and the Sembians while harrying all the northern Dales."

"That cursed little flyspeck Shadowdale remains unconquered." Fzoul grimaced briefly, fixing his baleful eye on the sharp spire of the Twisted Tower. "Doubtless the Great Lord permits that small land to resist our armies because he has some more subtle purpose in mind."

Scyllua bowed her head, expecting a sharp and painful rebuke. She had been given the task of subjugating Daggerdale and Shadowdale in order to close the three-sided trap that would have ensnared the elven Crusade in Mistledale. The elves and Grimmar had driven her army back north in defeat. But Fzoul's mind was evidently caught up in the next move, not the last one. The tyrant's eye turned from Shadowdale, and Scyllua dared to look up again.

"You may also note that the daemonfey have shattered the Red Plumes of Hillsfar," said Fzoul, "Now we must ask ourselves: What shall we make of this calamity that has beset the Dalelands and the old elven forests?"

Scyllua recognized the question as one that Fzoul would answer for himself. "Whatever the Great Lord wills, I shall do," she said simply.

"I know, my dear." The tyrant smiled coldly. "With the Great Lord's guidance, I have decided on Hillsfar."

That was no surprise. The First Lord of Hillsfar and the master of Zhentil Keep detested each other, and had been rivals for decades. Several years past they had tried to set aside their differences, arranging a secret accord . . . but neither Maalthiir nor Fzoul was the sort of man to live in a house where he was not the undisputed master. When they had met in the ruins of Yûlash a couple of months ago, they had met as enemies.

Fzoul continued, "While the daemonfey of Myth Drannor keep the Dalesfolk and the Sembians occupied, we have in our hands a golden opportunity to destroy a nearby rival. With its Red Plumes mauled and its Sembian allies in disarray south of the Ashaba, Hillsfar is mortally weakened. Sooner or later, the war between the elves and the daemonfey will be decided. Regardless of who wins, it suits me to sweep Hillsfar from the table while no other power can stop me from doing so."

"The daemonfey might be able to interfere, my lord," Scyllua said.

"Sarya has already shown that she regards Maalthiir as an enemy. If anything, we may perhaps earn her gratitude by completing the city's downfall."

Scyllua studied the map under Fzoul's hand for a time, already thinking about where the first blows would be struck and the details of a march eastward along the shore of the Moonsea. But she could see the glittering spires of demon-haunted Myth Drannor poised like a knife at her ribs if she attacked Hillsfar, leaving her right flank only a few dozen miles from Sarya Dlardrageth's city.

"The daemonfey have turned on everyone else, my lord. I must believe that sooner or later they will turn on us, as well."

"Perhaps." Fzoul shrugged. "I have communed with the Great Lord at length on this question. He has shown me that the daemonfey will not betray us before we complete the destruction of Maalthiir's power." Fzoul folded his thick arms across his chest, and nodded confidently. "There is a limit to the number of enemies Sarya Dlardrageth is willing to fight at once. We will not come to blows with the daemonfey this year."

Scyllua recognized the cold confidence in her lord's voice. When Fzoul spoke in such a tone, he was dealing in certainties. After all, as the Chosen Tyrant of Bane, it was given to him to know such things.

Scyllua bowed deeply. "Then I have only one question, my lord," she said. "Do you wish Hillsfar conquered or destroyed?"

☙ ☙ ☙ ☙ ☙

The House of Long Silences had changed little since the last time Araevin had set foot on its ivy-grown steps. He noticed that full summer had come to the Ardeep Forest; the woods were green and lush, and the air was pleasantly warm. It had been early in the spring when he and Ilsevele had traveled there from Evermeet, and the weather had been much colder and wetter then.

The house itself was an old palace of white stone, long abandoned. Much of the place was open to the sky, and mighty trees hundreds of years old grew up through the ruined chambers. Weathered statues of old elflords Araevin had never been able to put a name to gathered moss in ivy-filled alcoves, strangely sad and wise in their decay. A palpable hush hung over the forgotten palace, so much so that it was hard to speak in anything but a whisper.

Birdsong in the forest was rare and faint, as if the palace was not even really in the forest at all.

"What a sad place," Maresa said softly, running her pale fingers over a smooth stone balustrade. "Who would hide magical doorways in a tomb like this?"

"Long ago, it was the residence of a grand mage of Illefarn," Araevin said. "The great city of the kingdom stood not very far away, where Waterdeep now lies. Most of the doors in this palace were made long before it fell into ruin."

"Somebody comes," Nesterin said.

The star elf watched the dark doorway that had once served as the palace's front door. A somber sun elf knight appeared from the shadows, stepping into the golden dusk that had settled over the courtyard. He was tall and dignified, dressed in a long hauberk of silver mail. His hair was silvered at the temple, and bound by a narrow gold circlet.

"I see you have returned to the House of Long Silences, Araevin," the elflord said. He descended the steps and caught the mage's hand in a firm grasp. "It is good to see you again. Much has happened in a very short time, I hear."

Araevin offered a wry smile. "You don't know the half of it, Elorfindar."

"Then I look forward to hearing the tale from you." Elorfindar's eyes narrowed as he looked into Araevin's face, and he did not release the mage's arm from his grasp. "You have changed, Araevin. What has happened to you?"

"That is part of the tale." Araevin stepped back and indicated his comrades. "Allow me to introduce my traveling companions. This is Maresa Rost of Waterdeep; she is the daughter of Theleda Rost, who traveled with me some years ago."

"I remember," Elorfindar said. The elflord was too polite to allow his surprise to show—Maresa did not resemble her mother much at all, since Theleda had been fully human, and Maresa was most definitely not. "A pleasure to meet you."

"This is Donnor Kerth, a knight of the Order of the Aster and a servant of Lathander. This is Jorin Kell Harthan of Aglarond, and this is Nesterin Deirr, also of Aglarond."

Elorfindar bowed to each in turn. "Come inside, my friends. Not all of the house is a cheerless ruin. You are welcome here."

They left their mounts in the courtyard, where Elorfindar assured them they would be safe, and followed the elflord into the palace. Araevin had passed through the manor before, so he was ready for the eerie stillness of the place, but he felt his companions' steps grow slow and troubled as they followed. Then they came to a comfortable chamber that seemed brighter and less gloomy. Elorfindar invited them to sit, while he set out ewers of water and wine, and laid out a small spread of food.

"Now, Araevin, I think I am ready to hear your tale," he said.

"As you wish." Araevin sat down on a low couch, while Elorfindar reclined on another and his companions found comfortable places of their own. He told the elflord of his desperate efforts to counter the daemonfey threat, while the elven Crusade sought to bring Sarya Dlardrageth and her minions to bay. "And so here I am," he finished. "From Saelethil's Nightstar I have learned that the Waymeet—the Last Mythal of Aryvandaar—may threaten all of Faerûn. To address that threat, I must find the remaining pieces of the Gatekeeper's Crystal and seal the Waymeet against Sarya and her ally Malkizid."

Elorfindar examined the shard of the Gatekeeper's Crystal with interest. "I can tell it is an old and powerful device," he mused aloud. "I wonder . . . you said that the crystal is affiliated with the Waymeet?"

Araevin nodded. "If nothing else, the combined crystal allows its bearer to draw power from the Waymeet, no matter where he or she is. Its primary use is the sundering of wards, mythals, and other constructs of powerful magic."

"And it flies apart into its component pieces after its power is employed?" Elorfindar handed the shard back to Araevin. "It seems to me that the crystal's tendency to hurl itself across the multiverse is simply a reflection of its tie to the Waymeet. After all, the Waymeet touches on thousands of doorways spanning Faerûn, Toril, and the planes. I'd wager that the crystal uses that same network of portals to scatter itself."

"So its pieces would appear near gates leading back to the Waymeet?" Nesterin asked.

Elorfindar shrugged. "It is only a guess."

"That means we only have to find the right portals, and the shards will be right there," Donnor said.

Araevin shook his head. "You're forgetting that we've had a couple of months now for someone to stumble across the shards and carry them off from wherever they first appeared. But if Elorfindar's observation holds true, then we'll find that the trail begins somewhere near a Waymeet portal's terminus."

"Not so useful, if there really are thousands of doorways in this Waymeet," Jorin said. "But better than nothing, I suppose."

"Do any of the doors in this house lead to the Waymeet?" Nesterin asked Elorfindar.

The elflord nodded. "I know of one that will take you there. I can show you now, if you like."

"Might as well get to it," Maresa said. She stood and buckled on her sword belt. "I've never liked waiting, anyway."

Elorfindar led Araevin and his friends back into the silent halls of the house and turned down a shadowed corridor they had passed before. Every four paces, a tall blank doorway stood waiting. Each was nothing more than a stone lintel framing an empty place on the wall. Carvings of leaves and flowers, animals and scenes of nature graced each of the doors. The elflord passed several of the empty doors and stopped before one that was marked with a strange design of stars and dragons.

"This is it," he said softly. "I have never ventured into the Waymeet, so I cannot tell you what to expect on the other side."

"What do we do with our horses?" Donnor asked. "Do we take them with us, or do we leave them here?"

"Leave them for now," Araevin decided. "We can come back for them if we need them on the other side."

"I'll have them looked after," Elorfindar said. He touched his fingertips to the blank stone, and said a single word: *"Elladar."* Beneath his fingers, the stone seemed to melt away into a roiling gray fog.

"Thank you, Elorfindar," Araevin said. He nodded to his friends, and one by one they stepped into the fog and vanished.

"You need only repeat the password to activate the portal again," Elorfindar said. "Good luck, Araevin."

"Until we meet again, old friend." Araevin clasped his hand quickly, and turn and followed Nesterin into the misty doorway. There was a momentary darkness, a sense of movement in some direction that was not forward, up, or down . . . and he emerged.

He stood in a cathedral of glass.

The sky overhead was dark and starless. Underfoot, the ground was a sort of gray shale. But all around him stood walls and spires of luminous white glass. Great arching ribs of the stuff curved and met in a web of frozen light above him. Elsewhere serried ramparts of pearl marched in curved, sloping walls. The air was cold and still, but the crystalline castle seemed to whisper and sing in a constantly changing susurrus of sound. Maresa, Donnor, Jorin, and Nesterin stood nearby, silently taking in the sight. Their breath steamed in the chilly air, and their eyes were wide and rapt.

Araevin turned to examine the doorway behind him. It was a simple triangular arch between two swordlike spars of glass, its center gray and misty. Then he looked up and saw that the glass ramparts and spires extended for as far as he could see in that direction. The Waymeet wasn't a cathedral of glass, it was a *city* of glass, perfect and empty. And everywhere he looked, he saw the doors—asymmetrical interstices where sharp spires and slanting sheets met. Hundreds of them appeared in a single glance, each flickering with living magic.

"I had no idea," Araevin murmured. "It's immense!"

"Your ancestors didn't do anything by half-measures, did they?" Maresa said.

Jorin recovered from his awe long enough to turn his eyes to Araevin. "Do you have any idea which way to go from here?"

Absently, Araevin drew out the shard of the Gatekeeper's Crystal and raised it to eye level, speaking the words of a spell. It gleamed brightly, and in his mind he felt a distinct tug toward his right. "This way," he said. "I don't think it's far."

"So where are we?" Maresa asked Araevin. "Where is this place?"

"It's nowhere. This is a demiplane of its own."

"A what?"

"A demiplane—a small self-contained world that exists parallel to Faerûn. Much like Sildëyuir, but not anywhere near as large as that realm. The divine and infernal realms are places of a similar nature, but those of course are even more extensive than Sildëyuir." Araevin looked around. "I don't expect this one is much larger than what you can see from right here. Less than a mile across?"

"So where is it that this demiplane exists? What's outside of it?"

"You might as well ask what's on the other side of the stars when you're looking up into the sky on a summer night." Araevin shrugged. "The demiplane just ends. Outside you would find nothing but the unformed ether."

"That's horrible!" The genasi shivered. "Let's find your door and get back on solid ground before we fall through the floor or something."

CHAPTER FIVE

30 Flamerule, the Year of Lightning Storms

The walls and towers of the Waymeet formed a difficult maze, but it was not impassable. The place was not really designed to entrap travelers, it was just a very complex structure with few good points of reference. The clear space in which the portal to the House of Long Silences stood was part of a boulevard or avenue that curved around a striking cluster of tall spires that Araevin presumed to be the center of the Waymeet. Smaller "streets" angled away into the crystalline depths. They passed door after door along the way, and down each intersecting passage they saw additional rows of portals leading away into the luminous distance.

"Where could all these portals *go*?" Donnor muttered to himself. "There are *thousands* of them here. Faerûn must be riddled with gates!"

"Aryvandaar was a vast, long-lived, and wealthy empire," said Araevin. "Look at it like this: Even if various mages or lords of Aryvandaar only found reason to create ten new portals a century, you would expect to find almost a thousand portals here."

"I haven't been counting, but it seems like there may be more than that," the Tethyrian said.

Araevin frowned. "I think you're right. It seems there are even more than there should be." He paused, searching his mind for what the Nightstar had told him of the place. "Ah, that makes sense."

The others waited for him to continue. Araevin shook himself, bringing his attention back to his companions. "The *Fhoeldin durr* itself creates new portals. In the years since Aryvandaar's fall, it has continued to propagate portals throughout Faerûn—and into other planes and worlds, as well. That is why it has become so dangerous. Over the centuries, its expansion has weakened the barriers between the planes, especially in places where people created any number of portals of their own."

"Like Sildëyuir," Nesterin said. The star elf narrowed his eyes, studying the great artifice thoughtfully.

"Like Sildëyuir," Araevin agreed. "Or Netheril, or Myth Drannor in the dark years leading up to its fall." He paused to check his bearings, and turned toward a smaller alleyway leading off the large esplanade they had been following. "I don't think the mages who built this place intended for that to happen. They assumed that they or their descendants would be able to guide and govern the Waymeet's expansion and function over the centuries. But Aryvandaar fell, and this place was left to govern itself."

"Now that we're here, why don't you just take control of it like you did at Myth Glaurach?" Maresa asked. "Or just destroy it outright?"

Araevin shook his head. "I'm afraid the protections over this mythal are beyond my skill. That's why I need the entire crystal, so I can gain access to the mythal."

Jorin stopped suddenly, and knelt to look at something. "Araevin, what do you make of this?" he called.

The mage hurried over to his companion's side and looked over his shoulder. Near the footing below one of the portals a thick iron spike had been driven into the crystal, leaving a spiderweb of faint cracks that slowly leaked a luminescent blue fluid. Harsh runes and symbols inscribed in the spike glowed an angry red, just visible through the intervening crystal.

"Can you make out what the runes say?" Jorin asked.

"No, but I recognize the script. It's Infernal . . . the language of the Nine Hells."

"What do you think its purpose is?"

Araevin studied it for a moment, observing the delicate weave of the ancient elven magic and the bitter intrusion of the hellwrought spike. "I think it's pinning the portal open. Changing the portal's natural behavior by transfixing it with a corrupting spell."

Jorin looked up at him. "Should we remove it?"

"Go ahead and try, but be careful."

The ranger reached out to grasp the head of the spike, but he drew back his hand before he even touched the metal.

"It's hot," he explained.

He rummaged around in his pack and found a spare cloak to wrap around his hand, and he tried again. The spike didn't move an inch. Jorin shifted so that he was sitting on the ground, facing the portal, with his feet planted on the footing on each side of the spike, and grasped it with both hands. But still it didn't move.

Finally he gave up with a grunt of dissatisfaction and said, "It's anchored in there. We'll have to chip away the crystal or use magic to get it out."

"Leave it be," Araevin told him. "If we succeed in reuniting the crystal, it will not matter."

They hurried down the narrow avenue for another hundred yards or so, past more of the doorways transfixed with spikes. Then they turned a corner and came to something of a small square or open place amid the white spires. Great bands of iron had been riveted to the foot of one of the sharply soaring buttresses that leaped up into the interwoven spars overhead. As with the smaller spikes, it was also covered in fearsome lettering and glowed cherry-red with hellish magic. More of the iron bands were fixed to the crystalline walls and pillars nearby, and the whole area reeked of hot metal.

In the center of the small plaza stood a simple three-sided pillar, about fifteen feet tall, likewise clamped within spells scribed on hellwrought iron. Unlike the pearly white of the other crystal spars, it burned a bright blue. Araevin paused, searching the memory imparted by the Nightstar for details about the Waymeet.

"One moment," he said. "This is a speaking stone. We can speak to the *Fhoeldin Durr* here."

His companions exchanged puzzled glances behind him, but Araevin approached the blue pillar and set his hand on it. "Gatekeeper," he said softly. "Do you hear me?"

Nothing happened for a long moment, but then a dim flicker awoke in the depths of the pillar. The metal bands encircling the stone seemed to constrain the pillar's glow, smoldering brighter as the azure gleam danced more strongly in the pillar's depths.

A smooth, soft voice came from the pillar. "I am the Gatekeeper," it whispered. "I hear you, Araevin Teshurr."

"You know me?"

"I know anyone who addresses a speaking stone."

"Araevin, who are you speaking to?" Nesterin asked.

"The sentience of this mythal," Araevin answered him. "It is known as the Gatekeeper, because it guards the countless doors in this place."

"It's not doing a very good job," Maresa muttered.

"I am constrained by the infernal spells with which I have been bound, Maresa Rost," the pillar replied. "I have been prevented from fulfilling my purpose."

"What are these spells doing to you?" Araevin asked.

"The archdevil Malkizid seeks to subvert me. Already he can prevent me from closing the gates that his spells hold open. In time he will extinguish my consciousness altogether, and he will be free to use all of the powers of the Waymeet as he wishes."

"Is Malkizid here?" Araevin asked.

"No. But many yugoloths and devils who serve him are. You are in no small danger."

"Great," Maresa snarled. She shrugged her crossbow from her shoulders and laid a bolt in the rest, looking around anxiously.

Araevin thought for a moment, studying the blue gleam. "Are you required to report our presence to Malkizid or his agents? Or this conversation?"

"No, but that may not be true for much longer. Malkizid may be able to compel me to speak."

"I have a shard of the Gatekeeper's Crystal in my possession," he told the device. "I mean to find the remaining shards and use the device to undo the damage Malkizid's spells are causing. Can it be done?"

The pillar was silent for a time.

"Yes," it finally said. "But you will need all three shards."

"Do you know where the other shards are?"

"Not precisely, but I know which of my doors is closest to each shard," the voice in the pillar said. It hesitated for a moment then added, "Three nycaloths approach, Araevin Teshurr. They will be here in moments."

Araevin stole a glance over his shoulder, while his comrades nervously scanned the mist-wreathed crystal spars nearby. "Which door do we use?" he asked.

"I will indicate the portal you seek. Look to your left."

Araevin complied, and found that a flickering blue gleam danced in the crystal ramparts in that direction.

He glanced to his companions and said, "Let's go, before Malkizid's servants appear."

Quickly they hurried after the blue glow. As they neared

Final Gate • 81

the flickering light, it vanished from the crystal where it danced, only to appear a little farther on. No more than fifty yards from the plaza of the blue pillar, the light halted by a portal that stood near the base of another soaring buttress. Araevin was relieved to see that no infernal spike transfixed it. As they approached, the portal came to life, its milky surface abruptly changing into a smooth, pearly mist.

"Do you have any idea what might be on the other side?" Donnor said to Araevin.

"No," the sun elf admitted. "But this is the way I have to go."

He drew a deep breath, and stepped into the blank mists.

☉ ☉ ☉ ☉ ☉

From their campsite in the ruined manor house near the Pool of Yeven, Fflar and Ilsevele rode eastward along the south bank of the Ashaba, picking their way through lands that showed increasing signs of habitation the farther they traveled. The long, low rampart of the Dun Hills grew steadily closer, marching northeastward as if trying to beat them to Blackfeather Bridge.

The air grew hot and still as the day wore on. It seemed as if the forests, fields, and hills yearned for a cleansing rain, but the heat did not relent. Far behind them, to the west, thunderheads piled up on each other only to dissipate and reform, never coming any closer. They rode past a farmstead where dozens of cattle lay butchered out in the fields.

"Demons or devils," Fflar murmured. "Best keep on."

"All right," Ilsevele replied. She did not look long at the scene of the slaughter.

As they rode away, the sight still worried at the back of Fflar's mind, until it seemed like some accusing stare was fixed at a point between his shoulder blades.

There's no point in going back, he told himself. *You know what you'll find there. It's done, and any people there are beyond help.*

But finally he could stand it no more, and he stood up in the stirrups to look back at the ruined farm, several hundred yards behind them.

Mottled gray shadows raced through the undergrowth and bounded along the road behind the elven company.

Fflar stared for a moment, too horrified to even call out a warning. The monsters were doglike things as large as small horses, but thickly built. Chitinous plates armored their bodies, but for all that they were quick. Blunt, eyeless heads ended in enormous rasping jaws, from which long barbed tongues lolled. The nearest darted through the dusty shadows along the roadside only forty yards behind them.

Finally he found his voice. "Canoloths!" he cried. *"Run!"*

He spurred Thunder, and the roan stallion leaped ahead in a gallop. It galled Fflar to lead the flight, but he'd seen a dozen or more of the monsters in his single glance, and he didn't doubt that there were just as many that he hadn't seen yet . . . and if the creatures were herding them into an ambush, he wanted to meet it himself.

Ilsevele did not waste a moment before spurring Swiftwind right after him, and the rest of the Silver Guards were no slower. In the space of five heartbeats the small company was at a full gallop, racing along the dry, dusty trail. Two of the guards bringing up the rear unlimbered their bows and managed a few awkward shots at their pursuers, guiding their mounts with knees only as they twisted around to shoot at the closest of the canoloths. One of the monsters tumbled into a great cloud of dust, lamed by an arrow that caught its shoulder. Another broke away, shaking its head to dislodge the arrow embedded in its jaws. The rest began to fall off the pace, outdistanced by the elves' horses.

"I think we're losing them!" Ilsevele called.

"Watch out for an ambush!" Fflar called back to her. "These things are clever."

He turned his attention back to the road ahead, just in time to spot three canoloths leaping down out of the shadows from the higher ground on the right side of the road. One bowled over a Silver Guard and his mount, dragging the warrior down into the dust. The second came right for Fflar. Thunder whinnied and sheered away, almost throwing him, but the swordsman kept his seat and drew Keryvian. The canoloth darted after Thunder, lashing out with its hawser-thick tongue to lasso the horse's rear leg, but Fflar leaned back in the saddle and severed the tentacle-like member with a quick overhand cut. The monster roared and jerked back, only to be ridden down by another of the Silver Guards.

"Ilsevele!" Fflar cried.

He whirled around to find his charge, just in time to see her stand up in her stirrups and shoot a pair of arrows over Swiftwind's shoulder, skewering the third of their ambushers twice in the center of its open maw. The creature bucked and jumped, black blood spurting from its mouth, and Ilsevele hurtled over it in one smooth jump and kept going. Fflar galloped after her, and their remaining guards followed.

"Captain Starbrow!" cried one of the Silver Guards. "Illithor went down!"

Fflar risked another look over his shoulder. A hundred yards back down the road, four or five of the canoloths snarled and snapped in a murderous fury around the guard and the horse that had gone down.

"He's gone!" he snarled back at the escorts. "Keep on!"

Half a mile later, Fflar judged that they had outdistanced the canoloths, and signaled for the rest of the company to slow down. They eased first to a canter, then to a quick trot. The canoloths were nowhere in sight.

Ilsevele turned her mare and looked back the way they had come. "Illithor," she murmured. "*Aillesel Seldarie,* what an awful fate."

"There is nothing we can do for him now," Fflar said. He exchanged a long look with Ilsevele, and they continued on their way.

Only four miles farther on, they crested a steep hill and spied a large company of riders a few hundred yards ahead, encamped around an old roadside inn overlooking the Ashaba. Most of the cavalrymen were human, dressed in assorted surcoats of blue and white, with red-pennoned lances standing at the stirrup. Fflar held up his hand, and reined in. Beneath the tree-shadows at the top of the hill he was relatively certain that the cavalrymen below had not yet spotted them.

"I can't make out any device," Ilsevele said. "Are they Sembians?"

"It seems likely," Fflar said. He peered at the company ahead. "I don't know of any Dalesfolk cavalry that might be this far to the east. Of course, they're probably mercenaries in Sembia's pay, not Sembians proper."

"Even if they're only mercenaries, they'll report to someone with the authority to treat with us," Ilsevele said. "I suppose we have to start somewhere."

Fflar looked over to her. "They may have no interest in talking to us, Ilsevele. You know that."

"I know." She looked at the riders who followed them. "Seirye, you stay here with half the company. Be ready to cover our retreat with archery, in case we must flee."

Seirye, the young officer who was in charge of the Silver Guards, agreed with a nod. "We will be ready. Be careful, Lady Ilsevele."

"I will," she promised.

The Silver Guards detailed to accompany her down to the Sembian encampment fixed long white streamers to their lances, and she led Fflar and the others out into the open, riding slowly down toward the inn house.

Final Gate • 85

The humans below noticed them immediately. Men shouted and hurried to mount up and make ready for a fight, but as it became evident that only a handful of elves were approaching, the stir of excitement in the camp died down. After a few moments, a pair of human riders cantered out of the inn yard and rode up the road to meet the elves.

"I think this is close enough," Fflar observed. "Let's wait for those fellows to come to us."

"Very well," Ilsevele said.

She came to a halt in a spot about halfway between the hillcrest and the inn house. The Silver Guards waited nearby, watching the humans come closer. Fflar studied them as well. They were good riders, comfortable in the saddle. One was a stocky brown-haired man with a sweeping mustache, and the other was younger, with a long mane of fine yellow hair.

The two humans clattered up close to the elves, and reined in. They looked over Fflar and the others, traces of puzzlement in their eyes. Then the older man pointed at the white pennons hanging from the guards' lances.

"Is that a flag of truce?" he asked.

"It is," Ilsevele replied. "Will you parley with us?"

The broad-shouldered man shrugged. "Doesn't hurt to talk. Might I ask who I'm speaking to, my lady?"

"I am Ilsevele Miritar. I am a captain of the Queen's Spellarchers of Evermeet. This is Starbrow, and my guardsmen Aloiene, Deryth, Hasterien, and Sylleth."

"I'm Randil Moorwatch, of Elturel. This is my bannerman Teren. I am the captain of the Blue Griffon Company, formerly in the employ of Lord Borstag Duncastle of Sembia, now in the employ of Lord Miklos Selkirk of the same." The mercenary captain glanced up at the trees shadowing the hillcrest, and frowned. Fflar could imagine that he was asking himself how many more elves were hidden in the woods there. Then he returned his attention to Ilsevele. "Well, my lady Miritar, what is it that I can do for you?"

"I wish passage through your lines, and an escort to the commander of Sembia's army in these lands," Ilsevele said. Her Common had improved in the months since she'd left Evermeet but still held something of the melodious tones of Elvish in her accent.

"And what would you like to speak to our commanders about?" Moorwatch asked.

"We believe that the daemonfey are your enemy as well as ours. We wish to make common cause against the forces of Sarya Dlardrageth."

The human captain narrowed his eyes, thinking. "If by 'daemonfey' you mean the various hellspawned monsters roving around these little flyspeck Dales, then I can't say I disagree with you. But you're not thinking clearly if you believe you can talk the Sembians into helping you retake Cormanthor."

"But surely you must see—"

"It doesn't matter what I see," Moorwatch said, holding up his hand to interrupt her. "I'm not a Sembian, and this isn't my war. The Blue Griffons fight for good Sembian gold, and I've come to learn that our paymasters didn't get as rich as they are by giving away anything for free."

Ilsevele hesitated. Fflar decided to step in to help her. "Will you allow us to take up the question with your employers?" he asked.

The captain looked over to him. "This whole campaign is buggered beyond belief. We certainly didn't sign on to fight our way through hordes of demons, devils, and worse. I suppose I'll pass you through my lines, and send along Teren here with a dozen Blue Griffons to provide safe conduct. I warn you, though—if this is a ruse of some kind, it will go hard with you."

"No ruse," Fflar promised. "We have six—no, five—more who will join our party, with your leave." Illithor's journey had come to an end in the road a few miles back. They were one fewer than they had been.

"Very well," the human captain agreed.

Fflar glanced back at the woods and signaled the rest of their Silver Guards to join them, while Moorwatch arranged for a detachment of his men to mount up. In ten breaths Fflar, Ilsevele, and the rest of their small company were ringed by a score of vigilant Blue Griffon riders—seasoned sellswords of a much smarter appearance than Fflar would have expected of mercenaries. He took a moment to warn Moorwatch about the canoloths roaming the road a few miles to the west, and they set out with the bannerman Teren and his riders.

The young officer led them east along the river for a mile or so, while the mercenary guards conversed among themselves in low voices, sticking to their own native Chondathan rather than Common. Then they struck southeast on a wide trail that climbed up into the Dun Hills, veering away from the broad river vale behind them. Few people lived in the hills, but from time to time they passed lonely lime kilns and disused quarries.

"Where are you taking us?" Ilsevele finally asked Bannerman Teren.

"Tegal's Mark in Tasseldale, my lady," the young officer answered.

"Lord Selkirk is there?"

Teren shrugged. "It's as good a place as any to start looking. Lord Selkirk has been riding all over the southern Dales for a month now, trying to make some sort of sense out of things. If he's not in Tegal's Mark, it's likely that he'll pass through within a day or two."

"It's important that I speak with him as soon as possible," Ilsevele said. "One of my people died but a short time ago to see me to your lines."

"That's not up to me, my lady. I expect he'll call on you or send for you as soon as he can, though."

Fflar nodded to himself. It was nothing more than good common sense not to lead enemy emissaries right into your headquarters, after all. A skillful wizard could easily mark the place for scrying spells or secret gates later on, creating all sorts of trouble. He wouldn't have led a Sembian party straight to Seiveril without taking similar precautions against treachery.

They reached the small town of Tegal's Mark shortly before sunset, riding down out of the dusty hills into a fair green valley of apple orchards and small stone farmhouses. Tasseldale had not yet suffered much from the daemonfey, but that did not mean the war had bypassed the place. The town was ringed by the patchwork tents and shelters of Sembia's battered army, with many hundreds of men bivouacked in the fields and orchards nearby. More soldiers filled the dirt streets of the town. And all around the soldiers' camps sprawled the simple shelters and crowded wagons of refugees from Battledale, Mistledale, and the lands between.

Teren and his Blue Griffons led them into the town itself, threading their way through the narrow lanes with some difficulty. They finally halted by a fine-looking inn near the middle of the town. The signboard read simply "The Markhouse."

"I'll arrange quarters for you here," the bannerman said. "You can wait here until Lord Selkirk sends for you."

"We thank you, bannerman," Ilsevele said.

"I am afraid that you will have to remain here until we tell you otherwise, Lady Miritar. If you or any of your folk need to go out, you'll have to be escorted. We wouldn't want any misunderstandings."

Ilsevele nodded. "We understand."

The young officer nodded. "In that case, I'll see to your rooms, and notify the Silver Ravens that you are here and wish to speak with Lord Selkirk." He dismounted, handed his reins to another of the Blue Griffons, and touched his brow before striding into the Markhouse.

Fflar studied the inn. It seemed strong and well-built, which might be important if they had to fight in or around the place. He glanced back at the street behind them, noting the ways that led out of the town. With care, it might just be barely possible to get out from under the Sembians' hands if they needed to.

He felt eyes upon him, and looked up at a window in the upper floor of the Markhouse. A dark-haired human girl of striking beauty stood there, gazing coldly down on the elves in the courtyard. She regarded him with no expression at all for a long moment, and moved away from the window.

"We're in danger here," he said quietly.

"I know, but I mean to carry on as if I expect nothing but good faith," Ilsevele replied. "Still, I didn't expect to be put under house arrest."

"That's the trouble with crossing an enemy's lines under a flag of truce. You may find it harder to get out than it was to get in." Fflar smiled crookedly at her. "How long do we wait before we go looking for this Selkirk ourselves?"

"I'll give him two days," Ilsevele said. "After that, we'll see."

ॐ ॐ ॐ ॐ ॐ

Absolute lightlessness greeted Araevin on the far side of the portal, a darkness so complete that for one panicked moment he wondered if the portal had somehow hurled him into solid stone. He inhaled sharply—the air was very cold and dry—and staggered into an awkward crouch, fearful that he might blunder over some unseen precipice in the dark. His own sudden breath was the only thing he could hear in the blackness. Cold, rough rock greeted his fingertips, and he reassured himself that he was simply standing in an unlit cavern of some kind.

"Courage, Araevin," he murmured.

He fished a small copper coin out of his belt pouch by feel, and pronounced a simple light spell on it. The copper piece began to glow with a bright yellow radiance, dispelling the darkness around him so that Araevin could see where he stood.

As he had suspected, it was a cavern of some kind—a long, winding passageway that seemed to follow the bottom of a crevice, for the walls simply leaned against each other about twenty feet overhead. He turned to look at the portal behind him, and found that it was set in a square alcove hewn out of the living rock. Its rectangular lintel was carved with geometric designs that reminded Araevin of dwarven work. He examined the strange runes with interest, but before he could make much out of them, shadows filled the space within the lintel and parted suddenly. Maresa stepped through, rapier in one hand and crossbow in the other.

"Where in the Nine Hells—" she began, but then she remembered to move away from the door. She took several quick strides into the tunnel, making room for Nesterin, Donnor, and Jorin to follow her through. Araevin held his magical light aloft, and kept watch over the passageway while the rest of his companions joined him.

"We're somewhere in the Underdark, aren't we?" said Donnor. One thick hand rested on the hilt of the broadsword at his belt.

"I think so," Araevin replied. He murmured the words of a seeking spell, and frowned as the magic seemed to fray awkwardly beneath his subtle shaping. *Faerzress,* he remembered. The weird magical energy permeating the deep Underdark sometimes interfered with spellcasting. At the last moment he rallied and managed to finish the spell despite the strange interference.

The silent call of the second shard echoed from the darkness, somewhere not far off. "The Gatekeeper was right. We're close to the second shard," he told his friends.

"Thank Tymora for that, at least," Maresa muttered.

"Have any of you traveled in the Underdark before?" Araevin asked.

"I have, a little," said Jorin. "There are extensive caverns and passages under the Yuirwood, at least in places." He shivered. "I don't remember it being this cold, though."

Final Gate • 91

"I traveled through the upper reaches of Deep Shanatar two years ago," Donnor said. The Tethyrian grimaced. "I can't say I liked it much."

"Until today, I'd succeeded in avoiding the place," Maresa answered. Her pale hair hung still around her shoulders, unstirred by even the faintest breeze. In the depths of the earth, the magic of elemental air in her veins guttered as low as a dying candle-flame. "My mother never had anything nice to say about it. She told me plenty of stories of the horrors the Company of the White Star encountered down here."

"I remember well," Araevin said. It had been more than twenty years since he had ventured into the vast warrens beneath the Chionthar Vale with Belmora, Theleda, Grayth, and the rest, but he had not forgotten a moment of it. "Let's make sure that we all have light close at hand. If you get separated from everyone else, you'll want illumination."

They searched through their packs, and shared out the candles and tinder kits they carried. Donnor had a half-dozen sunrods, and divided those as well. Of course, Araevin and Donnor had minor light spells they could call on, too.

"We'll use our spells first, and save the sunrods for an emergency," Araevin suggested. "Now, as for the Underdark . . . above all else, we must stay together. This place is vast and featureless. Sound plays tricks on your ears, so that you may think a distant voice is close by, and someone only a stone's throw away might not be able to hear you even if you shout. I can't warn you enough about how easy it is to get lost, and how hard it is to be found once you're out of sight and earshot.

"You'll find that this place is more hostile than the worst desert you can imagine. We may get lucky and find fresh water, but food is almost nonexistent. We must conserve our rations and our water carefully, for as long as we are down here.

"Finally, this place is home to dreadful monsters such as aboleths, mind flayers, beholders, and worse. Many are drawn by light and sound, so we should try to stay quiet and use as little light as we can."

"Anything else?" Maresa asked, rolling her eyes.

The sun elf frowned, taking her question literally. "Oh, one more thing—we can't count on teleporting. There are magical emanations in the rock all around us that often ruin teleport spells. It should be our very last resort. Once we leave this portal, we have no easy way back to the surface unless we retrace our steps to this spot, or stumble across another portal somewhere else."

"Fine," the genasi said. "Let's get going."

Araevin glanced up and down the passageway, and turned toward his right. "This way, then. The shard is somewhere in this direction."

CHAPTER SIX

3 Eleasias, the Year of Lightning Storms

They marched for what seemed like an eternity through the cold gloom, following the passage through the miles-long crevice. From time to time the path broke out into open spaces where small cairns of stones marked the trail through vast, black caverns. Araevin guessed that their path followed some subterranean road or trade route. Fortunately, they encountered no other travelers along the way.

After several miles, Araevin called a halt, and they rested for a time in a small cave that led away from the main path. It was almost impossible to judge the passage of time. There was no sky to see, no wind to taste, no forest-sound to listen to. The Underdark was truly a timeless place, in the sense that time altered nothing in the utter darkness and silence. Every moment was the same as the one that preceded it, and countless moments before that.

"What a dreary place," Nesterin said quietly to him while their companions slept. "I can't believe that anyone, not even the drow, could endure it for long."

"This seems to be a desolate stretch of the Underdark," Araevin agreed. "Not all of it is so featureless. In other places there are titanic vaults where great forests of fungus grow, vast lightless seas, spectacular waterfalls miles high, even caverns lit by glimmering veils of wizard fire, like the midwinter lights of the far north."

"You have seen these things?"

"Only a few. And to be honest, for every secret wonder one finds in the depths, there are ten deadly perils. We are not made for a life so far beneath the earth."

Nesterin glanced up at the ceiling of their small cave, and shuddered. "I could go mad just thinking about the weight of the rock over my head right now."

"It's better not to dwell on it," Araevin advised him. He stood and stretched, rubbing his arms vigorously. Strangely enough, he wasn't as troubled by the pervasive chill of the place as he would have been before the *telmiirkara neshyrr*. He sensed the heavy cold of the stone sinking into him, but it seemed to have little power to sap his strength. His companions, on the other hand, clearly needed every blanket they carried in their packs. Next time we'll have to risk a fire, Araevin decided. "Let's rouse the others. I think we've rested at least a quarter of a day, and I am as anxious as Maresa to finish our work down here and leave this place behind us."

The small company broke camp and pressed on into the darkness, winding farther from the portal leading back to the surface. At one point they found that their road led through a tunnel hewn through a bed of solid rock. The entrance was marked with a squared-off archway with a distinctly trapezoidal outline. Strange old runes marked the heavy stone slabs that made the arch, interspersed with sharply geometric designs.

"Is that Dwarvish?" Donnor asked after studying the ominous archway.

"No," Araevin replied. "I'm afraid I don't recognize the language."

They continued through the hewn tunnel, and Araevin became conscious of a subtle change in the quality of the air. It was growing colder, bitterly so. And it seemed that the air felt more open, less constrained, even as the darkness grew almost impenetrable, muffling all sound and drinking in their feeble lights with endless and ancient hunger. He felt his companions tensing uncomfortably, shoulders tightening, hands straying closer to weapons.

"There's something up ahead," Jorin whispered. "The air's changed somehow."

"We know," Maresa answered him. "It's sort of hard to miss."

They emerged from the tunnel but saw nothing ahead. Then Jorin, who was in the lead, scuffed to a stop with a muttered oath and threw out his arm to stop the others.

"A sheer precipice," the ranger said. "Our road turns to the right and hugs the wall. Be careful, or you'll walk right off into nothing."

Slowly, they negotiated the turn. Araevin paused for a moment, staring out into the gloom. The light shining from his enspelled coin illuminated a great wall that towered up out of sight overhead and fell away into blackness underfoot. Their tunnel simply emerged in the middle of this vast vertical obstacle, and met a narrow ledge winding along the side of the empty space. Staring into the darkness, Araevin could feel in his bones that it was vast indeed, cold, silent, and still as the crypt. No rail or wall marked the edge of the drop. The ledge was simply a path about eight or nine feet wide cut from the side of the immense cavern.

"By the Morninglord," Donnor Kerth murmured. "It's titanic."

The illimitable darkness around them seemed to deaden sound, swallowing their voices as if to enforce its own silence on the intruders.

"I think you chose the wrong god to swear by," said Jorin. "I promise you this place has never seen a dawn, not since the making of the world."

"Donnor, do you have a light spell ready?" Araevin asked.

The human knight grimaced. "I prayed to Lathander for almost nothing else when I rose today."

"Cast one now, please."

The Lathanderite held out his holy symbol, a bronze sunburst, and spoke the words of his holy prayer. His symbol gleamed brightly and began to shine, but Araevin thought the light spell seemed noticeably weaker than he might have expected. It was not unusual for certain spots to suppress magic of different schools, and he could well believe that the abyss before them muted light spells. When Donnor's light gained its full strength, such as it was, Araevin stepped close to the edge and tossed his own illuminated copper into the darkness.

The coin spun lazily down into the dark, falling past a featureless wall that seemed to plunge straight down. It dwindled into the deeps, receding farther and farther. And it kept on going, a bright point of light that fell, and fell, and fell, until Araevin felt sick at the sight of it.

"Aillesel Seldarie," he breathed.

"By all the golden heavens, how far down does that go?" Donnor muttered.

"I counted thirty-three heartbeats before I lost sight of it," Jorin said. He shivered. "It must be miles."

"At least you'd have plenty of time to make your peace with the gods before you hit bottom," said Maresa. "You might even have time to eulogize yourself, too."

Giving the widest berth possible to the yawning darkness waiting on the left, they followed the ledge to the right. Araevin expected that they might travel a few hundred yards alongside the silent abyss before their path turned back into some smaller cavern or crevice, but as they walked the road simply followed the wall of the abyss, going on for what must have been mile after mile. From time to time the road climbed up or down a few steps at a time, and on a couple of occasions they passed by deep alcoves or niches cut into the rock wall at their right—safe resting places created by or for travelers who went that way, Araevin guessed. But what truly disturbed him were the staircases they passed on their left. Every so often they would come to a squat trapezoidal column in a landing of sorts overlooking the edge, marking the place where a set of steep, narrow stairs climbed up out of the measureless blackness below. Someone—or some*thing*, he reminded himself—had delved ambitiously in the cold black emptiness of the abyss.

After an eternity of marching alongside the abyss, they stopped and rested in one of the alcoves. For the comfort of his friends, Araevin covered the opening of the place with an illusion of barren rock, so that they could build a small fire from a little store of firewood Donnor and Jorin carried in their packs. A warm meal cheered them somewhat, but all too soon they had to allow their little fire to gutter down to glowing embers, and the darkness outside seemed to press in on them with an almost insatiable hunger. Without even realizing they were doing it, they fell silent and sat still listening to the sound of the dark, straining to catch even the tiniest hint of something from the vast space beyond their small refuge.

Araevin found himself crouching forward on the edge of his seat, his arms wrapped close around his body, an awful suspense hanging over him. He shook himself a little, and managed to bring himself around to look at his friends, only to find everyone else sitting silently in the dark, faces sick with dread.

By all the gods, what is this place? he wondered. What is it we think we're listening for? "Nesterin," he rasped. He cleared his throat, and tried again. "Nisterin, I think we could use a little music. Something to alleviate the darkness."

The star elf looked at him blankly for a moment, and nodded numbly. He drew a small flute from his vest pocket, and began to play—awkwardly at first, but then with a little more confidence and feeling. He did not try a merry air, but instead a small plaintive melody that nevertheless managed to break the unbearable tension. Soon enough they breathed easier and did not sit huddled anxiously against the blackness outside.

"The damnable thing about it," Donnor managed, "is that it's so weirdly *still*. It's a vast space out there, miles long, miles high, and in all that space there's not a breath of wind moving. We're on the side of a mountain thousands of feet high, and it's as quiet as the inside of a mausoleum."

"It's unnatural," Araevin agreed. If nothing else, he would have expected to hear the distant sounds of water on stone, or a faint susurrus of air breathing through rock. He started to speak, but Jorin hushed them all with a single curt gesture of his hand.

"Something is coming," the ranger whispered.

He sat near the opening of the ledge, listening intently. Araevin's illusionary wall kept any of their faint light from leaking out of the alcove, but that didn't mean they could not be heard. They all fell silent, and Araevin heard it too—a faint rustling, slow, deliberate, accompanied by thin wheezing.

Maresa glided over to crouch next to Jorin and peer through the wall. Unlike the elves, who could see well with little light but couldn't manage with none at all, the genasi could see a little even in absolute darkness—a gift of her elemental bloodline. She frowned in puzzlement, staring at something the rest of them could not see.

After a moment she looked back to Araevin and whispered, "It's a gnome of some kind, crawling along the ledge. He's sick or injured, hardly moving at all. What do we do?"

The sun elf frowned. In the Underdark, it was generally wisest to avoid any interaction you could. After all, who was to say that the wretch outside wasn't being hunted by mind flayers, drow slavers, or anything else imaginable? But it was simply unthinkable to let a person crawl alone through that fearful blackness. And there was at least some chance that they might learn something if they aided the fellow.

"Help him in," Araevin said.

Maresa nodded. She and Jorin stepped out onto the ledge, and a moment later they returned to the small alcove with the small, tattered traveler. He was indeed a gnome, only about three feet tall. His skin was gray, and he was bald, with short legs and long arms. Dreadful bloody bruises scored his knees and elbows. Even as Maresa and Jorin helped him into their shelter, the gnome's arms and legs moved in slow circles, still crawling, his small dark eyes focused on nothing at all as he wheezed and muttered in his own strange tongue.

"What happened to this fellow?" Nesterin asked, horrified.

"Donnor, can you do anything for him?" Araevin asked.

"We will see," the Lathanderite answered.

He moved beside the small wretch and studied him for a moment. Then, breathing the words of his healing prayers, he took hold of the gnome's gnarled hands. A warm golden glow appeared around Donnor's hands and slowly sank into the gnome's pebbly hide. The slow, autonomous clawing and scrabbling stopped, and the small creature heaved a ragged sigh of relief. In a few moments he came to himself and looked up at Araevin and his friends, his gray face taut with suspicion.

"Do you speak Common?" Araevin asked him.

"Not much. A little," the gnome croaked in a surprisingly deep voice.

"What is your name?"

"Galdindormm. I am called Galdindormm."

"Well, Galdindormm, I am Araevin Teshurr of Evermeet. My companions Maresa, Donnor, Jorin, and Nesterin. You are a deep gnome?"

"Yes. Svirfneblin, the deep gnomes, you call us." He tried to sit up but was simply too weak for it. "Why would you help me?"

"You were in need," Araevin answered. "That is enough for us. Though we hope that you might be able to tell us something about this portion of the Underdark we've wandered into. We are strangers to this place, as you can surely see."

The deep gnome made a thick sound in his throat, and for a moment Araevin feared the small creature was dying in front of his eyes before he realized that Galdindormm was laughing—a dry and harsh sort of laughter, but laughter nonetheless. "Why would surface-dwellers come to Lorosfyr? Do you have no ears for the whispers in the dark? Leave while you can, or my fate will be yours."

"I don't like the sound of that," Maresa snorted.

"Lorosfyr?" Araevin asked the deep gnome. "This place is called Lorosfyr?"

"That is the name for the abyss," the gnome croaked. "Lorosfyr, the Maddening Dark. It is a mighty vault. Many days across, many days around. It is accursed." The gnome shook his head and shuddered, his eyes growing distant as some inner fear caught his mind. "Ten thousand steps I climbed, crawling on my hands and knees, and still I can hear her calling me back. Do not let me go back to her, I beg you! Do not let me listen to her!"

"Who, Galdindormm? Who are you speaking of?" Araevin asked gently.

"The Sybil of the Deeps . . . Selydra, the Pale Queen . . ." Weakly the gnome raised his arms and buried his face, trying to hide from whatever memory tormented him. "She drank of my soul, strangers. And now she will come to drink of yours. There is no escape. No escape."

❧ ❧ ❧ ❧ ❧

Final Gate • 101

Warm, steady rain shrouded the towers of Myth Drannor, steaming and smoking where it fell on the forges and foundries the fey'ri had built amid the ruins. Sarya Dlardrageth enjoyed the sounds of raindrops hissing against hot metal and the harsh ringing hammer strokes of her fey'ri armorers at work. She had spent so many centuries immobile yet aware in the vaults beneath Hellgate Keep, and even though she'd been free for the better part of five years, she still reveled in simple physical sensations and freedom from confinement.

She stood in an old broken archway with her wings spread over her head, sheltering her face from the summer rain as she watched her fey'ri at work. Half a dozen of her demon-tainted followers worked to restore an ancient battle-construct to life. The secret crafts of weapon making and the building of arcane war engines were just as valuable to the old Siluvanedan way of war as swordplay and battle magic. Two of the more magically skilled craftsmen chanted and wove their hands in arcane passes, reweaving the old spells that had once powered the device. Others chipped away at countless ages of rust and corrosion, while two more of her fey'ri smiths were busy pouring molten iron into a sand mold, fabricating a new armor plate to replace one that was irreparably damaged.

Her son Xhalph towered behind her, his four powerful arms folded in two rows across his broad chest. "Is this truly worth the effort, Mother?" he asked. "The old warmachines are good for defense, but they are ponderous and slow. They're almost useless in the attack, especially when our foes cower a hundred miles away."

"It pleases me to have the war-constructs put back in working order," Sarya answered. "The automatons we've already repaired serve as a stout defense for our new capital when our legions are far away. And one never knows—we might yet find a way to bring them to the fight."

Xhalph inclined his head, accepting her explanation.

He was unconvinced but saw no point in arguing about it. Of course, he had most of the strength of his demonic father, a mighty glabrezu. Xhalph could crumple armor plate in his bare hands, or cleave a strong human knight and the horse on which he rode with a single blow of one of his heavy scimitars. But he overlooked the fact that few of Sarya's fey'ri possessed such a distinguished bloodline. He'd never needed old lore or skill at magic to master his foes, when pure physical ferocity sufficed.

Just as well, Sarya decided. Given his formidable physical prowess, an inclination toward arcane study or subtle plotting would have made him too dangerous to her. She had already been forced to destroy her son Ryvvik not long after the three Dlardrageths had been freed from the vaults beneath Hellgate Keep, simply because Ryvvik was gifted with a subtle and treacherous turn of mind. She would not like to do the same to Xhalph and start over again with new offspring.

A flutter of wings behind her caught her attention. "Lady Sarya, Teryani Ealoeth has returned from the Sembian camp," a fey'ri said, bowing before her. "She craves an audience with you."

Sarya frowned. Teryani was her spy and assassin in the midst of the Sembian army. Each time she ventured to leave the Sembians and report, she risked discovery . . . but Teryani was not the sort to waste Sarya's time.

"Very well. Have her join us."

The messenger thumped his breastplate in salute and sprang back up into the air, winging back to his post. He quickly returned with a strikingly beautiful fey'ri in tow. Teryani had a finely shaped face with large, dark eyes, hair of silken midnight, and a soft, coy smile that could incite men to kill when she willed it. She knelt before Sarya, and said, "My queen."

Sarya smiled coldly at the deference the girl showed, and motioned for her to rise. "Teryani, my dear. What brings you here?"

"I have news that seemed important, Lady Sarya. I saw Ilsevele Miritar ride into Tegal's Mark with the champion Starbrow, a little more than a day ago. They are waiting for an audience with Miklos Selkirk."

"Did you learn what business they have with Selkirk?"

"Miritar's daughter has been sent to work out a truce with the Sembians," Teryani said. "Moreover, I think she may hope to make an ally of Sembia."

The daemonfey queen hissed in irritation and shook out her wings with a quick snap. Without even thinking about it, she began to pace restlessly, a habit she had formed since escaping from the imprisonment of millennia. Teryani simply awaited her queen's will with equanimity, hands folded in her lap. She did not lack for courage, Sarya noted.

"You did well, Teryani," she finally said. "We must find some way to keep our enemies from collaborating against us."

"The Sembians are close to breaking, Mother," Xhalph observed. "Many of their mercenary companies have given up the battle already. As long as we refrain from attacking Sembia itself, there is little reason for the fat merchants who rule that land to pour more of their precious treasure into the Dales. Miritar will waste her time trying to convince them otherwise."

Sarya turned to gaze at her son with some small surprise. It was not often that Xhalph discerned a point at which restraint became a virtue, but he was right about Sembia. As long as she did not directly threaten the Sembians in their rich cities to the south, they would be inclined to write off the Dalelands as a bad investment.

"If they are as close to giving up the campaign as you think, then we should help to decide the issue for them," Sarya said. "Leave them be for now. While they count the costs of their campaign, we will turn our full strength against Miritar. But we must see to it that their negotiations lead to nothing."

"What do you wish me to do, Lady Sarya?" Teryani asked.

"If you can slay Miklos Selkirk or Ilsevele Miritar, and make it seem like an act of treachery by one side or the other, that should fix things nicely," Sarya said. "I suspect it would work better if you arranged for Miritar's death and affixed the blame to the Sembians."

"It will be as you wish, my queen." Teryani bowed again, acknowledging the command. Then she looked up to Sarya. "Neither the palebloods nor the Sembians will find cause to believe that we had anything to do with it."

"Good. I think I may have the perfect instrument for you to use in this work." Sarya smiled cruelly, implications dancing in her mind. "I will place at your disposal the services of the Cormanthoran drow. Use them to handle the slaying, and see to it that they are found to be in the employ of Sembians who wished Ilsevele Miritar dead . . . but did not want to be caught at it."

Teryani's dark eyes danced with mischief. "If I may be so bold, my queen, that is a subtle and brilliant ploy indeed. I will endeavor to carry it off as you have commanded."

"I have every confidence in you, Teryani," Sarya told her.

❖ ❖ ❖ ❖ ❖

Despite Donnor's healing spells, Galdindormm grew weaker. The small gray gnome passed in and out of consciousness in their small refuge against the darkness outside. Whenever he passed out, his arms and legs began to move with an awful life of their own. Araevin suspected that if they had not restrained the poor wretch, his own traitorous limbs would have dragged him to the edge of the precipice and toppled him over the edge in answer to the sinister call that still gripped him.

Araevin essayed a spell to break whatever curse lay over the gnome, but his magic did little more than reward the mortally exhausted gnome with a respite of peaceful sleep. And so Galdindormm died not long after crawling to their refuge, body and spirit spent beyond any hope of resuscitation.

Donnor arranged the deep gnome's limbs as best he could, and spoke Lathander's prayers over the body in the hope that death had brought some sort of release for the broken creature. When he had finished, he turned to Araevin and asked, "Do you know how his people would inter him, Araevin? I don't like the idea of leaving him with nothing more than a blanket to cover him."

"I don't know much about the svirfneblin, but I would guess that they are content to sleep under stone," said Araevin. He glanced around the alcove, and sighed. "Let's loosen some rock from the walls of this niche, and use it to build a cairn for him."

When they had finished, the gnome's body was covered with a mound of stones. Doubtless his own folk would have done better, but Araevin judged it as good as they could do given the materials at hand. He did not like leaving Galdindormm only a few feet from the oppressive darkness outside, but he resolved that if they ran into any more of the deep gnomes, he'd tell them where and how Galdindormm was buried. They would improve on the arrangements if it was important to them.

With Galdindormm seen to, Araevin took out his shard of the Gatekeeper's Crystal and weighed it in his hand. Perhaps it was the absolute quality of the darkness around them, but it seemed to him that the shard's pearlescence was brighter and more marked than before. A sign that the second shard was close? he wondered. To make sure, he cast another divining spell, seeking some sign of the shard's twin. The resonant tone in his mind was clear and close.

It was also straight down.

"Well," he murmured, "I suppose I was expecting that."

"The shard's somewhere down there, isn't it?" Maresa said, nodding at the still blackness beyond their narrow ledge. The genasi heaved a deep breath and smacked one fist against the stone floor. "Damn it all, I just *knew* it."

"I'm sorry," Araevin told his friends. "The signs are clear to me. I will have to descend into the abyss."

"You will try one of the stairways?" Jorin asked.

"I hesitate to rely on a flying spell. If I wandered a little too far from the wall, I might become lost in the void, unable to find my way back to the side. And eventually my flying magic would be exhausted." Araevin shrugged. "Besides, it seems to me that the stairs must lead *somewhere*. I would not be surprised to find that the second shard is there. It seems more likely to me that the shard would appear near some kind of feature, as opposed to a completely random spot on the floor of this great void."

"If it has a floor," Maresa interrupted.

"In any event, the shard is somewhere below, and the stairs lead down. If I don't find the shard at the foot of the stairs, I'll try my divining spells again. It's merely a matter of persistence."

"What about this Pale Queen the gnome whispered of?" Nesterin asked him. "He said that he climbed to escape from her. Descending the stairs would seem to lead us into her domain, whatever that might be." The star elf glanced at the cairn of stones they had raised over the corpse. "It wasn't the climb alone that killed poor Galdindormm. He was under the influence of some dark and deadly curse, I am sure of it. Neither you nor Donnor could break it, and that gives me no small amount of concern."

"What if she has the shard?" Donnor rumbled. "If she is a being of knowledge and power, she would surely recognize the importance of the thing, wouldn't she?"

Araevin nodded. "I think you are right, Donnor. I think I will find that this Selydra has the shard. Somehow I will have to get it from her."

They set out back the way they had come, heading for the last staircase they had passed. Araevin guessed that it was not more than three or four miles behind them. After they had walked for a timeless period through the silent darkness of Lorosfyr they finally came to the squat, oddly shaped pillar that marked the place where the steep stairs plunged down into the unthinkable darkness. Araevin hesitated a moment, staring down at the steps, and he began to descend.

The stone steps were cut into a sloping notch or crease hewn out of the abyss's wall. The staircase was about eight or nine feet in width, the steps about a foot tall and a foot deep. They were noticeably worn in the center, each step seeming to sag beneath the wear of the countless feet that must have passed that way—though who or what could have walked the dizzying path so frequently, Araevin could not say. He quickly realized that the simple act of descending the stairs required all of his attention. One careless step could result in an unimaginable fall. And it was more than a little physically demanding, so that not long after they started Araevin's thighs and calves burned with the effort of the descent.

"The question that occurs to me," Nesterin said softly as they shuffled and picked their way ever lower, "is how long it will take us to climb back up these stairs when we wish to leave. That is something I am not looking forward to."

"Speak for yourself," Maresa told him. "If climbing these damned stairs means leaving this place behind us, I think I'll find a way to manage it."

After a seemingly interminable descent, they came to a landing or switchback of a sort. Two more of the squared-off pillars marked the spot, each covered with more of the mysterious runes. The small company rested for a time at the landing, but it was bitterly cold, and their exertions had rendered them all too susceptible to the creeping numbness of the frigid stone and air. And worse yet, they were absolutely entombed in the dark—blackness above, blackness below, blackness all around them—with only a tiny little circle of cold and cheerless rock revealed by their inadequate lights. Araevin found himself entertaining the curious delusion that the world simply ended beyond their dim little sphere, and that the endless stairs were nothing more than an invention of the dark that faded back into nothingness once they had passed by. It was not a thought he cared for at all.

They tried to make a small meal of the rations they carried, but no one was very hungry. The weight of the abyss around them pressed close. Implacably silent, the stillness was like some awakened glacier of pure night. There was a conscious malevolence to the place that encouraged the mind to wander into despondency. After a time Araevin realized that the company had fallen still and silent again, straining to hear the sound of the darkness. Somehow he shook himself to motion again, and roused the rest.

"Come, my friends," he said. "I think it is not good to stay here too long."

"What did the gnome call this place? The Maddening Dark?" Jorin said. "I can see how it earned its name."

They started down the next great turn of the stairs, and dropped farther and farther from the level of the road's ledge. Each step jarred the legs until it seemed that the whole body dreaded the next footfall, but still they pressed on, winding deeper and deeper into the dark. Finally, when Araevin began to despair of seeing anything other than the few steps ahead and the few steps behind, the stairs reached a sort of broad ledge or shelf in the side of the abyss. It was impossible to see the full extent of the place, but strange old stone buildings brooded here in the darkness, guarding another switchback leading even farther down. Like the pillars above, the buildings were squat and square, with carefully worked geometric reliefs cut into the stones from which they were built.

"Some sort of guardhouse?" Donnor wondered aloud. "A watchpost to keep enemies from descending any deeper?"

"Whatever it is, it will have to serve as a campsite," Araevin decided. "We've been descending for too long, and this is the only shelter we've come across. I think we should rest before we attempt the next turn of the stair."

Nesterin studied the silent ruins looming up out of the lightlessness around them. "It seems an ill-omened place to me, Araevin."

"I know, but I don't want to be forced to make camp in the middle of the stairs. This will have to do." Araevin chose a structure that backed against the wall of the abyss, as opposed to one that stood on the open side of the ledge, and carefully peered into the square doorway. The chamber within was empty and cheerless, but at least the floor was level and it did not offer the opportunity to miss a step and plummet to one's death. "We'll sleep here, and press on when we're more rested."

CHAPTER SEVEN

5 Eleasias, the Year of Lightning Storms

Lord Miklos Selkirk sent for Ilsevele early in the morning of their third day in Tegal's Mark. A finely dressed Sembian officer delivered the news, requesting Lady Miritar and her retainers to follow him to the Sharburg—the town's small keep—after they had breakfasted and dressed. Ilsevele accepted the invitation with a gracious nod, and saw the courier to the suite's door.

After he withdrew, she turned to Fflar and said, "Well, it seems that Lord Selkirk has returned."

"I was beginning to wonder if the Sembians wanted to talk with us or not," he answered. In fact, he had found himself wondering whether the Sembians intended to hear them out at all.

"I trust there has been a good reason for the delay. Until I know otherwise, I choose to believe that our host has been absent." Ilsevele withdrew to her bedchamber to change, while Fflar found a handsome blue cloak to throw over his own tunic. Ilsevele soon emerged from her room, attired in a beautiful gold-embroidered dress of deep green over a chemise of sheer pale gray silk. Her long red hair was free to her shoulders, wavy and alluring, and she wore a slim tiara on her brow. The dress went well with her eyes, Fflar decided. Very well indeed. He couldn't recall ever having seen Ilsevele dressed up, and the effect was stunning.

She noticed his gaze and smiled awkwardly, smoothing her dress. "Is something wrong?"

"Not a thing," he admitted. "Lord Selkirk doesn't stand a chance."

She looked down and blushed. "Thank you, Starbrow," she murmured. "I simply want to let the Sembians know that I take them seriously."

They went down to the inn's common room, where the Sembian messenger waited, along with a small escort of half a dozen human guards. The Sembians had arranged for several carriages, even though the Sharburg was not much of a walk from the Markhouse. In a matter of minutes they rolled into the broad dusty courtyard of Tasseldale's chief castle, which had been crowned by the pennants of Sembia.

I wonder what the mairshars think of that? Fflar asked himself. The Sharburg was the stronghold of Tasseldale's constables, guards, and lawkeepers . . . but it seemed that the Sembian lords had evicted them when they chose the Sharburg for their headquarters.

"If you get the chance," he said to Ilsevele, "I think you should press the Sembians about their occupation of this dale. Don't let them think that you don't care that this town belongs to Tasseldale."

"I will not forget the citizens of Tasseldale, Starbrow," Ilsevele replied. She looked up at the pennants floating overhead, and drew a deep breath. Then the carriage door opened, and a coachman extended a hand to assist Ilsevele from the carriage.

A small party of Sembians waited for them in the courtyard, surrounded by a number of vigilant guards. At their head stood a tall, dark-haired man who wore lace at the cuff and collar. His hair was carefully arranged in tight ringlets, and his goatee was trimmed to an exacting point just a little below his chin, but Fflar could see at once that the man was more than a dandy. The rapier at his belt was a fine piece of steel with a well-worn hilt, and the set of his shoulders and easy confidence of his black eyes marked him as a man who knew his own strength.

"Good morning, my lady Miritar," the Sembian lord said, and swept off his hat in a gracious bow. "I am Miklos Selkirk, of House Selkirk. I am sorry that I could not meet you before now, but events in these troubled lands kept me away until a short time ago."

"I understand, Lord Selkirk," Ilsevele said. "It is those same troubles that led my father to bring his Crusade here."

She's very good at this, Fflar decided. Ilsevele possessed a natural poise that few elves could match, let alone humans, but at the same time she was sincere and direct. It made for a disarming combination. He quietly studied the Sembians observing her. They stood mute and unmoving, eyes wide, rapt. If they'd had suspicions about her, or duplicity in their hearts, those things were forgotten for the moment.

Ilsevele exchanged a few simple pleasantries with the Sembian lord, and Selkirk bowed and led them into the castle's hall. The windows were thrown open to the fine summer morning, and an impressive buffet was spread out on long tables along one side.

The Sembian made a point of helping himself to several small slices of cheese and a goblet of wine—demonstrating that it wasn't poisoned, Fflar guessed—and said, "Please, refresh yourselves if you like. I haven't had much opportunity for good meals lately, so I certainly intend to do so."

Ilsevele inclined her head and accepted some wine from a steward. "You are most kind, Lord Selkirk."

Selkirk studied her for a moment, then said, "While I am delighted to entertain such a beautiful lady of the *Tel' Quessir,* Lady Miritar, I am afraid I do not know what I can do for you. What does your father have to say to me?"

"We have no wish to fight you, not when our true enemy awaits in Myth Drannor," Ilsevele said evenly. "I would like to arrange a truce between our peoples. If we could reach some understanding, then my father would be freed to turn his full strength against Sarya Dlardrageth."

"I see," Selkirk answered. He looked down into his goblet and swirled the wine idly, thinking for a moment. "There are difficult questions to resolve between us, Lady Miritar. Regardless of the relations my father or I might desire with our northern neighbors, too many of my countrymen—including some with powerful voices in our realm's Great Council—will not be dictated to by an elven power in Cormanthor. We are here because those voices fear that your people will deny Sembia its natural and necessary growth."

"Do you think that Sarya Dlardrageth will permit that growth, Lord Selkirk?"

Miklos Selkirk snorted and shook his head. "Borstag Duncastle seemed to think so, but he is quite dead now. For my own part, I harbor no such illusions. Not after what I have seen in the last two tendays."

"Then you must surely see that it costs Sembia nothing to stand aside and allow us to try our strength against the daemonfey. If you husband your forces while we and the daemonfey weaken each other, your position can only improve."

"Unless you fail, and the daemonfey choose to make us the next target for their wrath." Selkirk smiled humorlessly. "Or succeed, and emerge stronger from the confrontation."

Ilsevele frowned and set down her own goblet. "You fear

our failure and you fear our success. But it seems to me that the current situation simply cannot be borne indefinitely. What would you have us do?"

"Defeat the daemonfey, and leave."

"I cannot make that promise, Lord Selkirk. We will not leave Cormanthor empty again. But I hope that we would be better neighbors than the daemonfey. We understand the notion of compromise, at least."

"You may find the concessions my countrymen demand difficult to meet. Our merchants want Cormanthor's timber, game, furs, even some of the forestlands to clear and settle."

"And you may find our demands equally difficult. We will not allow the outright conquest of lands allied to us—such as Tasseldale, here—or the ungoverned and reckless plundering of the forest's bounty." Ilsevele took a step forward, not allowing the Sembian lord to look away. "However, we are willing to strive in good faith to find common ground with you. We must put an end to the abominable depredations of the daemonfey. The bloodshed and horror of this awful season cannot be allowed to continue a day longer."

"The gods know that is true enough," the Sembian said quietly.

He set down his cup and paced away, hands clasped behind his back, to gaze out one of the hall's high windows. Fflar studied the set of the man's shoulders, the hint of fatigue and pain lurking beneath his polished exterior. It was hard to be certain, but he thought that the Sembian lord had the decency to be outraged by the murder and horror he'd seen.

Selkirk sighed, and faced Ilsevele. "Very well, Lady Miritar. You shall have your truce. My forces will not advance against Deepingdale or press any farther north than the positions they currently hold. If you can destroy the daemonfey, the world will be a better place."

"If you truly believe that," Ilsevele said, "then I have

something else to propose to you: Help us against the daemonfey. March alongside us and help us to burn out this evil from Myth Drannor."

Surprise flickered across Selkirk's face. "You have a bold turn of mind, my lady," he breathed. "I do not think you appreciate how difficult that will be for some of my countrymen."

"I understand, Lord Selkirk. But I suspect that elves and humans alike will find it much easier to trust one another once we have fought together in the name of what is right, as opposed to what is expedient."

"You may be right, Lady Miritar, but it is not in my power to agree to that. Extricating Sembia from this disaster of a campaign is what I came here to do." Miklos Selkirk shook his head. "Before I throw more gold and blood into the Dales, I will have to consult with my father in Ordulin . . . and likely some of the important voices in the Great Council, too."

"Then, with your permission, I will notify my father of our truce and await your decision about joining us against the daemonfey."

"Yes, of course," Selkirk said. "I will have word of the truce passed to all my commanders at once. And we will speak again soon about your bold suggestion."

❂ ❂ ❂ ❂ ❂

A dim sense of peril roused Araevin from a Reverie so deep and dark that he had almost begun to believe that he had died.

He struggled to wakefulness and discovered nothing but cold blackness all around him. The small lights they'd left burning in their camp had flickered out entirely during their long, cold sleep. *Why didn't someone strike a new light?* he asked himself. *Whoever was on watch would have needed something to see by . . . but did we even set a watch?*

"*Aillesel Seldarie,*" he whispered. The cold and exhaustion must have taken their toll on his mind! How long had they been helpless in the dark?

Light, he decided. That was the first priority. He fumbled through his pockets, searching for something he could throw his light spell on. But then he heard a sound, slow and deliberate—a faint creaking of stone, a small crackle as rocks pressed against each other. It was close by, somewhere only a few feet away.

Araevin froze, not daring to move. Something prowled just outside the square doorway of the stone structure. Something large sighed, a low, rumbling sound, and the stone creaked softly again. He held his breath, trying to discern what it was that moved outside their bleak little refuge.

The thing outside paused and held still. Araevin could see nothing, but he could *feel* it there, the subtle strain of something that leaned against the walls, the slight stirring of the otherwise motionless air. It's just outside the doorway, he realized. It's right here.

His fingers closed on the disruption wand holstered at his left hip. It was a potent weapon, but he dared not discharge it unless he knew none of his friends were in the way. But he drew it out slowly just in case.

The thing outside drew in a sharp breath.

It *sees* me! he realized.

Without another thought, Araevin rolled to his feet. *"Nharaigh lathanyll!"* he cried, casting his light spell on the wand in his hands. A sudden yellow radiance filled the room, throwing stark black shadows into the corners.

A huge, misshapen face filled the square stone doorway, peering at him with great round eyes. The face was *big*, easily three feet from chin to brow. It was a pallid white, the eyes black and huge, the lips fleshy and loose. Crooked yellow teeth as long as Araevin's hand glistened in its wet mouth. Then the creature screwed its eyes shut with a moan of distaste and jerked away, recoiling from the painful brightness.

"By Bane's black hand, what in the world was *that?*" Jorin, who lay closest to the open door, came awake in the blink of an eye. He scrabbled back from his bedroll, a short sword already in his hand. "Damn it, who had the watch?"

Maresa, Donnor, and Nesterin struggled to awareness more slowly than the Yuir ranger. They blinked in Araevin's light, fumbling to throw off blankets and find weapons.

"What's going on?" Maresa mumbled sleepily.

"Something is outside," Araevin replied, keeping his eyes fixed on the square doorway. "A giant of some kind."

"Giant?" the genasi muttered. She found her feet and backed away from the doorway. "What do we do?"

"Wait a moment," the sun elf said. "It recoiled from my light. Maybe it will move on."

His companions watched the doorway nervously, straining to catch a glimpse of what waited in the blackness. Nothing happened for twenty heartbeats, and Araevin began to hope that the creature had indeed given up on them. But then a wide, spadelike hand of pallid flesh reached in from the darkness, groping and fumbling toward them.

Maresa gasped in consternation at the size of the monster, and slid away from the door. The hand was easily as broad as Araevin's chest, with thick strong fingers as big as his forearm.

"Damn, it's big," she whispered.

The giant caught up a handful of Jorin's bedroll and dragged it outside, snuffling heavily. The companions backed away from the doorway, shoulder blades pressed to the far wall. Araevin caught a quick glimpse of the monster ducking down to peer into the building again—and the giant lunged violently for him.

Araevin fell back as the giant's fingers ground into the stone where he had been standing, splintering the rock. The creature rumbled in frustration, and grabbed wildly for Araevin again. Donnor caught hold of Araevin's arm and dragged him back out of the way.

"Watch yourself!" the Tethyrian snapped. "We're not likely to find another wizard down here."

Jorin, pressed against the opposite wall of the room, frowned and leaned away as the giant groped back in his direction. He crouched low under the groping hand, but then the giant suddenly fumbled closer. Without a word Jorin fell back flat, and jammed his sword into the meat of the creature's arm.

The giant jerked back its arm, flinging drops of blood against the doorway. It seemed to huff and whine in the darkness outside, but it did not roar, bellow, or curse as Araevin would have expected. Again stone creaked outside their small sanctuary.

"I think you drove it off," Maresa whispered. "Good! That'll teach it to go poking around in other people's business."

"I don't think we're that lucky," Donnor said, shaking his head. He looked up with a small frown on his face—and the roof above his head exploded in a shower of crushed blocks and mortar dust.

With two great shoves of its thick arms, the giant cleared the top courses of stonework out of its way like a man sweeping a table clear of dishes. Araevin covered his head against the flying debris, and when he looked up again the giant towered over their broken shelter, raising a colossal hammer of stone over its head.

Nesterin's voice rang out sharply in the darkness, and the star elf threw out a cloud of sparkling silver motes in the giant's face. It shook its head violently, trying to clear its vision from the brilliant pinpoints. Then Araevin pointed his disruption wand at the monster's face and barked out the command word. The cold black air sang with the shrill sound of the spell as a furious blue lance of energy slammed into the giant.

The creature reeled away, groaning . . . but then two more of the pale giants appeared. Hammers the size of

Final Gate • 119

hogsheads slammed into the old square blocks of the ledge house, knocking the place to pieces around Araevin and his friends. Donnor disappeared under a shower of masonry, while Nesterin barely dodged another block large enough to crush him like an insect.

"They're battering the place to pieces," the star elf cried. "We have to get out of here!"

Jorin darted through the doorway and instantly leaped aside to avoid a hammer-blow that would have driven him into the ground like a pile. Araevin waited a heartbeat for the giant outside to raise its hammer for another blow, and pushed Nesterin and Maresa out before the hulking monster could strike again. Then, rather than invite another hammer-blow, he quickly incanted the words of a flying spell and arrowed straight up through the collapsed roof.

Three of the pale giants surrounded their small safehouse. Now that he could see them entirely, Araevin found that they were horribly hunched creatures despite their great size. They went almost on all fours, with a curious hopping crouch that brought their faces down to not much higher than a human's height. Had they been able to straighten up, they would have towered over ogres or trolls. Yet for all their awkwardness they were surprisingly quick and deft. One battered at Jorin, Nesterin, and Maresa with great sweeping blows of its hammer, driving them back. Another methodically pounded the stone building into rubble, trying to drive Donnor out or crush the human knight where he stood. The last giant stared up at Araevin in surprise, astonished to find its quarry darting through the air.

Araevin flew back and down a little, and shouted out the words of a powerful spell. From his outstretched fingertips a brilliant fan of iridescent rays shot out, scything shoulder-high across the two nearest giants. Virulent green acid ate into doughy hide, searing orange fire leaped and scorched, and crackling golden lightning sparked and ripped through flesh. One of the giants, its flesh smoking from great black burns, recoiled one step too far and silently toppled into the abyss, vanishing into the darkness.

Crackling violet madness danced in the other giant's eyes. It dropped its hammer, clenching its fists against its head—and it looked up at Araevin and *screamed*.

The sound was indescribable, a mountain given voice. The mage was flung head over heels through the air to crash against the cold rock wall in a shower of rubble. Vision swimming, Araevin struggled to right himself and find a spell, any spell, to fend off the giant's next blow. But the magical madness of the purple ray had the giant in its grip. Rather than finish off the dazed wizard, the pale brute simply turned and bounded down the narrow stairs, fleeing back down into the dark.

"Araevin! Are you all right?" Nesterin called.

Araevin held up his arm and nodded, unable to frame any better response. He picked himself out of the rubble, while Jorin and Maresa darted at the first of the giants. They scored again and again with their blades, but the genasi's rapier and the ranger's short swords were not well-suited for the task of stopping a giant. The creature bled from a dozen pinpricks, but still it came on, swinging its heavy hammer in great whistling arcs.

I must help them, Araevin thought over and over again. But he was still shaking off the physical blow the giant's scream had dealt. He raised his disruption wand and pointed it at the monster's back, and somehow he managed to mumble the activating words through the haze that enveloped him. Another shrieking blue lance of force tore through the blackness, taking the giant high in the back and spinning it halfway around.

Jorin used that moment to spring in close behind the wounded monster and plunge his blade into the back of its knee. The giant snorted and fell heavily, its leg giving out beneath it. The ranger backed off, but not fast enough; with one backhanded blow the giant sent Jorin hurtling into the darkness.

Final Gate • 121

"Jorin!" Nesterin shouted.

The star elf leaped after the ranger, and caught a hold of his long cloak just as Jorin slid over the edge. Nesterin threw out his arms and legs, spread-eagled on his stomach as he struggled to keep Jorin from plummeting down into the darkness ... but behind him the crippled giant turned and raised its hammer.

Rubble shifted in the wreckage of their shelter, and Donnor Kerth suddenly stumbled out of the dust and debris at the giant's flank. He barreled into the monster's side and hewed deeply into its back. The giant turned again, and Araevin seared its torso with a brilliant stabbing bolt of violet lightning. The creature's face contorted in an unvoiced scream, and it slumped to the ground, just missing Maresa. Silence fell over the eerie battlefield.

"Aid me with Jorin!" Nesterin gasped to the others.

Maresa hurried over and grabbed another handful of the ranger's cloak, and the two managed to pull him back up onto the ledge.

Donnor limped over to where Araevin sat, his chest heaving. "I thought there were three of them," the cleric said.

"There were. One fell into the abyss. The other fled down the stairs, afflicted by a madness spell."

"Your doing?"

Araevin nodded. "Yes. The spell is unpredictable, but often quite effective. The third giant won't be back anytime soon."

Donnor nodded, and peered down the stairs leading into the dark. The Lathanderite stiffened, and took a step back. "Then what's that?" he asked.

Araevin stood up swiftly and looked where the Tethyrian pointed. Not far below them, a strange pale glimmer climbed steadily up the stairs toward their ledge. It almost seemed like a distant lantern carried by somebody ascending the terrible stairs, but it was close enough that Araevin could see that no one carried the light; it was simply a glowing white sphere, cold and small, arising from the depths below. Subtle tendrils of magic shifted slowly in his sight, whispering of dire power.

"It's no work of the giants," he told Donnor. "Warn the others."

The Tethyrian called a soft warning back to Maresa, Nesterin, and Jorin. Araevin watched the light come closer as his friends arrayed themselves at his back, prepared for anything. Cold and exhaustion were momentarily forgotten as they studied the strange glowing sphere.

"Should we fire at it?" Jorin asked Araevin.

"It will do no good," Araevin answered. "Wait a moment. It may not be hostile."

Jorin lowered his bow, keeping an arrow on the string. The sphere climbed to within twenty feet or so, just a few short steps down the stair, and it drifted up away from the steps, rising to their level. It was oddly cold in the pale glow of the orb. Lorosfyr was without warmth anyway, but as it drifted closer, Araevin felt as if what little warmth remained to him was being stolen away.

"Who are you? What do you want with us?" Donnor demanded of the glowing light.

It drew back slowly, giving an impression of cold, dispassionate scrutiny that Araevin did not care for at all. He sensed subtle divination magic at work, and frowned.

"It's studying us," he said.

The small globe hovered before them for a moment longer, then it sank back down into the depths. Soon it was gone from sight, though Araevin almost imagined that he could make out a dim gray glow from somewhere far below.

"A sending of the Pale Sybil?" Nesterin murmured. He looked over to Araevin. "Do we dare follow it down?"

Araevin simply nodded. "I intend to. After all, that is what we came here for," he told his friends.

☙ ☙ ☙ ☙ ☙

Moonlight danced on the pure waters of Lake Sember. Seiveril Miritar looked on the beautiful scene and found that he was heartened by the sight. It was a perfect summer night, warm and bright with the moonlight all elves loved more than words could easily express.

It was a good omen for the coming battle.

"The daemonfey approach, Lord Seiveril," Edraele Muirreste said. The girlish moon elf seemed far too small and frail to wear a warrior's arms, but appearances could be deceiving—behind those enchanting eyes lay a fierce determination and an uncanny capacity for bold, daring maneuvers and inspired leadership. Riding at the head of the Silver Guard, the great company of cavalry that had followed Seiveril out of Evermeet, Edraele was more dangerous than a full-grown dragon.

"I am afraid your eyes must be keener than mine, Edraele. I do not see them yet," Seiveril admitted.

The young captain pointed up into the clear skies above the lake, and Seiveril followed her gaze to a distant dark cloud of tiny winged figures . . . a darting, roiling stream that grew closer with every heartbeat. "You were right, my lord," Edraele said. "They are here, just as you predicted."

"The Seldarine favored my divinations. I only passed along Corellon's warning." Seiveril quickly inspected his armor of elven steel plate, more than a little battered and scored from months of campaigning against the daemonfey and their evil hordes. Then he glanced back to Edraele and touched his brow in salute. "Good luck to you, captain. Remember, you're not a rider tonight. It's not as easy to get out of trouble when you're fighting afoot."

"I haven't forgotten." Edraele sighed.

The moon elf was a rider of superb skill, the best Seiveril had ever seen. It seemed a waste to not allow her or her Silver Guard to mount up. But the daemonfey and their demons, devils, and such things were all winged, and even Edraele couldn't lead her lancers into the skies.

Seiveril hurried over to the place where Vesilde Gaerth and the battle-mage Jorildyn waited. Every company of the Crusade waited deep in the tree shadows, concealed from the flying foes winging toward them. Only a handful of volunteers remained among the lanternlit tents and shelters of the Semberholme encampment, doing their best to look like half-awake sentries who had no idea the daemonfey were about to descend on them.

"Are your mages ready, Jorildyn?" Seiveril asked.

The battle-mage—actually a half-elf, with enough human blood to sport a silver-streaked black beard—nodded once without taking his eyes from the menacing shapes descending from the sky. "My mages know their task," he said. "Whether the others will do as well, I cannot say."

"They will," Seiveril promised him.

He returned his gaze to the daemonfey. They had come close enough that he could make out the gleam of moonlight on their steel, and the larger and more ungainly shapes of vrocks and nycaloths scattered among the fey'ri warriors. The ancient magical wards guarding Semberholme kept infernal creatures from simply teleporting into the middle of the elven camp, and so the raid descending on them necessarily had to come from the skies. Otherwise the daemonfey and their demonic allies would have had to fight their way through miles of forest to get to Seiveril's army, losing any hope of surprise.

Not that they've caught us off our guard tonight, Seiveril reminded himself. "Thank you, Corellon, for your guidance this night," he whispered. "May our arrows fly swift, may our blades strike true, may our spells smite our foes and shield us from harm."

"As the Seldarine will," Vesilde said, finishing the ancient prayer.

"As the Seldarine will," Jorildyn answered too. The battle-mage took a deep breath, and said, "Here they come."

The fearsome shapes overhead wheeled and plummeted

down toward the camp. Many of the fey'ri were deadly sorcerers, and they announced the beginning of the attack by launching a terrible barrage of spells—searing fireballs, deadly purple bolts of lightning, and black rays of destruction that pierced soul and body alike. Demons and devils among the fey'ri scoured the ground below with their own deadly blasts of hellfire and abyssal plagues, enveloping scores of tents and shattering stones and trees like the hammer blows of titans. Thunderclaps split the night, echoing across the water. Flames roared and crackled, and overhead demons shouted in glee.

Even though Seiveril had expected it, he was momentarily appalled by the sheer ferocity of the attack. Some of those who had volunteered to play the role of sentries managed to send a few paltry arrows speeding up into the black ranks above. Others simply vanished in searing blasts of fire or were thrown like broken toys across the ground. But he set his horror and surprise aside for later, and barked out, "Now, Jorildyn! Now!"

From a hundred places scattered around the outskirts of the camp, elf sorcerers, wizards, war-mages, and clerics shouted out battle spells of their own, launching a ferocious barrage right back at the daemonfey. And alongside each mage or cleric, another elf armed with a wand, a staff, or even a scroll to read joined the effort. While only a few score elves in the Crusade were mages of any skill, many more had dabbled in the Art at least a bit—and even a raw apprentice could employ a wand. At Jorildyn's instruction, all the battle-mages under his command had shared their arsenals with any elf who could help, tripling the Crusade's magical power for at least a short time.

The night vanished in the brilliant blue glare of lightning bolts and the sullen red glow of fire-fountains burning through the daemonfey ranks. Scores of fey'ri burned and died in the skies over the empty camp, their blackened corpses tumbling to the ground or splashing into the lake.

"Well done, Jorildyn!" Vesilde cried. "Well done! Now it's our turn."

The Golden Star knight raised a horn to his lips and blew a single high note that echoed over the thunderclaps and roaring of the flames . . . and in response, more than a thousand archers bent their bows and let fly at the staggered fey'ri. More of Sarya's infernal warriors screamed and died in the silver storm of death rising up to rake them.

Fey'ri spellcasters threw a haphazard volley of slaying spells of their own back down at the elves below, while beating desperately for altitude. Many of Seiveril's wizards and clerics had necessarily given away their hiding places by hurling their spells up at the flying foe, and more than a few did not long survive after dealing their surprise blow against Sarya's legion. Half a dozen acid bolts and fireballs streaked down toward the clearing where Seiveril and his captains had gathered, but Seiveril had been waiting for that moment. In the space of an instant he raised a barrier of null magic, shielding his companions in a temporary cocoon in which magic, any magic, simply could not work. It shut off their own spellcasting, of course, but Seiveril decided it was easily worth the cost as spell after spell simply died a few feet before reaching him.

"Watch out for the demons and devils," Vesilde warned. "They'll simply attack with fang and claw if they realize you've taken away our spells as well as theirs."

"That's why I wanted your Knights of the Golden Star around me, Vesilde," Seiveril answered.

He watched anxiously for a short time as the fey'ri dueled his spellcasters and archers, trading spell for spell and arrow for arrow—but it was not a fair exchange, not by a long measure. The elves on the ground were hidden among the trees and ruins of Semberholme, and they outnumbered their attackers by three or four to one. The daemonfey had hoped to surprise a sleeping camp with a lightning-swift raid. They hadn't come to fight an army that was awake, alert, and ready for them.

Harsh voices cried among the ranks of the flying warriors, and the fey'ri turned away and sped back out into the night.

"It seems they've had enough," Vesilde said. The sun elf grinned, and clapped Seiveril on the shoulder. "Our camp is something of a mess, but other than that, your ploy was brilliant, my friend. I do not think the fey'ri will be quick to try our strength here again."

Seiveril breathed a deep sigh of relief, and allowed his null magic spell to end. "It's one thing to repel an enemy you expect," he said. "But we will not win this war by defending Semberholme. We will have to defeat the daemonfey on their chosen ground before this is all over, and I fear that will be a much more difficult task."

CHAPTER EIGHT

8 Eleasias, the Year of Lightning Storms

Araevin and his companions did not encounter any more of the pallid, hunched giants and didn't see the pale sphere again as they descended from the ledge into the deeps below. Araevin's legs felt stiff and numb, and no longer answered to him as well as he would have liked, but as exhausted as he felt, his friends seemed worse off. Every time he glanced back up over his shoulder at the comrades following him, grimaces of pain and concentration met his gaze.

How many days to climb back up to the top? he wondered. *Faerzress* or no, he'd be sorely tempted to try a teleport spell rather than face the daunting task of making their way back up the miles and miles of stairs on foot.

They marched on and passed another switchback.

As they turned back, Araevin decided that there was no doubt about it—some faint luminescence danced in the darkness below. In a short time, the light had grown bright enough that they could descry a strange city of sorts below. Like the watchpost on the ledge far above, the city rested on a great shelf in the side of the abyss. Its towers and buildings were square and squat, many with a distinct inward slant so that they seemed like flat-topped pyramids. The gray light emanated from dozens of strange pillars, each capped by a round sphere of crystal in which a faintly luminescent liquid swirled sluggishly.

"At last," grunted Donnor. Carrying fifty pounds of steel and sixty more of pack down the miles-long stairs had brought the human warrior to the very end of his strength, and he literally swayed with fatigue. "I am sick and tired of these damned steps. Anything would be better than more of this."

"Be careful what you wish for," Maresa told him. "The stairs might not look so bad once we get to the bottom."

The staircase began to cut through a serried row of terraces that overlooked the city proper. Araevin found something profoundly out of place. In the terraces stood the bare skeletons of trees, pale and leafless. He turned aside from the continuous descent, though it took a surprising effort of will to do so, and stiffly walked over to the nearest of the dead trees. He brushed his fingers over the desiccated bark.

"Apple trees," he breathed. "Impossible."

Jorin joined him, his face set in a thoughtful frown. "How in the world did these get here?"

Araevin glanced at the terraces, stretching for hundreds of yards to each side before vanishing into the dark. "I think they grew here."

"In this cold and lightless sepulcher? I can't believe that," Jorin replied. He shook his head. "They must have been brought down from the surface and planted here. But why go to such trouble to plant so many trees in a place where they would only die?"

"Because this place may not have always been as cold and lightless as it is now. Maybe it was not always like this."

"Then what happened to it?" Maresa asked.

Araevin shrugged. "I suspect we'll find out below," he said. He smoothed his hand over the dry, crumbling bark of the dead tree one more time and turned back to the steps. "Come on, we are almost there. Not many more steps now."

From the terraces overlooking the city, the great stair finally ended in a small plaza or square where one of the city's boulevards met the wall. Even with the gray light to lessen the darkness, the place was uncannily still and cold. They staggered out onto the square, stumbling and lurching as legs inured to step after downward step fumbled for the feel of level ground again. Araevin set his hands on his knees and rested for a long time before he decided he was ready to look around.

Jorin was right to call this place a sepulcher, Araevin decided. The place had all the animation and warmth of a thousand-year-old tomb. Empty black windows and doorways yawned on all sides, silent streets and alleyways rambled off into the shadows, and the pale and broken limbs of dead trees jutted up over the stone streets. The stonework was strange to him. Like the pillars marking the steps and the way posts on the road far, far overhead, they were marked with intricate geometric patterns—zigzags and squares, triangles and trapezoids.

"Is this dwarven stonework, Araevin?" Maresa asked.

"None that I recognize, not that I am any expert in such things."

"Who else would live down here?" the genasi asked. "Who were these people?"

"I don't know, Maresa. It's beyond my experience."

"They were humanlike, at least," Nesterin observed. "They cut steps to suit the legs of people five or six feet tall. And the windows and arches in the buildings look like they're proportioned for humans, orcs, or elves."

"Not the giants, then," said Donnor. "They would have built the place to suit their own size, not ours."

"Well, which way from here?" Maresa asked Araevin.

The sun elf surveyed the silent boulevards leading off into the shadows. Arbitrarily, he decided to follow the largest of the boulevards their staircase met. It marched off into the darkness as if the maddening descent above simply continued straight on in a level road.

With a few creaking joints and stifled groans, they set off into the cold ruins of the city. But they had only traveled a block or two when two of the pallid, crouching giants padded into the road ahead. Araevin set his hand on the wand holster at his hip, and his companions rustled softly as they eased weapons from sheaths and spread out, ready for a fight.

"Do we strike first?" Maresa asked.

"No," Araevin decided. "Let's see what they do."

The dark-eyed giants moved closer, eyes fixed on the small party but not a trace of expression on their faces. They wore sarks of small stone discs and carried enormous hammers like the giants Araevin and his companions had fought on the ledge watchpost. For a moment Araevin feared that they were simply going to lumber up and attack, but the creatures halted a good distance short of them and silently beckoned.

"It seems we're expected," Maresa observed. "Good. I think I'm too tired to fight anyway."

The giants turned and led the way, guiding the mage and his companions through the empty streets of the city. They walked for a few hundred yards, following twists and turns of the road. Then the strange creatures brought them out into a square before a large, rambling palace. A whole row of columns carved in the likeness of ancient human warriors fronted the citadel, looking out over the city beyond like a phalanx of stone. And standing beneath the columns, a company of human-seeming guards stood quietly before their stone champions, imitating their impassive watch. Two more of the giants waited there as well, but the whole assemblage stood motionless, speechless, simply watching Araevin and his friends approach.

"I don't like this at all," Maresa murmured. The genasi scowled, searching all around for easy avenues of escape.

"Araevin, the guards are not alive," Donnor Kerth said. The Lathanderite stared at the warriors in their ancient armor, his face set in a determined scowl. "They are undead of some kind, I am sure of it."

"I can see it," Araevin answered.

In fact, Araevin could clearly distinguish the necromancy that pulsed in their cold veins in place of living blood. He hesitated, unwilling to approach any closer. He had never held with necromancy, and in fact had avoided the study of the black arts for all the long years at Tower Reilloch. It was an unwholesome thing to make the dead answer one's bidding. Yet having come so far, they did not have any choice other than to go on.

"I think that someone here wishes to parley, not fight," he told the Lathanderite. "But remain on your guard nonetheless."

"Don't worry about that," Donnor said with a snort.

They followed the two giants into the square before the palace, and there six of the cold warriors took up the task of escorting them into the palace proper. They climbed up a wide set of shallow steps leading to the palace's gate, and followed them inside. The interior was resplendent. Columns of beautiful pale marble veined with gold marched through the halls, and richly appointed rooms gleamed in the dim light of low-burning lanterns worked in the shape of flowering vines.

They came to another great hall, and found a pale queen waiting for them on a small dais.

She was white-skinned, with a complexion that reminded Araevin of snow on some distant mountaintop. Even Maresa was not so perfectly colorless, since the genasi possessed the faintest tinge of blue-white, like a high cloud in a springtime sky. The queen's flesh, on the other hand, had a strange cold luster like polished marble. Her hair was long, black, and straight, bound by a simple fillet of silver on her brow. She wore a flowing gown of white that was gathered at the torso in an ornate silvered brocade, and a long, slender rod of black platinum lay across her lap.

"Welcome to Lorosfyr, Araevin Teshurr," she said. Her voice was soft and rich, with a purring accent that Araevin had never heard anywhere else. "I am Selydra, whom some call the Pale Sybil. May I offer you refreshment? The Long Stair is a difficult path."

"You are most gracious," Araevin said carefully.

Apparently she had observed them through the medium of the white sphere they had encountered on the stairs. He was not at all sure that it would be wise to dine at her table, but he certainly did not wish to offend her within the first few moments of meeting her. He offered a slight bow.

Selydra smiled coolly, as if she were amused by his caution, and made a small motion with her hand. A lantern in the shadows at the side of the hall brightened, revealing a small banquet already set out. Divans and cushions were arranged nearby. She descended from her dais and led the way to the table.

"Please, eat and drink your fill," she said over her shoulder. "Travelers are a rare treasure in this place, and I have always been fascinated by the World Above. I am eager to hear how you came to the Long Stair."

Araevin hesitated. He was indeed hungry and thirsty, but he reminded himself of the deathless warriors who stood watch at Selydra's door. "If you will allow us, my lady, my comrade Donnor would like to speak a small prayer before we eat," he said to Selydra. "It is our custom."

The Pale Sybil inclined her head, though Araevin thought he sensed a flicker of irritation in her gaze. "By all means."

Araevin glanced at Donnor, and to his credit the cleric understood perfectly without another word. He stepped forward and spread his arms over the banquet, looking up to the ceiling, and he murmured the words of an ancient Lathanderite prayer—followed rather subtly by a divination to determine if everything was safe. After a moment, he nodded.

"As Lathander rises," the cleric finished. "We may eat now."

Araevin and his friends helped themselves to the strange viands laid out for them—dark slices of some sort of broiled meat, small salty fish that were completely eyeless, a coarse gray bread, and even a few small, tart, blood-red fruits that he had never seen before. Cold, pure water and decanters of a black wine accompanied the meal. Selydra simply helped herself to a goblet of the wine, and reclined on a divan while Araevin and his friends shed their packs and sampled her table.

"What realm of the surface do you and your companions come from, Araevin?" Selydra asked, sipping at her wine.

"I am from Evermeet. Donnor Kerth, here, hails from Tethyr. Jorin and Nesterin—" Araevin nodded at the Yuir ranger and the star elf—"come from the land of Aglarond on the Sea of Fallen Stars. And Maresa is a native of Waterdeep."

"I have heard of these places," Selydra murmured, "but I have never seen them. Only a rare picture or two in the tomes of my library. How strange."

"You named this city Lorosfyr, my lady," Araevin said. "Who built it? What is the story of this place? And why do you choose to dwell here?"

"It is an intriguing mystery, isn't it?" Selydra said. She studied Araevin with that same amused half-smile on her lips, and Araevin sensed a deep stirring of something within her, a whisper of avidness, hunger, that she carefully concealed. "This was once a city of humankind. Long ago a race of great wizards fought and lost a terrible war in the surface lands. To escape the vengeance of their foes, they fled into the farthest depths of the Underdark, and founded hidden cities such as Lorosfyr."

"But why here, my lady?" Jorin asked. "How could they survive in this place?"

"Long ago, Lorosfyr basked in the daylight of magical suns," Selydra said. "This place was once a great, shining realm of golden mists, brilliant as the morning. I imagine that during its day it was not at all unpleasant."

"What happened to it?" said Araevin.

"A disaster befell the place many centuries ago. The spells sustaining light and warmth in this great darkness failed." Selydra shrugged. "I have not discovered the cause. I came here years ago in the hope of uncovering the secrets of Imaskari magecraft, and I have never managed to unravel the story of the city's end. Whatever doom came to this place, it fell so swiftly upon the people who lived here that they made no record of it."

"You are a student of the Art, then, my lady?"

"I am," the Pale Sybil admitted. "As are you, Araevin Teshurr. Now, I confess I am quite curious as to why an elf mage of such skill would venture into Lorosfyr."

Araevin did not glance at his companions, though he felt their eyes upon him. "I believe that you have come into possession of a shard from a magical crystal," he said. "I have great need of it, my lady. I was hoping that I could persuade you to allow me to make use of it for a short time."

If Selydra was surprised, she did not show it. She simply sipped again from her goblet, studying Araevin over the golden rim of her cup. "Unless I am mistaken, you also have a shard of this same crystal," she said. "It may be, Araevin Teshurr, that I would like to make use of *your* shard for a short time."

"It is a matter of great urgency, my lady. Thousands of lives may depend on this. I will be happy to explain."

Selydra rose to her feet. "And I will be happy to listen, and perhaps try to persuade you of my own need in turn. We are reasonable mages, and I am sure we can reach an agreement. But I can see that you and your companions are absolutely exhausted. Before we examine this question at any length, I must insist that you rest. Recover your strength, and enjoy my hospitality for a time. We can take up more serious matters tomorrow." She paused, her dark eyes fixed on Araevin. "I think there is much we will learn from each other."

Araevin started to protest, but thought better of it. He had the feeling that pressing Selydra on the question would get him nowhere. The Pale Sybil meant to enjoy her role of gracious hostess. Regardless of how reasonable she seemed at the moment, he had no way of knowing what she might or might not be capable of. He thought of the broken gnome Galdindormm, moaning in terror with her name on his lips.

Patience, Araevin, he told himself. He inclined his head to the Pale Sybil. "Of course, my lady," he said. "I look forward to our next conversation."

"As do I," Selydra answered. She motioned to the silent warriors standing nearby, and the creatures drew closer. "My servitors will show you to a comfortable set of apartments. You will have everything you need there, but I am afraid I must ask you to refrain from wandering about. While my swordwights should suffice to protect you here within the palace, you will find that there are many perils in Lorosfyr."

She gathered up her sleeves and slipped her pale hands within, and glided away into the shadows of her palace. Araevin watched her go, his lips pressed together in a frown. The ancient warriors regarded him with their dead, unblinking gazes, a pale light glimmering in their haunted eyes. One extended an arm, indicating a passageway leading somewhere else in the shadows.

"I don't trust her for a moment," Donnor said. "This

whole place reeks of necromancy. And stranger, darker arts too, I think. We're in danger here."

🙵 🙵 🙵 🙵 🙵

His features hidden beneath a well-worn hood, Fflar turned into the alley running behind a merchant's residence near the back of the Markhouse, and he paused for a moment to make sure he was not followed or observed. Then he quickly scrambled up to the roof of a shed leaning against the merchant's house and vaulted over the tall fence that separated the inn's smokehouse from the merchant's alleyway. A couple of conveniently located trees made it an excellent way to slip in and out of the Markhouse without being seen.

Fflar ventured into the common room and spent a short time there listening to a lutist strumming her instrument while he indulged in two goblets of good wine. He was just about to leave a tip on the table and head upstairs to his room when the dark-haired girl, the bewitchingly beautiful girl he'd seen watching from the window five days ago, appeared in the room.

Her face was heart-shaped and perfect, her hair black and straight as a river of pure night, her figure almost elf-slender but alluring beneath a snug gown of royal blue. She fixed her eyes on him, and her lips pursed in a small smile. Ignoring the stares of the mercenary captains and lordlings who filled the taproom, she glided over to Fflar's table and seated herself without waiting for an invitation.

"Well," she began. "You have a habit of taking long walks in the evening, don't you?"

Fflar did his best to keep a faintly bemused expression on his face. He could sense at once that he was badly out of his depth; he had no skill for fencing with words. "And you have a habit of watching me," he answered. "Who are you?"

"I am Terian. You are Starbrow, are you not?"

"That's what they call me," Fflar said. "Why have you been spying on me, Terian?"

"Now that is a truly ironic accusation, coming from an elf who's spent each night skulking about in the alleyways and shadows, eavesdropping on the whole town."

"If there's something you want to say to me, better say it soon. Otherwise I think I'm going on up to my room."

"Forgive me, Starbrow. I meant that to be clever, not rude. I truly do admire your directness."

Fflar leaned back in his chair, regarding the girl skeptically. "All right, then. What do you want, Terian?"

She tossed her hair and glanced around the room, and she moved closer, setting one slim hand on his forearm. "You are being watched, Starbrow. Ilsevele Miritar and all of the elves in your party, too."

"By you, apparently."

"I am being serious. Selkirk is not negotiating in good faith. I fear he may be plotting to take Lady Miritar captive and use her against her father."

Fflar narrowed his eyes. "How do you know that?" he demanded.

Terian raised a finger to her lips. "Not so loudly. I am in the service of a Sembian lord who believes that peace with your people is the only path that can lead us out of this disaster. He has sources of information close to Selkirk who have warned him of the prince's duplicity."

"Who is your master, then?"

"I can't tell you that." The girl frowned, chewing on her lower lip. "But . . . I think I might be able to arrange a meeting. Your delegation is to meet with Selkirk tomorrow afternoon, correct?"

"No, in the evening. He returns from Ordulin late in the day."

"The evening . . . even better. You will need to slip away from the delegation before they reach the Sharburg. There is a manor on the east side of the town that belongs

Final Gate • 139

to the Elgaun family, of Yhaunn. Meet me there one bell after dusk."

"Let me guess. I should come alone?"

"One elf slipping out is hard enough to hide. I think you would have a hard time if you brought any more of your warriors. But suit yourself." Then Terian leaned across the table to brush her lips against his.

Fflar was so startled he didn't even think to protest. Then she whispered in his ear, "For the sake of those who are watching us. Let them think you have an assignation of a different sort tomorrow." Then she pushed away and disappeared into the crowded taproom, with only a single mischievous glance over her shoulder for a good-bye.

"I haven't agreed to anything," he murmured to no one in particular. There was trouble brewing, he was certain of it, but if the girl had been telling the truth . . . then Ilsevele was in danger.

He shook his head and sighed. He didn't trust this Terian at all. Fishing a few coins from his belt pouch, he left them on the table and returned to the rooms set aside for the elven embassy. He replayed the whole mysterious conversation in his head several times before he reached the door to their rooms, but still he couldn't make any real sense of it.

Fflar rapped three times on the door and was admitted by the moon elf Seirye, leader of Ilsevele's party of guards. He found Ilsevele waiting for him, her arms folded across her chest and anxiety creasing her brow.

"Starbrow!" she said. "Where have you been? I was beginning to fear that some misfortune had befallen you."

"No such luck, I'm afraid. No one noticed my stroll through the town. Well, no one who took offense, I suppose."

She glared at him and nodded at the door leading to her room. The other elves in the suite were doing their best to find other things to occupy their attention. Fflar glanced at Seirye, who offered a small grimace of sympathy. Then he followed Ilsevele into the smaller room and waited as she closed the door. Still, he was surprised as she rounded on him and set her hands on her hips. "Next time, *ask* before you slip out into the night! Do you have any idea of what could happen if the Sembians caught you spying out the town?"

"I am charged with keeping you safe, Ilsevele. To do that I need to know what's going on around us. We're deaf, dumb, and blind as long as we wait here." He studied the floorboards between his feet. The last thing he wanted in the world was to anger Ilsevele.

"But you couldn't tell me before disappearing for so long?" Ilsevele demanded. "I was worried sick about you!"

Worried about me? Fflar looked up sharply and met her eyes, green as the spring. By the Seldarine, she is beautiful, he thought. She'd never been one to hide what was in her heart, and right now her worry for him left him dumbstruck. He found himself gazing at a faint dusting of tiny freckles across her cheekbones. They lent her features a girlish innocence that entranced him, until he realized that he was staring at her. Something in his gaze must have given him away, for a strange expression flickered across her face, and she suddenly turned and moved away to gaze out the window of leaded glass.

What are you doing? he demanded of himself. You do not have the luxury of mooning over this girl!

The silence grew uncomfortable, until Ilsevele cleared her throat and spoke. "Well?" she said. "As long as you were out there flirting with peril, did you learn anything useful?"

"I didn't pick up much from the tavern talk of the soldiers," he admitted, glad for the chance to speak of something straightforward and unambiguous. "But something else came to my attention while I was looking around the town. A human girl named Terian approached me in the taproom downstairs. She was the one I saw watching us from the window the day we arrived here."

"The dark-haired one?"

"Yes. She told me that Selkirk intends treachery, and that she can put me in touch with Sembians who wish to deal honestly with us. Terian said that she could arrange a meeting with her patron for me, tomorrow evening during the banquet." Fflar smiled awkwardly. "Of course, it would involve slipping out of your sight again."

Ilsevele let the last remark pass. Instead, she asked, "Do you think she can be trusted?"

"I have no idea at all. But I suppose I won't find out for sure unless I take her up on her offer."

"The Sembians would notice your absence. But I suppose you could take ill." Ilsevele studied him for a moment. "Can you think of a reason why you should not see what she and her mysterious master have to say?"

"It takes me away from your side. If anyone intends mischief toward you, it might be easier if I am not around."

Ilsevele's eyes flashed. "I think I can manage to look after myself for a short time."

Fflar raised his hands in surrender. "You asked," he said.

❦ ❦ ❦ ❦ ❦

Sarya Dlardrageth soared through the luminous spires and columns of the Waymeet, impressed despite herself. She had been born in an age when the works of elves were spectacular on a scale that the folk of latter years could scarcely have comprehended. But even she had never set foot in an undisturbed work of ancient Aryvandaar. The Waymeet embodied the boldness, daring, and skill of the ancient Vyshaan Empire, capturing in its living crystal a song of elven might that filled her heart with pride and approval.

"You will live again," she promised the cathedral of glass. "I will give you the opportunity to discharge your ancient purpose again. I swear it!"

Xhalph, flying at her side, glanced at her with puzzlement on his face. She did not respond to his unspoken questions. Soon enough she would show her son what their ancient forefathers had accomplished with this place.

She followed a single curving spar down toward the center of the complex, and alighted before a towering pillar of blue crystal—now shackled and bound by cruel bands of hellwrought iron. Malkizid awaited her there, caressing the harsh runes incised in the metal with his talonlike hands.

"Ah, there you are, Sarya," Malkizid said in a voice of pure music. The archdevil wore his natural form: a tall and regal shape seemingly sculpted from living marble, with vast gray-feathered wings and talons in the place of his hands. His noble mien was marred by the black, seeping wound that gave him the name of the Branded King. "What brings you here?"

"I have been trying to summon you all day," Sarya snapped. "Where have you been, Malkizid?"

"Here. I am nearly done with my work. It is only a matter of time before the Gatekeeper is broken to my will . . . and we will be able to employ the Waymeet for great things indeed, dear Sarya." The archdevil made a small gesture, and sent tongues of angry red flame jabbing deep into the blue crystal before him. The Waymeet itself trembled in agitation, and the keening sound of crystalline agony thrummed through the cold air. Malkizid nodded in satisfaction and turned his full attention to the daemonfey queen. "How fares your campaign against the army of Evermeet?"

"The accursed palebloods set a trap for us at Lake Sember," Sarya snarled. "I lost ninety of my fey'ri warriors, and they are irreplaceable."

"Whereas my own minions destroyed in your service are of no particular concern to you."

The daemonfey queen shrugged. "I would prefer not to lose devils and yugoloths unnecessarily. Why waste my strength? But it is true that the legions at your command are much more numerous than my fey'ri. You have an easier time replenishing your warriors than I do in replenishing mine."

"So you wish me to provide you with yet more of the yugoloths and devils who answer to me? To increase your infernal legions still more so that you may sweep away all the enemies who beset you?"

"Yes. The palebloods can be broken. Victory is within my grasp!"

"Possibly," the archdevil admitted. Blood trickled from the awful brand in his forehead. "But I decline to reinforce you again."

"What?" Sarya hissed. "Can you not see how close we are, Malkizid? What sort of treachery is this?"

Malkizid allowed himself a small, cold smile. "My dear Sarya, you might recall that in the beginning of our association, I told you that the day would come when our relationship would have to be . . . re-examined. I think that day is at hand."

"What do you mean by that?" Sarya demanded.

"Before I provide you with any more aid, Sarya Dlardrageth, you will bow down before me and take me for your lord and master. To help you remember your oaths to me when you leave this place, there will be certain arrangements made that will bind you inextricably to me."

"I will not!" the daemonfey queen snarled. "The Dlardrageths call no power master, fallen one!"

"You truly think so?" Malkizid sneered. "Whom do you think taught your uncle Saelethil the spells he knew? Or what of your forebears, the lords of House Vyshaan? They all groveled before my throne, and in return I gifted them with unimaginable power." The archdevil paused, savoring Sarya's wrath. "I have many such gifts to offer you, Sarya. And you would gain everything you ever desired. I have no desire to be the king of Cormanthyr. Rule as queen in Myth Drannor, subjugate or destroy any of your neighbors that you like. I will help you to do these things . . . if you swear fealty to me."

"Find yourself another slave, Malkizid. Our alliance is at an end." Sarya whirled away, her black wings snapping out behind her. She took three steps back toward the portal when Malkizid spoke again.

"As you wish," he said in his sweet, perfect voice. "But if that is your decision, I shall withdraw from your service the devils of Myth Drannor—they answer to me, you know—and the yugoloths I have provided you over the last six months. How long do you think you will be able to fend off Seiveril Miritar's Crusade with two-thirds of your strength removed?"

Sarya hesitated. "I still command the loyalty of hundreds of demons," she said. "I do not need you, Malkizid!"

"Are you so confident in the weavings of your mythal spells, Sarya? You are certain that you will have no further need of my assistance in maintaining the defenses you have raised over Myth Drannor?" Malkizid caressed the pommel of his greatsword, tracing with one talon the sinister runes graven on the blade. "Or do you think that I might have instructed you to weave your spells in such a way that you would need my assistance to continue them? How long will your 'loyal' demons remain in your service once Seiveril Miritar and his paleblood mages wrest control of the mythal away from you?"

"Let me punish him, Mother," Xhalph rumbled. "His arrogance cannot be borne!"

Malkizid threw back his head and laughed out loud, a rich and melodious laughter that hinted of the celestial he had once been. "You think to challenge me, half-demon? I slew princes of your kind ten thousand years before you were spawned! Now be silent, for I am not done speaking with your mother."

Xhalph set his hands on the hilts of his scimitars and took a step toward Malkizid, but the archdevil simply looked at him. The awful bleeding mark burned into Malkizid's visage gleamed with dark power, and Xhalph halted in mid stride, his eyes blank and unseeing.

"I should strike off one or two of your arms while you stand there. That might teach you to show respect to your betters," Malkizid said to the mesmerized daemonfey.

"Kill him if you must, but do not maim him," Sarya said. "He is of no use to me crippled."

"Perhaps you are right." Malkizid turned his attention back to Sarya. "So, dear Sarya, what is it to be? Shame, defeat, a bitter existence of crawling through the shadows, tormented by the knowledge that you might have been queen over Cormanthyr for a thousand years? Or would you prefer power unfettered, the might to defy your enemies, a dark and glorious reign as my favored emissary to the world of mortals? It is no more or less than the arrangement I had with your Vyshaan forebears, after all. But it matters not to me. Should you decline, I will find another to elevate in your place."

Sarya stood fuming, more furious than she had ever been in her thousands of years of life. But Malkizid had judged her all too well. Without the infernal monsters he provided to serve as her warriors, she would not long fend off the Crusade of Evermeet. And she could not bear the thought of spending the rest of her days hiding from her enemies, never daring to strike at them, never claiming openly the inheritance that was *hers*.

Grinding her teeth in anger, she turned back to Malkizid and slowly prostrated herself before him. "I will take you as my lord and master," she spat. "But you must give me the strength to destroy my foes once and for all!"

"Of course, dear Sarya, of course," Malkizid said. "You will find that I am generous with my gifts." He reached down with one taloned hand and elevated her chin. "Now rise. I require you to offer me a token of your loyalty, if you will. And it may be instructive to Xhalph to witness your fealty."

Sarya climbed to her feet and looked up into the pale marble face of the archdevil. Malkizid's black eyes burned with a hot hunger that left little room for evasion. Even though her hands shook with rage, she began disrobing in submission to her lord.

CHAPTER NINE

9 Eleasias, the Year of Lightning Storms

Storms swept through Tasseldale late in the afternoon, deluging Tegal's Mark with sheets of rain and a spectacular display of summer lightning. But as the afternoon faded toward dusk, the thunderheads marched off to the southeast, and the heavy rain slackened. In the evening, when Ilsevele and the rest of the Crusade's embassy climbed into the carriages waiting to take them to the Sharburg, Fflar slipped away with the aid of a potion of invisibility.

He found Elgaun Manor a quarter-mile or so from the center of the town. The road climbed up a wooded hill past a small shrine to Chauntea, and the manor house stood at the hilltop. Fflar passed through a small, unguarded gate of wrought iron that marked the lane leading to the manor. He noticed that his invisibility potion was beginning to wear off as he approached the manor. Good, he thought. Let Terian wonder how he had slipped away from the Markhouse.

He climbed a short flight of stone steps to the manor's front door. It was a handsome house of native fieldstone, with a broad veranda framed by great dark beams of Cormanthyran hardwood. He'd asked about the Elgauns during the day. They were a wealthy Sembian family from Yhaunn who often summered in the Dales.

I doubt that it's the Elgauns I'm here to meet, Fflar decided.

He set his hand on the door and pushed it open. A shadowed foyer stood within, tastefully appointed with several fine paintings. He could make out a staircase leading up to the second floor, and various anterooms and parlors opening from the front hall.

"Terian?" he called softly.

No one answered him. Frowning, he started forward into the room . . . but then he heard a faint creaking sound from the shadows under the staircase.

Bowstring!

Quick as a cat, he threw himself backward out of the doorway, where he stood silhouetted against the evening sky outside. Bows snapped and sang in the darkness, and arrows pelted at him. One stuck quivering in the door not five inches from his face, a second hissed past his ear and sailed out into night, and a third struck him on the right side of his chest—but bounced from the shirt of mithral mail he wore under his tunic. A slower man would have died in that doorway, but Fflar was just quick enough to spoil the unseen archers' aim.

Cursing savagely, he yanked the door shut behind him. Arrows thudded into the wood of the other side. "Stupid, stupid," he muttered. "You walked right into that one!"

Now what? He could make a run for it and reach the cover of the manor wall. Or he could sidle around the side of the house and head away in an unexpected direction. But whatever he did, he would have to do it quickly.

Make it something they're not expecting, he decided. With one swift motion he drew Keryvian. He counted to four, and he threw open the door and leaped back into the hall.

He found himself face-to-face with two drow archers, hurrying up to the door with bows in hand. The dark elves halted in astonishment, fumbling to draw and shoot. Fflar threw himself at the first archer and cut him down with a great overhand swing of Keryvian that struck sparks from the marble floor after laying the assassin open from collarbone to groin.

The second drow backed up two steps and shot. Fflar tried to spin out of the way, but the arrow caught him high in the left arm. The range was so close that the archer drove the shaft completely through mail, flesh, and mail again, transfixing Fflar's arm. Fflar cursed and stumbled, but he finished his spin within sword reach of his foe and skewered him through the middle with a single deadly thrust. The dark elf groaned and slumped to the ground.

Drow? What in the world are drow doing here? Fflar leaned over the dying archer at his feet. "Who sent you?" he demanded. "Who are you working for?"

Stealthy footsteps rushed up behind him. Fflar whirled and raised Keryvian just in time to block a murderous thrust from a third drow, who snarled in frustration and launched a furious attack. The fellow was armed with a slender rapier, and his swordplay was blindingly quick. Keryvian was really too heavy to fence with, especially with a wounded arm, and Fflar narrowly avoided at least three deadly thrusts in the space of as many heartbeats.

"Die, lightwalker!" the drow hissed. He launched another vicious thrust at the center of Fflar's belt buckle, but Fflar turned aside and let the rapier's point glide past him, slicing a neat furrow in his tunic. He was far too close to make use of Keryvian's point or edge, so he simply smashed the baneblade's pommel into the drow's face. Teeth shattered and bone crunched. The swordsman staggered in his tracks, until Fflar took his head off with a backhand swing.

Panting in the shadows of the manor, Fflar looked around for any more assailants, but none appeared. Before he could think about it, he set down his blade and snapped off the arrow shaft in his arm. Then he yanked it clear and threw it to the ground, stifling a ragged cry of pain. He hoped it wasn't poisoned. Drow knew more about poisons than anybody had a right to.

"Another kind of assignation, indeed," he muttered. If he ever got his hands on Terian, he'd wring her pretty neck.

Three dead drow in an empty manor—a manor he was lured to, specifically at this very time. Why in the world would drow want him dead? Of course, they had to be working for Terian, that was a given. Or she was working for them. But for what purpose? He stood silent for a moment, trying to puzzle it out, and it came to him.

"Damn it all to the Abyss," he snarled. "Ilsevele!"

Without another thought he rammed Keryvian back into its sheath, then turned and dashed out into the evening. In the lane outside, he reached into his vest pocket again and found another potion bottle. Ilsevele had insisted that he should be prepared for almost anything before setting out for his mysterious appointment, and so she had given him several of the more useful potions she and the others had brought from Semberholme. Fflar took a moment to make sure he had the right one and drank down its contents. Then he leaped up into the air.

The magic of the potion carried him up into the sky. Whooping in surprise and sudden panic, Fflar spun wildly in midair and nearly landed even quicker than he had taken off, but then he got the hang of it. In a matter of moments he was arrowing over the rooftops of Tegal's Mark, streaking toward the Sharburg.

Treetops and streetlamps streaked by under him. Fflar saw a handful of people in the streets below look up in amazement, pointing and shouting as he sped past. The roaring of the wind in his ears drowned out their words. It might have been wiser to try to circle the town or perhaps fly a higher, slower arc, but he was beyond such concerns. If the Sembians didn't like him flying over the town, they could damn well take it up with him after he was certain that Ilsevele was safe. His arm burned and tingled, blood flowing freely from the arrow wound, and Fflar found his vision beginning to swim drunkenly.

It's just the potion, he told himself. Flying is too much for the senses, especially after you lose a little blood. But his arm ached and burned with a strange cold sensation that he didn't like at all.

"Fight it off a little longer," he snarled at himself. "A little longer."

The towers of the Sharburg loomed before him, and he saw the high windows of the banquet hall where Selkirk had received them before. He angled down and swooped in at the castle, flashing across the battlements so swiftly that the sentries walking there could only stare dumbfounded. Then he threw his arms up over his face and barreled through the nearest of the windows in a shower of breaking glass. He glimpsed dozens of Sembians, Ilsevele and her guards, even a quartet of musicians, all frozen in amazement. Then he overshot them all and slammed into a vintner's table, sending bottles and fine glass flying everywhere.

"What in the world—?" Miklos Selkirk snarled. He surged to his feet, his hand leaping for his sword hilt.

"Starbrow!" cried Ilsevele. She stood too, and started toward him.

Fflar's vision reeled from side to side, and he hurt all over. But somehow he found his way to his feet. "Ilsevele," he groaned. "It's a trap! A trap!"

Ilsevele whirled around, seeking a threat. Around her, Sembians and elves scrambled to their feet, all looking wildly from side to side. She turned to Selkirk to demand an explanation—and behind her, the quartet of musicians calmly set down their lutes and bitterns, and raised deadly wands instead.

Fflar threw himself into motion, racing crookedly across the floor. The musicians were simply too far, but he launched himself headlong toward Ilsevele just as the assassins barked their commands and unleashed a storm of fire and lightning in the crowded hall. He managed to fling her to the floor as a brilliant blue-white bolt burned through the air where she had been standing, charring his back instead. Hot white agony seemed to pick him up and throw him down again, leaving him contorted on the hard stone floor. Screams of panic and mortal agony filled the air, amid the angry roar of searing magical flame and the deafening *crack!* of lightning bolts exploding in the elegant hall.

Ilsevele picked herself up and drew a wand of her own from the sleeve of her beautiful gown, now torn and blackened. She aimed it at the nearest of the assassins and cried out, *"Elladyr!"*

A coruscating bolt of white energy shot out and caught the fellow in the center of his chest, flinging him head over heels through the smoking wreckage of the bandstand. The others responded with another barrage of spells that wreaked even more carnage in the hall.

"Defend Lady Miritar!" Fflar croaked.

He rolled to all fours and shook his head to clear it of the ringing and the dizziness. It didn't work, but he planted one foot on the ground and levered himself upright, drawing Keryvian. The banquet hall was nothing less than screaming, smoke-wreathed pandemonium, the equal of any battlefield he had ever set foot on. Several of the Sembian lords, led by Selkirk himself, rushed the bandstand and struck up a furious melee with the surviving assassins.

Ilsevele whirled and fired her wand again, this time at a crossbow-wielding sniper who appeared on one of the upper balconies overlooking the hall. The thundering lance of white energy smashed the balcony to pieces, dropping the fellow to the floor below in a cascade of rubble.

Fflar turned, looking for any other threat, just in time to see an assassin dressed in the livery of a wine steward stealing up behind Ilsevele, a wavy-bladed dagger in his hand. But the young captain Seirye, so badly burned and charred that he couldn't even hold a blade in his gnarled hands, simply lurched into the knife wielder and held him up for a crucial moment. The blade flashed once, then twice, and Seirye sank to the floor, still clawing at the killer's tunic. But the young elf's valor was not in vain. Before the knifeman could pull himself free, Fflar staggered over and took his arm off at the shoulder with one wild, off-balance swing.

"Drow! They're drow!" cried one of the Sembians.

Fflar glanced down at the man he'd just downed, and saw the magical guise slip away with the assassin's death. In place of a round-faced, unremarkable human, an ebon-skinned drow with red eyes lay staring sightlessly up at him.

"I could have told you that," he muttered to no one in particular.

Keryvian rang shrilly on the stone floor. He looked down, surprised that he had dropped the blade. He leaned over to pick up the sword, but lost his balance entirely and crumpled to the ground beside his blade. *Fight it! Fight it!* he raged, trying to find the strength to push himself upright again. But all he managed to do was roll weakly onto his back. He found himself looking up at the proud banners that hung in the upper part of the hall, now burning merrily from the fireballs and lightning bolts that had been loosed in the attack.

The hall seemed to fall silent. The ringing of steel on steel faded, and no more thunderbolts or roaring blasts of flame split the smoke-filled hall. The battle was over, and a dozen drow warriors lay scattered here and there on the floor, still dressed in the tatters of their disguises.

"Starbrow! Starbrow!" Ilsevele rushed up to him and fell to her knees at his side, grasping his hand in hers. Tears streaked her face. "What happened? Are you hurt? What's wrong?"

"Arrow in the arm," he managed. "I think . . . I've been poisoned."

"You saved me," she murmured. "Just like the time you faced the ghost in the vault. You saved me again, Starbrow."

"I couldn't let you get hurt, Ilsevele," he said. He was so tired . . . all he wanted to do was close his eyes and sleep. "I couldn't bear it."

"I know." Ilsevele smiled through her tears, and she leaned over him, her hair of fiery red cowling her face and his, and kissed him deeply, passionately, her hands cupping his face and lifting him up to her. "Stay with me, Starbrow," she whispered between her kisses. "Don't die, not now! Stay with me."

Somehow he found the strength to reach one hand up to her face, to caress her perfect face and brush away her tears. Then he laced his fingers in her hair and gently pulled her down to kiss her again, to feel her breath mingling with his, her lips warm and soft.

"I won't die," he whispered to her. "I've found what I came back for."

Then he fell away into darkness, still lost in her emerald eyes.

☉ ☉ ☉ ☉ ☉

Araevin and his companions passed the night, such as it was, in a princely suite. Ornate lanterns of gold ringed the room, but the dim lanterns did little to push back the encroaching darkness outside, and nothing at all to alleviate the bitter cold. They eventually had to make use of the sleeping-furs waiting atop the great round beds, even though Araevin's skin crawled at the dusty age of the covers. He couldn't avoid the impression that he was wrapping himself in the cerements of the grave.

After what seemed like an age in the dimly lit apartments, two of Selydra's pallid warriors came for them. Araevin and his friends followed the Lorosfyrans through the long, echoing corridors of the palace for quite a distance. Shadows gathered in each doorway they passed, fleeing their light slowly and reluctantly. They came to a winding staircase and climbed up a floor, and their grim guides led them out into a courtyard of sorts. A tall white tree grew in a knurled knot of clawlike branches and leaping roots. Not a single leaf graced its sharp branches, but here and there dark red fruit like drops of blood gleamed in the darkness.

Araevin surveyed the rest of the court carefully, and found a blank trapezoidal archway a short distance to his left. A portal like the one above, he realized. That might be useful later.

"The Pale Sybil comes," whispered the dead warrior.

From another passageway leading into the courtyard, a ghostly pale light grew. Selydra drifted into the courtyard, still dressed in the raiment of silver and white in which she had first greeted her guests. Two of the hunched giants followed behind her, stooping to fit in the hallway. She paused, studying Araevin and his friends, her face set in a look of smooth, cool bemusement.

"Welcome, travelers," she said. "I trust your sleep was restful?"

"Nothing tried to kill us," Maresa said. The genasi made a show of gazing around the courtyard, admiring the stonework and the barren white tree. "What a strange tree that is! We don't have any like that back in Waterdeep."

"It is a sussur tree," Selydra answered her. She seemed amused by Maresa's insincerity. "It is rare indeed, growing only in those places where *Faerzress* exists in sufficient strength to nourish it. The tree subsists on the magical emanations of the Underdark."

"Interesting," Araevin murmured, feigning a calm he did not feel. "I have never seen anything quite like it."

"I have found that Lorosfyr is full of unsuspected wonders," Selydra said. She approached the company, and the sussur tree whispered softly as she came near. "So, Araevin, you have said that you have an urgent need for the gemstone in my possession. What is so pressing that you would leave the surface world and come here to find my shard?"

"I must sunder a very old and powerful mythal," Araevin said. "Demonspawned sorcerers have seized the ruins of Myth Drannor for their stronghold and are protected by its ancient spells. Thousands of people will die or fall into slavery if I fail to stop them. No place in—or below— Faerûn will be safe."

"I am not unmoved by your plea, Araevin," Selydra said. She descended into the court by the tree and sat on a stone bench, brushing her midnight hair away from her face. "But the artifact that has found its way into Lorosfyr could be gainfully employed here. You have no doubt noticed the swordwights who attend me here. There is an entity in this lightless place that consumes life and magic. These poor wretches were devoured by the hungry power in this old city. I think that the device you describe may hold enough magical power to finally slake the slayer of this city."

"You have escaped harm so far, my lady," Nesterin observed.

"Only because I have learned to . . . shield myself from its attentions, you might say."

Araevin found himself glancing up at the impenetrable darkness over their heads. The courtyard was open to the sky, as it were. The vast and airy reaches of the monstrous vault soared for unseen miles above his head, and the darkness pressed down on him with a weight that was almost tangible.

"The Maddening Dark. . . ." he murmured.

"It is alive, and it hungers," Selydra said. "It devours its victims so slowly that they never even know they are being consumed. Truly, it is a wonder you made it down the Long Stair alive." She folded her feet under her, and returned her attention to Araevin. "It would seem that we are at an impasse, then. I have need of your shard, and you have need of mine."

"I will return you a shard as soon as I can," Araevin said. "The Gatekeeper's Crystal separates after each use, but I am reasonably confident that I can locate at least one of its pieces not long after I employ the device. I will bring it to you as soon as I can."

"But if I have understood what I have learned from the shard in my possession, there is at least some chance of a much more violent separation, is there not? The three pieces might literally be scattered across the cosmos." Selydra pursed her lips. "Even a mage of your skill might find it difficult to locate a piece after such an event."

"If I cannot bring you a shard after I use the device, perhaps there is something else you might want? Some means of paying you for the use of the device?"

"The shard is virtually unique, Araevin. It is priceless. What might you offer?"

"What would you want?"

"Something of similar magical power, at the very least. Some artifact that I could use to content the hunger and keep it at bay for decades, perhaps centuries."

"I am afraid I don't have any such artifact to give you, Selydra," Araevin said.

"Ah, but I know where you might obtain one on my behalf," the Pale Sybil said. She smiled, stroking her chin with her fingers. Her nails were pale lavender. "In the Buried Realms under Anauroch lies a vault created by the unliving thaluuds, the so-called tomb tappers. I have reason to believe that a magical scepter was collected by a thaluud and taken to this vault. Bring me that scepter, and I would relinquish the shard I now hold." The dark-haired sorceress paused, thinking. "I would prefer to have the scepter before surrendering my shard, but I suppose I might relinquish my shard first if you were willing to accept a geas to ensure your return with the scepter."

Araevin was certain he did not want to give Selydra the power to command him through a magical geas. He remembered all too well Sarya Dlardrageth's domination over him only a few short months ago. Mind-enslaving magic was something he had no desire to subject himself to.

"No, I am not willing to accept a geas."

Selydra stood and paced away, her mouth turned down in a subtle scowl. "As I said. We are at an impasse. Neither of us will be the first to part with a shard."

"A single shard is not of much use to me. I suspect yours is not much use to you. Only in combination does the Gatekeeper's Crystal achieve its full potency."

"But we still must answer the question of whose problem we address first." Selydra folded her hands in her sleeves, and studied Araevin for a long moment with her dark eyes. Not a hint of white showed. There might have been the faintest suggestion of a violet iris around a large, black pupil, but otherwise her eyes were as cold and featureless as Lorosfyr itself. "You intrigue me, Araevin," she finally said. "Why don't you join me at my table tonight? I am eager for news of the world above, and I will be happy to hear you out at greater length. Your companions can rest and enjoy the hospitality of my palace, while you and I perhaps find some common ground in our appreciation of the Art. In turn, I may persuade you to consider my own . . . needs."

Araevin thought he knew what sort of persuasion Selydra had in mind. The Pale Sybil watched him considering her offer, her lips pursed in a subtle smile. He felt the eyes of his companions on him as they awaited his answer, but there really was no alternative. He could not openly spurn her.

"Of course, my lady," he said. "I will await your summons. In the meantime, my friends and I wish to see more of Lorosfyr. I am eager to read with my own eyes the stories this forgotten city might tell."

"As I have told you, Araevin, Lorosfyr is most perilous. You and your companions would do better to remain in my care."

"The apartments you have provided us are quite comfortable, my lady, but we are prepared to take our chances," Nesterin answered. "Some mysteries invite the traveler onward, regardless of the danger."

"So they do," Selydra breathed. "I must insist that you proceed with an escort of my warriors, and you must not go where they tell you not to go. But if this is your wish, I will not deny it." She folded her hands before her waist, and turned her dark eyes back to Araevin. "I will send for you when you and your friends return."

❂ ❂ ❂ ❂ ❂

Five days passed after the defeat of the daemonfey raid against Semberholme, and still Seiveril waited for some word from Ilsevele. He could feel the tides of summer turning, the forest's subtle hints that the hottest days were already behind them. He dared not march against Myth Drannor while there was still any possibility that the Sembians might rediscover their allegiance to the daemonfey cause, but he could not wait much longer. Time was not on his side, and so he prayed to the Seldarine for guidance while hoping for his daughter's return. He was deep in prayer when his guards summoned him to the lakeshore.

"What is it, Felael?" he asked the captain of his guard.

"The moonset, Seiveril," Felael replied. Somber and serious for a wood elf, Felael had become the leader of Seiveril's bodyguard after Adresin's death. He was not quite serious enough to put much stock in titles and honorifics, though, and rarely called Seiveril by anything other than his given name. "Watch the waters across the lake."

Selûne's silver light threw a soft, shining path leading toward the dark shore of the western side of the lake. It was a peaceful scene, and Seiveril wondered what was wrong with it. Then he saw what had caught Felael's attention. A white-winged ship followed the moonlight's path across the water, sailing gracefully through the silvery medium as if wind, water, and night were all one and the same.

"A ship of Evermeet," he breathed.

The ship seemed to meet the lake's waters, and its sails shifted to catch a breeze that rose up to greet it. Seiveril waited on the shore as the vessel glided toward him. As it drew closer he could make out the beautifully garbed lords and ladies of the court, so radiant it was hard to look on them.

Do we all look like that when we come so swiftly from the Emerald Isle? he wondered. Then he saw Amlaruil standing by the rail, dressed in silver and white, her long, dark hair untroubled by the ship's passage. She saw him awaiting her, and raised a hand in greeting. The ship glided to a stop, and the elves who crewed it quickly set out a slender ramp to the shore.

"Welcome to Semberholme, my lady," Seiveril said, bowing.

The Queen of Evermeet descended the silver ramp and set foot on Cormanthor's soil. As her foot touched the ground, her radiance dimmed noticeably, and a faint frown flitted across her face. But she set it aside at once, and greeted Seiveril with a warm smile.

"Lord Miritar,' she said, "I am glad I found you here. I am afraid I cannot tarry long."

"Are you certain? I would like nothing better."

Amlaruil smiled sadly. "Evermeet misses me already, Seiveril. I must return this night."

So it is true in part, Seiveril thought. It was said that Amlaruil could not leave the isle. Though her appearance in Semberholme was proof that she could, it seemed that she could not remain away for very long.

Final Gate • 161

"What can I do for you, then, my lady?"

"I have brought you a warning and a gift, Seiveril. First, the warning: A great and terrible battle draws near. I have seen it. Here in this ancient forest the fate of our people is to be decided, and it will be decided in a matter of days. You must not fail in your crusade, and yet I have also seen that you cannot triumph in Myth Drannor."

The elflord shrugged. "I will make the attempt anyway. I have to."

"You hold all of our fates in your hands, my friend. If you should fail . . ."

"If I fail, you must destroy every gate remaining in Evermeet, Evereska, and any other realm of the People that you can find. And you will have to Retreat absolutely and forever from these lands. You will have no other choice."

Amlaruil gazed on him for a long moment. "You have seen what I have seen, then," she said.

"I have."

"Then there is nothing more I can warn you against. You will succeed, or you will fail. But before you march on Myth Drannor, there is the gift I mentioned."

She looked up at the ship and nodded. A moment later a young elf maiden descended to the shore, carrying a small silver sapling swaddled carefully in its own earth.

Seiveril looked on the tiny new tree, and his breath caught in his throat.

"Is that—?" he whispered.

"A sapling of the Tree of Souls, yes. Only one other exists in the world, and that one is in the keeping of my son in his hidden realm." Amlaruil took the sapling from the girl and placed it in Seiveril's hands. "It is my fondest hope that you will have the opportunity to plant this in Myth Drannor. Until that day, guard it carefully—for it will guard you in turn."

"Guard us? How?"

"Carry it with your army as you march. It exerts a powerful influence for many hundreds of yards, keeping demons and other fiends at bay, guarding our own People against their attacks. The sapling will not utterly bar a demon's approach, but it will not be able to teleport itself anywhere nearby."

Seiveril looked at the fragile plant. He could feel something in the young tree, but he was not sure what. "This small sapling has such power?"

"In a way, it is a living mythal. But you must treat it with great care, Seiveril. No one can say when or if the Tree of Souls will bud again. Each sapling may be the last."

"It seems far too precious to carry into battle, Amlaruil."

"It is, Seiveril. But if you are to have any hope for victory, then I think you must have it. Guard it with all your care."

"I will," Seiveril promised.

"Good." Amlaruil glanced over her shoulder at the setting moon. Its lower limb already touched the dark treetops across the lake. She sighed and looked back to him. "I must go now, Seiveril. I fear that we will not meet again."

"That is not true," he told her. "If we do not meet again in this world, then perhaps we will walk together in Arvandor."

"In Arvandor." The queen smiled again, and she leaned forward and kissed Seiveril's cheek. She turned away and hurried back up to her ship. "Sweet water and light laughter for the rest of your days, Seiveril Miritar."

"And to you," he replied.

He watched as the white ship began to move away, its sails sighing as they caught a new breeze and filled out again. Dancing away across the silver moonpath, the shining hull rose higher and higher in the water until finally it broke clear altogether, speeding westward toward the moonset and far Evermeet beyond.

Seiveril watched the ship until it disappeared from sight. He looked down at the precious silver sapling, still in his cupped hands. So fragile a vessel for the hopes of our people, he mused. Then he carried it back into the warm shadows of the forest.

"Felael, send for Thilesin," he said to his guard captain. "I have a task I cannot trust to anyone else."

The wood elf gazed on the sapling, his eyes wide with wonder. "She is already here, Seiveril," he finally said. "She arrived while you were speaking with Amlaruil. She said she has urgent tidings for you."

Seiveril looked up, and found Thilesin waiting for him. A priestess of the Seldarine, she was a serious and quiet sun elf who had proved herself indispensable as Seiveril's adjutant and secretary, helping him to keep track of the countless details and tasks necessary to wield the Crusade against the enemies of the People. He carried the young tree to her.

"I can think of no better steward for Amlaruil's gift," he told her. "You must see to it that this tree is well guarded at all times. Ask each of our companies for a true and faithful warrior to help you. This is an honor and a duty that all of our folk should have a hand in."

Thilesin took the sapling, her eyes shining. "I will see to it," she whispered.

"Now, what news did you have for me?"

The cleric lifted her gaze from the small sapling, the taut frown of worry returning to her face. "There has been an attempt on Ilsevele's life, Lord Seiveril. She was not seriously injured, but several of our people died. No one knows more than that right now. There are whispers of drow assassins, Sembian conspiracies, and even treachery on the part of our own emissaries. In any event, Ilsevele and the others are now being held in the Sharburg under guard."

Seiveril took a step back and threw out a hand to steady himself against the trunk of a shadowtop. Were the Sembians so full of hate that they could not abide the idea of sharing Cormanthor with elves? Or was this some machination of the daemonfey, an effort to make sure that Ilsevele's mission failed? He felt his knees growing weak. Five years ago he had lost his wife, and he knew he did not have the strength to bear another loss.

"Who died?" he managed.

"We do not know, my lord. But Lord Theremen's people were certain that Ilsevele survived, if nothing else."

Seiveril looked down at the silver sapling in Thilesin's hands. There lies our hope, he mused. In Myth Drannor lies my destiny. But not yet, it seems.

"Call for the captains," he said wearily. "We march on Tasseldale before the sun rises."

CHAPTER TEN

10 Eleasias, the Year of Lightning Storms

Fflar opened his eyes in a small stone room, illuminated only by a single slitlike window. He hurt all over, and there was a febrile tremor in his arms and legs that left him feeling as weak as a kitten. Where am I? he wondered. What happened?

For a time he couldn't put anything together, and simply stared up at the brilliant daylight pouring through the window. Then his brow furrowed in recollection. There was a fight, he remembered. A lonely manor house on a hill, arrows in the dark . . . the banquet! The dark elf assassins!

"Ilsevele!" he gasped.

"Peace, Starbrow. I am right here."

Fflar turned his head and found Ilsevele sitting on a wooden chair by the head of the bed on which he lay. A rough abrasion scored one of her cheekbones, and she'd cut away some of her beautiful copper-red locks—most likely because they'd been singed beyond repair, he supposed. But she regarded him with a soft, shy smile and set one cool hand on his forehead. "I think the poison has run its course. We feared the worst, but Lord Selkirk sent a cleric of Tyr to tend to our wounded, and he spoke powerful healing prayers over you while you lay senseless. For that, at least, I am grateful."

He looked past her shoulder, and saw several of their comrades waiting nearby—Aloiene, Deryth, and three others. But Seirye, Hasterien, and Jerien were not present. I saw Seirye die, he reminded himself. Did Hasterien and Jerien fall as well? He remembered other elves falling in the fury of the battle spells and swordplay.

"By the Seldarine, what a disaster," he breathed. "Where are we now?"

"The Sharburg. We're being held in one of the towers. The Sembians say it's for our own protection." Ilsevele grimaced. "I pointed out to Lord Selkirk that I would be quite well protected in the camp of my father's army, but he hasn't seen fit to allow us to leave yet. There are a number of guards just on the other side of that door."

"We'll leave any time you like," Fflar promised her.

He started to throw off his blanket and rise, only to realize two things at the same time—first, he was still quite weak, and second, he was not wearing a stitch of clothing. While elves did not concern themselves quite as much as humans about that sort of thing, he suddenly found that he was not so willing to abandon his modesty with Ilsevele watching him.

He fell back into his covers, and he remembered everything. *She knelt over me and wept when I was hurt. And she kissed me, and I kissed her too.* All of the sudden, his heart was hammering in his chest, and he could feel his face flushing with embarrassment. He looked up suddenly in alarm. "Ilsevele, I think I—did we?"

Final Gate • 167

She smiled down at him, and her eyes sparkled with delight. "Yes, we kissed," she said, and she leaned close to kiss him softly again. "I knew what I was doing, and I meant what I said," she whispered to him.

"I don't know what to say," he answered. In fact, he did, even if he did not want to admit it. Even as his heart danced with the words she breathed into his ear, a dark and ugly knot of guilt grew under his ribs. Seiveril had trusted him to guard Ilsevele, not to steal her heart. And he had dealt with Araevin in an even worse way, hadn't he? Even if Ilsevele and her betrothed had quarreled lately, he hadn't waited a day before stepping into his friend's place. How could he ever look Araevin in the eye again?

"What is it?" Ilsevele asked.

He couldn't bear to say what came next, but he had to. "Ilsevele . . . what about Araevin?"

"Do you think it is any easier for me?" A shadow flickered behind her eyes. "I wept for hours, Starbrow. But I came to realize that I have been growing apart from Araevin for years now. And lately he has been growing apart from me, much more so in the last few months. He has left me behind him, and I do not understand him anymore."

"He is my friend."

"I know. And I hope that somehow he still will be. But this is my choice, Starbrow, and it is my responsibility as well as yours. Who can tell their heart what to feel?"

"I didn't mean for this to happen."

Ilsevele laughed and said, "Perhaps that is exactly why it did." Fflar started to respond, but she simply laid her fingers across his lips and drew back. "No more for now. You still need rest, and we have all the time in the world to make sense of this. I am not going anywhere, and neither are you."

Fflar started to protest, but Ilsevele pushed him back into bed with one hand, and he resigned himself to resting a little longer. Sleep—full, unconscious sleep, in the helpless manner of humankind—claimed him for a time.

When he woke again, the sunlight streaming into the room was dim and golden with the approaching dusk. He felt much stronger, and Ilsevele allowed him to rise and dress himself. He found that the elves' arms and magic devices were in the keeping of their captors. He was just starting to examine whether the narrow window in their chamber could be widened with some judicious removal of stonework when a sharp knock came at the door.

Miklos Selkirk and several of his Silver Ravens entered the room. "Good evening, Lady Miritar," the Sembian lord said smoothly. "I think it is time that we had a word."

"It appears that I am at your disposal, Lord Selkirk," Ilsevele answered, with just the subtlest inflection of bitterness in her voice.

Selkirk grimaced, but he pulled a plain wooden chair out from under a table by the door and seated himself. His guards took up places just behind him.

"Your father's army is marching," the Sembian began. "My scouts are not entirely sure, but it seems that Seiveril Miritar is marching east, along the south bank of the Semberflow. If he meant to attack Myth Drannor, he'd be on the other side of the Semberflow and he would be heading north. I can only assume that he means to attack Sembia."

Ilsevele sank down onto a couch with a stricken look on her face. "He must have heard of the attempt on my life."

"I had nothing to do with that."

"I believe you," Fflar told him. "But you are holding us here like prisoners. What else do you think Seiveril Miritar would do?"

"I will have no choice but battle if he continues. And if I must fight, I see no reason to allow you to return to your people with knowledge of what you've seen here." Selkirk raised a hand to forestall Ilsevele's protest. "You will be treated honorably, of course. I am not a savage, and I will not allow you to come to harm under my protection."

"If you continue to hold us, you will only confirm my father's fears," Ilsevele said sharply. "If you have any hope

Final Gate • 169

of avoiding a battle, you must let go. My father is coming here for my sake, and my sake only. When I am no longer in danger, he will turn aside. He does not want to fight you, Lord Selkirk."

The Sembian lord nodded. "I think that is true, too. In fact, I am willing to risk allowing you to report on my strength and dispositions, because I hope to avoid the fight altogether. But before I consider setting you free, I need to know something. What happened last night? What exactly was your Captain Starbrow doing before he made his dramatic entrance? What game are you and your people playing at?"

Ilsevele glanced at Fflar. He met her gaze steadily. He was done with fencing with words. The truth was a better answer than anything else he might think up, and he wouldn't have been surprised if Selkirk had some way of ferreting out a lie anyway. He straightened up and faced the human lord.

"Two nights ago, I was approached by a young woman, a human, who asked me to meet her at the house of the Elgaun family—a manor on the outskirts of town," Fflar said. "She claimed that she had proof that some among your folk were negotiating in bad faith. I agreed to come, and so when Ilsevele and the rest of our companions went to your banquet, I slipped away unseen to meet my mysterious friend."

"I did not deal dishonestly with you," Selkirk said stiffly.

Fflar shrugged. "I felt that I had to hear her out if there was any possibility that she had information about a plot against Ilsevele."

"What happened after that?"

"When I arrived at Elgaun Manor, I was ambushed. Several drow were there, waiting for me. I managed to kill three of them and make my escape—though I caught a poisoned arrow for my trouble. I realized that I had been drawn away from Ilsevele, so I drank a flying potion and raced to the Sharburg as fast as I could. You know the rest."

Selkirk rubbed his jaw. "I'll have my men search the manor at once. Perhaps they'll turn up something. Did this treacherous lady of yours give her name?"

"Yes," said Fflar. "She called herself Terian."

The human lord looked up sharply at the moon elf. "Terian? Short and slender, with long black hair and a face that would stop a man's heart?"

"You know her?"

"I only met her once, a few tendays ago," Selkirk said. "She was in the company of a noblewoman named Senda Dereth. I hadn't heard of either of them before, which struck me as odd. I know most of the highborn folk of Sembia, Cormyr, and the Dales too, for that matter. Both ladies were speaking with Borstag Duncastle when I came upon them."

"Who is Duncastle?" Ilsevele asked.

"A very wealthy merchant of the sort that we in Sembia call 'lords,' and a member of my country's ruling council. He was the power who was behind Sembia's involvement in this war." Selkirk frowned, fixing his dark eyes on the scene in his memory. "Duncastle was found dead the day after the daemonfey openly revealed their strength and turned against our army in Battledale. His eyes had been cut out, and Terian was nowhere to be found."

"You believe she killed him?" Fflar asked.

"She went alone to his tent, and his guards admitted no one else that night. I looked into the matter myself, because the murder of a powerful lord is certainly of interest to the Overmaster." Selkirk stood up and began to pace, chewing his lip absently as he considered the puzzle. "I presumed that she had decamped after murdering Duncastle, but it seems that she has been skulking around since. I wonder what other sort of mischief she has been up to? For that matter, who is she really? And who is she working for?"

"She managed to slip a dozen drow assassins into the middle of your army," Fflar pointed out. "Who would be able to persuade drow to take on such work?"

They fell silent, considering the question. Then Ilsevele spoke up. "I think you have been dealing with a daemonfey, Lord Selkirk," she said. "Terian must be a fey'ri in Sarya Dlardrageth's service. Some of them are shapechangers of great skill, after all. And Sarya would certainly be interested in making sure that negotiations between my father and your father never bore fruit."

Selkirk stopped his pacing and looked hard at Ilsevele. "Damnation, but that fits," he said. "How many other daemonfey spies have been whispering a word here and a word there in order to set my countrymen against Evermeet?"

Ilsevele fixed her bright green eyes on the human lord and said, "Lord Selkirk, you are not our enemy. Our enemy hides in Myth Drannor. Regardless of what you decide to do, my father is going to march on Sarya Dlardrageth and destroy her once and for all. Now, are you going to stand aside and let him do his work? Or do you want to continue as Sarya's dupe a little longer?"

Fflar shot a quick look at Ilsevele, surprised by her forcefulness. Then he looked back to the human lord to gauge the effect of her words. Selkirk glared at Ilsevele, and his face flushed red. "You need not remind me of how Sembia found herself entangled in this whole disastrous enterprise. I do not like to be made a fool."

"What are you going to do about it, then?" Fflar asked.

Selkirk took a deep breath. "You are free to go," he said to the elves. "I will have your weapons and other belongings returned at once. But I have a favor to ask of you."

"What is it?" Ilsevele asked.

"Take me to see your father. You trusted me enough to come to Tegal's Mark, so I can trust him enough to go to Semberholme—or meet him on the road between here and there, I suppose, since he seems to be on his way here." Selkirk grinned fiercely, and set his hand on the rapier hilt at his belt. "I think Sarya Dlardrageth has a few things to answer for."

❧ ❧ ❧ ❧ ❧

The forgotten city of Lorosfyr was terrible and magnificent at the same time. Araevin and his companions wandered along empty boulevards and past proud towers whose curiously squared doorways and windows stared down on them, black and forbidding. Two files of six swordwights each marched on either side of the small company, escorting them at all times. Cold, dead eyes sunk in faces of pallid flesh stared back at Araevin when he studied the creatures. The only sound they made was the soft creak of molded leather and rasp of green-pitted bronze as the dead warriors followed the travelers.

Araevin drew his cloak closer around his shoulders and paused to study the façade of a public building rising above them. It seemed to be a library, or perhaps a courthouse. He started toward the steps leading up to the dark doorway, but two of the swordwights moved to bar his path. With a shrug, Araevin turned away.

"Are you really going to accept Selydra's invitation?" Nesterin asked him in a low voice.

Maresa scowled fiercely. "Tell me you're not going to bed that spell-spinning vixen, Araevin!" the genasi hissed. "She'll stick a knife in you or poison you or worse the minute you let down your guard. I can see it in her soulless black eyes!"

"I do not trust her any more than you do, Maresa," the mage answered. He also kept his voice down. The swordwights did not appear to be listening in, but that didn't mean it would be wise to speak too freely in their presence. "I accepted her offer because I was not ready to offend her by declining."

"She seems to be interested in you, Araevin," Nesterin offered. "I hesitate to suggest it, but perhaps if you played along, you might find a way through this impasse."

"Or he might find that her bed is the most dangerous place in this city," Maresa retorted. "Have you seen the way she looks at him? She hungers after Araevin, Nesterin. She has evil designs on him, I am sure of it."

Araevin held up his hand, interrupting the conversation. "I think I have found what I am looking for," he said.

They had reached a courtyard close to the edge of the abyss, with a tall citadel or palace overlooking it. The plaza was ringed by a colonnade of angular pillars, each scribed with the strict runic script of the long-dead city. Statues of forgotten heroes stood among the columns, each gazing sadly out toward the center of the court, where a great geometric mosaic of green, white, and purple tile gleamed in the dim light.

"What? What is it?" Donnor asked. The Lathanderite spoke over his shoulder, keeping his eyes on the swordwights.

"One moment," Araevin answered. He took a deep breath and examined the place, searching for any hint of secret enchantments or hidden wards. He could feel the whispers of old power in the place. Before him the mosaic glowed with the familiar hues of portal magic ... strange and overly intricate to Araevin's experience of such things, but a dormant portal nonetheless. He wove a spell of revealing, examining the magical doorway built into the tiled floor of the court. "I thought so."

His friends waited. Behind them, Selydra's swordwights watched impassively. "There is a portal network within this city," Araevin said. He nodded at the mosaic, and lowered his voice. "We can return to the palace any time we like. For that matter, we can go anywhere the portals reach."

"Can you tell where all of the portals are?" Jorin asked.

"Yes, though I couldn't begin to guess what might be waiting for us on the other side of each door. I think I've already seen several of the portals, though."

"So what do you propose?" Nesterin asked.

Araevin shot a look at the swordwights surrounding the company. "I think it is clear that anyone who employs servants such as these cannot be trusted. Our hostess intends to ensnare me if she can. Instead of waiting for her to spring her trap, I think we should try for the shard."

"We won't be welcome in Lorosfyr for very long," Donnor observed.

"Good," said Maresa. "It's cold and it's dark and I *hate* this place. I'm with Araevin."

Jorin, Nesterin, and Donnor exchanged looks, and nodded. "We agree," the Lathanderite said quietly. "How do we begin?"

"Stand on the mosaic," Araevin said.

He led his friends to the center of the courtyard and paused on the delicate tile. The swordwights followed, but only two of the creatures actually stopped on the mosaic itself. Araevin took a deep breath, and began to work a portal-waking spell.

Selydra's minions fixed their dead gazes on him but did not intervene. Evidently, the Pale Sybil had not instructed the creatures to stop Araevin from casting spells that did not obviously violate their instructions. That will change in a moment, he decided. Beneath his outstretched hands the blue, green, and purple chips that made up the old mosaic awoke to luminescence. Confidently Araevin grasped the metaphysical presence of the gate and reshaped its governing rules to suit his needs.

"Be ready," he warned his friends.

The mosaic glowed brighter, and suddenly seemed to vanish beneath their feet. There was an instant of motion, and Araevin and his friends were standing in the courtyard of the sussur tree, in front of the portal he had seen before. The two swordwights who had been standing on the mosaic when Araevin cast his spell stood alongside them. Despite their lifeless silence, the creatures were quick to realize that the travelers were no longer where they were supposed to be. The two Lorosfyrans raised their halberds and rushed at Araevin, but Jorin and Donnor intervened. In the space of ten heartbeats Araevin's friends cut down the undead creatures.

The sun elf quickly swept the courtyard with his eyes, thinking. He settled on a hallway leading into darkness on the far side of the plaza.

"This way," he said, and he loped across the flagstones under the white tree and took the steps at the far end two at a time, descending into a long passage that ran deeper into the palace. Whatever else happened, he did not want to linger too close to the sussur tree and its null-magic aura.

The small band hurried through the dimly lit corridors, past huge empty chambers and echoing halls. Araevin paused every few yards to stretch out with his senses, seeking some hint as to the direction of the second shard. It was close, he could feel it, yet it was not clear which passages might lead him closer to his goal. They broke out into another courtyard, this one a narrow cloister surrounded by high walls, and headed for the hallway that continued on the far side.

They were halfway across when dozens of the swordwights poured into the court ahead of them. Araevin halted, and started to retreat the way they had come—only to meet more of the creatures following them, with one of the pallid giants shambling up behind.

"Well, I did not think that Selydra would be truly surprised if we tried for the shard," Araevin said.

"Damn the luck," Donnor grated. The Lathanderite took a deep breath and dropped the visor of his helm. "Forward or back, Araevin?"

"Forward," Araevin answered.

He turned back to seal off their pursuers with a spell, but a strange white radiance abruptly glimmered in the ranks ahead of them. Streamers of pale mist collected in mid-air and coalesced into the form of the Pale Sybil. Cold fury blazed in Selydra's eyes as she glared at the travelers caught in the center of the courtyard.

"I had thought better of you, Araevin," Selydra hissed. "While you took your rest in my hall and dined at my table, you plotted treachery of the basest sort! Why, you are nothing more than a common thief." She drew her scepter of black platinum from the folds of her dress and motioned at the bronze-armored swordwights accompanying her. "Slay all but the mage," she commanded. With dull rasps the creatures drew their weapons and rushed at Araevin and his friends.

"Donnor, keep her minions at bay!" Araevin barked. "Leave Selydra to me."

She faced Araevin, her dark eyes narrowed. Araevin did not strike at once, instead waiting to counter whatever spell the Pale Sybil attempted. Selydra hesitated as well, doubtless intending a similar strategy. For a moment neither mage began casting, and they watched each other warily as Araevin's comrades leaped forward to meet the silent rush of the Pale Sybil's minions. Steel rang against bronze as battle was joined.

"It seems that one of us does not have the measure of his or her foe," Selydra said softly. "Let us find out whom." With a small scowl, she began to speak an enchantment designed to ensnare Araevin's mind and bend his will to hers.

Araevin hastily incanted a negating spell. For a moment Selydra's voice seemed to whisper enticingly in his ears, but then the enchantment unraveled and dissipated. He waved his hand to brush away the fading embers of her spell and gather himself for the next enchantment, expecting another attack on the heels of the first.

"I see you are not so easily taken, Araevin," Selydra called. "I knew you would prove a worthy adversary!"

"I have no wish to be your slave," Araevin answered.

He began a spell of his own, summoning out of the darkness a whirling chain of emerald-glowing links. The chain crackled and hissed with an oddly grating sound, growing louder and stronger as it emerged from the shadows over Selydra's head. With a confident turn of his hands he shaped the emerging spell and moved to catch the Pale Sybil in a tightening globe of magical energy.

Selydra frowned and attempted a counterspell. But she failed to excise the spinning green chain that settled around her. Araevin sensed victory—the spell chain would make her own spellcasting nearly impossible if she allowed it to bind her. But at the last moment the enchantress abandoned her attempt to cancel the spell with her own Art, and instead flicked her platinum scepter out to parry the tightening chain. In the space of an instant Araevin's spell chain vanished, its energy absorbed by Selydra's scepter.

"A potent spell," the Pale Sybil murmured.

A dark look flickered across her cold and perfect face. She wove her hands sinuously together and muttered powerful, perilous words. The very stone around Araevin's feet seemed to groan in reply, and from her outstretched fingertips a sickly purple ray lanced out.

Araevin recoiled in alarm and barked, *"Iorwe!"*

In the space of an instant he slid out of the path of the lambent ray, conjuring himself a dozen feet from where he stood. The Sybil's spell arrowed past him to strike one of her own warriors dueling Jorin on the opposite side of the courtyard.

The luckless swordwight crumbled into dust and bits of pitted bronze.

Jorin spared a quick look over his shoulder and grimaced. "Bane's black fist," he muttered. "That was too close." The ranger twisted out of Selydra's line of fire and engaged a new foe.

Ignoring the destruction behind him, Araevin responded by fanning his fingers out before him and invoking the brilliant, many-colored rays of his prismatic blast. Rays of blazing red fire and crackling yellow lightning shot past the Sybil, and the beam of emerald poison she parried with a graceful flick of her glossy black scepter.

That's the second time she's saved herself with the scepter, he thought. Clearly it was enchanted to absorb magic. He would have to figure out how to get it away from her.

Thinking furiously of the spells he had ready that might serve, he prepared himself for her next attack.

But Selydra did not strike immediately. She studied him avidly for a moment, perhaps considering her own tactics.

"Enough," she said. "I think you are perhaps a little too dangerous to toy with any longer, and I am growing hungry."

Araevin started to speak a defensive spell, but Selydra fixed her eyes on his and opened her mouth wide, looking for all the world like she was giving voice to a silent scream, and inhaled deeply. Shadows dark and potent seemed to rush into her open mouth, and Araevin felt *something* in him tear free from his body and fly to her. The Weave tore away from his grasp, and spells held in his mind faded and vanished as the Pale Sybil literally drank them from his soul.

Appalled, he took several steps back and staggered to a knee. He could see it as a visible phenomenon: a nimbus of ethereal silver light ringed his body, but over his heart it streamed out toward Selydra like a plume of white sand driven by a wild wind. It should have been intensely violent—the wind should have roared in his ears, his hair and clothes should have whipped and flapped in the force of that ethereal blast—but Selydra's hunger was something that was not at all physical. Even as tatters of his soul seemed to tear loose and fray in the awful storm, Araevin suffered in silence, the blackness of Lorosfyr's night still and cold around him.

"What *are* you?" he gasped.

"You are strong, Araevin," Selydra said. Her voice was a deadly moan. "I have rarely encountered your equal. You will sustain me for many long years, I think."

"Araevin!" shouted Maresa. "Fight it off! Do something!" She snapped a shot at the Pale Sybil with her crossbow, but the quarrel struck an invisible shield around Selydra and shattered.

She is a vampire of some kind, Araevin thought. *She drinks souls and magic, not blood.* Any spell he had that might guard him from such an insidious attack was gone already, consumed by the Pale Sybil in her hunger. More were being ripped from him with every moment, and he could feel himself literally fraying away. In the space of moments she would tear his soul free from him, and that would be his destruction.

"Magnificent," Selydra crooned. Her eyes blazed with a sinister purple light, and there was a feral cast to her face that had not been there before. "Not since I consumed the archmage Talthonn have I tasted such as you!" She stalked closer, reaching out one white hand as if to hold him in place through sheer force of will.

Fight it, he told himself. *Saelethil Dlardrageth taught me something about battles within the soul, if nothing else.*

With great cry of anguish, Araevin threw all of his heart, his will, into battling Selydra's consuming hunger. For a moment he stemmed the awful tide, and in the space of that instant he lashed out with a blinding bolt of lightning. It was a deadly enough spell in its own right, but all he really wanted to do was to drive her back and gain a moment to gather himself.

Selydra drank the spell the instant it left his fingertips, and laughed in evil delight. "Surely you can do better than that, Araevin! Have you no more powerful spells than that left to you?"

Araevin's other knee gave out, and he found himself kneeling on the cold tiles. *Think!* he raged. *She will simply consume any spell you hurl at her. How else to strike back, to break her deadly grasp?*

A sudden intuition sprang to his mind. Desperately clutching at the remnants of his magical power, Araevin conjured up a wreath of deadly green flame around his fist. It was a spell meant to smite an enemy, but deliberately he brought his smoldering hand up and set it against his own breast. Searing emerald pain exploded against his chest—but then it vanished at once, drawn away by Selydra's black hunger.

A tiny green flame sprang into life above the Pale Sybil's heart. She frowned and looked down in puzzlement—and the small spark burst into a roaring sheath of emerald fire. She shrieked in pain and staggered back . . . and with that her connection to Araevin was broken, and the black consuming void ceased with the suddenness of a slamming door.

Araevin toppled forward as his soul seemed to snap back into his body with startling force. He heaved a great sobbing breath and clutched a hand to his burned chest, momentarily defenseless. But Selydra was engulfed in green fire, wailing like a banshee. Somehow she managed to gain enough control to rasp out the words of a countering spell and extinguish the flames.

Wreathed in acrid emerald smoke, almost doubled in on herself, Selydra glared at him. Her face twisted in a murderous fury. "I will have you yet," she hissed. She barked out the words of a teleport spell, and vanished.

Araevin pushed himself to his feet, looking around for any sign of the enchantress. The Pale Sybil's warriors pressed Donnor, Maresa, Nesterin, and Jorin from all sides. Several of the hunched giants lumbered up after the dead warriors, huge mauls gripped in their massive fists.

"There are too many of them, Araevin!" Nesterin cried. He wheeled and gave voice to a piercing shriek that blew several of the undead warriors into shards of bone and crumpled bronze plate. Jorin and Donnor fought furiously side-by-side, giving ground as they backed out into the courtyard.

"Leave that to me!" Araevin took a deep breath, trying to find his strength again, and took a quick look around. Selydra's servants crowded both the doorway through which he and his friends had entered, as well as the passage she had emerged from—there was no easy escape in either direction.

He wasn't about to let that stop him. He faced one wall of the narrow court, and deliberately incanted his next spell. Parting his hands slowly, he phased a six-foot wide plug of the wall into nothingness, creating a safe passage out of the courtyard.

"This way!" he shouted, then he hurled himself through into the still, silent chamber beyond.

One by one, his comrades broke away from their own fights and hurried after him, abandoning the cloister to Selydra's minions. Donnor was the last one through, pausing before the gaping hole to brandish Lathander's sunburst and blast a half-dozen of Selydra's warriors back into the true and final death from which they had been called.

"To dust with you!" the cleric shouted. "Return to your graves, warriors of Lorosfyr!"

Jorin and Nesterin reached out to pull Donnor through the hole. Several of Selydra's giants reared up before the opening, mauls raised over their heads, but Araevin made a single curt gesture, and the stonework phased aside by his passage spell suddenly returned to its rightful place. With a rush of displaced air and an echoing *boom!* he walled off their pursuers behind them.

"Well done, Araevin," Nesterin said. The star elf wiped blood from a shallow cut across his forehead. "Our enemies are confounded, at least for a moment. Now what do we do?"

"We find the second shard," Araevin answered. "We're not leaving Lorosfyr without it."

☙ ☙ ☙ ☙ ☙

The smoke of burning fields left a yellow-gray pall over the Moonsea's shores. Scyllua Darkhope saw little point in the destruction, really. The grain was shoulder-high and close to harvest. It would have been better to capture Hillsfar's fields rather than fire them. But at least the burning induced the folk of Hillsfar's westerly farms and hamlets to flee east to the city proper, carrying panic, despair, and disease within the distant city walls and clogging the roads for miles.

"All is in readiness, High Captain," reported Marshal Kulwarth. A fierce soldier who had been born among the barbarians of the Ride, Kulwarth was in charge of Scyllua's cavalry. Other marshals led her archers, ogres, footsoldiers, and spellcasters. "We await your order to attack."

Scyllua gazed at the simple ditch-and-dike the Red Plume brigade had thrown up across the road in front of the village. She could not quite make out the towers of Hillsfar itself, but she could see twisting ribbons of smoke rising a few miles to the east, where parts of the city were said to be burning still after the daemonfey raid. Four days before, she and her army had crushed the Hillsfarian garrison at Yûlash, driving the Red Plumes out of the ruined city. Within two days, perhaps three, she would lead her army against Hillsfar itself. The renowned Red Plumes of the city were broken and leaderless, and the paltry collection of mercenaries and peasant levies thrown into the path of the Zhent advance would not delay her long.

"Your orders, High Captain?" Marshal Kulwarth asked again.

"Send the ogres and the footsoldiers against the center, with the support of the spellcasters. Give them a short time to allow the attack to develop, and lead your cavalry against the enemy left flank. You will shatter the Red Plumes and drive them into the sea. I will lead the flanking attack personally."

Kulwarth thumped his fist to his breastplate and grinned. "I am honored, High Captain. It will be as you say." The scarred barbarian rode off, barking orders, while Scyllua settled her helm over her head and drew on her gauntlets.

Horns blared and drums rolled ahead of her, and phalanx after phalanx of the Zhentilar infantry started forward against the Red Plumes in their hasty fortifications. Ogres in heavy hauberks of mail, armed with maces and axes the size of small trees, waded among the human and orc warriors. Scyllua expected that the infantry alone would suffice to break the Hillsfarians... but she wanted to *annihilate* the Red Plumes, and that meant cutting off their retreat with her cavalry.

The sounds of battle drifted back from the ramparts, while the Zhentilar horsemen sat impassively watching. Then Kulwarth had his trumpeters sound their commands. Scyllua led the way as the cavalry rode south, moving away from the center of the fight. When she judged that they had circled far enough, she stood up in her stirrups and let out a high, piercing cry: "Warriors of Zhentil Keep, *follow me!*"

Brandishing her scalloped blade, Scyllua Darkhope wheeled her pale white hellsteed in one tight circle and spurred the nightmare across the trampled fields before the Hillsfarian position. Blue fire fumed from the nightmare's nostrils and struck from the ground at each hoof beat, wreathing Scyllua in the hot stink of brimstone as she dashed out in front of her soldiers. Few of the cavalrymen at her back could keep up with her, but she did not concern herself with what was happening behind her back. In front of her the Red Plumes of Hillsfar were arrayed for battle, and she meant to conquer or die.

Arrows hissed past her, and a couple glanced from her armor of black plate. One even pierced her left leg just above the greave, skewering the meat of her calf, but Scyllua shoved the pain out of her consciousness with a single shrill battle cry. There would be time to worry about her wounds later. A foolish wizard hurled a blazing ball of fire right at her and her hellish mount, but the High Captain of Zhentil Keep rode through unscathed—no flame found in Faerûn could harm her nightmare, and her armor was magically warded against fire.

"For the Black Lord!" Scyllua screamed.

She hurled herself over the warriors of Hillsfar, striking off the head of a Red Plume who tried to spear her as she rode past. She threw herself into the middle of the biggest knot of Hillsfarians she could see, and for twenty red heartbeats she laid about her on all sides, taking arms and cleaving skulls in a bright and perfect battle-madness. Her steed kicked, tore, and spumed blue fire everywhere her sword did not reach, and together they worked awful destruction.

"Kill her! Kill the captain!" cried the Hillsfarians around her.

On all sides Red Plume veterans hurried to attack her, hoping to strike down the leader of the Zhent army while Scyllua fought recklessly and alone. But then the rest of the cavalry caught up to her, sweeping into the gap her impetuous charge had ripped in the Hillsfarian line. The Zhentilar cavalry broke like a black thunderbolt over the Red Plumes' defenses and swept them away.

In the end, a small number of the Red Plumes managed to escape. Half a dozen Hillsfarian war galleys arrived on the shore late in the afternoon and carried off a few hundred of the surviving soldiers. Scyllua killed her last Red Plumes of the day while her nightmare plunged steaming belly-deep in the cold waters of the Moonsea, chasing after the enemy soldiers floundering toward the waiting ships. Only then did she allow her warriors to lead her back to the shore.

Kulwarth greeted her on the rocky strand. "We have about one hundred prisoners, High Captain. What do you wish done with them?"

"Put the badly wounded ones to the sword. Send the rest back to the slave markets in Zhentil Keep."

"As you command, High Captain." Kulwarth struck his breastplate again in salute.

"One more thing, Marshal. Have our spellcasters send word to Lord Fzoul. Tell him that we are victorious. The Red Plumes are driven from the field." Scyllua doffed her helm and shook out her short-cropped hair. "We march on Hillsfar tomorrow."

Final Gate • 185

CHAPTER ELEVEN

11 Eleasias, the Year of Lightning Storms

Exchanging messages by magical couriers, Miklos Selkirk and Seiveril Miritar agreed to meet at an old manor atop a hill in Battledale, twenty-five miles north and west of Blackfeather Bridge. Selkirk arranged for Ilsevele and her remaining escorts to be set free, asking only that she allow him to accompany her to Battledale. And so as dawn broke over the broad gray downs stretching east from Tegal's Mark, Selkirk and Ilsevele rode out from the Sharburg together, with their escorts intermingled.

The overmaster's son brought only seven of his Silver Ravens with him, since Ilsevele's party was reduced to herself, Fflar, and six of her own bodyguards. Fflar decided that he approved of Selkirk's good faith, though he certainly hoped that they would not run into any roaming bands of daemonfey or marauding demons with such a small company. Fortunately, the miles passed without trouble. Few people lived in that part of Battledale, and the daemonfey war had largely passed by the rolling hills and lonely farmsteads of the area.

Shortly before dusk, they sighted the crumbling walls of Orskar Manor. The old house had been abandoned for more than a century, and little remained except the shell of its sturdy stone walls. Open grassy fields surrounded the place, crisscrossed by tumbled-down walls of fieldstone. Fflar spied a small company of elves waiting at the top of the hill, horses grazing in the fields near the old ruins.

"It seems your father is already here," Selkirk observed to Ilsevele. The Sembian studied the surroundings for a moment and allowed himself a small smile. The broad hillsides around the place offered little cover for a company of warriors to lurk unseen nearby, so it was a good spot for a parley. "Let us go on up and join him. I wouldn't want to keep him waiting."

"I am sure he is anxious to meet you, Lord Selkirk," Ilsevele assured him.

She tapped her heels to Swiftwind's flanks, and the horse picked up her step and cantered easily up the old lane leading to the house. Selkirk followed a length behind her, his big coal-black charger streaked with dust from the long ride. Together they clattered into the old drive of the manor, while Fflar contented himself to follow close on their heels. Elves in dappled green and gray cloaks trotted out to take the riders' reins and steady their mounts as they dismounted and stretched their legs.

"Ilsevele!" Seiveril Miritar appeared, standing on the steps of the old veranda. He wore a tunic of gray silk over a coat of bright mithral mail and carried his long-handled silver mace at his hip. He trotted down the stone stairs and caught his daughter in a strong hug. "Thank the Seldarine that you are safe. I worried about you every day."

Final Gate • 187

"There was no need for that!" Ilsevele said with a smile, and kissed her father on the cheek. "I am well enough, as you can see."

Fflar swung down from his horse and took a deep breath. *Seiveril and I need to have a long talk about Ilsevele,* he reminded himself. In the right and proper course of things he would have asked the elflord for his permission before courting Ilsevele, but somehow events had conspired against that sort of formality, hadn't they? And what if Seiveril decided that he did not approve? What were he and Ilsevele to do then?

All of the sudden, Fflar found that he was not as relieved to be back with the Crusade as he had thought he would. *Do it soon,* he told himself. *The sooner the better.*

"Starbrow! You are up and about." Seiveril grasped Fflar's hand and squeezed his shoulder. "We heard that you were injured. I am glad to see you, my friend."

"A little drow poison. I'm much better off than the fellow who stuck me with it." Fflar managed an uneasy smile, wondering what to say next, but Ilsevele rescued him.

"Father, this is Lord Miklos Selkirk, son of Overmaster Kendrick Selkirk of Sembia," she said. "Lord Selkirk, this is my father, Lord Seiveril Miritar of Evermeet."

The elflord and the Sembian appraised each other. Then Selkirk swept off his hat and bowed. "Lord Miritar. I thank you for receiving me," he said. "Before we say anything else, I must say this: I deeply apologize for the attempt on your daughter's life while she was my guest, and I am sorry for the deaths of her guards. I would sooner have died myself than permit harm to come to guests at my table. I beg you to tell me if there is any way in which I can begin to set this right with you."

"Well said, Lord Selkirk," Seiveril answered. He reached out and took the Sembian's hand in the human fashion. "Ilsevele sent word of what happened, and she does not hold you to blame for it. Neither will I. The fault lies with the daemonfey and their assassins, not with you."

Selkirk held Seiveril's eyes for a long moment, and nodded. "In that case, please accept my condolences for those who were killed. We will be more vigilant for treachery of that sort in the future."

"I understand." Seiveril turned to indicate the others waiting with him. "Allow me some introductions. My daughter you know already, as well as our battle captain Starbrow. This is Lord Theremen Ulath of Deepingdale."

Selkirk inclined his head to the half-elf Dalesman, who regarded him with a carefully neutral expression. "I have known Lord Ulath for some time."

"And this is Jorildyn, the leader of our battle-mages. Vesilde Gaerth, my second, could not be here this evening. He is leading our march."

Selkirk nodded to each of the elves in turn, and introduced his own companions. "My Silver Ravens," he said with pride. "Like me, they believe that Sembia should be something more than a counting house. Perhaps someday we'll make it so."

Seiveril indicated a simple shelter that had been set up in a small grove behind the ruined house. "If you'll follow me, Lord Selkirk, I think we have much to talk about. I am afraid we did not bring much with us, but we have a little food and drink if you would like refreshment."

"I am grateful."

Selkirk, Seiveril, Ilsevele, Theremen, and Fflar adjourned to the shelter. It was simply an open-sided tent arranged over the simplest of furnishings—a pair of old stone benches left from the ruined manor, facing each other around a small table that held plates of bread and sliced fruit along with ewers of cold water and wine. Fflar found that he was more tired than he had thought, and wasted no time in helping himself to some of the food and a deep goblet of clean water. Selkirk and Ilsevele followed suit.

After quenching his thirst, Selkirk held his goblet in his hands and looked up at the elflord. "So your army is marching east. Mine is marching north. In a day or two

Final Gate • 189

they're going to meet somewhere a little south of Essembra. What happens then?"

"I intend to turn toward Myth Drannor," Seiveril answered. "You have returned my daughter unharmed, and I do not now believe that the attack against her in the Sharburg was any fault of yours. As Ilsevele has told you, I have no wish to fight your army. Sarya Dlardrageth is my foe."

"As it so happens, I intend to march on Myth Drannor as well," Selkirk said. "The events of the last few days have convinced me that the daemonfey are simply too dangerous to ignore. I am going to do my best to drive her out of Myth Drannor."

"It would seem wise to combine your efforts, then," Ilsevele said.

"So it would," Selkirk agreed.

Theremen Ulath cleared his throat. "I do not presume to speak for you, Lord Seiveril, but I must say this: Deepingdale will not fight alongside Sembia so long as Sembian soldiers occupy any of the Dales. Mistledale, Battledale, and Shadowdale hold the same opinion."

"These are your lands the daemonfey are terrorizing," Miklos Selkirk said sharply. "You will not fight for your own countrymen?"

"We will not fight to deliver our countrymen from one conqueror to another, Lord Selkirk."

Miklos Selkirk straightened up, and anger flashed in his eyes. Fflar exchanged a quick look with Ilsevele and read his own fears clearly enough in her face: Hope for an alliance against the daemonfey has come down to this. Selkirk gathered himself for a sharp retort but held back, considering his words. He studied Theremen Ulath closely, and after a long moment, he spoke. "I do not like to be compared to the daemonfey, Lord Theremen. But you should know that I will withdraw our armies from the Dales once the daemonfey are dealt with. You have my word on it."

Theremen frowned, weighing Selkirk's offer. Fflar held his breath, hoping that the lord of Deepingdale would not find that the right occasion to speculate about whether Selkirk was the sort of man who would honor his word.

Finally, Theremen asked, "Your Ruling Council will allow you to withdraw, Selkirk? They have paid well to hire the army that occupies Tasseldale and Featherdale. I must believe they will insist on a return for their investment."

"Some will protest," Selkirk admitted. "But I will not lose the argument, for two reasons. First, Borstag Duncastle was leader of the faction in our Ruling Council advocating a more direct . . . involvement . . . in the Dales. As it so happens, he no longer has much to say on the subject.

"Second, and more important, it is apparent to me that the Dales are much more valuable to us as trading partners than troublesome conquests. Sembian policy follows Sembian gold, Lord Ulath. As long as you refrain from throwing Sembian merchants out of the Dales, we'll refrain from using our soldiers to guarantee their interests."

"It isn't likely to be as simple as that," Theremen said in a low voice.

"I know it," Selkirk said. "There will be quarrels, differences, difficulties. . . . But I'd much rather deal with Lord Miritar than Sarya Dlardrageth, and Lord Miritar would much rather have me for an ally than an enemy. Keep those two truths close to hand, and we'll manage."

"Does that satisfy you, Lord Ulath?" Ilsevele asked.

The lord of Deepingdale looked to Seiveril. "Will the elves stand with us if Lord Selkirk's countrymen fail to honor his word?"

The Sembian lord scowled, but he kept his silence. Seiveril did not look at him. "We will guarantee the freedom of the Dales," he told Theremen. "But I am confident that it will not come to that."

"It won't," Selkirk said. "But I must warn you that if you ask each and every Dale if they're willing to let Sembia

Final Gate • 191

help them fight their war, we will spend the rest of the year talking over this table. Now, do we have an enemy in common or don't we?"

"Remember Mistledale," Theremen said to Seiveril. "That must be answered too."

"Mistledale?" Selkirk asked.

"Mercenaries in Sembian employ pillaged portions of the middle Dales. More than a few Dalesfolk were robbed or killed by your sellswords, Lord Selkirk," Fflar explained. He'd seen the aftermath of the fighting during the retreat to Semberholme.

"The Sable Wyverns of Arrabar," Selkirk said. He stood and gazed out over the long shadows of the sunset. "I know what you are speaking of. For what it is worth, I gave no orders for the pillaging of these lands. But I can't say that Borstag Duncastle—or his 'advisors'—did not. I should have done more to put a stop to that."

"The sellswords responsible must be dismissed from your service immediately," Theremen said. "They are murderers and thieves. Dalesfolk fighting under my banner will fall on the Sable Wyverns at the first opportunity."

"As I understand it, Dalesfolk have already fallen on the Chondathans, Lord Theremen," Selkirk said. "The folk of Glen delivered a sharp defeat to the Sable Wyverns before the daemonfey unleashed their demons against us. But I will have the survivors placed under arrest. I deplore their atrocities as much as you do."

Seiveril glanced at the lord of Deepingdale. "Is that enough, Theremen?"

The lord of Deepingdale grimaced, but he nodded. "You have no idea of what I will have to do to explain myself to my neighbors. But I am satisfied. I will march with you."

"Then I consider myself satisfied, too," Seiveril said. He looked over to Fflar. "Starbrow, what is the best way to attack Myth Drannor?"

Fflar took a deep breath. He had anticipated that question for days. He had half-hoped that Araevin would return with some potent magic to make the task easier, but he didn't know if they could wait on Araevin's mission any longer.

"Give me parchment and a quill," Fflar said. "I'll start by sketching what I recall of the city."

◈ ◈ ◈ ◈ ◈

The empty chamber on the other side of the wall led to one of the long, lightless passageways of the palace. The still, cold air was stale, and dust lay thick on the old mosaics of the floor. Araevin and his companions looked up and down the passageway, but they did not see or hear any signs of pursuit.

"Which way now, Araevin?" Jorin asked.

"I am not sure," the mage answered. "The second shard is still below us, but I don't know where we can find a descending stair."

"Pick a direction and go!" Maresa snapped. "It won't take Selydra's slaves long to figure out where we must be."

"Left, then." Araevin set out at an easy run, loping down the hallway with a wand gripped in his left hand. He could already feel his strength returning, but he would not care to fight another magical duel yet.

Is that what happened to the swordwights? he wondered. Did the Pale Sybil consume them too? That would make her centuries old, perhaps millennia. Who could guess how long she had ruled over the cold, changeless dark of Lorosfyr?

Araevin's guess was better than he thought, for the travelers came to a spiraling staircase leading deeper into the palace.

"This way," he said, and started down cautiously.

It was possible that Selydra might think he was heading for the Long Stair and the way back to the surface world, but he had to believe that the Pale Sybil would expect him to try for the shard and seek to stop him.

They were halfway down when the muffled blasts of vast wing beats followed them into the stairwell. Araevin hesitated, then turned to face the threat pursuing them, whatever it was. Donnor Kerth drew his broadsword and moved to the topmost step, crouching behind his shield. Jorin unslung his bow and laid an arrow on the string.

"I don't like the sound of that," the ranger muttered.

"Steady, my friends," Araevin said.

He took a deep breath, and their pursuers appeared. The things were taller than ogres, with black batlike wings and faces of rumpled, eyeless flesh. Nests of fanged tentacles sprouted from the center of their hunched torsos, writhing and snapping. The horrors dropped down on the small company in a single swift rush, clawed fists and slavering lamprey-maws reaching out of the darkness.

"Courage!" Nesterin cried, and he loosed an arrow at the nearest of the monsters.

The white-fletched shaft sank into the blank, rugose head, and the beast sagged to the steps. It floundered awkwardly, plucking at the arrow, but Donnor darted up three steps and hewed at it with his broadsword. Jorin peppered the next of the monsters, killing it in midair. The creature dropped heavily to the steps and rolled, sweeping Donnor off his feet and carrying him back down the stairs.

Maresa's crossbow sang out, and Araevin let loose with his disrupting wand. A bright blue beam of shimmering thunder blasted back up the stairwell, pulping the creatures' foul, purple-black bodies and rending great shadowy wings. More of the horrors crumpled to the steps or floundered into the curving wall, but still others came on. Before Araevin could find another safe target for his wand, one of the monsters vaulted over the struggling Donnor and hurled itself against Maresa. It caught the genasi with one taloned hand and dragged her close to its torso so that its slick, snapping jaws could fasten themselves to her.

"Get off me!" the genasi shrieked. She dropped her crossbow to the steps and yanked out a poniard with her free hand, slashing wildly at the tentacle-maws groping for her flesh.

"I'm here!" Nesterin drew his own sword and threw himself into the monster's reach to bury his point in its side. Thick black blood welled up from the creature's wounds. It shuddered so violently that it wrenched the star elf off his feet, and shook itself free of the blade and released Maresa, flapping back up into the air. The genasi snarled a savage curse at the monster before retreating away from the winged horrors.

A few steps above Araevin, Donnor struggled to his feet and hacked the creature fumbling at him to pieces, while Jorin ducked, dodged, and shot arrow after arrow at the hovering monsters above.

"More are coming!" the ranger cried.

"I see them," Araevin answered. He dropped down a step or two and drew out a pinch of sulfur from a small pouch at his belt. Rolling the yellow powder between his fingers, he quickly incanted a fire spell and hurled a small red bead of flame up the stairs. "Fall back!" he warned his friends.

Blades flashing furiously, the company managed to back down a dozen more steps, while the many-fanged horrors pressed down the broad stairwell after them. Then, with a stone-shattering roar, Araevin's fiery bead detonated behind them. A searing wave of crimson fire scoured the stairwell above, consuming the creatures outright. Shrill shrieks of pain filled the stairs above, only to die away in awful, wet mewling.

"Come on!" Araevin called to his friends. "We should keep moving before more of Selydra's minions follow us."

They reached the floor below, and found a great hall with passageways leading in several directions. Araevin paused only a moment to glance down each before he chose a high bevel-vaulted passage leading to his left. He could sense the second shard, almost as if he heard some small and distant sound that he could follow if he concentrated on it. Moving with more confidence, he led his companions through several empty rooms and past strange well-like pits that punctuated the lower passages.

They came to a dark doorway guarded by strong and terrible sigils, evil runes that glowed with power when they came too near. Araevin studied them and spoke a countering spell to suppress the door's defenses. Then he led the company into the chamber beyond—a round conjury with a low ceiling, its floor pocked with five more of the black wells spaced around its edges. In the center of the chamber a small stone podium stood, and on that podium rested a small iron coffer. Even through the locked iron box Araevin could sense the presence of the shard.

"There," he said. "The shard is in the chest. I can feel it."

Maresa scowled at the small coffer, one hand clamped to her side where the winged monster's lamprey-jaws had gouged her flesh. "I don't suppose we can just walk off with that," she said. "It's trapped with magic, or I'm an ogre's stepchild."

Araevin peered closer. "It is," he said. He could see spell shields glimmering around the coffer . . . a potent conjuration held in abeyance, something tied to the odd black wells ringing the room. He did not doubt that something very unpleasant would be unleashed the instant the iron box was disturbed. "Give me a moment to puzzle out this—"

A bone-chilling moan cut off his words. It was a horrible sound, a sort of thin high wailing that turned the blood to ice. He whirled, searching for the source of the cry, and found streamers of ebon mist surging up out of the wells. Tortured faces appeared in the foul fog, roiling and shifting in the liquid darkness. Each cloudlike entity seemed to be composed of dozens, perhaps hundreds, of the screaming souls, and as they streamed up into the room they shouted, cried, wailed, begged, and threatened in a multitude of voices, until all Araevin wanted to do was cover his own ears and try to shut out the awful sounds.

"Araevin!" cried Jorin. The ranger pointed at the well

opposite the doorway, on the other side of the shard's pedestal. "The Pale Sybil!"

The mage turned again, and there Selydra hovered in the air, her black eyes blazing with cold fury. A spectral wind sent her robes wildly streaming around her body, and a corona of frigid white fire enveloped her. "I am not so easily defeated, Araevin Teshurr!" she snarled. "The souls of dead Lorosfyr hunger for living flesh to consume. I have promised them yours!"

Jorin raised his bow and shot, but his arrow glanced from an unseen barrier ringing Selydra. She laughed in dark scorn, and raised her arms. From all sides the streaming waves of mangled souls gabbled in hunger and rushed forward, leaping out at Araevin and his companions. Then Selydra began to chant a terrible spell, forming a spiderlike blot of inky nothingness between her hands.

"Donnor! Light!" Araevin cried. He readied himself for the Pale Sybil's spell.

She hurled the living blot straight at him, but the sun elf managed to bark out a counter charm and interpose a flickering wall of tangible magic, angling the sinister missile away from it. The thing shattered his shielding spell on the instant it made contact, but it deflected away from him and plowed into the wall of the vault. A shock of outraged stone jarred the entire chamber, shattering the mosaic floor and starting a net of jagged black cracks in the ceiling above. Araevin reeled and almost fell.

"Swordwights are coming!" shouted Maresa. Araevin risked a glance over his shoulder and saw her back by the archway leading into the vault, side by side with Jorin as they held the gap against Selydra's undead servants. "We're surrounded!"

Araevin looked back just in time to see a wall of whirling black soul-stuff reaching out for him with ethereal talons, plucking at his breast. Dozens of contorted faces leered and hissed at him, a visage of pure madness. He threw up his arm to ward off the fearsome apparition—and the chamber exploded with brilliant daylight.

Donnor stood behind him, legs thrown out shoulder-wide, his cupped hands high over his helmed head. Above his outstretched arms spun a blazing orb of molten gold too bright to look at.

"Part this eternal night, Lord of Morning!" the cleric shouted. "Drive away the shadows that beset us, and shield us with your holy radiance!"

The dead souls of Lorosfyr wailed in anguish and shied away, repelled by the blistering light. The looming apparitions simply dissolved into streamers of dark mist, recoiling from the cleric. Selydra threw up an arm to shield her eyes, even as she reached out with one hand to wrench her blot of destruction out of the wall. More brick and stone disintegrated as the small manifestation of *nothingness* worked its way free.

"Your conjured sun will not avail you, priest!" Selydra hissed. The enchantress threw out her hand in Donnor's direction, and the bubble of twisting, tortured space jumped forward in answer to her command.

"Aillesel Seldarie!" Araevin watched the deadly missile advancing on his friend, frozen in helplessness. He had no more spells that could counter or parry Selydra's annihilating sphere. Furiously he cast around for something, anything, to defeat the Pale Sybil's magic.

Donnor Kerth grimaced and shifted his shield from his shoulder, interposing the warboard. "Araevin, what do I do?" the cleric shouted.

"Keep away from it!" Araevin answered. It was not a good answer.

Selydra's sphere was much quicker and more agile than the armored cleric, and even if Donnor did stay away from the damned thing, she would turn it against another of his companions.

Selydra smiled in cold satisfaction, amused by Araevin's dilemma. "You have no answer to my spell, High Mage?" she taunted him.

Araevin wheeled back to face her, beginning to summon the power for a fierce attack if he could not find a way to banish her deadly orb. Many spells vanished with the death of their creator, after all. But then his eye fell on the slender black scepter hanging from the Pale Sybil's hip.

In a lightning-swift flash of inspiration, he changed the spell he was casting and instead shouted the words of a straightforward telekinesis spell. He snatched the Pale Sybil's magical scepter—the scepter with which Selydra had absorbed or deflected some of his best spells—from her belt in one quick move, summoning the device to his hand. Then, before Selydra could begin to even frame a protest, he turned his back on her and used the telekinesis spell to hurl the slender rod of black platinum right at the spinning sphere of nothing.

"You fool!" Selydra screeched.

The sphere's fearsome touch destroyed the rod, and the rod's potent negation magic dispelled the sphere. Two powerful forces that were never meant to meet struggled with each other for one impossible heartbeat, and sphere and rod together exploded in a tremendous blast of raving purple energy. Jagged rifts of fractured reality flailed out from the site of the concussion. One grazed the Pale Sybil's left side, and in the blink of an eye she was wrenched away and hurled into some distant plane.

"Araevin! What did you *do?*" Maresa cried. She leaped aside from one sharp-edged rift that swept past her. "How in the Nine Hells does this make things better?"

The sun elf shook his head, trying to brush off the ringing metaphysical concussion that still echoed between his ears. He finally managed to steady himself on his feet. "Stay by me!" he called to his companions. "If we are caught in a rift, we all must be caught together!"

Jorin and Nesterin exchanged dubious looks, but they quickly backstepped from the warriors of Lorosfyr—many of whom had already been scythed to pieces in the blast, or who stood around stupefied without the Pale Sybil's direction. Araevin's companions gathered close, warily watching for any reality-shards that might come their way, while the mage searched for a warding spell to deflect the rifts.

"Araevin, the chest!" Jorin called.

Araevin looked back at the pedestal on which the iron coffer rested. To his horror, a flickering discontinuity drifted down toward it, spinning lazily end over end like a piece of a broken mirror. He was out of time.

"Get ready! We will teleport away from here!" he snapped.

"I thought you said you couldn't teleport in the Underdark," Maresa protested.

But Araevin did not answer. Instead he hurled himself at the pedestal, ignoring the fraying spell wards that surrounded it. Recklessly he scooped up the small iron coffer from its resting place and leaped back. The powerful conjuration he had sensed on the shard unleashed itself all at once. Above the pedestal a great and terrible monster began to take shape, a thing of fiery tentacles and clustered eyes—some sort of demon dragged into the vault of Lorosfyr by Selydra's spells. But broken pieces of discontinuity scythed toward the monster.

In a distant part of his mind, the mage in Araevin wondered what would happen when a monster in the process of transitioning itself from the netherworlds encountered a drifting planar rift. He chose not to find out. Praying to the Seldarine that he did not fumble his words, he barked out his teleport spell and pulled himself and his companions out of the disintegrating vault and into a maelstrom of waiting blackness.

✦ ✦ ✦ ✦ ✦

Hundreds of campfires flickered faintly along the wooded hillsides on each side of the dusty cart-track the humans called Rauthauvyr's Road. The Sembian army had chosen to pass the hours of darkness three miles south of Essembra, the only town of any size at all in the broad land of Battledale. Most of the townsfolk had fled south to Tasseldale several tendays ago, unwilling to become Sarya Dlardrageth's subjects. For her own part, the daemonfey queen could not have cared less what the folk of Battledale thought of her dominion. They were simply irrelevant to her calculations.

On the other hand, the army of Sembia was *not*. She ground her teeth, galled at the thought that she had to account for the interference of a human realm in her affairs. But that was the simple truth of the diminished age in which she now found herself, wasn't it? She had humbled Hillsfar and enticed Zhentil Keep away from the board, but despite her best efforts, Sembia was still a force to reckon with.

"How strong are they?" Sarya asked her warmaster. Mardeiym Reithel stood nearby in the darkness, along with half a dozen more of her fey'ri captains and lords. The daemonfey watched the humans from a circle of standing stones half a mile from the Sembian camp.

"A little more than seven thousand, my lady," Mardeiym said quietly.

Sarya scowled and returned her attention to the foe that worried her far more than any army of human sellswords—the army of Seiveril Miritar. In the forests a short distance from the human camp gleamed the soft light of scores upon scores of elven lanterns. The two armies marched only a mile or two apart, ready to come to each other's support should one come under attack.

"What of Miritar's army?" Sarya asked.

"Four thousand elves, including many elite warriors and champions. Another fifteen hundred Dalesfolk march under Miritar's banner. We do not know much about the Dalesfolk, though."

"The palebloods are weak, and the humans are mercenary rabble," muttered Xhalph. "We could break the Sembians in short order, I'd wager."

Final Gate • 201

"I am not so sure, Lord Xhalph," the warmaster said carefully. "While it is true that you shattered a number of the Sembian mercenaries when you struck them near the Standing Stone, I think that many of these fellows are sellswords of a better quality. They are certainly better led now under Selkirk. The Sembians may prove more tenacious than you think."

"In other words, all the mercenaries who were going to flee have fled already?" Sarya did not attempt to conceal the acid in her voice.

Mardeiym did not respond. The warmaster had learned to tread lightly around the daemonfey queen and her son over the last few days, as had most of the other fey'ri. If he wondered why Sarya fumed with black fury or why Xhalph's habitual bloodlust had grown into a storm of murderous violence that exploded at the least provocation, he was clever enough not to say so. If Sarya believed that Mardeiym or any other fey'ri had the least suspicion that she had been forced to kneel to Malkizid, she would have killed him in an instant. She would have torn him to pieces with her own naked talons.

I will not be your thrall for long, Sarya silently promised the archdevil. If Malkizid thought the Dlardrageths would take him for their lord and master, then he was a fool. Sarya intended to dispense with Malkizid's help as soon as she could . . . but she would have to defeat the armies of Evermeet and Sembia first, and for that she needed the archdevil's help for a little bit longer, as much as it galled her to admit it.

When I have crushed my enemies, we will see who is the master and who is the slave, Sarya told herself for the hundredth time. I will carve out Malkizid's heart for his arrogance and his presumption!

But first she had to defeat the enemies at her doorstep.

"We could strike them tonight with our assembled fey'ri and demons," Jasrya Aelorothi mused aloud. "In but a short time we could bring five hundred fey'ri and half again that number of demons, yugoloths, and devils to this place."

"We have taught our enemies to be wary of sudden attacks," Mardeiym answered her. "They have been careful to fortify their encampment at the end of each day's march. I advise against attacking either encampment with anything less than our whole strength."

"Are we to simply allow them to march on Myth Drannor, then?" Jasrya snarled at Mardeiym.

"For two more days, that is exactly what we will do," Sarya said. She turned away from the distant points of firelight and lanternlight to her assembled captains. They fell silent, sensing that she had arrived at her decision. "We will harass them, of course. Our demons will harry their march—kill stragglers, waylay scouts, and teach them to fear being out of sight of their banner. But we will not try their camp again, not yet, anyway."

"Where do you intend to give battle, then, Mother?" Xhalph asked.

Sarya leaped across the menhir circle with one easy snap of her wings, and pointed out over the forests to the north. "There," she breathed. "The Vale of Lost Voices. We will meet Miritar and his human allies in the Vale of Lost Voices."

Final Gate • 203

CHAPTER TWELVE

16 Eleasias, the Year of Lightning Storms

The Crusade marched through the lush forest, a river of diamond and sunlight in the warm green shadows. Seiveril rode at their head, caparisoned for battle. He did not expect to meet the daemonfey yet—after all, Myth Drannor was still sixty miles ahead of him—but a sudden demonic ambush was more than likely, now that he had led his warriors out of the ancient wards of Semberholme.

Seiveril guided his mount to one side of the hidden elven road along which his warriors marched, and paused to watch his warriors pass. His guards formed a wary ring around him, watching for any sign of daemonfey attack.

"The Sembians are keeping up?" he asked Edraele Muirreste.

"We could march to Myth Drannor and back twice in the time it would take them to get there," the young captain said. She failed to suppress a restless flick of her head. Edraele was simply not made for standing still. "I suppose they're still moving north, if that's what you mean. Rauthauvyr's Road is about two miles east of us here, but we're still in touch with the overmaster's banner."

"Good," Seiveril said. Should Sarya Dlardrageth attack the Sembians, Seiveril could join them quickly . . . and if the daemonfey struck at him, he intended to fall back toward the Sembians and bring both allied armies into the battle in that fashion.

For three days they'd marched north through the forest, paralleling the Sembian march along the road. A contingent of elven captains and spellcasters marched with Selkirk, while a whole company of Sembian officers and Silver Ravens remained close by Seiveril's banner. The hope was that the exchange of trusted captains would make it easier for the leaders of the armies to coordinate their efforts when battle came. Seiveril did not know if the arrangement would work out, but any measure that reinforced cooperation over rivalry would go that much farther toward keeping their swords pointed at the daemonfey instead of each other, and that was no small thing. On the other hand, he had spent almost no time in Ilsevele's company since the two armies started on their way north, simply because she was the elf the Sembian leaders knew the best.

He turned his attention to the warriors passing him by. Several strong companies of wood elf scouts were already well in front of the vanguard, and a mile or more ahead of him. First came the Vale Guards of Evereska, grim and purposeful, shining silver in their mail hauberks. The Evereskans noticed Seiveril watching, and hailed him. "Miritar! Miritar!" they called, raising their arms in salute.

Final Gate • 205

"Quietly, now!" he answered them. "Let's keep the daemonfey guessing about our whereabouts instead of shouting out where we are."

The Evereskans passed into the tree-shadow, vanishing in the gloom. Behind them rode a large contingent of Seiveril's own Silver Guards, who saluted both him and their captain Edraele. Seiveril watched them pass, and Starbrow joined him, riding up from the rear of the column. The moon elf looked over the march and nodded in approval.

"We'll be on the other side of the Vale of Lost Voices by sunset," he said.

"I suppose Sarya has decided to wait for us in Myth Drannor," Edraele observed. "Still, I'd like to be sure of that. With your permission, I think I'll catch up to my company and see to our scouts." Seiveril nodded to her, and the small moon elf tapped her heels to her horse's flanks and cantered after the Silver Guard.

"We should make sure to provide the Sembians with plenty of guides for their crossing of the Vale," Seiveril thought aloud. "I doubt that their rear guard or siege train will make it all the way across before sunset, and I would not want the guardians of the place to mistake our human allies for enemies."

"Easier said than done. More than a few of those who rest in the Vale died fighting the Sembians' forebears. Human armies in Cormanthor rouse old and watchful spirits." Starbrow fell silent, and watched the Crusade's companies and banners glide swiftly by without further comment.

"Something troubles you, old friend," Seiveril finally said. "What is it?"

The moon elf looked down at the reins in his hands. "Seiveril, there is something I need to tell you."

Something in his friend's voice warned Seiveril that he would not like what followed. He turned his mount in a half-circle so that he faced the tall moon elf, and looked into his face. Starbrow avoided his eyes, instead looking out over the Crusade marching past.

"What is it, my friend?" Seiveril asked.

"Not here." Starbrow glanced around at the elf guards who watched nearby, and led Seiveril a short distance away. When they were out of easy earshot of the other elves, he looked around one more time, and took a deep breath. "I don't even know how to say what I have to say," he muttered, more to himself than to the elflord.

"For what it's worth, I've often found that it's easiest to just come right out and say the thing you're most afraid to say."

"I know it." Starbrow wrestled with himself a little longer, and he brought his eyes up to Seiveril's. "I have fallen in love with Ilsevele. And I think she is in love with me, as well."

Seiveril simply stared at Starbrow. He had heard every word clearly enough, but taken together they didn't make sense. "I do not understand," he managed.

"I don't either. I did not mean to, Seiveril. It just . . . happened."

"She is betrothed to Araevin, Starbrow. They are to be married."

"I know."

"Well, then, you must be mistaken," Seiveril said. The more he thought about it, the more confusing he found the whole conversation. "I know you have shared many dangers with her in the last few tendays. Perhaps you have misconstrued something she said or did. It happens all the time."

Starbrow sighed and looked away. "I know my own heart, Seiveril. I don't think I'm mistaken about what I feel there."

"Have you said anything to Ilsevele about . . . this?"

"I don't think I've made myself clear, Seiveril. Ilsevele and I both feel this way. She has given me her heart, and I have given her mine." Starbrow looked away to the east, and Seiveril followed his gaze. She was there, somewhere, riding alongside Selkirk by the Sembian banner. "When I look into her eyes, my spirit sings. And I see something in her eyes that tells me she feels the same way, and I feel like I want to leap into the sky and fly. How could I be mistaken about something like that?"

"But Ilsevele is so young," Seiveril protested. "I am her father, and you are centuries older than me. I know that doesn't mean much for our people, but still . . ."

"I've lived about one hundred and thirty years, Seiveril. I may have walked in Arvandor for centuries, but now the Elvenhome is only a dream to me. I can't remember it anymore."

Seiveril shook his head. What did I expect when I called him back to life after so long? he asked himself. He was not just a hero in a story, after all. He was a living man, and life has its own tumbling and crooked course to it. No one knows where it might lead from one moment to the next. He realized that Starbrow was waiting for him to speak, and he sighed.

"Starbrow, I do not know what to say. I did not foresee this."

Starbrow found the confidence to look Seiveril in the eye again. "I want your blessing, Seiveril." He waved his hand at the warriors marching past. "This war will end someday, and I might live through it. If I do, I think that my path will lead me to Ilsevele's side . . . and hers to mine. I need to know that you approve."

"Approve?" Seiveril said hoarsely. "Starbrow, you have known each other only for a single short season. Ilsevele has already promised herself to Araevin. He is a fine man, and they have waited many years for the day of their marriage to come. And you were married too, were you not? It seems hard to approve of something that seems, well, impetuous at the least."

"I can't tell you what has passed between Ilsevele and Araevin. I suppose you will have to ask her if you want to know." Starbrow shrugged awkwardly. "As far as my own marriage, Sorenna survived me by a century or more. She took another husband after the Weeping War, Seiveril. Death parted us, you might say. And I think that when she finally came to Arvandor, we did not walk together any longer."

Seiveril thought of Ilyyela, his own wife. He had reached out to speak to her spirit in Arvandor, hoping to bring her back to life, but she had refused to come back. He knew with the certainty of the stars in their firmament that she waited for him in the Elvenhome, and that they would be together there when his own work in Faerûn was done. He looked at Starbrow, his friend and comrade-in-arms, and he saw in the moon elf's eyes the shadow of an old pain indeed. *How happy would I be in Arvandor if Ilyyela loved another?* Seiveril asked himself.

"In Myth Glaurach, you told me that I hadn't been called back to fight one battle," Starbrow said. "You told me that I had been called back to *live,* for as long as chance dictates. When I look in Ilsevele's eyes, I know why I came back. I came back to meet her, even if I didn't know it the night you summoned me from Arvandor."

"Enough." Seiveril raised his hand, forestalling Starbrow's words. "It is still too unexpected, Starbrow. And this does not seem to be the time—"

"Lord Miritar! Lord Miritar!"

Seiveril looked around behind him. Edraele Muirreste galloped back down the forest road, standing in her stirrups. She waved to him as soon as she caught sight of his banner.

"Selkirk of Sembia asks for you. The daemonfey await us in the Vale!"

Starbrow glanced at him, and back to the captain of the Silver Guard. "How strong are they, Edraele?" Starbrow called.

"Two thousand or more. The fey'ri legion is there, along with many demons and devils!"

"I suppose we'll have to speak about Ilsevele later." Seiveril grimaced, realizing that he was actually grateful

Final Gate • 209

for the opportunity to turn his attention to less confusing matters. "I did not expect Sarya to make a stand outside Myth Drannor's walls."

Starbrow shrugged. "I had a feeling we weren't going to get to Myth Drannor without a fight."

❖ ❖ ❖ ❖ ❖

As it turned out, Araevin's teleport spell was very nearly a fatal mistake.

Instead of conjuring himself and his friends safely to the cavelike sanctuary near the top of the Long Stair, he botched it badly. The small company was scattered for a mile or more in the lightless dark. Araevin himself appeared alone a good six or seven feet in the air above the narrow roadway, and gave his knee a painful wrench on landing. Jorin and Donnor arrived in the sanctuary, but Nesterin was half a mile distant in the opposite direction and wound up clinging to the ledge with white-knuckled hands, having been dropped right at the edge of the awful precipice. And Maresa herself did actually appear out in the middle of the dreadful space, but fortunately arrested her fall with her elemental gifts. They all finally found their way to the small, cold cave above the abyss, warded by the best spell shields Araevin could manage with the last of his strength.

When they finally roused themselves, Jorin prepared the best breakfast he could from the haphazard collection of belongings they had managed to bring out of Lorosfyr with them, while Donnor illuminated their small refuge with Lathander's golden light. Then the cleric addressed their various injuries, salving bruises and sealing cuts with his healing spells. He even managed to ameliorate the abominable ache in Araevin's knee.

"Don't ask me how we managed it, but we are all alive and reasonably hale and whole," the cleric muttered when he finished. "By the Morninglord, I thought that I had seen my last dawn. When Selydra hurled that black orb at me . . ."

"Try finding yourself alone, falling in total blackness." Maresa hugged her arms close to her chest and shivered. "Is that what Ilsevele meant when she said that teleport spells sometimes don't work as well as they ought to, Araevin?"

"More or less," Araevin admitted. "Strange magic permeates the deep places of the world. It can scatter a teleport spell, as I demonstrated for you. That is why I was hesitant to try it, unless I thought we had absolutely no other choice."

"I think I'll be happy to walk the next time you offer to whisk us off somewhere in the blink of an eye," the genasi said. "Speaking of which, I think I'm about ready to walk on out of here. I've had all of the Underdark that I care for."

"Back to the portal, then?" Jorin asked Araevin.

"I think so, but I am not sure. The Waymeet is not safe any more." Araevin thought of the infernal monsters that haunted the place, and the fiery iron brands driven into the living crystal. He did not know if the devils guarding the Waymeet had determined which door they had used to leave, but the last thing he wanted to do was walk right into an ambush. "I want to make sure that I know where we're going before we chance it again."

"Can you sense the direction to the third shard now?" Nesterin asked.

"Let me try."

The sun elf rummaged through his pack for a moment and drew out the first shard of the Gatekeeper's Crystal. Then he opened the iron coffer from Selydra's vault. The Pale Sybil's shard rested inside on a bed of black velvet. He lifted it out carefully, and held it beside the first shard. The dagger-shaped fragments glowed with a soft lavender radiance even in the brightness of Donnor's light spell. Araevin noticed that the glow grew stronger the closer the shards were to each other. Taking a deep breath, he fitted the two together. He felt a sharp jolt of power flow through his hands, magic old and strong indeed, and the two pieces were bonded together as if they had never been parted. He couldn't find the slightest seam to mark the place where they joined each other.

"Amazing," he murmured.

Cradling the joined crystal on his lap and closing his eyes, he chanted the words of a simple seeking spell and opened his mind, casting about for any hint of direction. The crystal in his hands began to shine brighter, and seemed to stir or whisper, filling the chamber with a strange high note like the ringing of a glass he might have tapped with the edge of a knife. Araevin felt his friends watching him, silent and intense.

At first he felt nothing in answer to his call. But then, faint and far off, he sensed an answering note. He reached out to catch it with his mind's eye, but no matter how he imagined the third shard, he couldn't derive any idea of where it was in relation to the cave on Lorosfyr's edge. He could tell that it was distant, but not in what direction it might lie.

"Well? Where is it?" Maresa asked.

"Not nearby," Araevin answered. He frowned and tried to listen closer, hoping to learn something from the quality of the ringing note, but it was beginning to fade. "I do not think it lies on this plane of existence."

The others exchanged sharp glances. "Where is it, then?" Donnor asked.

Araevin raised his hand for silence, still straining for the last whispers of his seeking spell. He had half-expected something like that, and he was not unprepared. As the faint ringing of the crystal faded, he freed one hand from the Gatekeeper's Crystal and reached into the pocket of his cloak, where he kept his spell components. Casting a pinch of powdered glass above his head and muttering the words of a powerful spell, he invoked a vision.

"Where is the third shard?" he demanded. *"Where?"*

The chamber darkened and whirled away as the vision snatched him away from his body. He felt an instant of dizzying movement, a great leap of awareness that sent his perception racing outward through silver nothingness at the speed of thought itself, and he found himself standing on a barren, dusty plain. The sky was dark with black, racing clouds that flickered with an angry orange glow, as if great fires seethed within. Thunder crackled and echoed around him, and the air was desperately hot and dry. Around his feet, shriveled black thorns clawed their way from the dust, waiting for rain that never came. Jagged peaks as sharp as swords fenced the distance.

"Where am I?" he asked the harsh desert.

Nothing answered him, but he sensed something behind him. Turning slowly, Araevin beheld a mighty citadel of black glass. It soared skyward from the depths of a forest of dead, twisted trees. In one small tower a white light flickered, enticing him. The shard! he realized. But then the awful plain and the terrible castle reeled drunkenly, and vanished in an instant.

He gasped and jerked awake, his skin hot and dry even in the numbingly chill air of the abyss. For a moment he flailed in surprise, but strong hands caught his arms and steadied him.

"Easy, Araevin! You are back," Jorin said. The Yuir ranger knelt on his right, and Donnor Kerth at his left.

"You have seen the shard?" the cleric asked.

Araevin drew in a deep breath. "Yes. It lies in an infernal plane. Some hell or another beyond the circles of our world."

"Of course," Maresa muttered. "Maybe Bane himself is keeping it in his vest pocket. Why not?"

Donnor grimaced. "Are you sure?"

"There was a dry plain of sharp stones . . . clouds of fire in the sky . . . a dark and strong fortress. It was an awful place." Araevin passed a hand over his eyes. "I know what I saw, Donnor."

The company fell silent. Maresa shook her head and stood, keeping her thoughts to herself for once. Donnor's armor creaked as he eased back against the wall, his stubbled jaw clenched in thought. Nesterin and Jorin watched Araevin and waited.

"So . . . what do you intend now?" Nesterin finally asked. "Will you try for the third shard?"

"I have to. I have no choice."

"Myth Drannor is that dangerous in Sarya Dlardrageth's hands?" Donnor asked.

"It's not Myth Drannor—though that is certainly perilous in its own right. The true danger is the Waymeet, the Last Mythal. Ilsevele's father could set a cordon around Myth Drannor and imprison the daemonfey within its bounds forever if he had to, but I can't allow Malkizid to master the Waymeet. The consequences would be awful."

"So we need to venture into the Hells to get this last shard." The Tethyrian looked up at Araevin and nodded. "Very well. It can't be that much worse than Lorosfyr."

Araevin dropped his hands to his lap, and began to wrap the two joined shards in a cloth for storage in his pack. "I said it before we came to Lorosfyr, and I will say it again: None of you have to come with me. It is not your task."

Maresa shot Araevin a hard look and snorted. "I'm not done with Sarya Dlardrageth. I'm not about to give up now."

"The lower planes are vast and deadly. Can you find your way to the shard?" Nesterin asked.

Araevin looked at his friends. Cold, battered, and exhausted even after their comfortless rest in the cave at the edge of Lorosfyr's deadly dark, they still chose to go on. His heart could break at their quiet courage.

"I can find the shard," he finally said. "But I think we will have to return to the Waymeet to reach it."

❂ ❂ ❂ ❂ ❂

Soft and still, morning found the armies of Evermeet, the free Dales, and Sembia arrayed for battle at the edge of the Vale of Lost Voices. Rather than pressing forward to meet the daemonfey after a long march, the elves and Sembians had decided to rest for the night and join battle on the following day. The time was at hand. Banners hung limp in the cool air, and spears and helms gleamed in the gray mist. Fflar heard little other than the faint rustle of armored men shifting their footing or the occasional cough in the ranks. Heavy, brooding clouds overhead promised rain before long.

"The daemonfey are still here," Ilsevele murmured. She sat on her roan mare Swiftwind, dressed in her full battle armor. She and Fflar waited together beneath the twin banners of Seiveril Miritar and Miklos Selkirk. The two leaders intended to begin the day standing together. "After last night, I expected them to retire."

"I didn't," Fflar murmured back.

The daemonfey had harried both the Crusade and the Sembians throughout the night. Demons stealing through the darkness with blood dripping from their fangs, spells of stabbing fire or corrupting blight hurled from the dark skies above, sudden deadly rushes to hack down those standing guard . . . Fflar had seen horrors such as that before, in the last days of the Weeping War.

It would have been worse without the Tree of Souls. Carefully set in the earth at the center of the elven camp, the tree's aura made at least a few hundred yards of the Vale relatively safe from demonic attack. The only problem was that the sapling had no great influence unless it was rooted in the earth, which meant that it had to be concealed and guarded quite carefully. It was also dangerously vulnerable while the army was on the move. Fflar was frankly glad that Thilesin was charged with caring for the tree. The responsibility was more than he would have cared for.

"Why here?" Ilsevele said. "The daemonfey have the smaller force. Why not stand in Myth Drannor itself if they're going to stand on the defensive?"

Fflar studied the lay of the battleground. "Sarya sees some advantage here that she won't enjoy if she waits for us

Final Gate • 215

to get any closer," he answered. "This open land certainly favors her flying warriors and winged demons. We won't be able to hide under the trees here."

Ilsevele reached out with one hand and found his, squeezing it in her archer's grip. "I fear this will be a terrible day, even if victory is ours."

Fflar could not disagree. He followed Ilsevele's gaze across the gray downs. The fey'ri legion stood in disciplined ranks, a little less than a mile from the elf and human armies. They would have been outnumbered almost ten to one by the allied army . . . but the restless horde of fiendish monsters tripled their strength. Tall, skeletal bone devils brandished their barbed hooks, insectile mezzoloths clacked their mandibles and jabbed their iron tridents in the air, and vulturelike vrocks crouched and slavered beneath their cowls of shabby gray feathers. Sarya's forces were outnumbered still, but each demon, devil, or yugoloth in her army was an engine of supernatural destruction that could slay dozens of mortal warriors with impunity. The question was whether the elves and Sembians had sufficient spellcasters and champions among their ranks to deal with the hellspawned monsters before they shredded the two armies. And Fflar simply did not know the answer to that question.

"Well, what do we do now, Miritar?" Miklos Selkirk said. He and Seiveril sat on their horses nearby, studying the battlefield ahead and making their plans. "Do we stand here and receive their attack, or do we strike first?"

"Sarya's army stands between us and Myth Drannor. I am afraid that places the burden of action on us," Seiveril answered him. "I certainly don't want to have to encamp again and fend off her demons through another night."

"Tempus knows that's true enough," Selkirk agreed. The Sembian prince had dispensed with his waistcoat and rapier, donning a suit of ebon half-plate covered in elegant gold filigree. A long-handled battle-axe hung at the pommel of his big black charger.

The elflord looked over to Fflar. "Starbrow, what do you think?"

Fflar studied the sky, absently wondering if rain would help or hinder the allied armies in the fight to come while he considered his answer. "I think that Sarya picked this place because she wants to beat us in a battle of maneuver, not overwhelm us with a headlong assault. She will wait for us to make our move, so we might as well get to it."

"As we planned, then." Selkirk drew a deep breath, and leaned over to grip Seiveril's arm. "May Tempus, Lord of War, favor us."

"*Aillesel Seldarie*," Seiveril said in reply. Then he turned in the saddle of his own mount, and called out, "Signal the general advance!"

Horns cried out in the still air, the high ringing tones of elven trumpets mixed with the deeper, flatter notes of the humans' horns. Drummers in the Sembian ranks started up with a stirring count, and the armies moved out together. Instead of maneuvering separately, elf and human warriors marched alongside each other. Between companies of Sembian soldiers or mercenaries trotted files of Dalesfolk longbowmen and elf archers. Across the field, wherever human swordsmen or knights went, elf archers and mages followed. Fflar smiled in grim satisfaction as he watched the two armies combine into a single mixed force. It was disorderly and imprecise, and it took time to execute, but instead of having both armies trying to join each other, the Sembians simply marched ahead in well-spaced ranks while the elves—faster, more disciplined, and quicker to react—did the work of finding their places between the human ranks. The fey'ri would find no enemies unprotected by powerful elf or Dalesfolk bows.

"Be careful," Ilsevele whispered to Fflar. She leaned over from Swiftwind and kissed him lightly. "The daemonfey will be looking for you."

"And you," he said in answer. "You won't stay out of the fighting for long, I fear."

"I know."

Ilsevele turned Swiftwind away from the banner and urged the horse into an easy canter, riding back to where the Silver Guard of Elion and hundreds of Sembian cavalry waited, a few hundred yards behind the two standards. She had been placed in charge of the allied armies' reserve—not because it was any safer there than elsewhere on the battlefield, but because it was an assignment of crucial importance. Seiveril trusted no one else beside Fflar to choose the moment to fling the allies' last strength into the fray, and he needed Fflar to lead from the front in this fight.

Sehanine, watch over her today, Fflar prayed silently.

"Forward the banner!" Seiveril shouted, and Fflar spurred his mount into an easy walk. Instead of hiding their standard, the elflord and his guard marched in plain sight near the center of the army, surrounded by the Knights of the Golden Star, the Moon Knights, Selkirk's own Silver Ravens, and the Evereskan Vale Guards, who were the best troops to be found in either army. Fflar glanced over his shoulder one more time. Ilsevele took up her spot at the head of her warriors, who stood watching in a double line of horsemen.

"Beware the fey'ri!" someone cried near Fflar.

He looked back around, just in time to see the whole daemonfey legion taking to the air, along with scores of the demons, devils, and other such things that could fly. The wing beats echoed like thunderclaps across the downs. They climbed higher, making ready for the strike to come. Below the winged warriors and monsters, the rest of Sarya's motley array howled, shrieked challenges, and gnashed fangs, eager for the taste of mortal flesh. More than a few of the Sembian mercenaries slowed their pace, shrinking from the prospect of getting anywhere near the foul monsters. But still the combined armies moved on.

"Spellcasters, ready your defenses," Seiveril called.

The leading companies drew within two bowshots of the daemonfey horde, and heavy brazen horns sounded deep in the enemy ranks. All at once, the leash was slipped, and the cacophonous tide of hellborn monstrosities surged forward to meet the advance. Bulldoglike canoloths as big as draft horses bounded across the field, barbed tongues lolling from their terrible jaws. Mezzoloths clacked and hissed, leaping over the wet grass with astonishing speed for creatures as big as ogres. Fflar reached up to close his visor over his eyes, and drew Keryvian in one smooth motion. The sword burned with bright blue fire, sensing demonblood nearby.

"Archers! Mages! Take them!" Selkirk called.

Streaking balls of fire sailed out of the Sembian ranks, along with flight after flight of white arrows. The demons and the rest responded with infernal spells of their own, scouring the ranks of the human and elf warriors with ripping blasts of scarlet lightning and worse. Then the fey'ri overhead dropped down low and added their own deadly sorcery to the barrage of hellwrought spells and blights searing the field. The battlefield erupted into waves of roaring fire, booming thunderclaps, glowing shields and barriers, as on both sides hundreds of clerics, wizards, and demons hurled magic at their foes or sought to parry enemy strikes.

"Tymora preserve us," Miklos Selkirk muttered, so softly that no one more than ten feet away could have heard him.

Humans and elves died by the hundreds in that awful moment, charred to smoking corpses, blasted into bloody pieces, or smothered beneath life-snuffing necromancy. But fey'ri burned and fell out of the sky, while demons screamed in rage at spells that destroyed them or hurled them back to their own foul plane.

"Demons! Demons among us!"

An uneven wave of sulfurous bursts all around the standards announced the appearance of demons and devils by the hundreds, teleporting themselves to attack the twin standards. Elves and humans cried out in alarm or screamed in mortal pain, while the fiendish creatures roared, hissed, or bellowed in obscene laughter. Fflar swore savagely and closed up with Seiveril, guarding the elflord's back. In the skies above them the fey'ri legion climbed back above bowshot and soared over the allied army.

"It's the Lonely Moor again!" Seiveril shouted to Fflar. "They are trying to surround us!"

"That didn't work before," Fflar replied. "The daemonfey are up to something else!" Then he found himself hurled out of his saddle by a deafening thunderclap.

His horse screamed once in mortal agony, and the ground hit him like a giant's hammer. For a moment he stared into the sky, his head swimming. The demons came after the standard despite our guards, he realized. Then he rolled to his hands and knees and pushed himself upright.

Seiveril was nowhere in sight, but all around him the elf knights of the Golden Star fought furiously against dozens of demons—fire-wreathed things that looked like black skeletons, hulking toadlike hezrous that filled the air with their noxious reek, even buzzing chasme demons that flitted over the ground like monstrous flies. Sun elf knights battled the monsters, swords aglow with holy fire, while blazing arrows streaked from spellarchers' bows and elf battle-mages hurled destruction in a dozen forms. Human warriors fought beside them, spending blood and strength with an extravagance that awed Fflar. Even though few wielded weapons that could harm a devil or a demon, still they stood shoulder-to-shoulder with their elf comrades.

"Dieee, elfff!"

A darting chasme swooped toward Fflar, knifelike claws extended to impale him. Its buzzing, chittering voice stabbed like daggers in his ears, but Fflar leaped to meet the creature and sheared off its arms and half its head with one great upstroke of Keryvian. The sword rang shrilly with its first kill of the day.

"You'll have more than enough today, old friend," Fflar said to his sword.

To his right a hezrou clawed an elf knight out of the saddle and stooped, catching the unfortunate warrior's head between its huge, wet talons. It leered at its victim, needle-like fangs dripping in anticipation—and Fflar sliced into it from its side, hewing great black cuts in its quivering flesh. The hezrou let loose a gurgling wail and collapsed. Fflar reached down and dragged the wounded warrior to his feet.

"Watch yourself, friend!" he called.

The sun elf clamped one hand over his side and nodded, shaking, behind his visor. He stooped to pick up his sword, and turned back to the fray. Fflar turned, seeking the next threat.

Metal scraped and creaked nearby.

"Now what?" the moon elf warrior murmured.

He looked toward the sound, and for a moment didn't see anything at all—it was coming from behind the line of demons and fiends fighting savagely at the army's front. But a flash of lightning and sharp thunderclap slashed through the ranks, clearing his field of view.

Tall, ponderous iron shapes lumbered up out of the demonic ranks. They were shaped like elves dressed in ancient armor, their fists encased in huge spiked gauntlets. Each was fully ten feet tall. Bright blue flashes sparked from the joinings of their armor and glowed behind their expressionless visors. For a moment he thought they were lumbering up to attack Sarya's demons from behind, destroying them against the swords of Evereska's Vale Guards. But the fiends simply ignored the old elven constructs. With mindless determination, the battle golems raised their fists and struck down elves and humans alike.

What new deviltry is this? Fflar wondered.

The war-constructs were old elven work, he could see that easily enough. But they fought for the daemonfey—scores of them. Arrows splintered on their rusted breastplates, swords broke, spears shivered, and even spells seemed to be of no avail against the relentless new enemy.

Fflar looked down at Keryvian in his hands. "Come on, old friend," he said. "I think we have a long day ahead of us."

With a bold battle cry, Fflar charged at the first of the daemonfey battle golems.

CHAPTER THIRTEEN

17 Eleasias, the Year of Lightning Storms

Araevin and his companions made the trek from the refuge-cave at the top of the terrible stairs to the portal leading back to the Waymeet in one long hike. They encountered no other travelers along the way, reinforcing his original impression that this was a very remote part of the Underdark indeed. They did not even rest for food or drink until they made the turn into the wall of bedrock and left the vast, silent dark of Lorosfyr a good half-mile behind them.

"Good riddance to that place," Maresa said. No one argued with her.

Some time later—it was impossible to tell in the changeless dark of the underworld—they reached the blank-faced portal, set deep in its squared alcove of stone. The place looked much as they had left it. He peered down the tunnel snaking away into the darkness, and looked back the way they had come.

"We've marched for quite some time, and I feel like we should rest before entering the Waymeet again," he said to the others. "But this is a bad place to make camp. Anyone or anything using this tunnel couldn't help but walk right into us."

"Then let's not take the chance," Jorin said. "I'd rather deal with what might be waiting for us on the other side of the portal than pass another day in this sunless place."

"I'm with Jorin." Donnor squared his shoulders, shifting the weight of his armor. "I think we should press on."

"Very well," Araevin agreed. He considered the blank portal for a moment, thinking. How long had they been in the Underdark? Six or seven days? Or even more? And what had the servants of Malkizid accomplished in that time? "I think we should take some precautions, though. I will conceal us with a spell of invisibility. Some demons and devils can see through spells of that sort, but perhaps it will help us to avoid unnecessary trouble."

"I will speak a prayer for Lathander's protection, too," Donnor said.

Araevin moved his hands in the arcane passes of the spell and murmured the familiar words, while Donnor chanted his own prayers. In the space of a few moments his companions grew translucent and faint. The cleric's protective spell left no visible sign, but Araevin felt a reassuring warmth on his shoulders, almost as if he stood in the bright sunshine of the World Above. Satisfied that they were as ready as they were likely to get, he turned back to the portal and woke it with another spell.

"Follow me," he said to his companions, and he strode into the gray mists.

As usual, there was an instant of darkness and a flutter in his stomach as if he were suddenly falling, and he emerged in the Waymeet. He stopped dead a step inside the doorway, appalled.

Half the Waymeet had been consumed by the hot black iron of infernal magic.

Like some torturer's machine, the rune-scribed iron bands affixed to the pillars and columns of the crystalline cathedral had chewed their way deeper into the fragile glass. It almost seemed that a second, parasitic Waymeet was being built over the first, riveted to its skeleton. The pearly luminescence of the whole structure had died away to a lifeless dull gray, and the air was hot and acrid.

"By the Seldarine," he murmured.

The portal whispered at his back, and Donnor staggered into him. Araevin flailed for balance, and his outstretched hand brushed against one of the metal bands. Searing heat scorched his flesh, and he yanked back his hand with a stifled cry. In the space of a moment, Jorin, Nesterin, and Maresa filed out of the doorway after the cleric.

"Bane's brazen throne, but someone has been hard at work here," Jorin said. The Yuir ranger scowled fiercely. "Is this as bad as it looks?"

"Araevin, what happened to his place?" Donnor asked.

"Malkizid's servants have increased their efforts. We have less time than I thought." Araevin did not give his friends much time to get over their shock. "Come on. I want to see if the Gatekeeper can help us, and our spells will not hide us for long."

Stilling their questions, his companions hurried after him while he quickly retraced the path leading back to the plaza of the speaking stone where he had questioned the mythal before. At one intersection they found a pair of barbed devils crouched atop ramparts of iron-scarred glass. The spine-covered monsters kept watch over the path below, but Araevin managed to double back and go around the creatures. He simply wasn't certain that he could rely on the invisibility spell to fool the devils.

With no more close calls, they came to the open space where the speaking stone stood. Iron plates had been riveted to each side of the triangular pillar, encasing the crystal in a cruel coffin. Not a glimpse of the original crystal showed through the plating.

"Damnation," Araevin murmured. "I should have expected that."

"Have the devils finished their work here, then?" Nesterin asked.

Araevin studied the scene, searching for the subtle strands of magic that pervaded the structure. Angry reddish-gold threads of infernal power coiled around the original weavings of the ancient mythal, strangling vines that slowly tightened their grip on the living artifice that hosted them. At first he feared that Malkizid's cruel siege was complete, and that nothing remained of the original spells the hellish sorcery replaced. But then he sensed a dim blue pulse, soft and shallow.

"Not quite yet," he answered the star elf. "It took the high mages of Aryvandaar a hundred years to raise this mythal. It's not entirely corrupted yet."

"Another tenday or two, and they'll have the whole thing riveted shut in those rune-covered bands," Maresa said. "What happens then?"

Araevin did not answer. Instead he moved closer to the speaking stone, examining the iron driven into its face. He hesitated to interfere with the spells burned into the metal for fear of announcing their presence to the power or powers behind the device, but he could see at a glance that the Gatekeeper was barred beneath the metal. After a moment, he decided that it was more dangerous to delay within the Waymeet than it was to risk a disturbance.

"Watch for Malkizid's servants," he warned his friends. "I am going to try to reach the Gatekeeper."

He felt quick glances at his back, but his comrades didn't question his judgment. Blades whispered out of their sheaths as Donnor and Nesterin drew their swords and set themselves at Araevin's shoulders, while Maresa and Jorin found good places to crouch in the shelter of soaring spars of iron-banded glass. Trusting that his friends would warn him if anything threatening appeared, Araevin quickly considered the spells ready in his mind and settled on a powerful spell of unjoining. It was the most potent counterspell he knew, which worked by rending spells into their component parts. He thought it might separate the diabolic curse from the Waymeet, at least in that one corner of the edifice.

He hummed a strange atonal tune and wove his hands in the sinuous passes of the disjunction. *"Estierren nha morden!"* he called out, and plunged his mind into the tangled skein of magic in front of him.

He brushed his hand to one side, as if to clear away the foul clinging webs of the devilish magic, while holding the original magic in place with his other hand and fierce concentration.

Iron shrieked in protest. Araevin was so intent on his work that he did not even notice the heavy plate facing him come loose until Donnor muttered an oath and dragged him back three steps. The sinister runes cut into the plating blazed an incandescent orange for one long moment, and they grew dull and dark.

The iron cladding over the speaking stone peeled away and toppled to the hard paved ground with hideously loud clangs. The revealed crystal was pitted and cracked, leaking tears of blue from the places where iron bolts had been driven into its surface.

"Mask's sweet night, Araevin, could you have made any more noise?" Maresa demanded. But then the genasi fell silent, for the speaking stone guttered into a weak, fitful life again. A tiny candle-flame of pure light danced and flickered in the shattered facets of the stone.

"Gatekeeper, can you hear me?" Araevin asked urgently. "Are you there?"

"I . . . hear you . . . Araevin Teshurr . . ." the speaking stone replied. "Speak quickly . . . I do not have much strength."

"I have the second shard of the master crystal. I divined the location of the third shard, but it lies in one of the infernal planes. Can you direct me to a portal that will take me to its location?"

"Yes . . . but you must hurry. Your spell . . . has not gone unnoticed."

"I thought that might be the case. Which door do we need?"

"Turn toward the center . . . at the next intersection. It will be the third arch . . ." A faint blue gleam briefly flickered across the face of a broken pane on the far side of the open space, illuminating the way. "Good fortune to you, Araevin Teshurr . . . I fear that we will not speak again."

"How long can you endure, Gatekeeper?" Nesterin asked.

"Not much longer . . . Nesterin Deirr . . . a few days, perhaps . . . Go now! Many devils come . . ."

"That's good enough for me," Maresa said. Turning in a quick circle to clear her back, she started across the square. She spared Araevin a quick look and jerked her head at the corridor marked by the failing blue gleam. "Come on, let's not wait around to see exactly what it means by 'many.'"

Araevin nodded, and backed away from the speaking stone. The broken iron cladding at its foot would certainly reveal that someone had been there, and if the Gatekeeper was right, the devils infesting the place would know that a skilled mage had worked magic to communicate with the mythal. *Malkizid will be looking for me*, he realized. *Well, perhaps he will not think to look where we are going.*

"Araevin, come on!" Maresa hissed.

He turned and ran after the genasi, while his companions joined him. Abandoning stealth for speed, they ran down the passageway until they reached the intersection, perhaps fifty yards past the plaza of the speaking stone. He took a quick glance at the lay of the Waymeet around him, and pointed to his right.

"That way," he told his friends.

The third portal was already waking as they skidded to a halt in front of the alcove sheltering it. This time the mists forming in place of the blank doorway had an ugly, roiling red-orange hue to them.

"I don't like the looks of that," Jorin said quietly. "Is this the right doorway, Araevin?"

Araevin quickly examined the portal. He could feel the tug of the third shard, a constant pressure in his consciousness whenever he focused on it. There was no mistaking it. It was the right door.

Behind them, something gave voice to a shrill, furious scream. Araevin glanced around at the cry, searching the crystalline corridors for the pursuers that must be following by now.

"I think they've found my work at the speaking stone," he said to his friends. "This way, quickly! And may the Seldarine protect us."

He stepped into the angry portal and vanished.

☙ ☙ ☙ ☙ ☙

The smoke of countless fires choked the Vale of Lost Voices.

Fflar couldn't remember how any of the blazes began, really. Most likely it was a simple consequence of fire spells and lightning blasts hurled recklessly across the field after a long, hot summer. But even if the daemonfey and their infernal legions had set the grass of the vale alight through the pure accident of battle, the wildfires had become one more enemy for the Crusade to contend with. Walls of blinding smoke partitioned the battlefield into dozens of furious skirmishes, most of which were being decided outside Fflar's sight or knowledge. The horses of the elven cavalry and the Sembian dragoons were growing so panicked and skittish that many riders had been forced to fight afoot. And Fflar had seen too many elves and humans who had perished horribly in hungry red flames, too badly wounded to escape.

He stumbled into a clear space in the fighting, and took

a moment to wipe the hot, stinging sweat from his brow. His arms quivered with fatigue, and he was not as steady on his legs as he would have liked, but so far he had avoided any serious injuries. On the other hand, he had lost sight of the banner again. Fflar took a slow, careful look around his surroundings, trying to peer through the hot embers and billowing gray smoke that danced and streamed wildly in the hot breeze. "We might as well fight in a burning house," he muttered to himself.

"Starbrow! Another war-golem!"

Fflar wheeled at the call. He fought alongside a small band of spellarchers for the moment. In the early afternoon Seiveril had sent him to the aid of the Deepingdalesfolk, hard-pressed on the far left of the fight. Fflar had killed several demons and yugoloths while aiding Theremen Ulath and his warriors, but it seemed to be taking the moon elf champion the whole of the rest of the day to fight his back across the vale.

"Aim for the legs!" he shouted. "Immobilize the thing!"

He didn't know where the daemonfey had found scores of battle-constructs, but the ancient devices certainly hadn't made the fight any easier. They were ponderous and slow, so heavily armored that it would take a siege engine to wreck one. And they crackled with electricity, hurling lightning across the battlefield with abandon. But he'd discovered that they could be brought to the ground much more easily than they could be destroyed, and once on the ground, sword blades and spear shafts jammed into their joints prevented them from rising again.

Of course, we'll have to get around to dealing with all the immobilized ones sooner or later, he told himself. But for the time being, the war-golems were a threat best avoided. While warriors worked to bring down the daemonfey machines, demons and fey'ri were all too likely to launch sudden vicious attacks against the distracted elves and humans.

The archers near him whispered their spells and sent their enchanted arrows winging into the ancient iron war-golem. The thing simply continued ahead, insensitive to whatever damage the arrows caused. Metal groaned and creaked.

"Keep at it," he told the spellarchers, but he kept a wary eye on the fuming smoke nearby.

There! A pair of black, slimy babau demons appeared in the smoke, silently rushing the archers while they concentrated their fire on the war-machine.

"Behind you!" Fflar called to them, and he raced over to intercept the monsters.

One archer spun and fired arrows blazing with holy white fire at the nearest of the demons. The silver shafts stuck quivering in the thing's gaunt ribs, searingly bright. Demonflesh withered and smoked, and the thing shrieked in agony. Plucking at the arrows embedded in its body, it stumbled to the ground. Its companion sprang forward in one quick leap and gored the archer on its single curved horn, burying the point in the elf's belly. It shook its head free of the dying spellarcher, fangs bared in the pleasure of the kill—and Fflar reached it. He ducked under one wild swing of its taloned hand and severed its leg at mid-thigh, and when the demon screeched and toppled over, he smashed Keryvian across its chest. The baneblade's blue fire flashed and burned with cold, blinding light.

"Die, hellspawn!" the moon elf roared.

He wrenched his blade free of the smoking corpse. Behind him, the war-golem lurched to a halt and fell over, its legs pinioned by elf arrows buried in the knees and hips. Two of the elf warriors ran up with broken spear shafts and jammed them into the golem's shoulder joints, immobilizing its arms as well.

"Well done!" Fflar called.

The smoke parted for a moment, and he glimpsed the twin banners of Seiveril Miritar and Miklos Selkirk flying a short distance away. Ranks of elf and human warriors waited there for the next demonic assault, a rampart of defiant steel against the setting sun. That had been the way of the battle all day long; islands of desperate soldiers gathered around the champions, bladesingers, battle-mages, wizards, or clerics who could stand against the hellspawned servants of Sarya Dlardrageth.

Not much daylight left, he decided. Against any other foe, the end of a day of hard fighting might have brought some small respite. The warring armies would break apart, withdraw to their respective camps, and gather their strength for the next day. But Sarya's demons and battle-constructs were tireless, and they would allow the allied armies no rest. *We'll still be fighting when the sun comes up again . . . if we don't break during the night.*

"Rally to the banner!" he told the archers who followed him. "Pass the word along if you see anyone else."

"We're behind you, Starbrow," one of the spellarchers answered. "Lead the way."

With five of the archers at his back, Fflar made his way toward the two standards flying side by side, picking through the smoke and burning brush. Fey'ri and winged demons darted and swooped in the skies overhead, but not too low—they'd learned to be wary of elven bows, at least during daylight. When darkness fell, it would be a different story.

Not far from the small rise where the heart of the Crusade stood gathered, he found Ferryl Nimersyll and many of the Moon Knights of Sehanine Moonbow. Most were torn by demon claws or burned by sinister magic. But others carried fearsome wounds across their faces, flesh deeply scored in the same strange pattern over and over again. Ferryl himself had the same wound as his warriors, but the thin hole punched in his breastplate looked like a sword thrust to Fflar. Crumpled yugoloths and a few broken fey'ri completed the scene.

"By the Seldarine," the first of the spellarchers said, her face white and sick. "The Moon Knights. They're all dead."

"Ferryl," Fflar said. A skilled warrior, but also a compassionate one, wise beyond his years . . . Fflar would miss his wry smile and quick humor. He knelt and composed Ferryl's features as best he could, arranging his arms over his breast. So many of the Moon Knights slain? he thought dully. Thirty knights of Evermeet, overwhelmed in the middle of battle. Fflar sighed, wondering how many more such tales the day held for the Crusade.

"At least they did not fall alone, Starbrow," the archer said. "There must be a dozen dead mezzoloths here."

"Ferryl was slain by no mezzoloth," Fflar said grimly. He looked around, taking in the wreckage of the Moon Knights. They had been among the Crusade's finest, but it was clear they had met an enemy beyond their skill. He had seen such things during the Weeping War, when some mighty fiend or another had taken the field against the army of Myth Drannor. "A lord of the Nine Hells, I think. Sarya Dlardrageth has emptied the lower planes against us."

"How can we defeat foes of such power, Starbrow?" the spellarcher asked him.

"We will find a way, I promise you."

They searched among the last of the Moon Knights in case any of the knights still lived, but to no avail. With his heart as dull and cold as lead, Fflar quietly gathered his small band and led them the last couple of hundred yards to the twin banners. He expected some new enemy to lunge at them out of the smoke at any moment, but to his surprise they reached the battered ranks of the main body without any more fighting.

The Evereskan Vale Guards and Silver Ravens of Sembia still ringed Seiveril's banner, along with the Silver Guard of Elion—Seiveril had summoned the reserves into the battle long ago. Fflar parted from the spellarchers and made his way to the banner.

Seiveril and Ilsevele stood there. Both seemed tired but otherwise unhurt. Fflar gave a sigh of relief that he didn't

Final Gate • 233

even realize that he had been holding, and moved up to clasp Seiveril's arm.

"I'm back," he said simply. "The left is holding, but the Dalesfolk have had a hard time of it. I don't think they can do much more than stand their ground for now."

"Starbrow!" Ilsevele looked up to him, and reached up to kiss him softly, holding him as tightly as she could in their armor. "I was beginning to fear that something had happened to you. You were gone for an age!"

"The fortunes of battle," he told her. "How has it been here?"

"We have been standing around the sapling," Seiveril answered. "The daemonfey and their fiends tried to break us five times this afternoon, but we fought them back each time." The elflord looked exhausted, but a fierce light still glowed in his eyes. "I expect they'll try again soon. On the right, several of the Sembian companies broke early in the day, but Lord Selkirk rallied the rest. They're standing for now, too. But the wood elves tell me that warbands of drow are gathering in the forest nearby. I think they're waiting for darkness to join the daemonfey assault."

"Drow, too?" Fflar grimaced. He should have expected that after the attempt on Ilsevele's life in Tegal's Mark. Clearly, Sarya had reached some accommodation with the drow clans lurking in the Elven Court. Just when it seemed that the battle might be in hand, Sarya came up with another arrow to shoot . . . which reminded him of something else that Seiveril needed to know. "Seiveril, I have some more bad news. Ferryl Nimersyl has fallen, along with many of the Moon Knights. I came across them just a few minutes ago. I think a new foe has taken the field against us—a lord of fiends, perhaps."

"Do you think the one Araevin spoke of is here?" Ilsevele asked.

"So Sarya's mysterious ally has finally shown himself," Seiveril said. He glanced up at his smoke-blackened banner, hanging limply overhead. "Perhaps that explains why we are fighting demons and devils at the same time, when they are the fiercest of enemies. Some prince of the nether planes commands the creatures to serve together."

"Is there some way to turn them against each other?" Ilsevele mused. "If we can slay or banish the leader, will the devils abandon Sarya's cause?"

"That won't be easy." Fflar looked out over the smoldering fires of the vale and set a hand on the hilt of Keryvian. He'd challenged an infernal lord once before, hadn't he? Of course, he did not know if the Army of Darkness had disintegrated after he had pierced Aulmpiter's heart with Demron's last baneblade. Myth Drannor had been destroyed anyway. But this was a different time and a different enemy. Maybe there would be a different outcome.

"Lord Seiveril!" Jorildyn called. The grim battle-mage had his left arm in a bloodstained sling but still carried his tall staff in his right. "The daemonfey are gathering to our front!"

The elflord glanced at Fflar and Ilsevele, then drew a deep breath. "So it begins again," he said softly. "Let us hope that the Seldarine smile on us for a sixth time today."

✦ ✦ ✦ ✦ ✦

A little more than one hundred miles north of the battle in the Vale of Lost Voices, the army of Zhentil Keep was encamped around the walls of Hillsfar. Near the cold waters of the Moonsea, the rain had been steady all day, leaving the roads outside the barred gates rivers of ankle-deep mud. It was not enough to hinder the movements of armies—it was not the spring melting, after all—but it was certainly sufficient to make the common footsoldiers miserable and preclude any attempts to fire the city for at least a short time.

Careless of the cold water streaming through her armor, Scyllua Darkhope stood by the edge of the growing camp and studied the city's formidable walls. It would not be easy to storm Hillsfar. Death did not frighten her, and the casualties of any assault were simply of no concern, but she could not ignore the fact that zeal alone could not guarantee a successful attack. She did not like to admit that even in the silence of her own thoughts, but it was evident that the city's fortifications were a significant obstacle. The Black Lord admired valor and rewarded devotion, but he *demanded* obedience. If she were ordered to take the city, she would have to take the city. Failure was not an option. Given the choice between valor and success, she must choose success. That was the lesson she had learned in the aftermath of her failure in Shadowdale earlier in the summer.

Even though the first lord's tower was in ruins and the Red Plumes soundly beaten, the walls of Hillsfar were reasonably intact and held by better than a thousand of the city's warriors—plus two or three times that number of poorly armed and ill-trained militia, who hardly counted. The ramparts towered almost sixty feet in height, and ringed the city's hilltop so that any assault must first struggle up the hillside just to reach the foot of the wall. The gates were protected by strong gatehouses with flanking towers, and the Hillsfarians had been careful to keep their city's immediate surroundings clear of anything that might offer cover. No, Hillsfar was best taken through siegecraft, treachery, or magic.

Or terror, Scyllua decided. Her pale nightmare could carry her over those walls. It might be instructive to the defenders of the city if she led a raid of sky mages and blades against Hillsfar in the dark of the night.

"High Captain?" Marshal Kulwarth trotted up to her elbow, ignoring the mud splashing around his feet. "The Hillsfarians have sent out an embassy. Lord Fzoul intends to receive them at the Golden Manticore. He requests your presence."

"Very well. Take charge of the field fortifications. We have already lost one battle this summer through insufficient entrenchment. It will not happen again."

Kulwarth struck his fist to his chest and strode off, barking orders at the soldiers who toiled in the rain. Scyllua turned her back on the forbidding walls and strode purposefully back toward the main road leading westward along the Moonsea's shores. While no buildings stood within bowshot of the city walls, a few scattered outbuildings, farmhouses, and workshops hugged the roads leading away from the gates. The old inn house known as the Golden Manticore served as the Zhents' command post.

Scyllua hurried up the steps to the inn's common room and strode inside. She found Fzoul Chembryl warming his hands by the hearth, attended by six of his handpicked bodyguards. The Chosen Tyrant of Bane glanced to the door with a small, cold smile.

"Ah, there you are, Scyllua," he said. "How do your preparations proceed?"

She knelt before him and lowered her head. "We have thrown a cordon around the city, Lord Fzoul. I have ordered our soldiers to entrench for a siege."

Fzoul nodded, looking back to the fire. "How long do you think it would take us to reduce the city by siege work?"

"It depends on the magic the Great Lord sees fit to place in my hands, my lord. With the spellcasters and monsters under my command now, we could undermine a wall or destroy a tower and mount an assault in a tenday. If we directed more powerful magic to the task—enslaving a dragon to destroy a gate, perhaps, or summoning earth elementals to pull down a wall—we could storm the city within a day. If our spies' reports are accurate, we can overwhelm the garrison once we breach the walls."

"I agree with your assessment." Fzoul drew back from the fire and pulled on his heavy gauntlets. He wore a breastplate of black mithral emblazoned with the emerald fist of Bane and carried a large mace at his hip. From time to time he liked to take the field in command of his armies. "However, there is a new complication. I have learned that the daemonfey and their infernal legions are even now engaged in a great battle against the armies of Sembia and the Crusade of Evermeet."

Scyllua looked up at his stern features, her attention sharply focused. "Who will win?" she asked.

"My divinations are inconclusive. The issue seems to be in doubt." Fzoul flexed his hands in the gauntlets, working his fingers into the leather and steel. "I think that it would be useful to issue promises of support to whichever side wins. If Sarya defeats this attack, I do not think the Sembians will throw good coin after bad. They will abandon the middle Dales, and Sarya will remain the mistress of Myth Drannor for some time to come. If I show her that I mean her no harm, I think she will keep herself quite busy on her southern frontiers. On the other hand, if the elves triumph, it would be good to demonstrate that I have an interest in what happens in the middle Dales . . . and that I must be given a seat at the victors' table when the fighting is done."

"What of Hillsfar, my lord?"

"Why, wait and watch, my dear Scyllua. The mere fact that they seek to treat with me indicates that they fear defeat. And as our Great Lord teaches us, to fear something is to give it power over you." Fzoul motioned for her to rise, and turned away from the fire. "Bring in the Hillsfarian," he told the sergeant of his guards.

They waited together in silence for a short time before the guards returned, leading a short, stocky man with broad shoulders, a shaven head, and a dark, pointed goatee. He wore a fine red coat with a broad lace collar, and his wide mouth was set in a carefully neutral expression. "Lord Fzoul," he said with a bow. "I am Hardil Gearas, High Warden of Hillsfar. I have come to request your terms."

"Terms?" the tyrant replied. He arched an eyebrow. "I do not see the need to bargain with you, High Warden. I will obtain everything I require in a few days anyway."

The Hillsfarian remained calm, though a small trickle of perspiration beaded on his brow. "Then we might as well make the best resistance we can. You may indeed be able to take our city, but if we have nothing to lose by fighting to the last man, you may find the price of your victory steeper than you like."

"I am not without compassion," Fzoul said, baring his teeth in a predatory grin. "Should you submit absolutely and immediately, I will spare the lives of Hillsfar's citizens."

"We are hesitant to throw ourselves on your mercy, Lord Fzoul. Most of my compatriots would frankly rather die than be dispossessed of everything they own and sold into slavery. In the absence of reasonable terms on your part, we cannot capitulate." Gearas licked his lips, and added, "It is customary to offer something in exchange for being spared the costs involved in a siege or assault."

Fzoul stroked his chin, studying the shorter man intently. "That is true," he admitted. "Very well, then. First, I require the dismissal of the Red Plumes from Hillsfar. You will be allowed to retain a small city guard and constabulary, under the supervision of my officers. Second, Hillsfar must cede all claims to the coastal lands from ten miles west of this spot to Zhentil Keep, including the ruins of Yûlash. Third, your city will pay me tribute once per year . . . two hundred thousand gold crowns should suffice. Fourth, the former First Lord's Tower is to be rebuilt as a temple to the Great Lord Bane. I will appoint its high priest and clergy. Finally, I require the immediate delivery of First Lord Maalthiir. I will appoint a regent to govern in his place."

"I am afraid that we cannot comply with your last condition, Lord Fzoul."

The tyrant of Zhentil Keep scowled furiously, deadly wrath awaking in his eyes. "Are you certain of that?" he asked in a cold voice.

"Maalthiir has decamped. He left the city almost a tenday ago. I do not think that he intends to return."

Fzoul snorted in dark amusement. "I suppose that does not surprise me. So who governs Hillsfar in his stead, High Warden?"

"The Council of Lords is the acting authority in the city, Lord Fzoul. They share power with the remaining Red Plumes."

"I see. So which of those powers do you serve?"

"I am a lord of Hillsfar."

"Weren't you high in Maalthiir's service? Why did you not follow your master into exile, Lord Gearas?"

The high warden grimaced. "The First Lord departed abruptly, Lord Fzoul. He did not give me that opportunity."

"And so your fellow lordlings have rewarded you for your faithful service to Maalthiir by making you their envoy to me." Fzoul's dark eyes danced with malice. "Go back to your council of lords then, and convey to them my terms. You have one day to indicate your acceptance."

The high warden knew when he had been dismissed. He bowed again in silence, and left the Golden Manticore. Fzoul watched him go.

"A pity that I shall not have the opportunity to banter with Maalthiir one more time. But I suppose that he has chosen a fate for himself almost as hopeless as anything I might have concocted. The knowledge of what he has lost will consume him alive, and he will spend the rest of his days waiting for the time when he is found out."

"Should I make ready to attack tomorrow, my lord?" Scyllua asked.

"You will not need to, my dear. I have offered generous terms, and Hillsfar has no choice but to capitulate." Fzoul folded his arms over his chest. "For more than one hundred years Hillsfar has been the fiercest rival of Zhentil Keep. Now we have laid them low, Scyllua. Whatever else comes out of this season of chaos, I am already content with my gains."

CHAPTER FOURTEEN

18 Eleasias, the Year of Lightning Storms

Araevin stepped into a world of stinging dust and baking heat. He started coughing immediately and threw one arm over his eyes as he staggered away from the gate. The portal stood in a broken wall of black stone on the side of a steep hill. He reached out to steady himself, and found that the stones were hot to the touch. Overhead, the skies churned with black clouds, lit from within by searing flames. A harsh wind like the blast of a furnace scoured the landscape, driving streamers of the bitter dust past the shattered ruins around him.

"Where am I?" he muttered between coughs.

The ruins might have been some sort of keep or watchtower long ago, but had become little more than a foundation of heavy stones abraded smooth by dust and wind. He had to wonder who had thought to raise a portal in such a place. Jorin and Maresa staggered through the portal next.

"They're right behind us, Araevin!" Maresa called.

She drew her rapier and took up a position by the side of the portal, while Jorin hurried a few steps away and turned back to face the gate with an arrow on his bowstring. Nesterin appeared next, blade already in hand. He staggered away from the portal, and dragged Donnor through by one arm, catching the knight in mid-swing.

"Nycaloths pursue us!" the star elf shouted.

"Stand aside. I'll deal with the portal," Araevin answered.

He backed away a few more steps and chanted the words of a spell to temporarily seal the portal behind them. Refusing to allow the hostility of their surroundings to distract him, Araevin fixed his attention on the portal and hurried to complete the spell. The gray misty space between the portal's framing stones shimmered, as if something were about to emerge . . . and he finished the portal seal. In an instant the roiling mists of the gate reverted to cold, dead stone, bound under a glowing spiderweb of silver magic.

Maresa breathed a sigh of relief and sheathed her rapier. Then she glanced around the ruins of hot black stone and volcanic dust. "Out of the frying pan and into the fire," the genasi muttered.

"Will we be able to retreat through that portal when the time comes?" Jorin asked Araevin, eying the spiderweb of magic with concern in his gaze.

"Yes, I can dismiss the spell any time I want."

"Will the devils pursuing us be able to find another way to get through?"

"I don't know, Jorin. They might not know where this portal leads, and they can't find out as long as my seal holds. But I have no way of knowing if there are other portals nearby that they might use to follow us. Just in case, we would be wise to move on soon. My spell might have been noticed."

The Yuir ranger nodded. He slipped his bow over his shoulder and checked his paired short swords in their sheaths. "Do you know where we are?"

"I do not know much about the lower planes." Araevin rummaged in his vest for a handkerchief and tied it around his mouth and nose to help keep the grit out. "Donnor is a better guide than I am here."

"What's there to know?" Maresa said. "They're all hells of one kind or another, aren't they? Hostile, poisonous, and filled with supernatural terrors that can kill you in a dozen different ways. I think I understand."

"Trust me, there are important differences," the Lathanderite said. "Each lower plane has its own perils."

"So what is this place, then?" said Jorin.

Donnor studied the landscape beyond the black ruins. Jagged peaks marched along the horizon, and the angry red sky overhead flashed with fire and thunder. "It might be Avernus, first of the Nine Hells. Or perhaps the Blood Rift, an unstable plane that aligns with other infernal realms from time to time. But I think we are in the Barrens of Doom and Despair, an infernal plane that lies near the Nine Hells."

Araevin followed the cleric's gaze. "I think you are right, Donnor. The appearance of the place matches what I have read about the Barrens."

"And who or what resides here?" Maresa asked.

The Lathanderite wiped his brow with one gauntleted hand. The gray dust stuck to his sweat and left a broad smudge across his forehead. "Several dark gods have their domains here, Bane first and foremost," he said. "We would be wise to avoid those places if we can." Maresa rolled her eyes at that but did not interrupt him. "Other than the gods' realms, the Barrens of Doom and Despair are home to the fiends we call yugoloths or daemons. Expect to encounter things such as mezzoloths, canoloths, nycaloths . . . perhaps some devils outcast from the Nine Hells, too."

Final Gate • 243

Something the cleric said caught at Araevin's mind. He frowned, puzzling out the thought. From his very first encounter with the daemonfey in the halls of Tower Reilloch, they had relied on yugoloths of different sorts. At the time he had thought it nothing more than the expedience of summoning the creatures. Yugoloths were notorious as bargainers and mercenaries, easily persuaded to serve in a variety of evil causes. But Sarya had also rallied devils and demons to her banner, creatures that normally loathed each other. She was blood kin to demons, so it must have been Malkizid who brought his devils to her service. If Malkizid was an *exiled* archdevil, as Quastarte had told him, he might very well have established himself as a lord in some other infernal domain . . . accompanied by those devils who followed him into exile.

Just as he had known from the moment he beheld Lorosfyr that the second shard waited in its depths, he could sense the truth: The third shard was in Malkizid's domain.

"Malkizid," he murmured. "He seeks to subjugate the Waymeet. Of course the Gatekeeper's Crystal will be useful to him. At the very least, he would want to make sure that no one assembled the crystal and used it against him. So the Branded King keeps one shard safe in his domain."

"Araevin?" Maresa asked. "What are you muttering about?"

"Malkizid, Sarya's infernal ally. He has the third shard of the Gatekeeper's Crystal. This is his kingdom."

Donnor looked down and scuffed his boot in the dry, gray dust. "I haven't ever read of any such power in the netherworlds. But I recall hearing that there are many nameless devil princes or yugoloth lords who rule kingdoms in these planes. I would not be surprised if Sarya's ally is one of them."

"Does this alter your intentions, Araevin?" Nesterin asked. The star elf had followed Araevin's example and tied a cloth across his lower face to help against the burning dust in the air.

"No, I don't think so. We need to get to the shard and make our escape. But Malkizid certainly knows the importance of the crystal, so we must expect it to be well-guarded."

"Then let's get on with it," Maresa said. "The sooner we find the last shard, the sooner we can get out of this place."

The sun elf consulted the shards in his possession, seeking for the resonating tone of the third. He felt it almost at once, a clear and distinct ringing that seemed to come from somewhere not too far away. Checking his bearings against the sharp hilltop behind them, Araevin pointed across the dusty, cracked plains below.

"Then I think our path lies that way," he said.

☙ ☙ ☙ ☙ ☙

To Seiveril's surprise, the battle slackened early in the night. The fey'ri legion withdrew from the field, the few surviving war-golems pivoted and strode away from the allied ranks, and the depredations of the demons and devils came to a grudging halt. Some of Sarya's infernal minions prowled the night, seeking out the wounded and the stragglers, and from time to time shrieks of horror and mortal agony rang out of the smoke and darkness. But the daemonfey did not test the allied lines again and did not come within the influence of the Tree of Souls.

Seiveril stood at the head of his troops, staring into the darkness. The daemonfey were up to some sinister ploy, he was certain of it. But his soldiers were absolutely exhausted. They'd been fighting since shortly after sunrise. For that matter, he was no better off himself. He'd channeled every spark of divine power he could manage throughout the course of the long, bloody day, and when he exhausted his spells, he'd wielded his mace against the hellish horde until his arm trembled with fatigue.

He felt a presence behind him, and glanced around.

Starbrow and Miklos Selkirk approached.

"Good evening, Miritar," the human lord said. "I am glad to see that you are still with us. Too many aren't."

"I am glad that you have survived, too, Lord Selkirk. I am afraid I did not see much of the fighting over on your front. We were kept busy all day long."

"As were we. So much for the idea of fighting in concert. It's said that one's battle plan is the first casualty of any engagement, and I see now that it's true." Selkirk had started the battle by Seiveril's banner, but the fighting on the right had demanded his presence for most of the day. The Sembian shook his head. "If we didn't have some of your archers to help keep those flying sorcerers at bay, I think we would have been overwhelmed long ago."

"And if we didn't have your valiant swordsmen to keep Sarya's demons from teleporting into the midst of our archers, we would have fared poorly too," Seiveril answered. It was a little bit of an exaggeration—the Sembians had needed the elves' aid more than the elves had needed the Sembians' help—but it was reasonably true. If Sarya had been able to concentrate all her forces against the Crusade alone, with no human allies on the field, she might have succeeded in breaking Evermeet's army.

Selkirk gave a soft snort, understanding perfectly well who had helped whom. But he accepted the remark. "So what do we do now? I didn't expect the daemonfey to draw back at the end of the day."

"I don't understand it, either," Seiveril said. "We are at the end of our strength, and Sarya's demons have ten times our stamina. Why aren't they attacking now, when we are at our weakest?"

Starbrow limped up beside him. A fey'ri dart thrown from high overhead had pierced his foot in the last stand of the evening. With so many others in dire need of the clerics' attention, the moon elf had declined to have it healed, and settled for washing and binding it as best he could.

"The fey'ri are mortal enough," Fflar said. "They tire just like we do. If I had to guess, I'd say they withdrew to recover their strength. It doesn't make sense for Sarya to send the demons and devils at us piecemeal. She'll wait until the fey'ri and their drow allies are ready to resume the fight."

"There are demons prowling all over the vale in the dark," Seiveril observed.

"I can hear them," Starbrow replied. "But if we keep a guard up, I think we won't see another concerted attack until the fey'ri are ready."

"When will that be?" Selkirk asked.

Starbrow shrugged. "Assuming they'll recover their strength faster than we will, maybe three bells?"

Miklos Selkirk frowned. "Three bells won't be enough for my men, not with half on watch. But I suppose it's better than nothing. I'll go give the order." He offered a stiff bow—apparently, even the suave Sembian lord was at the end of his strength—and withdrew.

Seiveril watched him go and returned his attention to the darkened vale before him. "We seem stalemated, Starbrow. We can defend ourselves against the daemonfey attacks when we stand and hold our ground, but when we move, the fey'ri and their demons savage us. Sarya's forces are simply much more maneuverable than ours."

"The way you defeat a foe more mobile than you are is to make him defend something that doesn't move. The Army of Darkness pinned down the Akh Velar by striking for Myth Drannor. They made us fight the stand-up battle that favored numbers and ferocity over skill and mobility."

"Yes, but if we ignore the fey'ri and strike north, I fear that they would lay waste to the lands behind us. We might be able to get along with what we can carry on our backs, but I doubt the Sembians could march for long without their supply train. And dividing our forces would invite Sarya to concentrate against one or the other."

Starbrow rubbed his jaw, thinking. "Is there some other way we could counter the daemonfey advantage?" he wondered aloud.

The elflord considered the question. "What if we could contest their mastery of the sky?"

Starbrow looked at him sharply. "You have something in mind?"

"I think I do. You and I have an errand in the vale, Starbrow."

The moon elf nodded. "Better speak to Vesilde, then. I don't think the daemonfey will attack for a while, but if they do, the Crusade will need a commander."

They hurried back to the banner, Starbrow keeping up well enough despite his injured foot. Seiveril found Vesilde Gaerth and told the knight-commander to take charge of the Crusade's defenses while resting as many warriors as he could. Then he searched out Jorildyn, the battle-mage who led the Crusade's spellcasters—there might be a need for arcane magic where Seiveril intended to go.

As Seiveril was waiting for Vesilde and Jorildyn to set the Crusade's defenses in order, Ilsevele rode up on her gray destrier. She and Edraele Muirreste had managed to reform the Silver Guard of Elion as a reserve again, and the swift cavalry waited a few hundred yards behind the standard.

"Felael sent word that you are leaving the camp without your guards, Father," she said. "Are you sure that's wise?"

Seiveril glanced at Felael Springleap, who made a point of looking elsewhere. Felael had had a hard enough day already with trying to keep Seiveril from getting killed. Seiveril supposed he did not blame the wood elf too much for asking Ilsevele to have a word with him.

"We will not need to ride very far," said Seiveril, "and I hope we will not be gone for long. Besides, I'll have Starbrow and Jorildyn with me."

"So that all the leaders of the Crusade can be killed at the same time if Sarya's demons find you?"

"The fewer with me, the better," Seiveril said. "Besides, I have a feeling that the Seldarine may favor us this evening."

Ilsevele narrowed her eyes. "Where are you going, Father?"

Seiveril started to dismiss her question, but then he checked himself. She did not know it, but she had as much right to be with him as any of the others. "Now that I think on it, I want you to come with us, Ilsevele. This is something that you should see."

Seiveril, Starbrow, and Jorildyn found horses and mounted quietly. Seiveril took a moment to murmur a prayer for swiftness and stealth, weaving the magic of the Seldarine over their small band. Then the four of them rode away from the standard, heading north and west in the darkness.

Since most of the day's fighting had taken place around the elven and Sembian standards, within four hundred yards they had passed out of the battleground proper. Though the smell of smoke still hung heavily in the air, the vale grew silent and almost peaceful as they rode deeper in. They began to pass isolated markers of white stone, each covered in faded Elvish script that seemed to shine with a silver radiance when the moonlight glimmered through the overcast and smoke.

"These are burial markers," Ilsevele whispered.

"Yes. For many centuries, the People of Cormanthyr laid their dead to rest here. Long ago there was a battle lost in this place, and many warriors fell. Since that time it has been hallowed ground."

"It seems strange that the daemonfey would choose this place to fight."

"They probably revel in desecrating it," Seiveril said harshly.

They rode on in silence for a time. Whether his intuition had come from Corellon's mind or they had simply proven lucky, they ran into none of the Dlardrageth minions during their ride.

Finally, Seiveril spied a small structure of pale marble gleaming in the moonlight. It was a windowless rotunda of sorts, half-sunk into the loam of the vale amid a small copse of trees. A single door of dark iron barred its entrance.

"Ah, we are here," Seiveril breathed.

"What is this place?" Jorildyn asked.

"This is the ancient crypt of House Miritar. Many of my forebears—and yours too, Ilsevele—rest here." Seiveril dismounted, and faced the old monument. "I have not been here in more than two hundred years. A long time by any measure, I suppose." He was pleased to see that the tomb had weathered well in the passing centuries. Old enchantments had been laid on the place long ago to protect it.

"Why have we come here, Seiveril?" Jorildyn asked.

"Sarya Dlardrageth has shown a talent for employing ancient secrets against us. I think it is time that we returned the favor. There is help for us here."

The battle-mage nodded slowly in understanding. "I don't understand why you didn't summon the guardians of the vale last night," he murmured. "We could have used the help."

"I dared not do so until I had given them a chance to witness the valor of the Sembians," Seiveril answered. "Many of the warriors sleeping here regarded the humans as enemies during their living days. I was afraid that the guardians might not be able or willing to treat Selkirk and his men as allies. But the Sembians fought and died alongside elf warriors today, Jorildyn. And most of them did so with courage equal to our own. I think that will count for a lot in the judgment of the Vale guardians."

"Seiveril, be careful . . ." Starbrow warned. "The powers here are not to be lightly called upon."

"I know."

Seiveril strode up to face the rotunda's only door, while the others exchanged looks behind him and slowly dismounted. He whispered a small devotion to clear his mind for the labor ahead, and pressed his hands together before his chest. Then he began to chant a powerful spell, calling on Corellon Larethian's power and shaping the divine energy with his words and will. He sensed all around him the slow awakening of the vale. The wind shifted and grew strong, raking across the dry grass and fallen leaves with an icy touch. A pale corona began to flicker and burn around the ancient white stones of the place. He shivered and finished the incantation. Throwing his arms wide, he shouted, "Come forth, I beseech you! Come forth!"

A golden light seemed to illuminate the domed crypt in front of him, sunlight from some distant and unseen dawn. The radiance spilled out over the nearby glade. And a spectral form seemed to stride through the mithral-chased door. It was the shade of a noble sun elf warrior, dressed in the arms of Myth Drannor's Akh Velar. His red hair spilled out from under his helm, and his eyes gleamed with a brilliant light.

Behind Seiveril, Starbrow recoiled two steps in pure astonishment. "Elkhazel!" he whispered. "Is that truly you?"

"Greetings, Father," Seiveril said weakly. He swayed, suddenly exhausted beyond all endurance, but Ilsevele and Jorildyn hurried up to steady him.

"Seiveril, my son," the shade of Elkhazel said. Warmth filled his voice. "Fflar, my old friend. I am pleased to see you walk in Cormanthor again."

Seiveril looked on the visage of his father. "Forgive me for calling you from Arvandor, but the guardians of the vale are needed tonight. I hoped that you could intercede on our behalf."

"I am not angry, Seiveril," the golden spirit said. He drifted before the door of the Miritar crypt, ethereal mists streaming from his translucent form. His face was compassionate, but there was iron in the set of his mouth. "It is for needs such as yours that the ancient rites were first spoken. The daemonfey are an abomination in the sight of the Seldarine. Your appeal has been heard."

"You can aid us, Father?"

"Only within the bounds of the Vale of Lost Voices itself, and only for a short time. Call for me when you judge the moment to be right, and I will come with others who sleep here." Elkhazel Miritar offered a grim smile. "The Dlardrageths have transgressed against the memory of Cormanthyr. We await the chance to chastise the daemonfey."

"I will call for you," Seiveril said.

He studied the spectral visage, so familiar and yet so distant. Elkhazel had passed to Arvandor three centuries after Retreating to Evermeet, and a century after Seiveril's birth. Though he had become a lord of Evermeet, he had never ceased to grieve for the elven realm destroyed in the Weeping War. Seiveril remembered the old pain in his father's eyes, the wounded heart that had never wholly healed, and he felt his own heart aching with love and sorrow. Tears came to his eyes, and he made no attempt to stop them.

The ghostly elflord stretched one hand over his son's shoulder, and stood in silence. Then he looked up, and his gaze fell on Ilsevele. "Your daughter?" Elkhazel asked softly.

Ilsevele's eyes glimmered with tears, but she stood straight and looked her grandfather in the face. "I am Ilsevele, daughter of Seiveril and Ilyyela," she said. "I greet you, Grandfather."

The shade drifted closer and studied her face, his eyes shining with light. Then, slowly, he knelt and bowed his head before her, doffing his spectral helm. In the moonlight he seemed as faint as a forgotten memory, but the night fell silent as the shade paid her homage.

"I am sorry that we did not meet in life, granddaughter," he whispered. "You are the hope of Cormanthyr, Ilsevele. In your day our People will come into a new spring."

Ilsevele looked down on the shade of Elkhazel and frowned in puzzlement. "I don't understand," she said.

Elkhazel smiled. "You will," he said. Then he rose and

turned to Starbrow. "She is your hope as well, my friend. Across the centuries you have found the love you once lost, and it gladdens my heart to see it."

Starbrow stared at the visage of his friend, and struggled to speak. But the golden shade simply raised his hand in farewell and vanished in a single swift heartbeat. The four living elves were left standing in the glade before the Miritar crypt, and the night was still and warm again.

No one spoke for a long time. Jorildyn studied his three companions, his gruff expression lost in a strange and rare wonder. Finally he cleared his throat. "We should return to the Crusade, Seiveril. We don't know how much time we have before the daemonfey attack again."

"Yes, I suppose you're right," Seiveril admitted. He looked at his companions. "I think it would be best if we kept what passed here in this glade to ourselves for now. The shades of the dead are right about many things, but their words often have many meanings. Nothing is written yet."

Climbing into his saddle, he turned his horse's head back to the east and led the others away from the crypt of his fathers.

❦ ❦ ❦ ❦ ❦

It proved surprisingly difficult to measure time or distance in the Barrens of Doom and Despair. The sky was a featureless mass of low, roiling clouds, and the blowing dust frequently obscured distant landmarks. Clearly, this was a place where one could easily become lost. Without the distant call of the third shard to guide him, Araevin doubted that he could have managed to keep his bearings.

They started off by descending the treacherous hillside from the old ruin, slipping and sliding in dust and scree. Then they struck off across the plain itself, trudging across the windswept waste. On several occasions the surging fires overhead burned their way free of the black clouds, scouring the ground below like dancing waterspouts made of flame, but fortunately none of the fire-strikes fell close to them.

After several miles, they started to climb again, following a dry watercourse that snaked up into the razorlike maze of ridges. Near the foot of the defile they paused to drink some water and make a small meal from their rations.

"I am surprised that we have encountered no infernal beings yet," Nesterin said as they ate. "This plane seems virtually uninhabited."

"Don't invite trouble," Maresa growled. "I'm in no hurry to meet more demons or devils."

"It's the nature of the plane, Nesterin," Donnor said. "The domains of the evil powers in the Barrens are separated by vast stretches of wasteland. This place is not bounded like Sildëyuir. It goes on and on for countless thousands of miles. Not all of it can be full of evil creatures all the time."

"I think you spoke too soon," Jorin announced. The ranger stood a little behind the others, looking back the way they had come with a hand above his eyes. "Something is on our trail."

Araevin and the others stood and hurried to Jorin's side. The keen-eyed ranger was not mistaken; out in the open wastes a number of tiny, dark shapes that kicked up wind-blown arrowheads of dust were following them. Studying them for a long moment, Araevin decided that the creatures ran on all fours, but they were too far off to make out any more detail than that—though they were covering ground at a very good speed indeed.

"What are they?" Donnor asked. He gave up trying to see for himself, since his human eyes were the least keen of any in the small company.

"I can't say yet," Jorin answered. "Wolves of some kind? I count at least thirty, about a mile behind us."

"If they keep on like that, they'll be on us soon ," Nesterin added. The star elf looked over to Araevin. "We might be able to avoid them for a time by pressing ahead or scaling the slopes of these hills, but we cannot outrun them."

"What about using magic?" Maresa asked.

Araevin studied the defile for a moment. "I know a spell to raise a wall of ice, but I can't do it here," he decided. "It's not narrow enough. And I have doubts as to how long magical ice would last here, anyway."

"I hesitate to suggest it, but could we teleport away?" Donnor asked.

"Have you forgotten about our little misadventure in Lorosfyr?" the genasi demanded.

The cleric winced. Araevin shook his head. "That was due to the peculiar conditions of the Underdark, Maresa," he said. "But it would not be any safer here. In the first place, I haven't really seen the place we are trying to reach, and second, I don't know anything about how magic of that sort works in this plane. I think we'd be better off to continue up this watercourse and look for a place to make a stand."

They quickly gathered their packs and set off again, scrambling up the boulder-strewn ravine at the best speed they could manage. In level spots they stretched out their legs into a loping run, and in more difficult places they bounded from boulder to boulder, arms wide for balance. By the time they'd gone a quarter-mile, they heard the first sounds of their pursuers—a deep, raspy baying that drifted up on the hot wind whistling up the defile.

Not long now, Araevin decided.

They could press on and delay the inevitable for a few more steps, or they could make the best of it where they were. He paused to study the lay of the land. To his right old rockslides from the jagged cliffs above had created a tangled jumble of boulders that seemed as good as anything.

"Over there!" he called. "Get on top of the boulders."

He led the way as they scrambled up the defile's side and scaled several of the larger stones. On the downhill side they stood a good ten or fifteen feet above the valley floor, but it would not be hard for the creatures chasing them to get up on the gravel slopes above the slide and come down on them. Still, it was the best they could do. Donnor Kerth drew his broadsword and set himself at the uphill side of the boulder-top, ready to defend the easiest path from the valley floor, while Nesterin and Jorin readied their bows and Maresa unslung her crossbow. Araevin drew a wand from his holster and turned to face the oncoming foes.

A couple of hundred yards down the winding watercourse, the first of their enemies appeared. The creatures were monstrous hounds of some kind, with coal-black hides and eyes that glowed with an evil red light. Smoke and embers fumed from their heavy muzzles.

"Hell hounds," Donnor said grimly. "I think I will seek Lathander's favor for this fight." He started to chant a holy prayer.

The pack caught sight of the company standing atop the boulders and filled the canyon with their voracious cries. Without a moment's hesitation they streaked forward, bounding over the gravel and stone like black thunderbolts.

Jorin's bow sang its shrill note, followed an instant later by Nesterin's and the deeper thrumming of Maresa's crossbow. In the front of the pack, charging hell hounds folded up and rolled headlong in the dust, crippled by the arrows. For ten heartbeats the archers rained a furious shower of destruction against the fiendish creatures, killing or wounding a dozen of the monsters. Then Araevin judged the distance suitable for his wands, and began to alternate blasts of his disrupting wand with blistering lightning bolts from his wand. Hell hounds snarled with fury and roared in pain, hammered by the powerful concussive blasts or flayed alive by dancing lightning.

"They're still coming!" Maresa called.

The pack swirled around the boulders, snapping fiercely. Searing gouts of fire scorched up at Araevin and his friends. Araevin recoiled, throwing his cloak over his face against the fiery breath of the monsters below—but the withering blasts seemed weaker than he could have expected. Instead of charring skin and setting cloaks aflame, the hell hounds' breath left wisps of smoke rising from his clothes and angry red burns that were painful, but not serious.

"What in the world?" he said aloud.

"Lathander shields us against fire!" Donnor shouted. He was busy hacking down at the hell hounds who leaped and clawed for the boulder-top. As Araevin had feared, the hell hounds scrambled up the slope to get at the company. "I need some help here!"

"Keep shooting!" Araevin barked to the others.

He hurried to Donnor's side just as four of the monsters rushed the cleric at the same time. The Tethyrian lunged and spitted one on the point of his sword, while Araevin raised his lightning wand and blasted two of the others. But the last hell hound rounded on him with the speed of a striking snake and caught his arm between its fiery teeth, wrenching the wand out of his hand. Bones cracked under the terrible strength of the creature's jaws, and with a sudden sharp shake of its head it dragged Araevin off his feet and sent him toppling into a narrow crevice between two boulders.

Araevin suddenly found himself flat on his back, rock hemming in on two sides, as hell hounds snarled and leaped for him from all around. Burning teeth closed in on his left ankle, but he shoved the pain to one side of his mind and managed to grate out the words of his prismatic blast. Blinding light filled the space between the boulders, and a mingled roar and rush of fire, lightning, and other arcane energies echoed in the canyon. When he could see clearly again, the cleft was littered with dead or petrified hell hounds. He staggered to his feet, just as a hell hound he hadn't seen leaped at his back.

A silver arrow from over Araevin's head pinned the creature through the skull. Its lifeless body struck him across the shoulders and knocked him down again, but Araevin shoved the creature off him and found his feet again. He looked left, then right, but the hell hounds around him were dead or dying.

"They're running!" Jorin called. The ranger stood over Araevin's crevasse, bow in his hands. He looked down at the mage, and knelt to lean down and offer a hand. "Are you all right, Araevin? For a moment I thought we'd lost you."

"You nearly did," Araevin said. He took Jorin's hand with his left arm and let the ranger help him scramble back up on top of the boulder. Once he was sure of his footing again, he looked around. About a dozen of the hell hounds were in full flight back down the defile, leaping over the arrow-pierced bodies of their packmates. All around the rockslide more of the creatures sprawled, their bodies smoking as they cooled. "Thank you for that last shot, Jorin. I never saw the one behind me."

"Think nothing of it," Jorin replied. His face was red, and his cloak was blackened and smoking. "If Donnor hadn't warded us against fire, that would have been a lot worse."

Araevin limped over—his ankle hurt fiercely, if not as badly as his right forearm—and clapped the Lathanderite on the shoulder. "Well done, Donnor. Grayth would have been proud of you today, I think."

The human knight returned Araevin's grasp. "I thank you for that, Araevin. Now, let me see what I can do for your arm. I think you'll have need of it soon enough."

CHAPTER FIFTEEN

18 Eleasias, the Year of Lightning Storms

Dawn was still a short time away. Pale gray streaks lightened the eastern sky, but it was quite dark. All around Fflar, the elves and their human allies rustled and murmured to each other, quietly taking their places. To his left, he could make out the haphazard lines of the Dalesfolk, reinforced by a phalanx of elf footsoldiers from Leuthilspar. On the other side, the Sembians made up most of the right wing of the army. His foot ached, and he felt tired enough to lie down and fall into the senseless slumber of humankind, but Keryvian was still light on his hip.

Fflar found himself gazing to the rear of the mustering army, hoping to catch a glimpse of Ilsevele. Against her protests her father had assigned her to command the forces they were leaving behind. Too many soldiers were too badly wounded to keep with the Crusade and its allies, but if they were left behind without a strong guard, they would be easy prey for Sarya's bloodthirsty demons.

She has the Tree of Souls to protect her, he told himself. *She should be safe enough.*

Seiveril rode up and joined Fflar at the head of the Crusade. He followed Fflar's gaze to the warriors they were leaving behind and asked, "You are worried that the daemonfey will ignore us and fall on those we leave behind?"

"I don't like to divide our forces," Fflar answered. But there was no other way to draw the daemonfey into a stand-up fight, was there? He flicked his reins and turned back to face the mist-shrouded vale before the army. The fey'ri and their infernal minions were out there, likely preparing their own assault. "Is Selkirk ready on the right?"

"He just sent word that he is. What of Lord Ulath?"

"The Dalesfolk are ready on the left. And it seems that we're ready here."

Seiveril glanced up at the overcast sky. A few faint stars glimmered through the drifting mist. Then he set his helm on his head, and motioned to Felael Springleap. "Felael, pass the signal: Forward, all!"

Horns rang out, flat and low in the damp night air. From thousands of throats, both elf and human, a roar of defiance shook the Vale of Lost Voices, and the ground trembled with their footsteps. Fflar tapped his heels to his chestnut's flanks, and the horse snorted and broke into a prancing walk, eager to run. The smoke and mist drifted slowly across the battlefield, stirred by the faintest of breezes, and a fine cool drizzle fell, dampening the banners and warriors' cloaks.

They covered close to half a mile with no sign of the daemonfey army, and Fflar found himself wondering whether Sarya had thought better of meeting them in the vale. But then Jerreda Starcloak and a pair of her wood elf scouts emerged from the gloom before the marching Crusade, and trotted up to Seiveril. "The daemonfey are waiting about five hundred yards on your right front, Seiveril!" she called. "They're drawn up opposite your center. Demons and devils, just like yesterday. The fey'ri are there, but they haven't taken to the air yet!"

"My thanks, Jerreda!" Seiveril replied. The elflord looked over to his guard captain. "Felael, signal Lord Selkirk to hold in place. We'll wheel to the right and hit them straight on with our center."

"Yes, Lord Miritar!" the young captain answered.

He turned and called out more commands, and horns blared again in the morning. Seiveril turned his horse a few points to the right, and the Crusade followed, wheeling easily in the new direction. Fflar heard more signals off to the left, where the Dalesfolk and the elves marching with them had to jog to keep the line dressed. Some would manage it, and some would not; that was a simple fact of trying to maneuver large bodies of warriors on a battlefield.

"There they are!" a sun elf near Fflar shouted.

Fflar stood in his stirrups to see better. In the gray gloom ahead, a dark line of fearsome shadows waited. The hate and supernatural menace from the daemonfey army was as tangible as a thunderclap. The demonic tide roiled and surged ahead, eager for blood, while the fey'ri warriors took to the sky. In the darkness before dawn they seemed like great black crows, inky silhouettes against the lightless sky. He could hear their wing beats even over the footfalls and rustling and creaking of the Crusade on the march.

Seiveril brandished his mace above his head. "This is our time!" he shouted to all within earshot. "The dawn is coming, my friends! Today we break the army of the daemonfey and send their minions back to the Hells from which they came! Now, forward, all! *Attack!*"

With a great ragged roar, the armies of the Dales, of

Evermeet, and of Sembia threw themselves forward, racing over the cool wet grass. Fflar drew Keryvian and followed close by Seiveril.

"Archers, rake those hellspawn!" the elflord cried. "Clerics, ward the ranks! Mages, cast at will!"

Better than a thousand elves, and hundreds of Dalesfolk and Sembians, paused to loose their arrows at the monsters charging up to meet them. Many of the demons and devils among the Dlardrageth armies could not be harmed by mundane steel—but some could, and more than a few of the elf archers carried enchanted arrows. Monstrous shapes stumbled and fell beneath that terrible storm of arrows, but many more shrieked and hissed in defiance and leaped forward to meet the first ranks of the oncoming warriors. Huge bursts of fire and brilliant strokes of lightning crisscrossed the battlefield, banishing the night in flashes of white and sullen red.

The fey'ri arrowed past overhead, seeking to surround the army as they had before. Many shot arrows or threw darts as they passed over, while others contributed deadly spells of their own. Some of the daemonfey spells winked out or rebounded harmlessly, stopped by hasty spell-shields or countered by the Crusade's own spellcasters, but more hammered the elven ranks. All around Fflar blasts of fire and deadly gouts of acid seared man and beast alike, sowing chaos across the battlefield.

"Seiveril!" Fflar shouted. "It's time!"

The elflord had his eyes on the fey'ri. As they crossed overhead, he bared his teeth in defiance and raised one hand in the air. "Guardians of the Vale, I call on you!" he shouted. "Aid us against the fey'ri!"

For a moment, Fflar feared that somehow the spirits had not heard Seiveril in the chaos of the battle. Spells, arrows, and furious melees on all sides were all that he could see. But then, a golden light caught his eye. He glanced in that direction, and it seemed that a path of molten light had sprung up in the sky—but this dawn was breaking in the west, not the east. Out of the shining door a host of brilliant white warriors streamed forth. Hundreds of elf spirit-warriors appeared silently and ran to meet the wheeling fey'ri overhead, simply mounting into the air to grapple with their foes.

The fey'ri cried out in consternation and shifted their attacks to the Vale spirits. Fireballs and blasts of lightning scoured the celestial ranks. Some of the ghostly figures winked out, extinguished or driven off by fey'ri spells. But more of the spirits leaped up, attacking the daemonfey legions with swords of blazing light. Despite the battle raging around him, Fflar could not help but watch the spectacle in the sky above the furious clashing armies, and he was not the only one.

"Starbrow, look out!" Felael shouted. Fflar whirled around and found a nycaloth rushing up from behind him. The huge winged daemon leaped for him, claws hooked to tear out his throat, but Fflar spurred his horse and ducked under the scaly monster's swing. He spun in the saddle and lashed out in a backhand slash that dug a long, shallow gash across the nycaloth's shoulders. Holy fire blackened its flesh.

The nycaloth howled in agony. "You will pay threefold for that insult, elf!" it screeched.

It leaped into the air with one snap of its vast leathery wings, and dropped down on Fflar like the shadow of a mountain. But the moon elf took his baneblade in both hands and rose in the saddle to stab the point straight through the nycaloth's black heart. The creature fell on him, one clawed hand clenching its talons in his shoulder, and its fanged maw gnashed only inches from his face. Fflar managed to duck under the worst of the monster's weight and let the horse ride out from beneath. The nycaloth fell heavily to its side and moved no more.

Remember, you still have a battle to fight, he berated himself. The shining spirits of the vale won't keep you from having your head torn off by one of Sarya's demons.

"My thanks, Felael," he said, but the guard captain was no longer in sight. The battle had carried him away.

A chorus of sudden cries of dismay caught his attention. Fflar pulled the reins in that direction and spurred his horse forward. Seiveril's banner was under attack. Barbed devils and mezzoloths swirled around the standard, battling Felael and the rest of Seiveril's guards. The elflord himself laid about furiously with his silver mace, which flashed and thundered with holy enchantments. Without another thought, Fflar charged forward into the fray, and for a terrible instant he slashed and stabbed, and shouted defiance at the infernal creatures all around him.

He suddenly found himself standing in a space cleared of enemies, and briefly wondered if they'd driven off all their foes. He glanced at Seiveril, who was also looking for foes.

"Where did they go?" he asked the elflord.

"They drew back," Seiveril answered. He started to say more but suddenly stopped in mid-word. And Fflar felt a presence, a malevolence so powerful and close that his war-horse gave off a high shrill whinny of panic and shied away. He wrenched at the reins to keep the animal under control, and looked up to see what new terror had come to the battle.

A dreadful king with pale skin and great gray wings confronted them, bearing a terrible black sword. Dark blood seeped from a wound or mark on his brow, and a guard of devils and yugoloths simpered at his side. The infernal lord studied the two elves with a predatory grin.

"It seems that I must take matters into my own hands," he said. His voice was rich and musical, unbearably sweet. "Your Crusade ends here, Seiveril Miritar. I have raised up Sarya Dlardrageth as Queen of Cormanthor, and I do not intend to allow you to interfere with the work of fifty centuries."

"You are Malkizid," Fflar said.

The archdevil turned his black eyes on Fflar. "So I am, Fflar Starbrow Melruth. I well remember who you are and how you failed . . . though I have never forgiven you for destroying my servant Aulmpiter. I look forward to granting you a second death."

"I do not fear you, devil!"

Malkizid's cold smile failed. "Then you are a fool, mortal," he snarled.

The mark burned into his forehead began to smolder, and the Branded King advanced to meet Fflar and Seiveril.

❂ ❂ ❂ ❂ ❂

The rocky defile grew steeper and more narrow as Araevin and his friends pressed on from the scene of their battle against the hell hounds, until they finally found themselves toiling up a trail of sorts that switchbacked its way up to a bladelike saddle between the jagged hilltops. Here they found the first pitiful signs of vegetation that they had seen so far—black, iron-hard briars that clung to the deepest clefts in the rock. The wind grew stronger as they gained height, blasting at them with unpredictable and malicious gusts. Dust and grit coated their faces and hands, and clung to their garments.

With one last nerve-racking scramble, they reached the saddle proper and finally glimpsed what lay on the other side of their climb.

"That, I did not expect," Nesterin breathed.

"Me, neither," Maresa agreed.

The serried ridges continued on into the distance, their flanks scorched and bare. Immediately before Araevin and his friends, the steep-sided valley separating the ridge they had just scrambled over from the next was filled with a forest of sorts. The trees were black and dead—scorched by the dry heat of the Barrens, Araevin guessed, though he couldn't imagine how they had grown there in the first place.

In the center of the dry, dead forest stood a tower of blackened glass. Its needle-like spires soared above the barren branches, glistening darkly in the ruddy light. Araevin had glimpsed its like only a few times in his life in some of the most ancient places of elvenkind. The spiraling ascent, the slender buttresses that arched away from the tower, the fluid lines of the place . . . it was a citadel of the Crown Wars, a glimpse of elven castles from the dawn of the world. But the fortress was blackened, its crystalline substance scorched and cracked.

"Malkizid's tower," he murmured. "That's it."

"That has the look of elven work," Nesterin said, frowning. "Was this place made in mockery of the People? Or did elves once live here?"

"The Vyshaan of Aryvandaar," Araevin answered him. "They built the Waymeet, and they had dealings with Malkizid. They might have built the portal leading to this domain and raised a tower here."

"Elves lived *here?*" Maresa asked, incredulous.

"The Vyshaanti were more like daemonfey than elves, Maresa," Araevin told her. "They would not have been deterred by dealing with the evil denizens of the Barrens. I don't know if they actually dwelled in this place, but I would not be surprised to learn that they visited it often enough to see the need for a strong refuge here."

They fell silent, studying the old citadel and its dead forest, until Jorin cleared his throat. "We'd better start down from this ridgeline. We don't want to be seen."

The ranger led them down the steeply descending path that dropped from the barren hills into the dead forest. Sliding and scraping their way down the hillside, they finally reached the sparse cover of the desiccated forest. Their path grew easier as the slope lessened. When they reached the black woods, Araevin could see that the valley floor was choked with thick briars. Thorns as sharp and long as daggers gleamed on each side of the path.

Jorin led the company deeper into the forest, staying

on the trail. On several occasions winged fiends—devils or yugoloths, Araevin could not easily tell—flew overhead, croaking to each other in harsh voices. Each time he and his friends crouched down under the cover of the burned trees and sullen briars, getting as close to the thorns as they dared, and waited until the monsters flew off.

"Do you think they are looking for us?" Donnor asked softly after the third such encounter.

"I doubt it," Araevin said. "I think there would be many more devils prowling in this vale if they suspected our presence."

"That's reassuring," Maresa snorted. "They're going to figure it out sooner or later, you know."

Araevin did not answer her. When the danger passed, they climbed to their feet and continued on. After another parched mile of walking beneath the bare branches and black trunks of the old forest, they came to a small clearing where an old fountain basin had once stood. It was crowned by a statue of a winged angel transfixed by a sword. Immortal agony and despair gaped silently toward the sky. Rising above the trees a few hundred yards away, the nearest spire of the ruined citadel peered down on them.

"I've seen this before," Araevin murmured.

It was the place from which he had glimpsed the third shard's hiding place in his vision. He could not make out any gleam of light in the spire to announce the shard's presence, but that did not surprise him. Visions exaggerated things like that in order to convey information.

A broad balcony caught his eye. It ascended the outside of the spire for quite a distance before it came to a ruined edge. A dark doorway midway along its length seemed to lead to the tower's interior. A sudden inspiration came to Araevin then. He'd been wondering how they could slip inside the tower proper, since he assumed that Malkizid's minions would carefully guard what passed for the tower's gate. But it might be possible to make their entry from the balcony outside.

"There," he said, pointing out the balcony to the others. "We'll enter the spire from the balcony. Link hands—I'll teleport us all to the balcony."

"Is it safe?" Donnor asked.

"Nothing here is safe," Araevin admitted. "But I suspect that we may do better to trust in speed than stealth once we get inside. It will be very hard for me to conceal my presence."

The Lathanderite bowed his head and murmured the words of a prayer. Then he looked back up at Araevin. "I'm ready."

The mage reached out and seized his friends' hands, and spoke the words of his teleport spell with his eye firmly fixed on the tower's balcony. He felt the familiar icy plunge into blackness, an instant of disorientation . . . and he and his friends were standing high above the barren forest on a narrow balcony of ebon glass. Fortunately, it seemed sturdy enough to hold them all. Araevin had half-feared that it might give way beneath their weight.

Maresa glanced down to check herself, as if she expected that not all of her would have made the trip. Then she grunted in satisfaction and said, "Well, we're here. What next?"

Araevin quickly took his bearings. The citadel was really three distinct spires in one structure, winding around each other as if they had grown out of the ground in that form. About halfway up the height of the central spire, one of the two smaller ones branched off and soared out as a hanging minaret. The other, the one Araevin and his friends stood on, branched out a little bit higher. The whole edifice spurned the earth below, boldly leaping out over dizzying drops below with the support of long, slender buttresses. Beneath their feet loomed a drop of two hundred feet or more.

"This way," he said, and he led his friends to the doorway close at hand.

The archway was guarded by a warding symbol, glowing

red with malevolent magic. Araevin studied it for a moment and framed a negating spell to suppress it while they passed. Inside the spire, he found a chamber finished in red marble with gold veins. A broad stair circled up to the floor above, and another led below. The room was appointed as a conjury of some kind, with summoning diagrams inscribed on the floor and shelves filled with scrolls of sallow parchment.

The third shard whispered to him from somewhere above. Araevin started for the stairs leading up—but then Nesterin hissed in alarm. "There's a devil following us!" the star elf said. He stood by the archway leading outside, peering back the way they had come. "It's alighting on the balcony . . ."

Maresa drew her rapier and melted into the wall beside the archway. Nesterin and Jorin backed up, readying their bows, while Donnor found the best cover he could on the opposite side of the archway from Maresa and hefted his broadsword. Araevin found a good place in an alcove along the far wall . . . but then he heard a hissing, scrabbling sound coming from the downward stairs to his left. He looked down just as a trio of chitin-plated canoloths appeared on the stair, spiky tongues lolling from their barbed snouts.

A black-scaled shadow filled the archway. It was a towering devil, easily the height of a good-sized giant, though it was lean and lanky. A bladed tail whipped anxiously behind it, and the fiend gripped a long, barbed chain in its talons. Two great, curled horns crowned its fearsome visage.

"Stupid mortals," it gloated. "Did you think your sealing spell could hold us for long? You will soon learn—"

"Enough of this," Jorin said.

The ranger loosed his arrow and buried the slender shaft in the thick scales over the fiend's chest. The devil roared in pain and started toward the archer just as Maresa slipped in from the left side of the portal and skewered its hip—the highest part of the creature she could easily reach—with her rapier. The devil roared again and leaped away from her, ripping her rapier from her hands.

"Impudent insect!" the creature snarled. "I will eat your liver before your dying eyes!"

It lashed out in a blinding frenzy, whirling the huge barbed chain in its taloned hands. With one quick strike it wrapped the cruel chain around Maresa's shins and jerked the genasi off her feet, and with the other end it smashed the bow out of Jorin's hands. The monster wheeled and lashed its bladed tail at Donnor, striking the knight's shield with a resounding clang that sent him staggering to his knees.

"Araevin! The stairs below!" Nesterin shouted. He gave voice to a sharp atonal song that scoured the lean monster's side with a blast of blue power. An instant later he very nearly lost his left leg to the creature's bladed tail as it whipped around and lashed at him, slicing through his mail as if it were paper. The star elf cried out and fell, his leg buckling.

"I know!" Araevin answered Nesterin.

The canoloths below bounded up the stairs with startling speed for creatures so large and heavy. Doubled jaws, wide enough to bite a man in two, gnashed and slavered. He snapped out the words for an ice spell, sealing the top of the stairway with a glistening white wall. The ice shuddered as the monsters below hurled their strength against it, but it held.

The horned devil glanced once at the ice sealing the stairwell then fixed its hateful eyes on Araevin. "You are the mage who tampered with the speaking stone," it hissed. It began to gather a ball of green fire in one fist, but Donnor Kerth surged forward and laid into its black-scaled flesh with his broadsword.

"For Lathander!" the human knight shouted.

He turned and hewed at the devil's knee, cutting its leg out from under it. The devil threw out its wings for balance—knocking Maresa off her feet again, just as she disentangled herself from the end of the chain—and hopped awkwardly, trying to stay aloft. It hammered Donnor to the ground with one spiked elbow, and flicked its chain out at Araevin in an easy motion that would have shattered his skull if he hadn't ducked at the last instant. Instead, the chain whistled over his head and pulverized a divot of red marble out of the wall behind him.

The devil drew back for another strike, but a red-feathered quarrel sprouted behind its ear as Maresa's crossbow thrummed. From the floor she had quietly cocked her weapon and waited for the perfect shot. The towering fiend crumpled to all fours, fumbling to pull out the bolt with one taloned hand, but that brought its head within reach of Donnor's sword. The cleric surged up and clove the devil's skull in two with one huge overhand swing. Black blood sizzled and smoked on the dusty ground as the creature folded.

"Well struck, Donnor," Jorin said.

He stooped and retrieved his bow while Maresa reclaimed her rapier from the devil's corpse. Nesterin struggled to his feet, having improvised a bandage for his wounded leg by ripping the sleeve off his shirt and binding it tightly over the cut.

"How long will your ice wall hold?" the star elf asked Araevin.

"Only a few minutes. We must move quickly now." Araevin took a moment to cover the archway leading out to the balcony with a mass of gluey webbing, just in case the canoloths had a way to double back and climb the outside of the tower. Then he hurried to the stairs leading up. "Come on, my friends! The third shard is close."

Bruised and battered, Araevin and his companions rushed up the curve of the stairs to the next chamber. Two clicking mezzoloths appeared on the stairway above them, iron tridents clutched in their thick talons.

"Fight through them!" Araevin called.

The mezzoloths raced down the steps to meet them. One hurled its trident at Donnor, who ducked under the weapon

Final Gate • 271

and kept going. Jorin and Nesterin shot together, their arrows transfixing that monster long enough for Donnor to bound close and cut it down. Araevin handled the other one, blasting it into flakes of smoking ash with an emerald ray of disintegration. He did not even break stride as he leaped past the wreckage of the two infernal warriors.

They came to the top of the stair, and Araevin halted in amazement. The chamber filled the entire top of the spire. Despite the black ruin that had come to the tower, it was still majestic, soaring half a hundred feet above his head. In the center of the room hovered the third shard of the Gatekeeper's Crystal, suspended twenty feet above the floor by magic. A great shield of elemental fury enclosed the artifact—dancing bands of ruby fire, crawling arcs of blue-green lightning, spinning boulders covered in foot-long spikes of stone. The sound was indescribable as the flames roared, the lightning snapped and thundered, and the heavy stone spheres howled through their orbits.

"Selûne's starry eyes," Maresa said. She had to shout to make herself heard over the roaring that filled the room. "There it is, all right, but how do we get it?"

"Is that some sort of shielding spell, Araevin?" asked Jorin.

"Yes. A very powerful one, too," the mage replied.

Malkizid clearly commanded rare and potent magic indeed. Araevin studied the elemental sphere, picking out the complex weavings of arcane energy it was made of. No ordinary spell would suppress Malkizid's defenses . . . but high magic might. The difficulty was that the spell he had in mind could not help but draw a great deal of attention.

Speed, not stealth, he reminded himself. *Malkizid's servants already know we are in the spire. It's only a matter of time before the master of the house returns.*

"Stand back and guard the stairs," he warned his friends.

Then he raised his hands and began to declaim the opening verses of the *kileaarna reithirgir,* the spell of unbinding.

Power flooded into him, and he felt the room around him growing gray and unreal, insubstantial. Only he was real and solid, he and the fiery font of magic he coaxed from his heart and hands. The stone blocks of the chamber floor under his feet cracked and dissipated in granite dust, while the air around his body kindled into pure white flame.

Honing his will into pure purpose, Araevin threw his might against Malkizid's defenses.

✦ ✦ ✦ ✦ ✦

Malkizid and his infernal champions tore into the warriors surrounding Seiveril's banner like a hurricane of black fire. Shrieking, grinning barbed devils hurled themselves against the Evereskan guards and the Knights of the Golden Star and literally ripped seasoned elf warriors limb from limb. Mezzoloths clicked and buzzed in their hideously insectlike speech, dragging down Sembian riders and working awful slaughter with their red-hot iron tridents. In return, elf champions and Silver Ravens hurled themselves into the fray, trying to stem the onslaught. Everywhere gouts of fire and crackling blue rays of disruption hurled back and forth between Malkizid's fiends and their foes, leaving Seiveril's ears ringing with thunderclap after thunderclap and the insane roar of hellspawned rage.

The Branded King himself stalked through the elven ranks with avid glee dancing in his black eyes, slaying with spell and blade all who stood against him. Elves and humans who looked him full in the face reeled away, hands covering their eyes and mad shrieks rising from their throats.

"Seiveril Miritar!" the fiend shouted, and his voice shook the vale. "Face me!"

Seiveril's horse stumbled and foundered, dragged down by a mezzoloth that caught it by its hindquarters and broke its back. The elflord managed to free his feet from the stirrups and leap away as the animal screamed and fell. He banished the insectile daemon back to its hellish home with a spell of dismissal, and found Malkizid striding toward him, only twenty paces distant.

"Your doom is at hand, Lord of Elion!" snarled the archdevil.

"For Tower Reilloch!" Jorildyn appeared beside Seiveril and lashed out with ray of emerald destruction.

The battle-mage's spell caught Malkizid in his right side and blasted deep into his stony white flesh. Malkizid hissed in pain and twisted away, his ebon armor smoking. Seiveril immediately began to chant a spell of his own, hoping to overwhelm the mighty devil with a barrage of magic.

"Insolent mortal!" Malkizid roared.

He threw out one taloned hand and clenched it into a fist, speaking a word so evil that spikes of hot pain stabbed into Seiveril's ears. An unseen force crushed Jorildyn's ribcage like matchsticks. Blood burst from the half-elf's mouth, his eyes rolled up in his head, and he collapsed in a nerveless heap. The archdevil returned his attention to Seiveril—and Seiveril finished chanting his spell. A column of brilliant white fire stabbed down from above, pure and holy, engulfing the Branded King.

Malkizid roared in pain and ducked aside. He retaliated by turning his talons on Seiveril, reaching out to crush him in a fist of malice as he had just destroyed Jorildyn. Seiveril felt the horrible pressure of Malkizid's grip settling over his chest, tightening, buckling the elven steel of his plate armor. Dark spots danced before his eyes, and the elflord gasped for breath.

"Now, Seiveril Miritar, I send you from this world," the archdevil gloated.

"Not while I can help it!" Leaping over the body of a dead mezzoloth, Starbrow hurled himself against the Branded King. Keryvian sang with clean holy light as the moon elf launched a furious assault against Malkizid. The baneblade darted past Malkizid's guard to gash him once across the upper arm and a second time at the knee, but

Malkizid parried blow after blow that might have done real harm.

"Is that the extent of your swordsmanship?" the archdevil laughed.

Quickly recovering from the surprise of Starbrow's attack, he suddenly leaped forward and returned a dizzying fusillade of stroke and counterstroke with his great black sword. Starbrow left his guard just a little low for an instant, and the archdevil very nearly took his head off. The black sword whistled up in a deadly arc that the moon elf somehow ducked under—almost. Instead of decapitating him, Malkizid smashed Starbrow's helm, sending it spinning through the air, and stretched him out senseless, blood pouring from a bad cut across his forehead.

"Now, to finish this," the archdevil said.

He turned back to Seiveril, who was wrestling for breath on all fours. But then Malkizid hesitated, and tilted his head to one side as if listening for some faint, far-off sound. His feral grin faded, replaced by a scowl of anger so hot and fierce that Seiveril had to look away.

"What? Impossible!" the archdevil hissed. Then he vanished, teleporting away without another word. In the space of an instant, the concentrated malice and violence at the heart of the fiendish attack vanished as well.

Seiveril pushed himself to his feet, reeling with astonishment. *The archdevil simply left?* he thought. *What in the world is more important to him than what is happening on this battlefield?*

He was jarred from his confusion by a scream over his head. He looked up, and leaped aside as a mortally wounded fey'ri warrior plummeted into the ground almost exactly where he had been standing. The red-scaled daemonfey groaned once and fell still. Seiveril turned to search the skies for some clue as to where the fey'ri had fallen from or what might be happening above the battlefield.

The fey'ri were fleeing the fight. Speeding toward the north, they wheeled away from the Vale of Lost Voices and beat their leathery wings with all their might. The shining spirits of the vale guardians ran after them across the sky, swift and tireless, but it seemed that some of the fey'ri at least would escape to fight another day. Seiveril raised a shout of exultation and held his mace in the air. "The fey'ri flee! Strike now, my friends! We have them!"

Warriors all around him added their voices to his. From somewhere off to his right, scything rays of brilliant purple fire—some mage's work, Seiveril guessed—lanced into the sky and burned two more fey'ri out of the air. A little farther beyond them he saw a tight cordon of daemonfey withdrawing in good order, recklessly hurling powerful spells left and right to keep the vale's spirits at bay and discourage any mages below from interfering. It was too far to be certain, but Seiveril thought he glimpsed a slender feminine form amid the retreating band. So the queen of the daemonfey was retreating to her stolen throne, was she?

"Enjoy Myth Drannor while you can, Sarya!" he called after her. "I am coming to end your reign!"

Starbrow staggered to his feet, bleeding freely from the cut across his forehead. "Where did Malkizid go?" he managed.

"He left," Seiveril answered. He hurried over to help his friend, already speaking the words of a healing prayer as he reached out to steady him on his feet. "The fey'ri are withdrawing."

The moon elf's eyes cleared as the healing spell took hold. He looked after the retreating shadows in the sky, and surveyed the battlefield with one quick glance. "Some of the demons and devils are fighting on."

"If they can't fly or teleport," said Seiveril, "we'll surround them and deal with them one at a time."

A warm light flooded over the battlefield, and Seiveril looked to the east. The sun was climbing above the horizon, slipping into a narrow strip of open sky below the overcast. As the sunlight touched the field, the brilliant spirits of

276 • Richard Baker

the guardians of the vale grew dim and translucent. The spirits slowed their pursuit and hovered for a moment in the sky. Then, silently, they turned toward the sunrise and vanished in motes of golden light, striding back into the radiant forests of Arvandor. The last of the warriors looked down on Seiveril and touched the hilt of his sword to his lips in salute before he vanished, too.

"Thank you, Father," Seiveril murmured to the sky. He shook himself, finding new strength in his tired body with the bright golden light of dawn. "Felael! Sound the pursuit! We have more work ahead of us this morning!"

CHAPTER SIXTEEN

18 Eleasias, the Year of Lightning Storms

High magic blazed around Araevin like a mantle of white fire. Like heat rising from a blacksmith's forge, the incandescent power enfolding him left the chamber around him shimmering and dancing. The spire itself seemed to tremble with each word of the *kileaarna reithirgir*.

"Araevin! We are running out of time!" Donnor had to shout to make himself heard over the roar of the mighty magic in the room.

"You must hold them off a little longer!" he managed to shout back at Donnor, trying not to let his friend's warning distract him.

His companions fought a desperate skirmish to keep Malkizid's servants out of the room, but Araevin could spare them none of his power. Attacking Malkizid's elemental shield took all of his strength, and he feared that if he stopped to aid his comrades he would not be able to begin again.

Wielding lances of argent fire with his mind, he hammered at the defenses of the third shard. He struck at the orbiting boulders first, hurling them aside. The great spiked stones crushed masonry and shattered the tiles of the floor when they landed. Araevin risked a quick glance over his shoulder and saw that a pair of winged devils harried Nesterin and Maresa near the top of the stairwell. The next stone sphere that he tore out of Malkizid's warding spell he sent hurtling at the flapping monsters, crushing one against the wall.

The spinning bands of fire he dealt with next, using the shield's own waters to quench them. One by one he guided each arc of flame into collisions with the half-globe of shimmering water that revolved slowly around the center. Steam hissed and poured away from the elemental shield, giving Araevin a glimpse of the last defense—the vortex of wind. The furious cyclone sucked in the plumes of steam, growing cloudy as it did so. Lightning danced and crackled within.

"We could use your help, Araevin!" Maresa called.

The genasi fought with rapier in one hand and wand in the other, lunging forward to stab and slash, darting back to pummel her opponents with bright darts of magic. She was no mage, but she had skill enough to put a wand to good use. Unfortunately, more of Malkizid's servants were pouring into the room.

"I almost have it!" he shouted back to her. "Donnor, can you block the stair?"

The Lathanderite had been fighting a few steps down out of Araevin's sight, but he retreated back up into the chamber at the top of the spire. Black furrows raked his armor in at least two places, and his sword burned with furious white radiance. Seizing the golden sunburst of Lathander that hung around his neck, he raised it high and called out, "Lord of the Dawn, ward us from our foes!"

Hundreds of golden sparkles danced around the cleric, slowly beginning to grow larger and revolve around him. In the space of a moment, they flew and whirled too fast for the eye to follow, each one a spinning razor of golden light. With shrieks of anger, the infernal monsters trying to fight their way into the chamber recoiled, not before some had been slashed to ribbons by Donnor's spell.

"Finish your work, Araevin!" the cleric shouted.

Araevin turned his attention back to the shield of winds, the last barrier in Malkizid's elemental ward. Carefully he began to unbind the spell. The last shard hung in plain sight now, glowing softly with the proximity of its sister shards. He had only—

A font of ebon flame sprang up from the flagstones, almost directly beneath the floating shard. It blazed and danced in a shout of black power, and it took the shape of a tall, pale seraph as cold as marble. A seeping wound marked his forehead, dripping black blood.

"You believe you can defy me in my own citadel?" the pale lord snarled. "Your punishment will last a thousand years, fool!"

Araevin recoiled a step before the dark king's vehemence. "Malkizid," he murmured.

It seemed that the master of the tower had indeed returned. With a grimace of frustration, he allowed the *kileaarna reithirgir* to gutter out, not yet completed. He would need every ounce of his strength for the struggle to come.

The archdevil studied his face for a moment. "You must be Araevin Teshurr," he observed. His voice was eerily beautiful, even in the depths of his anger. "I see that the *telmiirkara neshyrr* has left its mark on you. A shame, since I might have made something of you otherwise." He bared his teeth in a feral grin, and the terrible wound across his brow began to gleam darkly.

"Strike, my friends!" Araevin cried.

He heard the sharp thrumming of bowstrings, and

arrows flashed at Malkizid. The archdevil parried one with a quick motion of his black sword, and simply stopped the others with his outstretched hand. Araevin wove his hands together and intoned the words of a powerful spell, conjuring a spellchain of green energy around Malkizid. The links settled closer to the archdevil, but Malkizid countered and shifted the spellchain away. In the blink of an eye it appeared around Jorin Kell Harthan, who was approaching the archdevil with his swords in his hands. The Aglarondan cried out in dismay and stumbled to the floor as Araevin's spellchain ensnared him instead.

"You are a fool if you think you can defeat me with your spells," Malkizid gloated. "Who do you think taught Saelethil Dlardrageth his lore? I tutored the Vyshaanti archmages when the world was young! You are not their equal."

Araevin ignored Malkizid's boasting and started on another spell, seeking something that the archdevil could not deflect. But Malkizid simply stared at Araevin. The brand above the archdevil's brow burst into black flame. It demanded Araevin's attention, and when the sun elf's eye fell on the brand Malkizid's towering malevolence and will struck him like a physical blow. Lines of fire seemed to burn themselves into Araevin's face as he stood transfixed by the archdevil's terrible visage. He felt his friends behind him fighting their own silent struggles against Malkizid's black stare.

Behind him, Nesterin cried out, "Corellon, it burns!"

"Corellon himself placed that mark on my brow, elf," Malkizid hissed. "You quail so after only an instant of the torment I have endured for twenty thousand years?"

Araevin ground his teeth and fought down the pain. He tried to grope his way toward a spell, any spell, but it was impossible. The grip of Malkizid's terrible will was simply too strong. He looked up at the third shard of the Gatekeeper's Crystal, spinning slowly within its cocoon of shrieking wind.

Final Gate • 281

So close! he thought. So close!

The archdevil stalked closer, shifting his grip on his ebon blade. Behind Araevin, Donnor let out a grunt of agony—but then the human stumbled through the verses of a holy prayer and invoked a ring of golden light. The light washed over Araevin harmlessly, but seared Malkizid's marble flesh and left a great smoking scar across the archdevil's torso.

Malkizid roared in anger and staggered back several steps. He wheeled around, fixing his attention on the Tethyrian.

"Insolent dog!" he snarled—and the terrible burning brand that filled Araevin's eyes vanished.

Gasping for breath, Araevin slumped to his knees. He could feel blood streaming from his wounded face, but the awful power that had held him motionless was gone. Fight it off! he railed at himself. I must do something before he destroys us all.

"The *ondreier ysele*," he murmured. The Word of Potency ... a comparatively simple high magic spell that added strength to lesser spells. From his knees, Araevin focused his mind and will and fanned the embers of power burning in his soul. Shining like a silver beacon, he shouted out the Word of Potency. The spire top rocked with its raw might.

"No!" Malkizid whirled back on him, raising his taloned hand to counter what followed.

But Araevin had judged his moment right, catching the archdevil at the exact moment his attention had been fixed on Donnor. Before Malkizid could raise a defense against the Word of Potency, Araevin struck again with a spell of integument. The Branded King vanished in an instant, hurled headlong into a dimensional prison that glittered once in the air where he had stood before fading out of view.

Nesterin stared in amazement. "You defeated him, Araevin!"

"No," Araevin gasped. "The dimensional maze will restrain him for only a few moments. We must be gone from this place before he returns."

He looked up at the shard, still waiting overhead, and tried to find the strength for a spell to deal with the remaining fragments of Malkizid's elemental shield. Think, Araevin! Think! he exhorted himself. There had to be a way.

Maresa looked over to Araevin. "Can you get it?" she asked. Red blood ran down her snow-white features from angry cuts across her face, but she was still on her feet.

"I don't have a spell to overcome the last shield."

The genasi glanced up at the shard, and frowned. "Only the wind remains?"

"Yes, I unbound the rest of the spell." Araevin staggered to his feet, still furiously searching for some way to deal with the elemental shield. If he couldn't come up with anything, they would have to retreat and try again later . . . but Malkizid would be waiting for them next time.

Maresa spread her arms wide, and lifted herself into the air. Without a moment's hesitation, the genasi levitated herself toward the sphere of shrieking, howling wind. Araevin stared in horror.

"Maresa, no!" he cried. "It will tear you to pieces!"

She ignored him and flew straight into the spinning gray globe. Araevin cringed, expecting to see her flung out of the elemental shield—but instead the winds seemed to simply part around her. Her long white air streamed softly behind her head as it always did, seemingly unaffected by the hurricane raging around her. She reached out and seized the last shard of the crystal, and just as swiftly dropped back down through the sphere of wind. She alighted next to Araevin, and extended the shard to him.

"Can we go now?" Maresa asked.

"How did you—?"

"I'm a genasi, you idiot, a daughter of the elemental air." Maresa looked over to the place where Malkizid had vanished. The dimensional prison was becoming visible again, brightening as it returned to reality. The archdevil would return in mere heartbeats. "If you have a way to get us all out of here, this would be a good time."

Araevin set his astonishment aside for later. "Quickly, join hands!" he told the others.

Nesterin and Donnor helped Jorin, who had been mauled by the errant spellchain, to Araevin's side. Taking Maresa's hand and Donnor's hand in his own, Araevin chanted the words of a planewalking spell. Even though he was numb and cold with fatigue, he reached into the deepest wellsprings of his strength and found the willpower to finish the spell.

The last thing he saw of the spire top was Malkizid emerging from the dimensional prison, his face contorted in pure fury. Then the Branded King's fortress vanished into silver, silent mist.

❦ ❦ ❦ ❦ ❦

The last rays of sunset painted the walls of Sarya's throne chamber a brilliant red-gold. Two days had passed since the defeat in the Vale of Lost Voices, and the weather had turned clear and warm again.

She stood facing the window, looking out over the tree-shaded ruins of the ancient city. She had first walked the streets of this place more than five millennia ago, when Arcorar, the Great Forest, was the name of the realm. She could still make out the faint suggestions of that old city, even though it had evolved over many centuries into Myth Drannor before meeting its end.

"The fey'ri are here, Mother," Xhalph said quietly.

She nodded and turned away from the view. Mardeiym Reithel and Vesryn Aelorothi had survived the battle in the vale, so she still had her general and her spymaster. But the bladesinger Jasrya Aelorothi was dead, killed by some human archer's lucky shot. Hundreds more of her fey'ri had died fighting against the guardians of the vale. Her legion had been reduced to no more than five hundred strong.

She studied her subjects for a moment. Mardeiym and Vesryn returned her gaze without expression, while Alysir Ursequarra's eyes burned with a fierce anger barely kept in check. The half-dozen remaining House lords did not meet her eyes.

"What news, Vesryn?" Sarya asked the vulture-featured sorcerer. "Have our guests arrived yet?"

"The armies of Evermeet and Sembia have encircled the city, my queen," Vesryn Aelorothi reported. "They are preparing fortifications to besiege us."

"I am not concerned," Sarya replied. She paced back to the window, leaving her back to her subjects. "The mythal protects us. I can destroy any paleblood or human who sets foot in Myth Drannor. Miritar and his human allies can bark and bay in the forest outside our walls for a hundred years."

"Then what was the purpose of fighting in the vale of Lost Voices?" Alysir Ursequarra demanded from behind her. "What advantage did you seek by abandoning the defenses of this city in order to meet our enemies so far beyond our walls? And how could you fail to anticipate that the guardian spirits of the vale would side with Seiveril Miritar?"

Sarya ceased her pacing and eyed the fey'ri over her shoulder. "I have always thought it foolish to teach my subjects to guard their thoughts in my presence," she said in a cold voice. "However, it is equally unwise to tolerate insolence. *I* rule here, Lady Alysir, and you exceed my tolerance."

Alysir Ursequarra threw back her head in defiance and set her hand on the hilt of her sword. "I only speak what all here think, Sarya Dlardrageth. If you believe that you can extinguish our doubts by destroying me, then you should do so. Otherwise, I demand answers."

"In that case, I choose to destroy you," Sarya said.

She whirled on the fey'ri and hissed the words to a dreadful necromancy. The fey'ri drew her sword and leaped for Sarya, conjuring a spell of her own to fling at her queen—but Sarya's spell proved the quicker. In mid-leap a fierce midnight flame erupted from Alysir's mouth, her eyes, even her finely scaled flesh. Her spell drowned in the horrible crackling darkness that consumed her, feeding on her body as if she were made of tinder.

The rebellious fey'ri crashed to the stone floor at Sarya's feet, screaming black fire. She found the sheer willpower and determination to claw herself two paces closer, while the awful black flames devoured her alive. Sarya smiled coldly and took a step back, remaining just out of Alysir's reach. The ebon flames were quite dangerous, after all, and could easily spread. In a few moments there was nothing left of Alysir Ursequarra but a charred skeleton encased in blackened mail.

Sarya extinguished the flames with a single curt gesture and returned her attention to the fey'ri lords that remained. "Does anyone else wish to question my authority?" she asked. None of the others spoke up. They simply waited in silence.

"As it so happens, I had several compelling reasons to try Miritar's strength in the vale," she continued. "First, the open terrain favored us greatly. We worked great destruction with the advantage of the skies in the early hours of the battle. Second, I did not care to allow myself to fall under siege here. Permitting Miritar to reach Myth Drannor struck me as something that might be seen as weakness in the lands surrounding Cormanthor, even if I felt confident that he could not storm the city in the face of my control over the mythal.

"As for the vale guardians, they have been quiescent for months. So long as we did not despoil the tombs—and you may recall that I gave exacting orders that no tombs were to be broken—they should have had no reason to trouble us. It seems clear now that Seiveril Miritar had some way to rouse the guardians against us, but we did not suspect that he could do any such thing." Sarya stretched her wings out with a sharp snapping motion, and folded them tightly to her back. "I remind you that this is *war*. We must be audacious, inventive, and resourceful. We set out half a year ago to avenge the wrongs of five thousand years and shake the foundations of the world. Did you think it would be easy?"

"We are with you, my queen," Mardeiym Reithel replied. He struck his fist to his breastplate and bowed his head. The remaining fey'ri lords followed the general's example, murmuring promises of loyalty and lowering their heads before her.

Sarya did not doubt that some at least harbored doubts much like Alysir Ursequarra's, but for the moment she chose to accept their words of fealty. If some of them had to be bent to her will through the fear of her wrath, so be it. She did not govern by their consent and she did not care to weaken her power over them by acceding to ultimatums.

"Mardeiym, I want you to mount a vigilant guard over the city," she said. "I have arranged the mythal to severely chastise any of our enemies who set foot in Myth Drannor, but I do not rule out the possibility that clever infiltrators may find a way to worm through the mythal's defenses. As for the rest of you, remember what you have seen today. I trust I will not have to repeat that lesson. Now leave me."

The lords and ladies of the fey'ri bowed again to her, and departed. Sarya refrained from pacing anxiously until they left. The audience chamber she had chosen for herself in Castle Cormanthor was too small. She could not stand confinement of any sort.

Her fey'ri were decimated, her enemies were allied against her, the drow had abandoned her cause, her city was beleaguered ... but she was not yet beaten. Myth Drannor was an unassailable fortress beneath her mythal weaving.

"I will teach the palebloods the cost of defiance," she muttered angrily. "They will rue the day they set themselves against me!"

"Ah, now that is the proper spirit." Malkizid's golden voice preceded the archdevil as a font of flickering black fire sprang up in one corner of the chamber. The dancing flame took on a roughly manlike shape, roiling and shifting, and it condensed all at once into the familiar form of the Branded King. "Truly, the Dlardrageths are made of stern stuff."

Sarya turned on the handsome archdevil, cold hate smoldering in her green eyes. "My determination owes nothing to you, Malkizid! You abandoned the field at the height of the battle. We might have won the day if you had not fled!"

Malkizid offered a slight shrug. "I discovered that I had matters to attend to in my own domain, Sarya." He set one hand on the arm of Sarya's throne, and smiled to himself as if amused by her anger. "Have you perchance recovered the shard of the Gatekeeper's Crystal from Nar Kerymhoarth yet?"

Sarya frowned. Malkizid had made no mention of the shard in months. What had brought it to his mind now? "I sent a small company of fey'ri to search for it, but they fell afoul of the serpent folk lairing in the undamaged levels."

"Send another company immediately," the archdevil said. "Make sure that they do not fail, Sarya. That shard has become important again."

"Why is that?"

Malkizid narrowed his eyes, perhaps measuring her distinct lack of deference. Sarya hoped that he understood how precarious his hold over her was. But the Branded King set it aside without comment, at least for the moment. "The mage Araevin Teshurr seeks to reassemble the Gatekeeper's Crystal. That is a weapon we do not wish to see in Seiveril Miritar's hands."

"He could destroy this city's mythal," Sarya said with a scowl. That was far and away her best deterrent against attack in Myth Drannor. If the mythal fell, the palebloods and their humans could storm the city. The monstrous denizens of the ruins would exact a price, of course, but she did not have sufficient fey'ri warriors or enslaved demons and devils to feel confident of repelling such an attack. "Has he found any shards yet?"

"One at least, possibly two," Malkizid answered. "I think it wise to make certain that he does not recover the remaining shards."

"I will put it in Teryani Ealoeth's hands. She has been most anxious to make amends for her failure to turn the Sembians against Evermeet's army." Sarya tapped her chin. "Yes, she should do. I will dispatch her tonight."

"Tell me the moment she finds the shard in Nar Kerymhoarth," Malkizid said. He offered her a mocking half-bow and slid back down into the shadows again.

Sarya stood still, looking at the place where Malkizid had made his exit. The Gatekeeper's Crystal was a powerful weapon indeed. Perhaps, if Teryani found the shard for her, she would no longer need Malkizid. Frowning in thought, she strode to the chamber door.

"Erraichal!" she called. "Have your Talons bring Teryani Ealoeth here at once."

The captain of her guard bowed once. "As you command, my queen," he said.

❦ ❦ ❦ ❦ ❦

Araevin and his companions rode into the Crusade's new encampment on the outskirts of Myth Drannor late in the afternoon. It was a warm, clear summer day, with a cloudless sky overhead, which had made the hard ride a little easier. It had taken them almost three days to catch up to the army of Evermeet, riding from the sacred forests of Semberholme more than a hundred miles to the south. It was the closest to Myth Drannor that Araevin could manage with his planewalking spell.

He asked the way to Seiveril's headquarters and was directed to the ruins of an old elven manor, hidden in a deeply forested hollow. Scores of elf knights and archers stood guard over the place, vigilantly scanning the skies and the shadows of the woods. Alongside the elves stood no small number of Dalesfolk—Deepingdalesfolk and a handful of Riders from Mistledale, if Araevin judged the heraldry right. He also saw a few Sembian banners standing next to the Crusade's own pennants, and shook his head.

I should have known that Ilsevele would succeed at anything she set her mind to, he reflected.

The guards standing watch over Seiveril's quarters recognized Araevin at once. "Mage Teshurr, you have returned!" one of the Knights of the Golden Star exclaimed. The fellow hurried up to take the horse's bit, while other elves did the same for Jorin, Nesterin, Donnor, and Maresa. "I think Lord Miritar will be glad to see you."

Araevin recognized the knight, a passing acquaintance from his days in the Queen's Guard long ago. "I thank you, Vessen," he answered. He swung himself down from his horse, while his friends followed suit. None were too proud to knead fists in their backs or wince as they walked off the effects of the long ride. Donnor and Jorin were the best horsemen of them all, but even the Tethyrian and the Aglarondan were saddle-sore. "Can you take me to Lord Miritar?"

"Of course," the sun elf replied. "This way."

Araevin and his friends followed Vessen into the old manor. The roof had long ago collapsed, leaving the place open to the sky, but the elves had fashioned a simple canopy of light canvas to serve as a shelter against rain and cleaned the dirt and debris of centuries from the place. The warrior led them to a room that had once been a spacious banquet hall. Seiveril waited there, along with Ilsevele, Starbrow, and Theremen Ulath of Deepingdale.

The silver-haired elflord strode up and gripped Araevin's arm with a fierce smile. "Well met, Araevin! You are exactly the person I was hoping to see."

"I did not expect to find you on the doorstep of Myth Drannor. Nor did I expect to find the Sembians fighting at your side." He turned to Ilsevele. "It seems that Ilsevele's mission must have met with some success."

Ilsevele dropped her gaze when he looked at her. "Lord Selkirk of the Sembia had the sense to see that the daemonfey were enemies to all of us. I had little to do with that."

Araevin released Seiveril's hand and moved to embrace his betrothed. She returned the gesture without looking into his face, and gave him a light kiss on his cheek before disentangling herself from his arms. The mage stopped in surprise and frowned. Had they quarreled that badly when they parted in Deepingdale? She did not seem angry, though. She seemed . . . resigned.

A cold ache knotted the center of his chest. "Ilsevele, what is wrong?" he asked softly.

"We will speak later," she answered, just as softly. "I am glad to see that you have returned safely, though." Then she moved past him to embrace Maresa, and warmly greeted Donnor, Jorin, and Nesterin. Araevin stared after her, then made himself turn and offer his hand to Starbrow, who stood nearby.

"Welcome back, Araevin." The moon elf gave him an oddly strained smile. "Did you find what you were after?"

"I did," Araevin replied. "I have much to tell you—all of you. But first, I'd like to know how you ended up here. When I set out the Crusade was defending Semberholme. Now you are besieging Myth Drannor. I have only been away for a month."

"Understandable," Seiveril said. He indicated several lightly built divans that were arranged around a small table to one side of the room. "Please, make yourselves comfortable. We will trade tales."

They passed some time exchanging news. First Seiveril and Ilsevele told the story of the defense of Semberholme, the embassy to Miklos Selkirk in Tegal's Mark, the daemonfey plot to turn the Crusade against the Sembians, and the eventual alliance. Seiveril went on to describe the

Battle of the Vale, and the victory over the fey'ri and their demonic allies.

"It was not without cost, I fear. We lost many warriors, and the Dalesfolk and Sembians lost even more. I am afraid that Ferryl Nimersyl and most of the Moon Knights perished, along with your colleague Jorildyn."

"Jorildyn is dead?" Araevin sighed. They'd studied together at Tower Reilloch for twenty years or more. He would miss the taciturn half-elf. "How did it happen?"

"He was killed by the archdevil Malkizid."

"Malkizid?" Maresa interrupted. "He was here?"

Seiveril and Starbrow nodded. "Yes, he took the field against us in the Battle of the Vale. But he suddenly abandoned the daemonfey army."

"I think that was Araevin's doing," Nesterin said. The star elf shook his head. "We wondered where the master of the house was. Now we know."

"You were in Malkizid's domain?" Seiveril asked. His brows rose in surprise. "What in the world were you doing there?"

"I suppose that now we should share our story," Araevin answered. He took a deep breath, and went on to describe their own travels—the expedition to the Nameless Dungeon, the passage to the Waymeet, the long dark quest in the blackness of Lorosfyr, and finally the perilous journey across the Barrens of Doom and Despair. When he finished, he produced the Gatekeeper's Crystal, complete with all three shards joined to make a three-pointed star. "The daemonfey know that I have at least one shard of this device now. They must suspect that I might have all three . . . though Sarya and Malkizid may not know how much the Gatekeeper aided us."

"Please excuse my ignorance, Araevin," Theremen Ulath said, "but now that you have recovered this device, what is it *for?*"

"I believe I can dismiss the mythal wards barring you from Myth Drannor."

Seiveril drew in his breath. "You can breach the daemonfey spells? How long will it take you?"

"Give me a short time to prepare, and I could attempt it this evening," Araevin said.

"The sooner, the better," Seiveril answered. "We should—"

"I don't agree, Seiveril." Starbrow held up his hand, interrupting the elflord. "We should assault the city the moment the mythal's defenses fall. Why allow the daemonfey any time at all to improvise other defenses or organize a retreat? Better to wait until we are ready to exploit Araevin's magic by storming Myth Drannor the instant Sarya's defenses fall."

Seiveril frowned with impatience, but he nodded. "I concede the point. The heavier our strike, the fewer will escape. At first light, then?" He looked over to Araevin. "Does that suit you?"

Araevin grimaced. "The longer we wait, the more that can go wrong. But I'll wait until you are ready."

"Very well. I must advise Lord Selkirk of our plans. Please excuse me. Araevin, I'm sure that Felael or Vessen can have your horses looked after and find you and your companions a place to rest somewhere nearby." The elflord stood and took his leave. Vesilde Gaerth and Theremen Ulath departed with him. They would have a long night's work ahead of them.

Starbrow lingered for a moment, but he left too after Ilsevele looked up at him and gave him a nod. *Now what was that about?* Araevin wondered.

"Mage Teshurr?" The sun elf Vessen appeared in the hall shortly after Seiveril left. "We've looked after your horses. I can show you to a place to rest, if you like."

Araevin faced his companions. "Go on ahead. I'll find you shortly."

"I can't promise that we'll save you any supper," Maresa jibed. She poked him once in the ribs then she, Donnor, Jorin, and Nesterin followed Vessen through a different doorway in the old ruin. Araevin watched them leave then turned back to Ilsevele. She still sat on one of the divans, looking down at her hands in her lap. Her hair, a dark copper-red in the shadows of the hall, was gathered in a long braid over her shoulder.

They remained there in silence for some time. Araevin stood gazing on her, and she did not look up at him. Finally he decided that he could not stand it any longer. "Ilsevele," he murmured. "Why—?" And he stopped, unable to ask the questions that were in his heart. Instead he said, "I did not realize you were so angry with me. I am sorry if I have hurt you."

She sighed and met his eyes when he spoke. "I am not angry with you, Araevin. I am sad, but I'm not angry."

A sudden cold certainty descended over him. "You are breaking our betrothal."

"I am."

"I know we have walked different roads in the last few years, Ilsevele, but I still hope to mend that." He waved his hand at the ruined manor and the darkening woods outside. "This will pass. We will have the rest of our lives to make things right."

"I do not think so. There is something more I must tell you, Araevin. You are not the only one in my heart." Ilsevele did not allow herself to look away from him. "I did not mean for it to happen. It has only become clear to me in the last few tendays. But I know that I cannot remain betrothed to you while my thoughts dwell on another."

"I—I do not understand." Araevin took two numb steps to the divan and sat down stiffly beside her. "How could your heart turn from me in a single season, Ilsevele? Did you feel this way when we walked together into Sildëyuir? When we passed the days of spring together in Silverymoon?"

"My heart did not turn from you, Araevin, yours turned from me." She looked away from him, and a tear ran down her cheek. "The passion that moves you now leaves no room for mortal love. You are no longer *Tel'Quessir*, but something more. When you remade yourself for high magic in the shadows of Sildëyuir, you left behind the communion of the People. I cannot sense your feelings, I cannot speak to you without words. If I close my eyes, I feel your presence as a blazing fire . . . but your heart is closed to me. And you cannot even see this for yourself."

"Ilsevele . . ." he said.

He started to tell her that it was not true, that he simply had not been paying attention, but he realized that she was right. He hadn't spent much time around many other elves since coming back from Sildëyuir, so he had not noticed the *distance* he truly felt. The communion elves shared with each other, the bond that tethered the hearts of the People together, was almost entirely lost to him. He felt as if he were hundreds of miles from Ilsevele, sensing her presence only as a dimly glowing ember, when he should have felt her sorrow and her fear for him as strongly as anything in his own heart.

You will count this a great gift for now, yet you will also know regret. This was the price of the eladrin's kiss.

Ilsevele looked up to his eyes again. "I felt this moment approaching for a long time, Araevin. It is not simply your . . . transformation into a high mage. I believe that we have been following different paths for a long time now."

He gazed at her in silence for a while. Finally he said, "We have been promised to each other for almost twenty years."

"The custom of our people," she said, with a wistful smile. "But I think if we were ever going to marry, it should have been long before now. We lost the passion, the wonder, of our first years together. It vanished into . . . familiarity. I served the queen in Leuthilspar, and you returned to your studies in Tower Reilloch, and our thoughts, our hearts, turned to the things that kept us apart." She reached out and took his hand. His golden skin was faintly luminous in the gathering dusk. "When I first began to harbor doubts, I regarded our long betrothal as a mistake. I thought that if we had married sooner, we would not have had so long to grow apart. But now I see the wisdom of the custom. Better to find out whether a marriage can stand the centuries we are given before the vows are spoken."

He frowned, considering her words. That first summer in the woods and glades of Elion . . . nothing had mattered to either of them except the moments they could spend alone. In the years since, they had found glimmers of that memory, but nothing that ever equaled it. Had he asked for her hand in marriage because he sensed that distance growing and hoped to overcome it? Or was it simply a matter of doing what was expected of him?

Still caught up in that thought, he asked, "Who is he, Ilsevele?"

Now she looked away. "Starbrow," she said. "I know it is sudden. I do not know what to make of it myself."

Araevin closed his eyes. At least it was not anything she had tried to conceal from him. After all, she had only met the moon elf a few months ago. He was reasonably sure that even in their first travels with Starbrow, when they had explored the daemonfey portals beneath Myth Glaurach, nothing more than friendship had passed between them.

"At least I am in good company," he muttered to himself. "I hope you find happiness with him, Ilsevele. You deserve it."

"I think you mean that, Araevin. And I thank you for it."

He sat in silence for a while, his hand in hers. It was not just the change brought upon him by the *telmiirkara neshyrr*. She was right. They had started to grow apart years ago. There was a moment only a few months ago when he brought Ilsevele to Faerûn for her first time, and the wonder of the wide lands in her eyes rekindled something of their old passion. But it seemed that had been little more than a glimpse of a memory.

"I should not have stayed in Reilloch all those years," he murmured.

"I do not believe that," she said. "You have done what you were intended to do, Araevin. You have become a high mage. And who can say what might have happened this year if you had not?"

He took a deep breath and looked into her eyes. She was beautiful in the moonlight, and his heart ached with a deep, hot hurt. But he could not say that she was wrong.

"You will always be dear to me," he said.

"And you to me," she answered. She leaned forward and brushed her lips against his. "I hope you can forgive me, Araevin."

He essayed a sad smile of his own. "I hope I can forgive myself," he managed.

Then they both stood, and found their way out into the warm night.

CHAPTER SEVENTEEN

22 Eleasias, the Year of Lightning Storms

Shortly before dawn, Araevin and his companions joined Seiveril by the forest manor. The Knights of the Golden Star surrounded them, along with the surviving Moon Knights and a chosen guard of bladesingers, spellarchers, and mages. Araevin felt keenly awake and alert despite the restlessness of his night. In Reverie his memory had insisted on wandering in places that he had shared with Ilsevele. Sometimes he envied the oblivion of human sleep. He knew that humans dreamed too, but they did not long remember their travels, did they?

With a few whispered commands, Seiveril and his captains led the gathered warriors into the dark of the morning. The great company moved through the forest in silence, broken only by the small rasp of steel and leather or the occasional footfall on the forest floor. From time to time Araevin glimpsed jagged shadows against the dark sky—the broken towers of Myth Drannor rising above the trees.

They came to a clearing in the forest, on the outskirts of the city itself. Araevin studied the spot, searching for the intangible presence of the mythal. After a moment, he nodded. "This will do," he said.

Seiveril held up his hand. The rustling around Araevin grew still as the elves and Dalesfolk who accompanied his small band stopped moving and melted into the shadows beneath the trees.

"Good luck, Araevin," he whispered.

Araevin narrowed his eyes, willing the unseen currents of magic to become visible to him. Slowly the majestic weaving of the city's mythal ghosted into view—a great edifice of tangible magic, golden and alive, crackling with unimaginable power. Sildëyuir and the Waymeet itself were the only things Araevin had seen that even began to compare. The mythal's field descended in a great curve from the sky over the center of the city and plunged into the ground not far from Araevin's feet like a vertical wall of swirling golden light . . . golden light that was shot through with venomous strands of reddish copper, interwoven through the living magic.

"Be ready to protect me," Araevin told his friends. "Sarya will sense me as soon as I begin, and I cannot believe that she will allow me to go about this without some opposition."

"Do what you must," Nesterin told Araevin. "We will guard you."

Araevin drew out the Gatekeeper's Crystal, and balanced the heavy stone in one hand, cupping his fingers around its points. The device glowed a brilliant violet-white, strengthened by the proximity of the mythal. He attuned his thoughts to the crystal in his hand, and he stepped into the shimmering light.

Sarya's defenses woke at once, lashing about him like whipcords of furious magic. But Araevin was ready for that. He shielded himself with the crystal, deflecting the daemonfey's spell traps. Then he carefully invoked the crystal's power. From his outstretched hand a shrieking column of violet-white energy shot into the mythal field, brushing aside the locks and wards that kept him from the mythal itself.

The city groaned in reply. A wild wind sprang up in the forest, roaring through the treetops, and the ground trembled under his feet. Araevin felt the strength of the crystal mounting higher, doubling and redoubling on itself, as the device sought to master Myth Drannor's ancient mythal. Tiny fissures of purple light began to appear in the conjoined crystal, and the shards vibrated in his hand.

"Araevin! The crystal!" Maresa shouted. "It'll shatter!"

"Not if I can help it!" he answered.

He threw his willpower at the crystal, reining it in, arresting the wild power of the device as it surged toward release. For a moment the contest hung in the balance, and Araevin feared that he had allowed the crystal to channel too much power into the mythal—but then he managed to mute it, smothering the device in his iron determination.

"Donnor, guard this!" he said, and handed the crystal quickly to the cleric. Donnor wrapped the incandescent crystal in a common blanket, and backed away.

Sarya's defenses lay shredded before him. Without her wards to keep him from excising her from the mythal, he was free to do as he wished. Araevin drew a deep breath and shouted out the words of the *mythaalniir darach,* the rite of mythal-shaping. Distantly, he realized that a sudden skirmish had erupted around him—devils and fey'ri attacked Seiveril's standard from all sides, emerging from the ruins to give battle. But he paid no attention to the furious fight growing around him, and plunged his percipience into the golden strands of the mythal.

One by one, he severed the sullen red strands that were twisted around the mythal's original work. As he had done in Myth Glaurach, he imposed a new set of governances to lock out Sarya. And he detected a subtle weaving of tarnished silver-black, an older grafting on the mythal.

The devils of Myth Drannor, he realized. This is the spell that holds them here.

With another sharp incision of willpower, he severed that one as well. The mythal itself was old and frail, but he could not do much about that. It might recover in time, or it might founder and fail. But at least no one else would be able to pervert it from its original intent, not without defeating Araevin's own locks first.

Suddenly exhausted, he slumped to his knees and let the mythal fade away from his sight. He realized that Donnor and Seiveril were close beside him, thumping his back in congratulations. "Sarya's spells are defeated!" the elflord shouted. "We can take the city!"

"Dozens of fiends just vanished, Araevin!" Donnor said. "Was that your doing?"

"I've sealed the mythal against Sarya," he said weakly. "Anything she summoned with its power has been dismissed. But be careful. I think there are a number of demons and devils in her service that aren't anchored to the mythal. You'll have to deal with them."

"We have learned a thing or two about that in the last couple of months," Seiveril answered him. He looked over to his guards and shouted, "Sound the attack! This day we retake Myth Drannor and destroy the daemonfey!"

Silver horns greeted the morning, and hundreds of elf voices shouted in reply. From somewhere in the woods to the east, harsher human trumpets echoed through the forest too, as the Sembians charged into the streets from the other side of the city. Seiveril squeezed Araevin's shoulder with his gauntleted hand, and led his warriors into the ruins of the city.

Araevin found his feet again as the Crusade swept past him, storming Myth Drannor. He took a deep breath, feeling his strength beginning to come back to him.

"Now we need to find a portal," he said to his friends. "We have to deal with the Waymeet."

❂ ❂ ❂ ❂ ❂

Fflar ran into Myth Drannor, Keryvian aflame in his hand. In one small part of his mind he wondered at the irony that had brought him to this moment. Other than skulking about the outskirts of the city with Araevin and Ilsevele a little more than a month ago, the last time he had set foot within the familiar streets had been almost seven hundred years ago. Then he had been fighting to defend it against a horde of savage humanoids. But now he led an attack to retake the city from the demonspawned villains who had made it their stronghold.

The Crusade swept into the city ruins, rushing past the empty stone skeletons of elven palaces and towers. Seiveril led the warriors of Evermeet deeper into the city, striking for the old towers of Castle Cormanthor.

"To victory!" the elflord cried, and he dashed across the rubble-strewn courts.

"What does he think he's doing?" Fflar muttered to himself, and he ran after Seiveril.

A company of fey'ri appeared before them, snarling defiance. The daemonfey warriors unleashed a barrage of deadly spells and fuming fire, hurling every sorcery at their command against the elves. Sinister voices snarled out the words of dark spells, fire roared and hissed in lethal waves across the street, and the very cobblestones charred and splintered with earsplitting reports.

It seems Araevin didn't unbind all of Sarya's demons, Fflar observed grimly. Some at least she must have summoned without the mythal's aid.

He threw himself flat on the hard ground, ducking under

a sizzling bolt of green acid that tore through the ranks around him. When he scrambled back to his feet, he found a vrock demon stooping on him, croaking in its harsh voice. Fflar blocked its filthy talons with a quick parry, passed its claws above his head as he spun beneath the monster, and finished by opening it from groin to breastbone with a leaping slash. The creature collapsed in a spray of foul black blood and gray feathers.

"Seiveril!" he called. "Where are you?"

He turned, looking for a new opponent. Elf knights, archers, and mages battled daemonfey swordsmen and sorcerers in a furious melee that stretched across the square . . . but the army of Evermeet was gaining the upper hand, and quickly. He spied Seiveril dueling a tall fey'ri general with curling black horns, plying mace and spell against the daemonfey's skilled swordplay. The swordsman fought with cold fury, stabbing again and again at the elflord, but Seiveril parried each stroke with his mace until he found a chance to step back and speak a spell. A blinding white flash seared the battlefield, leaving the swordsman reeling—and Seiveril stepped forward and broke his neck with one swift swing of his silver mace.

"Well struck," Fflar cried. He hurried to Seiveril's side. "Now stop fighting and start leading! You are in command here!"

Seiveril flashed an easy smile at Fflar. "I think we have them!" he shouted back. "On to Castle Cormanthor! That is where Sarya will be hiding!"

Fflar took his bearings with a quick glance and pointed toward the right. "Down that avenue, then. It's only a couple of hundred yards away."

"Warriors of Evermeet, follow me!" Seiveril shouted.

He shifted his grip on his mace and led the Knights of the Golden Star and his guards along the street. All around them, elves skirmished with fey'ri and monsters. Storms of arrows brought down anything that tried to take to the skies, and spells flashed and thundered on every side. They came to the broad plaza in front of the castle, where more of the fey'ri waited, and another furious skirmish erupted.

Fflar found himself beset by a fey'ri bladesinger who leaped down into the fray from the battlements overhead. Keryvian gleamed like white fire in the morning light, leaping to deflect the spells and sword-thrusts the bladesinger threw at him. She was quick and graceful, her ruby face set in a small smile of concentration as she flowed through the bladesinger's trance. Fflar finally managed a two-handed stroke in response. His opponent threw up her own blade to block the strike—but he was stronger than she was, and he beat through her guard and broke her sword against her upper arm, gashing her deeply. She drew in a sharp hiss of pain and staggered back, only to be lost as the battle swept her away.

The roar of angry voices and shrill ringing of steel on steel filled the air. He took a moment to smother the smoking acid-drops still clinging to his armor with his leather gauntlet, and looked around to find Seiveril.

The elflord fought on the steps of the castle's front gate. He raised his hand above his head and loosed a towering ring of holy white fire against the demons and fey'ri nearby, scattering half a dozen foes like ninepins. Then a hulking daemonfey, the four-armed monster Xhalph, appeared behind Seiveril in a burst of fuming yellow smoke.

"Seiveril! Behind you!" Fflar shouted.

Seiveril started to turn—but a hezrou demon a short distance in front of him caught his eye, and he began a spell of dismissal against it. Xhalph took one step forward and plunged three of his swords into Seiveril's back, grinning with bloodlust. Seiveril let out a cry and fell to his knees. The daemonfey prince wrenched his swords out of Seiveril's back with a great spray of bright red blood, and flung the broken elflord headlong down the steps of the castle.

"Seiveril!" Fflar cried. With no thought for the enemies around him, he hurled himself toward the castle.

Xhalph leaped down beside Seiveril with an easy bound.

He raised his swords to butcher the elflord, but Fflar roared out a wordless challenge. Keryvian flashed in white wrath, sensing the blinding fury in his heart.

Xhalph looked up and grinned, his mouth full of small fangs. "You wish to be next, hero?" he hissed. "I have not forgotten our duel of a month ago. We have unfinished business, you and I."

"You will not live out the day, murderer!" Fflar cried.

Xhalph readied his swords, preparing to receive Fflar's attack. Then a blazing white arrow streaked into the daemonfey's breastplate, taking him high on his left chest. The blow spun him half-around, but his armor took the worst of the impact. Xhalph roared once and reached up to snap off the shaft. Another arrow hissed toward him, and he threw up one of his swords in its path and batted it aside.

Fflar glanced to his side. Ilsevele knelt by her father, drawing her bow again.

"Xhalph, come!" Sarya Dlardrageth appeared in the empty doorway of the castle, dressed in her armor of black and gold. Ilsevele shifted her aim and loosed an arrow at her, but the daemonfey queen deflected it with a word and a gesture.

"Another time," Xhalph growled. The wounded daemonfey spared one fang-filled snarl for Fflar, and leaped back up the stairs and disappeared into the castle proper.

Fflar started after them, but Ilsevele's voice stopped him. "Starbrow!" she wailed. She cradled Seiveril in her arms, his blood streaming down the marble steps.

With one more glance after the fleeing daemonfey, Fflar turned back to Seiveril and hurried to his side. He stumbled to his knees beside the elflord. "Seiveril," he murmured.

Seiveril's face was pale, and blood flecked his lips. He breathed in shallow gasps. "Starbrow . . . my friend . . . I had hoped to walk with you in Cormanthor . . . when all this was at an end."

Final Gate • 305

"You will, Father. You will," Ilsevele promised through her tears. "We will summon a healer. Stay with us just a little longer!"

"I am afraid . . . that it is too late for that, Ilsevele. It is time . . . to walk in Arvandor instead . . ."

Fflar's eyes blurred with tears. He had seen too many warriors fall on too many battlefields to argue with Seiveril. "Ilyyela is waiting for you there, my friend." He reached down and found Seiveril's hand, and gripped it tightly. "There is nothing to fear. I know it."

The dying elf found a smile. "I saw Myth Drannor before I died . . . I am content. Ilsevele . . . you must finish what I have started here. Starbrow . . . live the life you have been called back to. You have surpassed any failures . . . you carry in your heart." He reached out and set Ilsevele's hand in Fflar's, and breathed one last time. " . . . Love . . ." he whispered, and his eyes closed forever.

"Father," Ilsevele murmured. She lowered him to the palace steps and sobbed over his chest. "Father!"

Fflar simply bowed his head. No words came to him. He clasped Ilsevele's hand in his and knelt in silence by Seiveril's torn body. He knew he was soon to leave this world, Fflar thought. He knew, and he set out to right the wrongs he could before he was called home.

"Rest, my friend," he finally whispered.

Ilsevele looked up at him, ignoring the tears that streaked her face. "Starbrow, the daemonfey," she said. "They fled into the palace. Sarya must have another portal inside."

"It would not surprise me," Fflar grated. He picked up Keryvian and climbed to his feet. The broken gates of the castle waited for him. "We cannot let them escape again, Ilsevele."

"Go, Starbrow!" she said. "I will finish the fight here." She stood, bow in hand, and raised it above her head. "To me, warriors of Evermeet! To me!"

Sehanine, watch over her, Fflar silently prayed. He

looked around and saw Jerreda Starcloak and two of her wood elves, who stood gazing at Seiveril with horror.

"Jerreda, follow me!" he said, and he turned and leaped up the stairs.

The wood elves tore their eyes away from the fallen leader of the Crusade and bounded after him. Together they dashed into Castle Cormanthor, blades bared.

Fflar could hear the sounds of battle echoing throughout the castle. He followed the first hallway he came to for thirty paces or so, and it opened out into a small chapel or shrine. The old symbols of the Seldarine had been removed, but a blank alcove behind the altar still shimmered with a thin gray mist.

"As I thought," he said. "It's a portal."

Jerreda recognized it too. "What do we do?" the wood elf princess said. "The daemonfey might have gone anywhere."

Fflar hesitated only a moment before deciding. "After them," he growled. Then he ran up and hurled himself through the gray mists.

✦ ✦ ✦ ✦ ✦

It did not take Araevin long at all to find a portal in Myth Drannor. The city was riddled with them. A brief search and a quick spell of portal mastery allowed him to locate a suitable gate and shift its destination to the *Fhoeldin durr*.

They emerged in a blind alley of the Waymeet, surrounded by a thin, acrid yellow fog. Riveted iron plate inscribed with red-glowing runes covered the walls and pillars around them. Lurid firelight reflecting from the low-hanging clouds that roofed the Waymeet illuminated the place, striking angry gleams from the scorched glass spars and columns that still survived.

"By Tymora, they've ruined the place," Jorin said. "Malkizid's devils have made it into some kind of infernal machine."

"Araevin, what is the purpose of all this? What is Malkizid trying to do here?" Nesterin asked.

"I am not sure," Araevin breathed.

He frowned at the sharp smell of hot metal in his nostrils and made himself study the evil runes driven into the ancient glass walls. Hellish sorcery pooled and churned slowly through the metal conduits, pinning the ancient elven mythal spells open in the same way that a vivisectioned animal might be opened for inspection. What more could the archdevil want with the device? Didn't he possess sufficient knowledge of mythalcraft to do what he wanted with the *Fhoeldin durr?*

Unless . . . Araevin peered closer, studying the mythal weave before him, and it came to him. The ancient weave of the *Fhoeldin durr* was spun by the Vyshaanti of Aryvandaar . . . and they had woven their mythal in such a way that it could not be changed from its purpose except by another scion of House Vyshaan. Malkizid, for all his lore and skill, was not a sun elf of House Vyshaan, and so he could not exert his mastery over the Last Mythal of Aryvandaar without first devising a means of overpowering those ancient restrictions. The iron runes were Malkizid's own mythal, a mythal the archdevil was building for the purpose of destroying the ancient concordance governing the *Fhoeldin durr* and replacing it with rules more to his own liking.

"It's a battering ram to break down the Waymeet's defenses," he told Jorin. "Malkizid is building a mythal of his own that will take over the governing of the Waymeet."

"How much time do we have?" Donnor asked.

"None," Araevin said grimly. "Malkizid's spell is complete. I can't excise his influence with the Gatekeeper's Crystal."

"So all this was for nothing?" Maresa shook her head and muttered a savage oath as she turned her back on the rest of the company and kicked at the iron bands on the wall. "What was the point?" she demanded.

Araevin looked again at the corrupted mythal around

him. Then he withdrew the Gatekeeper's Crystal from under his cloak and looked at the three-pointed star. Its substance had taken on a sullen reddish hue, but power still coursed through it. *The crystal still draws on the Waymeet for its power,* he thought. *Maybe* . . . "The crystal no longer commands the Waymeet, but it still channels the power of this place," he said to Maresa. "We must use the crystal to destroy the *Fhoeldin durr*."

"Like the way the Dlardrageths destroyed the wards over the Nameless Dungeon?"

"Yes. I think it's the only way."

The genasi gave him a skeptical look. Then she shook her long silver-white hair out of her face with a toss of her head. "I saw what the crystal did to that hillside in the High Forest," she said. "Is that what you're going to do here?"

"First we must find the center of the Waymeet," Araevin said.

Maresa and Nesterin led the way as they set out along a curving corridor that spiraled in toward the middle of the place. The foul smoke hanging in the air of the place burned the eyes and seared the nose, and it limited visibility to a few dozen feet. Araevin quickly realized that the smoke kept them from navigating toward the Waymeet's center, but at least it also served to help conceal them from any of Malkizid's servants unless they actually blundered into their enemies.

They came to an intersection, and Araevin studied their surroundings for a moment before pointing to the right. The genasi and the star elf started down the new passageway, stealing forward as quietly as they could.

Harsh voices croaked in the mist behind the company.

Araevin whirled just in time to see three mezzoloths emerge from the acidic fog just behind them, following the intersecting avenue. The bulky insectile creatures did not hesitate for an instant; the moment they caught sight of Araevin and his friends, they threw themselves at the travelers, clacking and chattering to each other.

Jorin shot one in the center of its chitin-covered torso, but the monster shrugged off the arrow and kept coming. The ranger stepped back, continuing to shoot as fast as he could bring arrows to the string. Green-feathered shafts peppered the fiends, but then the ranger had to drop his bow with a sharp curse and sweep out his swords, for the mezzoloths were on him. Araevin drew a wand from his belt and looked for a chance to strike back at the monsters, but Donnor threw out an arm.

"Go on!" Donnor growled. "Perform the rite! Jorin and I will hold them!"

The mage started to argue, but he could hear more fiends hurrying to the fray. If he allowed himself to be drawn into a skirmish, he might not get a chance to strike the blow that truly counted.

"Follow us as soon as you can," he said to Donnor, and he hurried back to Maresa and Nesterin. "Come on, we must do what we came to do."

Behind him, the Lathanderite turned to face the oncoming mezzoloths, with the Yuir ranger at his shoulder. He shouted a holy prayer to his deity and banished one of the monsters back to its own plane, sending it shrieking back to the hells in a shroud of golden fire. Then Araevin pulled himself away and ran on into the Waymeet, Maresa and Nesterin a step behind him. Angry roars and hisses filled the mist behind them.

The foundations of the walls and columns grew thicker as the three of them came into the center of the Waymeet. Here the fence of titanic crystal spears that formed the heart of the mythal reached hundreds of feet overhead, and not even the elves of ancient Aryvandaar could build such things without a sturdy footing. The bitter yellow mists cleared a little, affording them a good view of the cathedral-like space in the heart of the Waymeet. Bold spurs of glass crossed and crossed again overhead, creating a ceiling of sorts far above. Smaller ribs of crystal linked the great columns; the place was a spiderweb of glass.

Beneath a spiraling dome in the center of the structure stood another speaking stone, a column easily thirty feet tall, but like the lesser speaking stone Araevin had seen on the outskirts of the Waymeet, the master stone was also encircled by iron runes. Thick bands of black metal pressed Malkizid's hellforged spells deep into the crystalline flesh of the living mythal.

"This must anchor the mythal," Nesterin breathed. "What a magnificent work this Waymeet must have been!"

"Admire it later," Maresa said. She looked to Araevin. "So how do we do this?"

"Here, take this." Araevin brought out the Gatekeeper's Crystal and quickly disjoined it, separating it into its original three shards. He handed one piece to Maresa, and another to Nesterin. "We need to spread out and create three points of a triangle with the shards—the wider, the better. At the very least, we should surround the master stone there. When you are in position I will invoke the crystal's power and unbind the magic in this place."

"What happens to us when you do that?" Maresa asked.

"If the Seldarine smile on us, the damage will be contained within the shards' borders. You must be careful to stand outside the triangle, not inside."

The genasi nodded once. "I'm off, then," she said, and she sprinted across the open plaza, running past the chained speaking stone. Nesterin observed her course for a moment, then hurried off at a right angle, seeking to separate himself as widely as possible from both Maresa and Araevin.

A winged shape dropped down out of the tangle of poisoned crystal overhead, diving down toward the star elf. "Nesterin, above you!" Araevin cried.

Nesterin looked up, and threw himself to one side as the monster above him slammed into the ground where he had been standing. Stone split with piercing reports, reverberating through the Waymeet's chancel. The monster, a powerful green-scaled nycaloth, cast its baleful red eyes on Araevin.

"You spoiled my pounce, elf," it hissed. "You will pay for that when I finish with your friend."

It turned to spring after Nesterin, who rolled away and came to his feet with his sword in hand. Araevin blasted at it with a bolt of lightning, charring a broad black scorch across its shoulders. The monster roared and kept after the star elf. Nesterin lunged forward and stabbed it twice in its thickly muscled torso, but the nycaloth shrugged off the blows. It beat its wings once and leaped up to fix the talons of its feet in Nesterin's shoulders, and dragged him up off the ground.

"Let go of me!" Nesterin snarled. His sword dropped to the ground and bounced with a shrill ringing sound, and he struggled in the monster's grasp.

"Nesterin!" Araevin started another spell, but halted in mid-word. Any magic he hurled might strike his friend as well as the nycaloth. He settled for a simple magical attack that hammered small darts of arcane power into the nycaloth's chest, eliciting another roar from the beast. It rose higher, trying to get out of his range. Then Nesterin threw back his head and sang out a potent warding spell against evil. The nycaloth hissed and recoiled, driven away by the abjuration—and Nesterin fell twenty feet or more to the hard stone floor of the Waymeet's chancel. He landed badly and sprawled to the ground, grimacing in agony.

Araevin started toward him, but Nesterin waved him back. Blood seeped from his wounded shoulders, and his left leg turned at a bad angle.

"I can hold the shard right here," the star elf said. "Speak the rite, Araevin!"

Maresa appeared on the far side of the chancel, holding her shard of the crystal. "Is this good?" she called.

He glanced at the genasi, and back to Nesterin, and quickly backed ten steps, trying to position himself correctly. He raised his shard, and looked into it, seeking the combination of willpower and knowledge to trigger its power.

Icy needles scythed into him from behind, piercing his flesh like hateful icicles. Cold so intense that his nerves shrieked as if on fire stabbed into him at shoulder, neck, arm, and back. Araevin screamed once and staggered away, dropping the Gatekeeper's Crystal from hands suddenly too numb to hold it.

"You feckless fool! You would destroy a work twelve thousand years old? You are little more than a vandal!" Malkizid strode into the Waymeet's heart, emerging from the mist-wreathed pillars behind Araevin. His taloned hands clenched in anger, and the glass walls of the place shivered at the anger in his melodious voice. "I have worked for this day too long to allow you to ruin it, ungrateful whelp!"

Araevin groveled in agony, plucking at the icicles that transfixed him. Across the chancel, Nesterin pushed himself to his feet and pointed his own shard at Malkizid—but the archdevil made one sharp gesture of his hand and sent the star elf hurling into the glass walls behind him. Nesterin hit heavily and slumped to the ground, stunned. Across the chamber, Maresa took one look at Malkizid and leaped for cover, disappearing into the ribbed columns on the far side of the room. Malkizid snorted in amusement as she ducked out of sight.

"Where does the half-breed think she can hide from me?" he rumbled aloud. "I control all the doors in this place now."

Get up! Araevin exhorted himself. *I have to do something!*

Cold wracked his body, pinning him to the ground. He reached behind his back and drew the icicle out of his shoulder with a hiss of pain. Its tip was stained red. Then he felt for the one in the back of his neck. Warm blood ran down his collar, but only a trickle. The frozen dart had found muscle, not the great arteries or the windpipe. The searing numbness in his throat diminished, and he found he could speak again.

"Not yet," he rasped.

He stretched out his hand toward Malkizid and spat out the words of his iridescent ray spell. Blazing beams of emerald green and sickly violet washed past Malkizid, and the fiery orange beam grazed one wing. The archdevil's feathered wing smoked as the amber-red flames seared him.

Malkizid twisted away from the brilliant stabbing rays, sheltering behind his wings until the flames died away. He straightened up and bared his teeth at Araevin. "You have ceased to amuse me, Araevin Teshurr," he snarled. Araevin tried to strike again with another spell, but Malkizid proved faster. The archdevil intoned terrible words, and with one taloned hand inscribed an intricate set of arcane passes in the very air.

A shell of golden force surrounded Araevin before he could roll away. In the blink of an eye it began to tighten around him, folding him into an awkward ball and constricting. He lost the spell he was trying to speak, and fought for breath. He threw out his arms and pushed back, trying to keep from being crushed, but the relentless orb compressed tighter with his struggles.

"That is better," Malkizid said in his beautiful voice. "I shall enjoy watching you die, mage." Then something struck him just under the collarbone. The Branded King roared and stepped back, and Araevin glimpsed a crossbow quarrel quivering in the archdevil's flesh. Malkizid yanked it out—only the very tip of the bolt had managed to pierce his flesh—and threw it aside. He glared into the maze of iron-bound glass columns. "You shall die slowly for that, impudent whelp!" he called into the maze of the Waymeet.

For once, Maresa had the sense to keep her mouth shut. She did not answer, prudently remaining hidden. But behind the archdevil, Nesterin stirred slowly. Still trying to resist the crushing weight of the sphere around him, Araevin's eye fell on the shard next to the star elf. The ghost of an idea flickered through his mind.

Fighting to clear his mind of pain, he muttered the words of a simple message spell and whispered to the Sildëyuiren lord. "Nesterin! Take up your shard, and summon the Gatekeeper. The crystal may still commune with the mythal."

Nesterin looked up at Araevin, caught in the floating sphere, and nodded. He fumbled for his shard, and concentrated on the great master stone in the heart of the Waymeet. The shard began to glow in his hands, and a few stray gleams of light leaked out from beneath the iron bands encircling the great speaking stone.

Malkizid whirled to glare at Nesterin, and strode angrily toward the wounded elf. His second step stuck abruptly, throwing him off balance. From the stone floor of the Waymeet, a spear of crystal had suddenly condensed around his foot, arresting his movement.

"What is this?" the archdevil snarled. He looked down at the luminescent crystal encasing his ankles, and pure black fury twisted his face.

Flaring his powerful wings wide, he tried to wrench himself out of the solidifying crystal. The glassy stuff cracked and split, but more filaments condensed around him, clinging to his form like gossamer webs.

"Stop this, Gatekeeper!" he demanded. "I command you!"

"You are not my maker, Malkizid." The Gatekeeper's voice was a weak whisper that echoed among the columns of soaring glass. "I still have some small power to resist your demands."

"I will teach you obedience, then!" Giving up on efforts to wrench himself clear of the mythal's snowy threads, Malkizid abruptly vanished, teleporting away . . . but blue lightning flickered across the highest spires of the Waymeet, and the archdevil instantly reappeared in the same place. The Branded King roared in anger, and drew his black sword to slash at the filaments settling around him.

The ruined speaking stone quivered once, and the Gatekeeper whispered to Araevin, "I cannot hold him for long, Araevin Teshurr. I beg you to release me from this durance."

Final Gate • 315

Araevin struggled for each breath as the golden sphere crushed ever tighter. Malkizid finally wrenched himself clear of the Gatekeeper's crystal webs. He slashed his black sword in a fierce arc, gouging the glass pillars around him. "Insolent device!" he growled.

The force-sphere spun slowly and tightened more. Dark spots gathered in Araevin's sight, and needles of icy agony transfixed him. There was no more time. He had to chance everything on one desperate throw.

He stopped fighting the sphere and let it pin his arms to his torso.

The sphere squeezed in, eagerly pressing closer, but he'd bought himself an instant for a single spell. Awash in pain, desperately short of breath, still he found the concentration to wheeze the words for a minor teleportation. In the blink of an eye he huddled ten yards away, free of the crushing sphere. The shard he had dropped lay on the ground before him, and he snatched it up. From his new vantage he glimpsed Maresa crouched in an interstice of the soaring spars a hundred feet away, laying another quarrel into her crossbow. Scarlet blood streaked the side of her head, but the genasi still had her shard. She looked at him and bared her teeth in defiance.

The archdevil realized that Araevin had moved, and he wheeled in a quick circle, searching for the mage. But Malkizid, along with the master stone, stood between Nesterin, Maresa, and Araevin.

"Now," Araevin said.

He staggered to his feet and raised the shard of the crystal above his head, and in one swift instant of will and decision he triggered the ancient weapon's most fearsome power. Beams of brilliant violet fire shot out from the crystal in his hands, seeking the other two shards. A lopsided triangle of unbearable brightness burned between the points anchored by Araevin and his friends.

"No!" shouted Malkizid, and he leaped into the air, climbing toward safety—too late.

Everything inside the triangle defined by the shards of the crystal vanished in a furious blast of incandescent light. The Waymeet shrieked in protest, and shattered glass scoured the place like a rain of razors. Dozens of tiny slivers drove into Araevin's flesh before the concussion picked him up and threw him headlong into the wall behind him.

In the heart of the brilliance, the speaking stone burst apart in a fountain of blue-white power, uncapped and wild. The infernal iron bands restraining it charred into black ash and vanished. Malkizid himself staggered in the air, and wrapped his wings around his body to protect himself. Shredded by flying glass and seared by the supernal light, still the archdevil was not destroyed. He raised his head and looked on Araevin with pure hate, blood pouring from his brand.

"I will flense your soul for that!" he shrieked.

Then the terrible brilliance filling the triangle guttered out and vanished, drawn back into the uncapped speaking stone in the center. A wind of dust and glass howled into the glowing triangle as the unimaginable power of the *Fhoeldin durr* collapsed in on itself and drained out into nothingness. Malkizid was picked up and dragged into the vanishing stream of blue fire, then expelled screaming into the void.

One more bone-shaking detonation rocked the Waymeet, and the raving brilliance and thunder died away. A great three-sided patch of the ancient glass cathedral was dull, gray, and lifeless, absolutely devoid of power. Araevin groaned and let his head drop to his chest.

The Gatekeeper had been extinguished. It was only a matter of time until the Last Mythal of Aryvandaar died.

CHAPTER EIGHTEEN

22 Eleasias, the Year of Lightning Storms

Sarya Dlardrageth curled her hands into fists so tight that her talons drew blood from her palms, and screamed defiance at the metal and glass around her.

"I will not stand for this!" she shrieked. "I am the rightful Queen of Cormanthor! My House has waited five thousand years to claim what was stolen from us. We will return and drive our enemies from Myth Drannor. I swear it!"

Her eye fell on a dull gray column of crystal nearby, and with hardly a conscious thought she barked the words of a violent spell and smashed it to splinters of glass with a spear of purple force. The iron cladding that had covered the thing fell to the stone floor, and she seized the heavy plating with a telekinesis spell and hurled it headlong into another flickering portal, shattering its lintel into a spray of diamond dust.

"I will drink their hearts' blood for my wine before I am through with the lot of them!"

"And you will, Lady Sarya," the spymaster Vesryn Aelorothi said smoothly. He bobbed his head up and down like the vulture he so resembled. "But your just vengeance must wait for a little while. You must see to your survival first. You cannot exact satisfaction from the palebloods if you are caught now."

Sarya wheeled on the presumptuous fey'ri with murder in her eye. Briefly, she considered killing him for his insolence. "No one tells me what to do," she hissed. "No one!"

Vesryn bobbed his head again, and steepled his fingers in front of narrow chest. "Of course, Lady Sarya. Forgive me, I beg you, but we must not linger here."

There is little point in killing him, she decided. She could not spare the obsequious Vesryn, not when all that was left of her kingdom were Xhalph, Vesryn Aelorothi, three warriors, and two vrock demons. Mardeiym Reithel, her faithful general, was dead. Teryani Ealoeth had simply vanished, likely using her shapechanging talents to slink away. The daemonfey queen turned away and folded her wings, her back to the pitiful stragglers, and fought to master the blinding rage that surged and roiled within her dark heart.

Betrayed! she fumed. Malkizid promised that the spells he could teach her would make Myth Drannor unassailable. Yet the cursed palebloods had found away to destroy her reweaving of the ancient wards anyway. She was throneless again.

"Which way from here, Mother?" Xhalph rumbled. "Vesryn is right. We must decide swiftly. This place is disintegrating around us."

"I can see that!" Sarya snapped.

She studied the Waymeet's maze of portals and corridors with a fearsome scowl. She knew several doors that might lead to useful destinations, but something had happened to the ancient mythal only moments after she and her small entourage had emerged from the door leading back to Myth Drannor. All around her, portals were growing unstable. Some remained open continuously, others surged and closed unpredictably, and still more were guttering out into dull gray uselessness. Malkizid's work? she wondered. Or the work of the palebloods?

"We need a place where our enemies will not follow," she said aloud, "a place where we can rebuild our strength in secret. We must hide for now, and in time we will embark on a new campaign against the usurpers of our birthright—a campaign of stealth, subterfuge, and deceit. The next time we move against the palebloods, we will do so in secret. For now, we must survive." If skulking and hiding was all that she could do, then she would do it as well as she could.

"What of the refuge beneath Lothen?" Xhalph said. "Our enemies do not know of it."

"It strikes me as dangerously close to the wood elves of the High Forest, Lord Xhalph," Vesryn Aelorothi offered. "The palebloods will certainly use divination magic to sniff us out. It might be better to hide somewhere far away."

Xhalph did not often stand for correction from one of their lessers, but in this case he did not rebuke the vulturelike fey'ri spymaster. Even he had realized that sheer fury and bloodlust might not be the way to victory any longer. "The Abyss? I doubt the palebloods would follow us there."

Sarya shook her head. "I will not go to the Abyss in defeat. I have no wish to beg protection from a demon lord." There were some who might offer her refuge, but she would not allow herself to be made into a vassal again. She thought about it for a moment more and made her decision. "We will seek out a portal to some remote part of Faerûn . . . Chult, perhaps, or maybe the lands beyond the Unapproachable East. Come; we will find a speaking stone and make the Gatekeeper show us a suitable portal." And if they happened to encounter Malkizid, why, she might demand an accounting from the archdevil.

She unfurled her wings and leaped into the air, soaring easily over the mazelike arrangement of corridors and walls that made up the Waymeet. She spied the cluster of higher towers and spars that marked the center of the device, and banked in that direction. Below her, she spied several dead mezzoloths, sprawled out in one of the main boulevards of the place. What is going on in this place? she wondered. Is Malkizid at war with some other infernal power?

"There has been fighting here," Xhalph said. "Those yugoloths have not been dead long."

The actinic flash of a lightning-spell close by threw a harsh white glare across the Waymeet's towers and columns, followed an instant later by a sharp crack of thunder. Apparently, the fighting was not yet over. Sarya would have ignored it and continued on her way, but as it happened, her chosen course was leading her toward the place where the lightning had flashed.

"It's the master speaking stone," she hissed.

"Allow me, Lady Sarya," one of the fey'ri warriors said. "I will spy it out and see who is there."

"Very well," she agreed. "Be swift, and do not allow yourself to be seen."

The warrior murmured a spell to cloak himself in invisibility and hurried off toward the center of the complex. Sarya alighted on a high spar to await his report. The Waymeet rumbled with a deep, ominous groan, and not far off one of the high spires lost its footing and toppled over slowly, crashing to the ground with the shriek of twisting iron and the shrill sound of shattering glass. More portals flickered and went dark.

"I do not think we will be able to return to this place once we depart," Vesryn said quietly.

"It suits me for now," Sarya replied. "Presently, no one will be able to follow us through this place. That may turn to our advantage."

Final Gate • 321

She heard the beat of unseen wings, and her warrior returned. He allowed his invisibility to fade. "It is the paleblood mage, Lady Sarya," he reported.

"Araevin Teshurr?"

"Yes. He has several companions with him—a human, a half-breed, an elf of a kindred I do not recognize, and some other planetouched woman. They are in the square of the master speaking stone, as you said. They just drove off a small number of yugoloths and baatezu."

"The mage must have damaged the Waymeet," Sarya breathed. Malkizid had told her that he had gotten his hands on a shard of the Gatekeeper's Crystal. Was that sufficient to explain the destruction of the mythal around her? Or, for that matter, was that how the palebloods had dealt with her defenses at Myth Drannor?

"There is something more, my queen," the warrior said. "The mage, the strange elf, and the half-breed all are wounded. The strange elf and the half-breed can't walk without help. They are heading that way"—he pointed, indicating a course at right angles to Sarya's—"making for a portal."

Sarya glanced at her small company. She had eight who could fight, including the vrocks. Araevin had half as many, and two of them were hurt. She might not be able to undo what he had done to her mythal's defenses at Myth Drannor, but she could make sure that he paid for the trouble he had caused her.

"Then it seems we have one more enemy to deal with before we abandon this place," she said. "Lead the way, my warrior. Araevin Teshurr is mine."

❦ ❦ ❦ ❦ ❦

The battle for Myth Drannor had broken down into a hundred fierce skirmishes. Bands of elves, Dalesfolk, and Sembians hunted the streets, searching out the surviving fey'ri and infernal monsters summoned by Sarya

Dlardrageth. Many of those had vanished with the Araevin's reduction of the mythal, but some still remained, creatures that had been brought to Faerûn through means other than the mythal. Ilsevele did not intend to allow any of those to escape, if she could help it.

At noon she found a few moments of quiet and allowed herself to grieve for her father. He knew it was going to happen, she reflected. He understood the designs of the Seldarine, and he did not shy from the part he was given. The only thing that kept her heart from breaking was the thought that her father did not regret the time of his death . . . and he was once again with Ilyyela, whom he had loved for three hundred years. How could she begrudge him that reunion?

A rustle of armor brought her back to the streets of Myth Drannor. She looked up as Vesilde Gaerth, the slightly built warrior who led the Knights of the Golden Star, leaned against the ivy-covered wall beside her.

"You do not need to go on today," he said softly. "Stay by your father, Ilsevele. We can finish this for you and allow you to grieve."

"I know," she said. "But I feel that I must finish Father's work here, Vesilde. I will grieve for him later."

"Have you given thought to what follows this victory?" the elf knight asked.

"You have been my father's second throughout this war, Vesilde. It is up to you. You command the Crusade."

"I may have been Seiveril's second, Ilsevele, but I am not his heir. You are House Miritar now." Vesilde knelt beside her and took her hands in his. "This war ends today. The Crusade has accomplished its purpose; the daemonfey are broken. What will tomorrow bring?"

"We must make sure that Sarya Dlardrageth and any fey'ri who escaped are found and dealt with."

"You misunderstand me. After today, I trust we will deal with the daemonfey." The slight sun elf shook his hair out of his eyes. "I was speaking of what follows our victory over the daemonfey. Your father had a vision of what might take root here, Ilsevele. To him, this was not just a Crusade against the Dlardrageths. This was the Return, a homecoming to the ancient lands of our people. With his death, will that vision still come to be?"

She frowned, studying the lush green forests that had grown over the city. The day was growing warm, warmer than it would ever be on a summer day in Evermeet, even though the season was fading toward fall.

"I think I will stay for a time," she finally said. "If nothing else, I want to be certain that no enemies arise in our ancient lands again. I suppose there will be others who feel the same."

"But I do not, Ilsevele. Evermeet is my home. I followed your father here out of my love for him, and my desire to see justice done for the murders at Tower Reilloch." Vesilde frowned, searching her face. "I suppose what I am trying to say is this: If you believe in your father's Return, you must take up his banner. You must look after those of our People who hope to make Cormanthor their home again, you must treat with the human of these lands, and you must make sure that our foes are defeated and driven out of Cormanthor. That is what your father asked of you when he asked you to finish what he had started."

She stared at the knight-commander in horror. "I don't even know where to begin with that, Vesilde. Even if I did, would anyone follow me? My father was the one who stirred the hearts of thousands with his words and his courage."

"And those words need a new voice now, Ilsevele. I can think of none better than yours." Vesilde straightened up and offered his hand to her. "As far as how to begin, well, we have unfinished work here today, as you have said. Perhaps you should begin with that."

Ilsevele took his hand, and stood up. She did not know if she could lead the Crusade . . . but she did know that her father's dream, his words, had stirred her heart too. If she was the best hope for that dream to continue, then she would honor him by making sure it was not forgotten.

"We need to speak with Selkirk and the Sembians," she said, thinking out loud. "He needs to know of my father's death, and we must determine the best way to finish off the daemonfey."

Vesilde nodded. "I will have him summoned at once, Lady Miritar."

"Thank you, Vesilde," she said. She turned away from him and wrapped her arms around herself. She had much to think about.

Selkirk and his personal guard arrived soon. Dressed in his resplendent half-plate of black and gold, Selkirk carried a double-bitted battle-axe in his steel gauntlets. "Ilsevele!" he called. He strode up to Ilsevele and doffed his helmet. His face was streaked with sweat and dust. "I just heard about your father. I am truly sorry for your loss. He was a remarkable man."

"Thank you, Lord Selkirk. I know that he thought well of you, too." Ilsevele brushed her hand across her eyes, unashamed of the tears that gathered there. She would mourn her father properly, in time, but today she meant to finish the work he had started. That was the best way to honor him, and to give meaning to his death.

"Where did it happen?" Selkirk asked, his voice soft.

"The steps of Castle Cormanthor, not far from here. He was struck down by Xhalph Dlardrageth, the daemonfey prince." Ilsevele's voice shook, but she continued. "He lies in the Castle's main hall now, with Felael and the rest of his guards keeping watch over him."

"And the daemonfey?"

"Xhalph and Sarya fled. Starbrow and Jerreda pursued them." A bleak tide of fear for the warrior who had won her heart threatened to overcome Ilsevele. She bit her lip, determined to see the rest of the day through before giving into grief and dread. *He will return*, she told herself. *No one else she had ever seen matched his skill, and he had* not gone after the daemonfey alone. It was foolish to let fear of what might happen to paralyze her. "Our scouts believe they went through a portal in the castle. When I am sure that we have matters in hand here, I will follow him."

"Of course," Selkirk said. He looked at the old ruins around them. A tall shadowtop grew right in the center of what must have once been the common room of an inn, spearing through the long-vanished roof to spread its branches more than a hundred feet overhead. It was a pleasant spot, in its own way. "As far as I can tell, we have broken the daemonfey in the eastern half of the city. There is no organized opposition to our warriors, though there is plenty of skirmishing against stragglers and handfuls of fey'ri . . . and other monsters that seem to haunt this place."

"It is much the same for us," Vesilde Gaerth told the Sembian lord. "We have secured everything from this spot to the west. The daemonfey who remain are in hiding."

Miklos Selkirk flashed a bright smile in his dusty face. "Then it seems that we have won the day."

"Almost," Ilsevele said. "Some fey'ri will escape, but I intend to make sure that most of Sarya's warriors do not get away this time. This must be the last battle of this war."

"What do you propose, then?" Selkirk asked.

"First, we must throw a cordon of archers and mages around the outskirts of the city," Ilsevele answered him. She reached into her tunic and drew out a parchment map, a copy of one sketched by Starbrow a few tendays ago when her father had first asked him how to go about taking the city. She spread it out on the stone rubble of one of the inn's walls. "Many of our warriors already surround the city, but now we must tighten the net. We have set a watch from the Burial Glen to the Meadow, here. Lord Selkirk, if you agree, I suggest that the Sembian army sets its guard from the Meadow to the Glyr—that's the stream on the north side of the city. Lord Ulath and his Dalesfolk already watch the northerly approaches to the city, from the Burial Glen to the Glyr."

"Done," Miklos Selkirk said. "We'll need to make sure the companies we assign to that duty keep in contact with the sentries on each side. We don't want to give the daemonfey a way out."

Edraele Muirreste looked over at Ilsevele. "How will you prevent the daemonfey from simply flying away, Lady Miritar?"

Ilsevele glanced up at the summer sky overhead. It was a clear morning, with only a few high clouds. A trio of Eagle Knights wheeled slowly hundreds of feet above the city, riding the air currents on their great birds of prey.

"I think the job is in good hands already," Ilsevele said. "Our Eagle Knights guard the sky."

Daeron Sunlance hadn't been able to risk his giant eagles and their riders against the fey'ri legion, simply because he would have been so badly outnumbered in the air. But with the fey'ri legion shattered, his thirty knights could deal with the stragglers that were left. Chasing down small bands of fey'ri was an entirely different sort of task than dealing with Sarya's legion all at once.

Miklos Selkirk was already issuing orders to his own captains and Silver Ravens. "We'll have your cordon set quickly, Lady Ilsevele," he said when he turned back to her. "I presume you'll want to sweep the city after we set our net?"

Ilsevele nodded. "We must clear these ruins building by building, and roust out any fey'ri who are trying to hide from us. I suggest that we divide the work as follows: You and your folk begin in the east near the Street of Sorrows, Lord Selkirk, and push toward the west. We'll start in the Westfields—the Dalesfolk on our left, the army of Evermeet in the center and right—and work toward the east."

"If I may, Lady Miritar?" Miklos Selkirk said. He looked at the map scroll in front of her. "Let's place a strong company or two in the center, even before we start the sweep you suggest. We'll ambush any daemonfey trying to stay ahead of the search."

Final Gate • 327

"A good idea," Ilsevele agreed. "I'll have our Evereskan Vale Guards take up positions along the Street of a Dozen Dreams. They are our best footsoldiers."

"What of the other denizens of this place?" Vesilde Gaerth said. "There are undead, beholders, nagas . . . all sorts of monsters the daemonfey left for us to deal with."

Ilsevele thought for a moment. "If a monster flees, let it leave unless it is too dangerous to be permitted its freedom," she decided. "If it hides within its lair and does not emerge, report its location, and post sentries to make sure that no one blunders into it. Otherwise, destroy it. My father wanted this city cleansed of the evil that has crept into it over the centuries. I intend to see his wishes carried out."

◈ ◈ ◈ ◈ ◈

The fall from the nycaloth's talons had left Nesterin with a leg too badly broken to walk on, so the star elf put one arm around Araevin's shoulders and the other over Maresa's. Together, the three of them limped back the way they had come in search of Donnor and Jorin. Broken glass crunched under their feet, and from time to time the ground trembled. Each such tremor was stronger and lasted longer than the previous one, bringing more of the *Fhoeldin durr*'s magnificent columns and arches crashing down from above.

After the third quake in the space of five minutes, Maresa scowled up at the majestic glass balanced overhead. "Araevin, do we have time to retrace our steps all the way back to the door to Myth Drannor? What do we do if we get there and find that our gate has already burned itself out?"

"We'll use whatever portal we can find if we have to," the sun elf answered. "But I don't want to leave without Donnor and Jorin. The Seldarine alone know where they might end up if they choose a portal at random. It might be impossible to find them."

"It doesn't look too promising right now," Maresa muttered. "This place is going to kill us if we don't leave soon, Araevin."

A loud groan from overhead caught their attention. Araevin looked up and saw a slender arch of glass more than a hundred feet above waver, and fold to the ground. They staggered back out of the way just as a spar forty feet long crashed end-on into the floor with a deafening crash. Flickering pulses of violet-white energy sparked and streamed from the ruin.

A misshapen figure appeared through the shower of sparks, lurching toward them. "Araevin!" hissed Maresa.

"I see it," Araevin said.

He slipped Nesterin's arm from his shoulder and stood free, gripping a wand in his hand. They'd already had to fight off several yugoloths and devils stalking them through the Waymeet. The creatures seemed confused and leaderless without Malkizid to command them, but that did not mean that they weren't dangerous, especially given how battered and bloodied the three companions were.

Araevin raised his wand and aimed it at the creature coming closer. He started to speak its trigger word, but Nesterin suddenly lunged out and pulled his arm down. "No, Araevin! It's Donnor and Jorin!"

Through the acrid smoke and bright sparks, Donnor limped into sight. He half-carried Jorin, and the Aglarondan had a hand clamped to his side. Blood trickled through his fingers. Donnor helped Jorin to a spot where he could lean against the wall, and addressed Araevin.

"Is all this your doing?" he asked. "Did you use the crystal?"

"Yes, and yes," Araevin answered. "We destroyed the heart of the mythal—this place won't last much longer—and we caught Malkizid in the crystal's influence. He will not trouble us again for a long time, even though his minions still roam the Waymeet."

"We ran into some," Donnor said grimly. He took in

Araevin's bleeding wounds and Nesterin's broken leg with a single glance, and sighed. "I am afraid I can't do much for you here. Jorin was mauled by a pair of barbed devils, and I used most of my healing spells to help him."

"I will live," Araevin replied. He looked around at the glass and iron maze that surrounded them. "Let's find a portal that leads someplace remotely safe, and leave this place to fall in on itself."

"Don't be too picky," Maresa said. "I'll take anything that doesn't drop us in a dragon's lair or put us back in the infernal realms."

Araevin spied a portal that still functioned, and limped over to inspect it. He started to speak a spell of portal lore to see where it led, when something gave voice to a foul croak above him. He looked up, and saw a pair of vrocks stooping on him.

"The daemonfey!" he shouted.

He managed to speak a dismissing spell and hurl one of the vrocks back to its home dimension, but the other crashed into him and bore him down to the stone floor. Filthy talons raked at his chest and belly, clicking against the light shirt of mithral mail he wore under his tunic, while the vrock slavered and snapped at his face with its stinking beak.

Araevin saw a green flash in the middle of his companions, and someone cried out in pain as sizzling gouts of acid splattered the narrow passageway. Swords rang shrilly nearby, and more spells flew back and forth, but he was pinned by the demon tearing at him. One claw found the meat of his thigh and raked open his leg, and Araevin screamed in pain.

"You'll s-scream more when I r-rend your limbs-s from your body, m-mage," the vrock hissed in his face. "I will d-devour you alive!"

The mage struggled furiously against the demon. He was already injured and tired, and he had no strength left. The sharp beak grated across his cheekbone, and stabbed down again at his eye. Araevin avoided a gruesome wound only by throwing his arm up in the monster's way, and it seized on his hand and bit until bones crunched and blood flowed. With his other hand, he groped for his holstered wands. He found the one he was looking for and jammed it into the vrock's belly before shouting the command word.

A shrill column of bright blue force blasted through the demon's torso and flung the monster away from him. Araevin rolled to his feet, trying to make sense of the battle around him.

Nearby, Donnor Kerth fought against the daemonfey Xhalph. The tall monster rained blow after blow down on the Lathanderite's shield, the impact of steel on steel ringing through the walls of crystal and iron. Jorin, hobbled as he was, still fought one-handed against a wounded fey'ri. Nesterin traded spells with another fey'ri mage, while a pair of vrocks and a fey'ri swordsman tried to corner Maresa in one niche of the Waymeet nearby.

"Araevin! Do something!" Maresa called.

He took the wand in his hand and threw it to her. "Here! The command is *dalsien*."

Maresa snatched the wand out of the air and turned it against the foes stalking her with a malicious grin. "*Dalsien!*" she shouted, and the bright blue bolt of disrupting energy hammered one of her foes against the opposite wall.

Araevin started to speak a spell against the daemonfey prince, but a sudden flurry of wing beats descended behind him. "You have upset my plans for the last time, Araevin Teshurr!" snarled Sarya.

He turned to defend himself, but not before she reached out and grasped him with a fist that glowed blue-green with arcane power. Icy lightning hammered through Araevin, hurling him off his feet. He sprawled to the ground, thrashing uncontrollably as Sarya's spell burned and stabbed at him. He could not even scream.

Sarya smiled, and flicked her tail. "Now that is what pleases me, Xhalph! My enemies prostrate before me, helpless! How shall I repay this one for all the trouble he has caused me?"

"Get away from him, you foul harpy!" Starbrow commanded as he hurled into the fray, Keryvian burning like a white brand in his hands.

The moon elf roared a challenge and raced to Araevin's side, brandishing his sword. Beside him, the wood elf Jerreda raised her bow and with one skillful shot dropped the fey'ri dueling Jorin. Two more wood elves behind her met with fey'ri warriors and began furious duels of their own.

Sarya whirled with a hiss of surprise. She threw herself into the air just in time to avoid Starbrow's deadly blade, and beat her wings furiously for a margin of safety.

"Xhalph!" she cried. "Deal with this one!"

Starbrow looked down at Araevin, who was still wracked by the furious blue-green energy of Sarya's spell. With one quick motion he dipped Keryvian's blade down to touch Araevin's chest. The baneblade gleamed once, and the ancient counter-magic that Demron had forged into his mightiest weapon scattered the daemonfey spell into dissipating tendrils of fog.

"Keep Sarya off my back," he said, and he threw himself forward to meet Xhalph.

Araevin rolled to one side, trying to shake off the effects of Sarya's spell. He heard Maresa shout out *"Dalsien! Dalsien!"* expending the power of his disruption wand with lavish lack of regard for the work he'd put into the device. Blue bolts of power scored the air, and peals of thunder rocked the damaged Waymeet. Well, I can't think of a better way to empty a wand, he decided. Meanwhile Donnor bludgeoned the fey'ri mage with a glowing hammer of force and blasted at his foe with brilliant sunbeams.

He looked around for Sarya, and found her shaping a spell of abyssal fire between her hands. Desperately he threw out a counterspell and negated the blast before she could incinerate Starbrow or the rest of his companions. Sarya snarled in pure anger, and blasted at him with a hail of magical darts that he parried with a quick shielding spell. He replied by hurling a deadly green disintegrating ray at the daemonfey queen, but she simply spun away from it with a quick twist of her wings. The ray chewed through a spar of the Waymeet behind her, and with a screech of outrage the daemonfey queen fluttered away to avoid being crushed beneath the falling column. Araevin lost sight of her and took a moment to push himself upright.

Only ten feet from him Starbrow and Xhalph battled each other in a furious display of swordsmanship. Keryvian sliced the air with streaks of white fire, and Xhalph snarled a foul curse and gave ground under Starbrow's attack. Keryvian scored him once across the thigh and a second time along the ribs, leaving seared black wounds in its wake. The daemonfey roared in anger and struck back. Parrying Starbrow's one sword with the two in his lower arms, he lunged out in a scissors-cut with both upper blades.

"I will kill you!" Xhalph screamed.

Starbrow ducked beneath the strokes and stepped up under the towering swordsman's guard. It was too close for Keryvian, but instead of trying to hack or stab with the blade the moon elf set its edge to Xhalph's ruby flesh and whirled away, drawing a long, deep cut with Keryvian's razor edge. Xhalph stabbed at his back with his two left-hand blades, and Starbrow parried one behind his back with the baneblade and jumped away from the other, finishing his turn just as Xhalph drew back his left hands and lashed out with his right.

"Not this day, demonspawn!" Starbrow snarled, and he brought Keryvian whistling up in a vicious uppercut that took off Xhalph's lower right arm above the elbow and his upper arm a little above the wrist. Two of the daemonfey's swords went spinning through the air, and Xhalph's roar of rage changed pitch into a shriek of pain.

"Mother!" he cried. Blood splattering from the stumps, he spread his wings for balance and backed away from Starbrow. The moon elf swordsman threw himself forward and buried Keryvian in Xhalph's belly before the daemonfey could get out of reach. Xhalph let out another awful cry as Keryvian flashed into white incandescence deep in his flesh. Smoke pouring from his mouth, the daemonfey prince crumpled to the ground and fell still.

Sarya Dlardrageth appeared above Starbrow, eyes blazing in fury. She threw out her hand and sent the moon elf warrior flying head-over-heels into a wall of jagged glass.

"You will die for that, paleblood!" she screeched.

She started to incant a fearsome necromancy, summoning a black aura that crawled over her hands like something hungry and aware. Starbrow shook his head and started to pick himself up out of the rubble.

Araevin saw his chance.

Quick as thought, he wove a spell shield and threw it over Starbrow. Sarya finished her deadly incantation and hurled the crawling black fire at the moon elf—but Araevin's defense flared bright blue, and reflected the black fire back at the daemonfey queen. Sarya hissed once in surprise, and her own spell took her full in the center of her body. Avid flames of dancing obsidian sprang up all over her body, guttering from her very flesh, streaming from eyes, mouth, and even her ears and the joinings of her armor.

The daemonfey queen shrieked in pain and anger. *"I—will—kill you—for that!"* she cried. She arched over in agony, then started to sink, no longer able to stay aloft. Fluttering awkwardly, she crashed into the ground in a corona of ebon flame.

Starbrow rolled to his feet and started toward Sarya, but another fey'ri warrior leaped down to intervene. In the space of the blink of an eye, the moon elf and the demon-tainted warrior were engaged in a furious duel, blades flashing almost too fast for Araevin to follow. Meanwhile, Sarya managed to extinguish herself with a potent counterspell.

Her ruby flesh still smoked, but she was no longer being consumed by her own spell.

Araevin took a deep breath, and evoked the Word of Power, the *ondreier ysele*. Sarya flinched away and quickly raised a spell-shield of her own, guarding herself beneath a mantle of golden spheres that shimmered and whirled about her. Araevin recognized the spell; it was a potent abjuration, a defense against almost any spell. The daemonfey queen grinned maliciously, and started to shape another spell to fling at him.

Framing his spell in the Word of Power, Araevin hammered at her spell-shield with a reciprocal spell of his own. He seized her golden spheres, channeling all the energy of Sarya's own defense against her. With the strength of the *ondreier ysele* behind his reciprocal magic, Sarya's defense doubled and doubled again in strength. The golden spheres froze in their orbits, quavered once, and plunged into the daemonfey queen's body.

"No! *No!*" Sarya screamed.

Golden light burst out of her body, raving streams of magical power that burned away her flesh and melted holes in her brazen armor. She tried once more to leap into the sky, to escape her doom, but in mid-leap a golden ray destroyed her face. She shuddered once, and collapsed into a desiccated husk. Smoke curled from her motionless form.

Araevin collapsed to all fours himself, exhausted beyond all endurance. Between the Gatekeeper's Crystal, the encounter with Malkizid, and the final duel with Sarya, he was utterly spent. It struck him then that the sounds of battle had died away with Sarya's fall. No more sword strokes rang in the failing mythal.

Jerreda stood over the body of the last fey'ri warrior. She looked over to Araevin. "Is Sarya—?"

Where in the world did Starbrow and Jerreda come from? he wondered. He shook his head. However they had found him, their timing had proven impeccable.

"Yes," Araevin said with a groan. "Sarya Dlardrageth is dead."

Maresa knelt beside him and raised him up. "Come on, Araevin, you have to get us out of here. Which door do we use?"

"I cannot tell anymore. My magic is spent." He leaned on the genasi, too tired to take a step. Starbrow stood unbeaten before him, watching for any more enemies who might appear. Donnor supported Nesterin, with the star elf's arm over his broad shoulders, while the wood elves who had followed Jerreda and Starbrow tended to Jorin. Araevin looked around, still trying to make sense of the scene.

"By the Seldarine," he whispered. "Is it over?"

"Not until we get out of here," Maresa retorted. Another convulsion shook the *Fhoeldin durr,* and more portals winked out. Only a few remained intact. "Take your best guess, Araevin!"

He waved his hand at the closest of the portals. The battered company hurried over to the doorway, and somehow Araevin found the tiny spark of power needed to steady it. Praying that they were not about to gate themselves into the heart of a volcano or the palace of an evil god, he staggered through the door.

The Last Mythal fell into ruin behind them.

EPILOGUE

*20 Marpenoth, the Year of the Blazing Hand
(1380 DR)*

The splendid colors of fall covered Myth Drannor in a mantle of red and gold. The air had a crisp, fresh smell to it that never failed to intoxicate Araevin. He loved the autumn, especially when the days still remembered a hint of summer's warmth but the nights grew cold and clear. He doubted whether Arvandor itself had anything to rival Cormanthor in the fall.

He stood in the *Seldarrshen Nieryll,* the Starsoul Shrine. It was a ring-shaped colonnade in the heart of the city, open on all sides. In its center stood the Tree of Souls, whose slender silvery trunk reached almost twenty feet in height. Some among the coronal's advisors had suggested guarding it in a courtyard of Castle Cormanthor, or even concealing it in the woods outside the city, but

Ilsevele had decided that the tree was a gift to be shared by all of Myth Drannor's folk. Through the open archways of the *Seldarrshen Nieryll* anyone passing through the square around the colonnade could see the tree, or even step inside to feel its presence. The tree's own influence and the spell-shields Araevin had woven around the shrine protected it far better than mere walls of stone or doors of adamantine could ever have.

"Grow strong, grow tall," he said to the young Tree of Souls, resting his hand on its warm bark. Then he gathered up his staff and pack, passing from the sunlit center of the shrine through the cool shadows of the colonnade to the stone steps outside. He paused again to enjoy the sensation of the autumn sunshine, so clear and perfect that it seemed the sun itself could sing for joy. Around the *Seldarrshen Nieryll* the ceremonial watch of warriors handpicked from the Coronal's Guard stood in vigilant silence, but only a few steps away the People of the city carried on with their business. Dozens of craftsmen and masons worked on the new temple to the Seldarine that was rising on the opposite side of the square, merchants carried on with the growing commerce of the city, and children sang and shouted joyfully in their games. There was still much to do, of course—some parts of the ancient city would likely never be rebuilt. But Myth Drannor was a whole and living city again, and Araevin still shook his head in wonder every time that thought crossed his mind.

"You have woven well, Araevin," Ilsevele said softly. She stood watching him, wearing an austere dress of midnight blue velvet finished with a delicate embroidery of silver thread. A tiara nestled in her bright red hair. At her belt hung a long, slender scepter of platinum—the Ruler's Blade of Cormanthyr, in the hands of a coronal of Cormanthyr for the first time in more than seven hundred years. Ilsevele preferred to carry the ancient symbol in this form rather than as a five-foot warblade. "Are you certain you will not stay?"

He shook his head. "I think my work here is done, Ilsevele. The mythal is as sound as I can make it. The Tree of Souls is a stronger anchor than anything I might have been able to fashion. I can add nothing more."

"You do not have to leave just because you have finished, Araevin," Starbrow said. He stood beside his wife, her hand in his. He wore a silver fillet above his eyes, and Keryvian still rode on his hip—not only was he Ilsevele's prince-consort, he was still her chief champion and guard as well as the high captain of Myth Drannor's army. "You've earned a rest. The world outside this forest can look after itself for a little longer."

Araevin met his friends' eyes and smiled sadly. They'd been married five years, but a small part of his heart still ached to see Ilsevele with Starbrow. He was glad that they were happy, and he understood better how high magic had changed him, but that did not mean he did not regret some of the choices he had made.

"I think it will be good for me to travel new lands and see new things," said Araevin. "There are still a few roads in Faerûn I haven't put under my feet yet."

"Where will you go?" Ilsevele asked.

"The Sword Coast, first. I want to look in on Donnor, visit with Elorfindar, and perhaps see if I can't find Grayth Holmfast's sons in Waterdeep. Then Aglarond and Sildëyuir—I have work there that isn't done yet. After that?" He shrugged. "I think I'll search out Auseriel and see if I can't put my talents to use in Lamruil's hidden city. If he is raising a mythal there, I may be able to help."

"I can't imagine anyone who could help him more," Ilsevele said with a smile. "You are always welcome here, Araevin. I will not name another grand mage yet. As long as you live, you are Cormanthyr's grand mage, wherever you wander."

"Are we leaving, or not? I'd like to be on our way before it gets dark." Maresa Rost stood a little behind the elves, holding the reins of two horses. She wore her customary scarlet with a rakish feathered hat, and she folded her arms and rolled her eyes impatiently. Araevin smiled at her impetuousness. She was something of a kindred spirit, after all. Friends like Maresa had given him his own humanlike restlessness in the first place. "You've been saying good-bye for something like a tenday now, you know."

Ilsevele laughed out loud. "I suppose you're right, Maresa," she admitted. She moved forward and kissed Araevin's cheek. "Sweet water and light laughter until we meet again," she said.

"And to you," said Araevin. "I will see you again before too many seasons pass."

"We'll be waiting for you both." Starbrow clapped his shoulder and took his hand in a firm grip. "Fair travels, my friend," he said.

Araevin returned his handclasp and turned to Maresa. He swung himself up into the saddle of the roan, and patted the horse's neck. "All right," he said. "I am ready."

Touching his heels to his horse's flanks, he put Myth Drannor behind him and rode out to see where the road would take him.

Elvish Words and Phrases

Aillesel seldarie
A prayer that means "May the Seldarine save us."

Dalsien
"Thunder," a command word for one of Araevin's wands.

Elladyr
"Starstrike," a command word for a wand Ilsevele carries.

Estierren nha morden
Part of a spell intended to undo other spells.

Fhoeldin durr
Literally "the Thousandfold Way," but more often translated as simply "The Waymeet."

Iorwe
"Step aside," the words of a spell that blinks the caster a short distance.

Kileaarna reithirgir
"Unjoining the mystic Weave," a high magic rite that negates other spells.

Mythaalniir darach
"Mythal-shaping rite," a high magic spell.

Nesirtye
"Elsewhere," part of a spell that teleports the caster a moderate distance.

Nharaigh lathanyll
"Noontime sunlight," part of a strong light spell.

Ondreier ysele
"Potent declamation," or "Word of potency," a high magic spell that adds power to whatever spell the caster employs next.

Telmiirkara neshyrr
"Transfiguring spell-song," a spell that changes the essential nature of the caster.

FORGOTTEN REALMS®

THOMAS M. REID

The author of *Insurrection* and The Scions of Arrabar Trilogy rescues Aliisza and Kaanyr Vhok from the tattered remnants of their assault on Menzoberranzan, and sends them off on a quest across the multiverse that will leave FORGOTTEN REALMS fans reeling!

THE EMPYREAN ODYSSEY

BOOK I
THE GOSSAMER PLAIN

Kaanyr Vhok, fresh from his defeat against the drow, turns to hated Sundabar for the victory his demonic forces demand, but there's more to his ambitions than just one human city. In his quest for arcane power, he sends the alu-fiend Aliisza on a mission that will challenge her in ways she never dreamed of.

May 2007

BOOK II
THE FRACTURED SKY

A demon surrounded by angels in a universe of righteousness? How did that become Aliisza's life?

November 2008

BOOK III
THE CRYSTAL MOUNTAIN

What Aliisza has witnessed has changed her forever, but that's nothing compared to what has happened to the multiverse itself. The startling climax will change the nature of the cosmos forever.

Mid-2009

"Reid is proving himself to be one of the best up and coming authors in the FORGOTTEN REALMS universe."
—fantasy-fan.org

FORGOTTEN REALMS, WIZARDS OF THE COAST, and their respective logos are trademarks of Wizards of the Coast, Inc. in the U.S.A. and other countries.
©2007 Wizards.

FORGOTTEN REALMS

PAUL S. KEMP

"I would rank Kemp among WotC's most talented authors, past and present, such as R. A. Salvatore, Elaine Cunningham, and Troy Denning."
—Fantasy Hotlist

The New York Times best-selling author of *Resurrection* and The Erevis Cale Trilogy plunges ever deeper into the shadows that surround the FORGOTTEN REALMS world in this Realms-shaking new trilogy.

THE TWILIGHT WAR

BOOK I
SHADOWBRED

It takes a shade to know a shade, but will take more than a shade to stand against the Twelve Princes of Shade Enclave. All of the realm of Sembia may not be enough.

BOOK II
SHADOWSTORM

Civil war rends Sembia, and the ancient archwizards of Shade offer to help. But with friends like these...

September 2007

BOOK III
SHADOWREALM

No longer content to stay within the bounds of their magnificent floating city, the Shadovar promise a new era, and a new empire, for the future of Faerûn.

May 2008

ANTHOLOGY
REALMS OF WAR

A collection of all new stories by your favorite FORGOTTEN REALMS authors digs deep into the bloody history of Faerûn.

January 2008

FORGOTTEN REALMS, WIZARDS OF THE COAST, and their respective logos are trademarks of Wizards of the Coast, Inc. in the U.S.A. and other countries.
©2007 Wizards.

FORGOTTEN REALMS®

PHILIP ATHANS

The New York Times best-selling author of *Annihilation* and *Baldur's Gate* tells an epic tale of vision and heartbreak, of madness and ambition, that could change the map of Faerûn forever.

THE WATERCOURSE TRILOGY

BOOK I
WHISPER OF WAVES
The city-state of Innarlith sits on one edge of the Lake of Steam, just waiting for someone to drag it forward from obscurity. Will that someone be a Red Wizard of Thay, a street urchin who grew up to be the richest man in Innarlith, or a strange outsider who cares nothing for power but has grand ambitions all his own?

BOOK II
LIES OF LIGHT
A beautiful girl is haunted by spirits with dark intentions, an ambitious senator sells more than just his votes, and all the while construction proceeds on a canal that will change the face of trade in Faerûn forever.

BOOK III
SCREAM OF STONE
As the canal nears completion, scores will be settled, power will be bought and stolen, souls will be crushed and redeemed, and the power of one man's vision will be the only constant in a city-state gone mad.

June 2007

"Once again it is Philip Athans moving the FORGOTTEN REALMS to new ground and new vibrancy."
—R.A. Salvatore

FORGOTTEN REALMS, WIZARDS OF THE COAST, and their respective logos are trademarks of Wizards of the Coast, Inc. in the U.S.A. and other countries.
©2007 Wizards.

FORGOTTEN REALMS®

THE KNIGHTS OF MYTH DRANNOR

A brand new trilogy by master storyteller

ED GREENWOOD

Join the creator of the FORGOTTEN REALMS® world as he explores the early adventures of his original and most celebrated characters from the moment they earn the name "Swords of Eveningstar" to the day they prove themselves worthy of it.

BOOK I
SWORDS OF EVENINGSTAR

Florin Falconhand has always dreamed of adventure. When he saves the life of the king of Cormyr, his dream comes true and he earns an adventuring charter for himself and his friends. Unfortunately for Florin, he has also earned the enmity of several nobles and the attention of some of Cormyr's most dangerous denizens.

BOOK II
SWORDS OF DRAGONFIRE

Victory never comes without sacrifice. Florin Falconhand and the Swords of Eveningstar have lost friends in their adventures, but in true heroic fashion, they press on. Unfortunately, there are those who would see the Swords of Eveningstar pay for lives lost and damage wrecked, regardless of where the true blame lies.

August 2007

BOOK III
THE SWORD NEVER SLEEPS

Fame has found the Swords of Eveningstar, but with fame comes danger. Nefarious forces have dark designs on these adventurers who seem to overturn the most clever of plots. And if the Swords will not be made into their tools, they will be destroyed.

August 2008

FORGOTTEN REALMS, WIZARDS OF THE COAST, and their respective logos are trademarks of Wizards of the Coast, Inc. in the U.S.A. and other countries.
©2007 Wizards.